FLOWERBED OF STATE

A WHITE HOUSE GARDENER MYSTERY

FLOWERBED OF STATE

DOROTHY ST. JAMES

WHEELER
CHIVERS

This Large Print edition is published by Wheeler Publishing, Waterville, Maine, USA and by AudioGO Ltd, Bath, England.
Wheeler Publishing, a part of Gale, Cengage Learning.
Copyright © 2011 by Tekno Books.
The moral right of the author has been asserted.
A White House Gardener Mystery.

The text of this Large Print edition is unabridged.
Other aspects of the book may vary from the original edition.
Set in 16 pt. Plantin.

LIBRARY OF CONGRESS CATALOGING-IN-PUBLICATION DATA

St. James, Dorothy.
    Flowerbed of State/ a White House gardener mystery / Dorothy St. James.
        p. cm.
    ISBN-13: 978-1-4104-4076-1 (softcover)
    ISBN-10: 1-4104-4076-1 (softcover)
    1. Women gardeners—Fiction. 2. White House (Washington, D.C.)—Fiction. 3. Large type books. I. Title.
PS3619.T245W48 2011
813'.6—dc22   2011021723

BRITISH LIBRARY CATALOGUING-IN-PUBLICATION DATA AVAILABLE

Published in 2011 in the U.S. by arrangement with The Berkley Publishing Group, a member of Penguin Group (USA) Inc.
Published in 2012 in the U.K. by arrangement with The Berkley Publishing Group, a division of Penguin Group (USA) Inc.

U.K. Hardcover: 978 1 445 86546 1 (Chivers Large Print)
U.K. Softcover: 978 1 445 86547 8 (Camden Large Print)

Printed in the United States of America
1 2 3 4 5 6 7 15 14 13 12 11

For Jim . . .
the love of my life and partner in crime.

And for all the
dedicated men and women
serving at the local, regional,
state, and federal levels
without acknowledgment or fanfare —
you are the glue that
keeps this country together.
This book celebrates you.

ACKNOWLEDGMENTS

When I embarked on this writing adventure that had me delving into the behind-the-scenes life at the White House I never imagined the wonderful and gracious people I was destined to meet along the way.

First, a huge thank-you goes out to Amy Dabbs, the Tri-County Master Gardener Coordinator, for sharing her passion for organic gardening; Roger Francis, the Senior Clemson Extension Agent at the Charleston office, for his commonsense advice; and to the amazing master gardener volunteers who have welcomed me as one of their own. My garden has never looked so lush! And Mike Dixon, because of you, I'll never think of grass the same way again. I'm still trying to decide if that's a good thing.

Hazel Betts, docent at the Richard Nixon Library and Museum, taught me about the burgundy red floribunda "Pat Nixon" rose.

7

And the incredible Eddie Gehman Kohan, who reports all things food and garden related from the White House in her Obama Foodorama blog, kept me "in the know." Thanks to Congressman Henry Brown, Senator Lindsey Graham, and their dedicated staffs — especially Taylor Andreae in Senator Graham's office — for arranging tours, answering questions, and giving me a peek into the inner workings of the federal government. My book is richer because of you.

Sergeant David Schlosser, of the U.S. Park Police, you have my sincere thanks for taking the time to explain how the various agencies work together. I'm also grateful to the members of the Secret Service for answering all my odd questions and *not* arresting me as I stalked them around the perimeter of the White House during all hours of the day and night. I have to point out that the men and women serving in the Secret Service, the U.S. Park Police, and the D.C. Police are some of the most professional and dedicated civil servants I've met. Our nation's capitol is in great hands.

Enormous thanks go to Brittiany Koren for offering me the chance to bring Casey Calhoun to life. Brittiany, you're a great friend, a hard-nosed editor, and one of the best cheerleaders in the business. A big thank-you goes to Michael Koren for his understanding and patience for all those times Brittiany locked herself away in her office in order to help me hash out all the details.

Thanks also go to Marty Greenberg, Rosalind Greenberg, Larry Segriff, John Helfers, and Chuck Wiseman at Tekno Books for your support. I send my deepest gratitude to my editor, Natalee Rosenstein, at Berkley Prime Crime, for giving me the chance to tell Casey Calhoun's story, to Michelle Vega for guiding me through the process, and to the talented staff at Berkley Prime Crime who have helped turn my manuscript into the novel you hold in your hands today.

Last but not least, I'd like to thank the incredible authors in the Lowcountry Chapter of Romance Writers of America, Sisters in Crime, and Mystery Writers of America, whose unflagging support has kept me pounding away at my keyboard: especially Nina Bruhns, Margie Lawson, C. J. Lyons, Mallary Mitchell, Tracy Anne Warren, and Joanna Wayne for patiently listening and giving advice as I worked out plot problems and tilted at windmills while writing this book. I couldn't have done it without you!

CHAPTER ONE

Casey, child, I swear some days ain't good for nothing but spreading out on a lawn like fertilizer, Aunt Willow was known to sputter when everything but everything seemed to go wrong. And I don't mean annoyances like when the car gets a flat tire, or the bank misplaces your deposit. No, she had to be *really* upset. It was the closest I'd ever heard my pearl-wearing, julep-sipping Southern belle relative come to swearing.

She had thousands of odd sayings like that. So I had to wonder why that especially dire one kept worming its way through my head.

Lately, everything in my life was coming up roses. Or perhaps I should say *pink ruffled tulips,* since I was apparently lying facedown in a bed of them.

I carefully lifted my head. A blob of mud slid down the side of my nose and trailed across my cheek. A few inches away a shiny black ground beetle tipped its antenna in my direction. I watched as it traveled across the rim of a tulip bloom. Despite the dim morning light, I was able to take this all in without any trouble at all. But when I probed deeper, I couldn't figure out why the devil I was napping in a bed of flowers.

Slosh.

I wasn't in any obvious pain. *Not yet,* a frightened little voice in my head warned. I'd been here before, a long, long time ago. Not in a bed of flowers, but semiconscious and confused. *And hurt.*

Ancient history, I reminded myself.

But was it? Waking up in a flowerbed was by no means normal for anyone, right? And why couldn't I remember anything about how I got here? While I knew I should have stayed put until I could thoroughly assess what kind of trouble I'd gotten myself into, I wasn't in the mood to lie about waiting for anything else to happen to me. It took some effort to push up onto my wobbly hands and knees. Oh, what a mistake! Sitting up set off a firestorm of agony that radiated out from behind my eyes and shot down my neck.

I groaned and cradled my sore head in my hands. When my fingers brushed my left temple, I felt something warm and sticky. It

12

took several seconds to realize what I was touching.

Blood. *My* blood. And under that film of hot, sticky blood a lump was forming. Not good. Not good at all. I had just enough wits to know that landing in a soft bed of flowers shouldn't have done this kind of damage. Something else must have happened. Something *bad*.

My hands shook as they skimmed the muddy soil in search of my backpack. It was half-submerged in a mud puddle a few feet away. A couple of years ago I'd started growing habaneras in my kitchen window. It's amazing how potent a concoction one can make with a little extracted pepper oil. I always carried my own special blend of homemade pepper spray in my backpack.

I pulled off my gardening gloves and dug around in the soggy bag. The bottle of pepper spray was at the bottom, the worst possible location if this had been an actual emergency. *Not an emergency? If you're thinking you're out of danger, honey, you're deluding yourself,* chided my pesky inner voice, which sounded eerily like Aunt Willow this morning.

I shook my head, sending the world spinning out of focus. Odd images tumbled through my mind. A silver briefcase. A

13

man's black-and-white leather shoe with a distinctive design . . . like a lightning bolt. Just one shoe, mind you, not a pair. A plain coffee mug. My yellow rain slicker, which I was still wearing. The White House. And the First Lady of the United States, or FLOTUS, as the press called her.

Did I *know* the First Lady?

Slosh.

My knees sank into the cool wet earth as I sat back on my heels to take in my surroundings. I recognized the pale pink flowers hanging down from the saucer magnolias and the line of elm trees to the right of me. I'd personally assisted in planting the profusion of tulip and grape hyacinth bulbs I had — I cringed to notice — crushed.

"It's murder, you know," I'd told someone just that morning as I'd slipped on my bright yellow slicker raincoat. What a time to remember that and very little else!

As I sat there, staring at the soggy landscape around me, details from that morning slowly trickled back into my throbbing head. I remembered Gordon Sims's windowless office. The cinder block walls plastered with landscape plans and schedules. The most recent addition was the cheerful pink and yellow sketch for the upcoming Easter Egg Roll. The oldest, a plan for the grounds drawn up by Frederick Law Olmsted, Jr., dated back to 1935. Gordon, the White House chief horticulturalist, hadn't been around quite that long. But he had an uncanny ability to remember every single day of his nearly thirty years on the job with precise detail. I, on the other hand, had only three months' experience as his assistant.

The White House rose above the elm trees like a gleaming beacon of hope on the far side of Pennsylvania Avenue, and here I was slumped on the ground like an overwatered houseplant. One had to wonder how I'd managed to land such a prestigious position when I apparently didn't have sense enough to keep away from situations that ended with me waking up in flowerbeds in the middle of Lafayette Square.

Slosh. Slosh.

Earlier that morning Gordon had been at his desk reviewing a stack of purchase orders while complaining about the sorry state of his 401(k).

"It's murder, you know," I'd said as I breezed into the room.

"That sounds awfully melodramatic, Casey," he'd said, straightening his hunched shoulders. He swiveled his chair toward me and fingered his plain white coffee mug. His strong hands were timeworn, but his face looked boyish despite his fifty-five years. Only his silver hair gave his age away. "You've been reading those murder mysteries again," he accused, waggling his coffee mug at me. But I'd made him smile.

"Perhaps . . ." I narrowed my eyes and shifted my gaze back and forth across the room, trying out the mysterious look I'd been practicing in the mirror. I always had at least one crime novel tucked into my backpack, and I liked to imagine myself a modern-day, hipper, and much younger Miss Marple. Not that I'd ever had a chance to solve a real mystery.

I leaned toward Gordon and lowered my voice to a whisper. "Perhaps a bit of melodrama is needed. Those spiny devils are strangling our ruffled tulips. I won't be a minute."

"Won't be a —" He half rose from his burnt orange desk chair, its ancient springs screeching. "Casey Calhoun, you can't be seriously considering pulling weeds now."

"Have to." I hurried into the room next to Gordon's office and straight to the partitioned space that served as my work area. The windowless workspace was tucked away underneath the White House's North Portico and North Lawn. The carpenter's shop

16

was just next door. The low whirr of a power saw vibrated through the thick wall.

Down here, underneath the ground, was where the real work in the White House got done. We were the earthworms whose tireless efforts made it possible for the mighty oak to grow. I'd joined the ranks of the most dedicated bunch of workers I'd ever met. With a shared sense of pride, we all worked behind the scenes to keep the nation's most famous household running seamlessly.

My office area wasn't as dreary as one might expect in a basement setting. Floor-to-ceiling windows in the hallway just outside the door opened up into a sunken courtyard that doubled as a delivery area. If I needed a dose of natural light, I would prop open the office door and let the sun shine in. That is, when I wasn't in such a hurry.

I kicked off the brand-new black pumps my roommate, Alyssa, had picked out for me, and I slipped on the pair of worn loafers I kept in a caddy beneath my desk. Alyssa had also picked out the dark gray Ann Taylor suit complete with pencil skirt I was wearing. Without her, I'd happily wear a comfortable old pair of khakis or jeans every day of my life. A fate worse than death to Alyssa's way of thinking.

"You're serious about this? You're going to Lafayette Square? Now?" Gordon's voice carried through the wall. I seemed to be the only one who could alarm him just as easily as I could make him laugh.

"There are just a few of them in the flowerbed, but you know how quickly the mile-a-minute weed spreads. A mile a minute." Naturally that was an exaggeration. But not by much. "I noticed them when I came in this morning. They weren't there when I left yesterday. I'm sure of it."

Gordon stepped into my small partitioned office, crossed his arms over his chest, and watched as I scurried about, his silver eyebrows furrowed. "Send someone from the crew. Sal usually gets in early. And you know he's got a soft spot for you. I doubt he'll even grumble when you tell him to pull weeds in the dark and in the rain."

Granted, it was early. With the recent change to daylight saving time, sunrise was still a solid hour away. And it had been raining all night. The windows in the hallway outside my office looked as if they'd been shrouded with a heavy black cloth. Gordon was right. I shouldn't be doing this. But I had to do *something.* Sitting at my desk waiting for the meeting to start was going to make me lose my mind.

I pushed aside one of the large display boards I'd made for this morning's presentation and grabbed my backpack. The display was ready. I was ready. There was really nothing left for me to do before the meeting. In three hours I would give my first presentation to the First Lady, which was the reason I'd been struck by this sudden manic need to make Lafayette Square perfect. When I got nervous, I gardened.

"Just don't show up with mud on your skirt," Gordon called after me as I rushed down the passageway, past the chocolate shop shrouded in rich, dark cocoa scents, and into the basement hallway that led away from the workshops and offices buried beneath the North Portico of the White House. I hurried, not toward the main building, but to the double doors on my right that opened into the sunken courtyard and the North Lawn.

It was still drizzling. A freezing wind rushed in from the north, pelting my face with the cold rain from one of winter's last gasps. Fresh green buds had already set on the trees. Cherry blossoms were just starting to brighten the capital city with their festive shades of pink. I smiled and waved at Fredrick, the bulky guard on duty at the northwest gate.

"Keep an eye out for the new batch of crazies," Fredrick stuck his head out of the guard hut to warn me. He had a head of bright red hair and cute round cheeks that were in conflict with his massive arms and broad chest. "They showed up last night and started harassing anyone they could find. We broke it up, but we expect they'll be back."

"What are they protesting now?" I liked to be prepared in case one of them started lecturing me while my hands were half-buried in a flowerbed. Some protesters viewed any member of the White House staff as part of the problem. That's free speech for you. I'm all for it as long as no one tramples my flowers.

"Apparently they're against the President's meeting with the bankers this week." He scratched his chin and shrugged. "Didn't read their literature."

I spotted about a dozen protesters setting up at the edge of Lafayette Square, the seven-acre public park situated across the street from the White House's iron gates. The protesters had arrived dressed in drab rags and burlap sacks. Several placards were scattered on the ground around them as they stood under streetlamps chatting and sipping their Starbucks coffees.

I made my way through the security gate and crossed Pennsylvania Avenue, passing by the group without incident. At this early hour, most of Lafayette Square was still empty and shrouded in deep shadows and fog.

Beyond the banking protesters, a sleeping woman hunched down in her makeshift tent. That was Connie, a nuclear arms protester who for the past three decades had lived in front of the White House among her large handmade poster board signs.

In no time, I arrived at the far side of the park and the flowerbed where the mile-a-minute weeds with their distinctive triangular leaves had taken root. They'd wrapped their tentacles and curved barbs around the long ribbon leaves of the newly planted pink ruffled tulips. Like tiny hands, the weeds were slowly but surely choking the life out of the showy flowers.

I unzipped my backpack and placed it on the ground so I could rummage through it. After pulling on my work gloves, I unwound the vines from the tulip leaves and teased their spider-vein roots from the soft, black earth. Ever mindful of my upcoming meeting, I took extra care to keep from splashing mud on my suit or pantyhose.

The steady motion of my hands, along

with the sounds of the city slowly coming awake, soothed my nerves. Soon, I was one with the flowers, trees, and chilly rain still falling from the ebbing storm. I was so totally lost in my work that I barely noticed the man dashing in the direction of Pennsylvania Avenue and the White House.

Everyone in Washington, D.C., always seems to be in a hurry running here or there. I think he glanced my way. His suit may have been black. He wore a dark-colored baseball cap low on his head. But come to think about it, there had been something odd about him. He'd been carrying a silver briefcase.

I shuddered. Just thinking about that shiny briefcase made my heart thump against my chest. A large, icy raindrop slapped my cheek, jolting me back to my present predicament. I rubbed the sting as I struggled to piece together the puzzle.

SLOSH.

I didn't end up facedown in a flowerbed by accident. Which meant someone must have either hit me or pushed me there. And if that was the case, my attacker might be lurking somewhere nearby. What if he saw me moving and was coming back to finish me *off?* That's what usually happened in the crime novels I read — the killer sticks around the scene of the crime to make sure he did the job right.

My insides clenched. I held my breath and prayed Gordon had been right in thinking I'd been reading too many murder mysteries lately. Though I didn't want to, I turned my head and peered over my shoulder to see if anyone was sneaking up behind me.

Despite the deep shadows cast by the elm trees and the stormy fog, I spotted a blurry black blob jogging toward me, splashing through the puddles. The killer!

I shouldn't have ignored that sloshing sound I'd been hearing. But to be fair, with my thoughts jangling about in my head like loose change, I was having trouble figuring anything out, much less paying attention to odd noises. But everything suddenly turned crystal clear.

The sloshing I'd heard had been from his boots.

I could feel it in my bones. He was coming back to make sure I stayed planted in the mud.

Why would anyone want to kill me? I'm a gardener. An assistant gardener, at that! Never mind, he'd already hit me once. With his silver briefcase, I think. I tightened my grip on my bottle of homegrown pepper spray, which suddenly felt inadequate. It was in a travel hairspray bottle that didn't have much of a range.

I should have bought a better bottle. I should have called for help right away. I dug around in my backpack for my cell phone. I found my garden shears, a small spade, the novel I'd been reading. Where was my phone? I should have stayed put. I should have kept my head down in the mud until I understood exactly what was happening. And now it was too late . . .

SLOSH. SLOSH.

He was directly behind me. His presence loomed like a heavy hand pressing down on me. I turned just as he grabbed my arm.

What transpired next happened so fast perhaps I should skip over it. It's not really that interesting. And, well, I didn't exactly live up to Miss Marple's standards.

I screamed like a girl. Who wouldn't? Adrenaline surged through me. Throwing my arms out, I leapt to my feet and pressed the plunger on my pepper spray bottle. Who could blame me? I kept squirting the man with my fiery concoction until he grabbed my wrist and twisted it with such force my hand went numb and the bottle dropped to the ground.

He was dressed from head to toe in villainous black. Black military boots, black combat pants, black flak jacket, even his hair was the color of the midnight sky. Not only that, a large assault rifle was slung over his shoulder and a menacing pistol jutted out from a black leather leg holster.

I tried to twist away from him to break his crushing hold on my wrist. I'd learned in a self-defense course I'd taken in college that the purpose of pepper spray is to blind your assailant long enough to escape him. I'd even perfected my quick dodge technique during the class's mock attacks. I should have been able to sprint several blocks away by now. But I couldn't go anywhere because this gun-toting bully stubbornly refused to play by the rules and let go of me.

Why wouldn't he let go? In a blind panic, I let loose a Xena Warrior Princess battle yell and landed a bruising kick to his shin.

"Ow!" he shouted, but his grip held firm. I kicked him again.

With a disgusted grunt, he twirled me around until my backside was pressed against his muscular legs and chest. He cinched his arm around my waist, pinning me so close to him I had no hope of using any kind of leverage against his brute strength.

"Let go," I wheezed.

"Not until you stop attacking me." He

swore under his breath while I twisted and turned and wore myself out. "This is what I get for playing the Good Samaritan, a hell-cat with claws. If you don't stop scratching me, I swear I will —"

"Wait a minute." He thought *I* was attacking *him?* I'm the good guy here. What would make him think I would willingly attack anyone? "Wait a minute."

As soon as I stopped kicking and punching and, yes, scratching him, he released his crushing hold. I stumbled forward a few steps before regaining my balance. Breathing hard, I grabbed my knees and tried to sort out what had just happened. Was it possible I'd overreacted? He hadn't actually attacked me. He'd only touched my arm. I was the one who'd —

"Let — let me get this straight," I huffed, still unable to fully catch my breath. "You're not trying to kill me?"

He didn't seem to be listening. With his shoulders hunched forward, he clamped his straight white teeth tightly together. Hopping on one foot, he cursed his existence and mine. I winced. His bloodshot, unfocused eyes were watering like a faucet because of me. He was blinking wildly, clearly suffering because I'd reacted too quickly and had thoroughly doused him with the potent, red-hot pepper oil.

Despite his arsenal, he didn't look that much like a killer, not really. His muscular yet trim physique was much more reminiscent of a heroic Roman warrior. His square jaw spoke of strength. His brows, though creased with intense pain, suggested a man of compassion and, I hoped, forgiveness. Because he wasn't a killer. His distinctive black uniform identified him as a member of the Counter Assault Team, which was no ordinary branch of the Secret Service, but its most elite military arm.

"You — you're Secret Service?" I asked, suddenly hoping I was hallucinating. Assaulting a Secret Service agent was most likely a felony.

"Yes," he hissed through gritted teeth.

Even if it wasn't a felony, I was sure blinding a Secret Service agent wasn't something Gordon or Ambrose Jones, the White House's chief usher, would likely forgive. I rushed to my backpack and quickly found my environmentally friendly, BPA-free water bottle. Moving as fast as possible, I unscrewed the lid and tossed the water into his face.

He gave a startled yelp when the icy water hit him.

"Give me that." He grabbed the water

bottle and dumped the remaining water on his mottled forehead and brow. The cold water caused him to shiver like the leaves on the saucer magnolia trees above us. Then he scrubbed his eyes with his coat sleeve. He still looked miserable. The skin around his eyes was puffy and turning an angry shade of red, but he didn't seem to be blinking as furiously anymore.

"Thanks." He dropped the water bottle and grabbed my shoulders. He squinted at me, his eyes unfocused. "Are you okay?" he demanded, his voice unnaturally calm considering the situation.

I nodded.

"Answer me. Are you okay?" he repeated. Apparently, he couldn't yet see well enough to make out my gesture. "Do I need to call EMS?"

"No," I croaked, and quickly cleared my throat, which burned as if I'd been shouting at the top of my lungs for hours.

"Good." He released me and started to pace. Limp, step, limp, step. Turn. Limp, step, limp, step. He stomped with that awkward gait through the middle of my flowerbed. The helpless tulips and fragrant grape hyacinths were no match for his heavy boots.

I winced both for my plants and for him.

He wouldn't be limping if I hadn't kicked him. He wouldn't be growling with every step if I hadn't blinded him with my pepper spray. He stumbled a couple of times, proving his eyesight wasn't even close to being back to normal. But I had enough experience with men's egos to know to keep my mouth shut. An apology right now would not be appreciated.

He stopped at the edge of the flowerbed. "Before I radio for backup . . ." he began, before turning his gaze heavenward. Muttering a curse to the heavy clouds above, he dredged his fingers through his wavy black hair. "There's no way around it. I'm going to have to file a report about this . . . this . . ." he grumbled more to himself than to me.

In my three short months at the White House, I'd seen the Counter Assault Team, or CAT, as they liked to call themselves, only a few times. They were one of the least visible segments of the Secret Service. They traveled everywhere with the President like the Secret Service agents who dressed in neatly pressed suits. But unlike their suited counterparts, CAT agents didn't make regular security sweeps of the President's Park.

"And look at this." He held up a loose

wire that had been attached to his earpiece. "You've broken my radio."

I'd always found the regular Secret Service agents easy to work with. They always had a smile and a polite manner. Not one of them had ever growled at me.

CAT agents, on the other hand, only ventured outside their tight protection circle when they were taking part in a training exercise or responding to a specific threat against the First Family. They were a very serious group.

I doubted I would fare well in his report. While mentally drafting my résumé, I started to move away from him to gather my backpack and gardening tools. He snagged hold of my arm. "Let's start with you giving me some basic information, like your name."

"Casey — Casey Calhoun." My heart was really pounding now. I wished he'd just shoot me and put me out of my misery. His grip tightened on my arm. "I'm Gordon Sims's new assistant." Everyone knew Gordon. He was a fixture, a one-man institution. But the agent's pained expression remained unchanged, which only made me more nervous. Was it possible? Did he not know Gordon? "I — I'm a gardener."

My slightly eccentric but altogether lovable aunts, Willow and Alba, and Grand-mother Faye back in Charleston, South Carolina, had instilled in me a love of gardening as well as an absurd fondness for ice cream desserts. But I suspected he didn't care to hear about any of that.

I decided to take the initiative. "I'm kind of in a hurry. So if it's okay with you, I'd like to clear up this misunderstanding as quickly as possible. I have a meeting sched-uled with the First Lady this morning to present my plans on how to transform the White House gardens into the White House *organic* gardens."

"We'll see about that." His red-rimmed gaze traveled up and down my mud-caked legs. I had a sinking feeling he was plotting to make my life at the White House a living hell. I bit the inside of my cheek. He couldn't really get me fired, could he?

He narrowed his bloodshot eyes and leaned toward me. "Now tell me, Ms. Cal-houn, why did you attack me?"

CHAPTER TWO

I chewed my bottom lip and wished I'd stayed in my little cubicle, letting the tick, tick, tick of the institutional clock that hung on the concrete block wall chip away at my sanity. The ticking was in my head now, counting down the minutes before my meeting with the First Lady was scheduled to start.

"Well, I'm waiting," the unhappy agent said.

"Really, I didn't attack anyone," I drawled, my voice dipping a little deeper into my Southern heritage than normal.

His dark brows rose with incredulity.

Undeterred, I flashed him my winsome, slightly crooked smile I'd tempered with a healthy dose of humility. "You see, I was protecting myself from whoever hit *me.* I'm sorry for it, but I'm afraid it was you who got in my way, Agent . . . Agent . . ."

"Special Agent Turner," he supplied, his

brows furrowing. "*I* got in your way?"

"Yes." I nodded, glad to have cleared that up. "We can talk more about it later. Right now I have to prepare for my meeting with the First Lady." This wasn't a presentation I could easily postpone. The White House Grounds Committee, a collection of nationally renowned nurserymen and horticultural professors, would also be present to provide their input. I needed to make a good impression. Showing up caked in mud wouldn't be the best place to start. "I'll need time to clean myself up." There would be no saving my mud-stained pantyhose. And my new pencil skirt had suffered several mud splatters as well. Perhaps I could —

"Nice try, Ms. Calhoun. But you can't just brush what happened under the rug. This is a serious —"

"I'd rather plant it in a garden. It's good natural fertilizer, you know."

He didn't laugh.

"I'm going to have to report what happened to you and what you did to me. Come along." He scooped up my backpack from the ground and headed toward the White House.

Stunned, I just stood there watching Turner's determined stride, my backpack swinging in his hand. He wasn't even going to

33

discuss what we should do? He wasn't going to let me explain why it was imperative that I make it to my meeting on time?

Filing a report and filling out reams of paperwork could wait. Certainly he understood that. Besides, paperwork had never been my strength. I liked to think of myself as a woman of action, a woman who rolled up her sleeves and got the job, any job, done — as long as that job didn't include paperwork.

Assistant Usher Wilson Fisher, with his slicked-back hair and hawk-like nose, was constantly following me around, waving sheaves of forms that I needed to fill out for this or that. I cringed as I pictured the mountain of paperwork Mr. Fisher would find for me from his oversized filing cabinet dedicated strictly to his official forms.

"Perhaps we can work something out," I called to Special Agent Turner. He kept walking. I gathered up the gardening gloves, bottle of pepper spray, and water bottle from the muddy ground before trotting after him. "Give me an hour — two at the most — with the First Lady. I promise you, this is a very important meeting. Members of the Grounds Committee have flown in from all around the country to listen to my report."

He stopped in the middle of the red brick path and glanced at his watch. "What time is your meeting?"

"Nine thirty."

"It's seven twenty-three," he reported with the kind of precision that, if Mr. Fisher had been listening, would have had him puffing up with pleasure. "That gives me two hours."

"Don't forget my clothes. I can't go into the meeting looking like this," I said as I caught up with him. I flapped my dirty garden gloves, hoping to emphasize my point. "I'll need to get cleaned up, not to mention the time it'll take to set up my presentation boards. I figure that should take at least an hour."

Apparently the sorry state of my clothes was of no concern to him. He turned away, seemingly much more interested in the protesters gathering ahead of President Bradley's banking summit. The crowd had more than doubled in size since I'd passed them earlier. They looked like a harmless bunch, most of them dressed in a ridiculous hodgepodge of old ripped and worn clothes and burlap sacks. And yet Turner stared at them as if he were watching a hive of assassins.

"Someone attacked you, Ms. Calhoun.

35

And it happened on government property. That is something the Secret Service takes very seriously. For all I know, what happened to you might be connected to . . ."

I waited for him to finish.

He didn't.

"Connected to what, exactly?" I wanted to know. I'd always felt extraordinarily safe at the White House. Being surrounded by a state-of-the-art security system and teams of highly trained agents, it was easy to forget that there were individuals and groups out there that wanted to harm the President, disrupt the governmental process, or simply make the six o'clock news.

Turner rubbed his sore eyes. "Nothing specific. We just need to be careful."

Had he answered too quickly? "Is there something going on that I need to be worried about?"

He started toward the White House again. "Every member of the staff is a link in the chain of security. Every one of us must play our part in assuring the President's safety. So you have to ask yourself, Ms. Calhoun, what did you do to make yourself a weak link in that chain this morning? And did you cause the chain to be broken?"

"I don't think I —"

He turned toward me. "These are vital

things we have to assess. If there has been a breach in security, wouldn't you want us to know about it right away?"

"Yes, but —"

"Jack! There you are!" Special Agent Steve Sallis called as he lumbered across the grassy lawn. He ducked under a low-hanging branch of a nearby elm to get to us. Special Agent Janie Partners was on Pennsylvania Avenue, speaking with one of the protesters. I knew both Steve and Janie. They were members of the Secret Service's Presidential Protection Detail, or PPD. They'd often stop and chat with the gardening staff whenever they had a free moment. Steve was a handsome man with blond hair and an easy smile. He was wearing his regular nondescript black suit. And Janie, who always tried to be a little different, was sporting black hair today and wearing a black pantsuit with a red, white, and blue silk scarf. "What brings you outside the iron fence? Thatch was beginning to wonder if you'd gone AWOL." Steve's tone was light, joking, and very different from Turner's take-no-prisoners manner.

But then Steve got close enough to see my handiwork imprinted on Jack Turner's face. His grin dropped. His hand went instinctively toward the holster inside his suit coat. "What's happened?"

"There was a . . . um . . ." Turner kicked a red brick paver with his combat boot. "An incident."

"A what?" Janie asked as she jogged up behind Steve.

"Incident. An incident," Turner repeated, the mottled red skin on his face darkened. "It's nothing."

Nothing? Getting conked on the head didn't feel like nothing to me. I coughed my disagreement, which earned an even deeper scowl from the all-too-serious Special Agent Jack Turner.

"I mean, I have it under control," he clarified. "I would have reported in, but my radio's on the fritz."

That's when Steve noticed me. "Good God, Casey, what happened to your throat?" He caught my chin and tilted my head back slightly so he could get a better look.

"My throat?" Sure, it hurt to talk. But it was my head that was throbbing. "Someone hit me . . . I think."

"Well, it looks as if someone tried to choke you as well."

"That's going to leave quite a nasty bruise," Janie added.

"Jack, you didn't —" Steve positioned himself in between Special Agent Turner and myself as if he believed I suddenly needed protection.

Turner simply stood there looking as if he'd wished he *had* strangled me.

"Someone tried to mug me, I think. It's kind of hazy right now." I rubbed my sore head. "But he didn't get anything. At least I don't think so."

"Ms. Calhoun, we were headed inside, were we not?" Turner tapped his watch's crystal. "You had mentioned something about being in a hurry."

"Yes, of course."

After assuring Steve and Janie that I was okay, I followed Turner back toward the White House. I made it only a few steps before I noticed one of the elm trees just off the path. It was a younger elm. Its lower branches would be trimmed away as it grew taller. But until then, its limbs arched up like candles in a candelabrum. When an older tree died or became diseased in the park, it was replaced with a younger specimen like this one.

The trees in Lafayette Square, representing over two hundred different species, were all lovingly tended and kept well groomed. That was probably why the rough condition of this particular tree jumped out at me. Several of the lower branches on its left side had been broken. Some of the snapped twigs were lying on the ground. Others hung limply from its trunk, attached only by a few wood fibers and narrow strips of bark.

"I'll catch up," I told Turner and stepped around a park bench and over the fallen branches to inspect the damage. It must have been caused by last night's storm, I told myself. But the winds from the storm had been blowing consistently from the north.

Turner didn't go on ahead without me, not that I really expected he would. But I was surprised when he followed me under the tree.

"What's wrong?" he asked.

"Probably nothing. The storm, perhaps. I'll send my crew out to take care of the mess and make sure they clean up these breaks where the branches have been torn off so the trunk won't rot."

"Okay. Shall we go?"

I told myself to leave it, to walk away. I didn't have time to figure out why a couple of broken branches were bothering me. I still had to answer Turner's questions, assure him that I hadn't endangered the President, and then get to my meeting on time.

40

And yet . . .

If a fierce northerly wind had snapped off the branches, the jagged stubs left on the tree's young trunk would have ripped in the opposite direction. And the branches on the ground would have fallen on the south side of the tree, not the north.

It almost looked as if someone had backed his way through the lower branches, breaking them off as he went. Where the grass began just a foot or so away, I spotted a short trail that dug up the thick sod in some places as if a sizable object had been dragged under the elm's canopy and through the lawn beyond.

Without even thinking about it, I followed the trail. My curiosity simply refused to let this go. Turner followed. Steve and Janie had joined us again. All three of them looked about as confused as I felt.

"Did you happen to read this morning's security briefing?" Janie asked Turner.

He nodded. "That's why I decided to do a quick sweep of the public parks as well as the outside perimeter."

"They sent us to interview the anarchists over there." Steve hooked his thumb over toward the protesters.

"They're an angry bunch," Janie said.

"But do you think they're involved?" Turner asked.

"Involved in what?" I asked over my shoulder.

None of the agents seemed willing to give me an answer.

"It looks as if the rain's finally stopped," Janie said after an awkward silence.

The trail ended near a public trash can. Beside it, I found a dark blue leather ballerina flat with a large buckle over the toes — a sensible but expensive shoe — lying in the wet grass. I'd tried on several similar pairs when shopping with Alyssa over the weekend. I'd liked the style and its comfort. But Alyssa had insisted I buy the black designer pumps with the half-inch heel, saying style trumped comfort.

I picked up the ballet flat and turned it over in my hand. It was my size. Why would someone leave one shoe behind? And why was the shoe at the end of this odd trail?

The back of my neck prickled. It felt as if a memory was trying to find a path through my pulsing headache. "There's something wrong here," I said aloud.

"What do you mean?" Turner asked.

"Another plant out of place?" Janie suggested with an indulgent smile.

"No. This shoe." I held it up.

"Garbage," Steve said, dismissing it. "It's

amazing what people leave behind. I'll never figure it out."

I had to agree with him. I'd worked as head gardener for two public gardens before taking this position, and I'd encountered all sorts of discarded items, which commonly included puppies, dirty diapers, baseball caps, and shoes. So why did this shoe in particular make me feel uneasy? Perhaps it was because my brain had recently been jostled about. Or perhaps being attacked had scared me more than I was willing to admit. My nerves had been fried to the point where I was seeing danger everywhere and in everything, including broken limbs and discarded shoes.

"I don't have time for this," I said, shaking my head with dismay. I took the shoe to the nearby trash can. I was about to toss it into the metal bucket when I saw it . . . *her.*

A woman.

The ballet flat slipped from my suddenly numb fingers and splashed as it landed in a puddle. I stood there too shocked to move, too frightened to make a sound. All I could do was stand there and stare into the round trash can and at the woman who'd been stuffed inside it. Her knees were pulled to her chest. Her head bowed as if she were meditating. Someone had wedged a brightly flowered tote bag into the trash can with her.

She was dressed in a hauntingly similar dark gray suit and matching skirt. Her hair, like mine, was long and light brown. She'd styled it in a tight bun at the nape of her neck, a style I'd long admired but had never been able to perfect.

I barely noticed when Turner approached from the side. With his hands clasped behind him, he leaned over the trash can. "Radio this in, Steve. We'll need the D.C. Police out here."

I appreciated his calm manner. I clung to it, hoping a measure of his steadiness would rub off on me, because my entire body was beginning to tremble. I feared if someone were to touch me right then, I would shatter into a million pieces.

Turner reached into the trash can and carefully tilted the woman's head back so he could feel for a pulse. I prayed he'd find one.

But I knew in my heart we were too late. The woman's glassy eyes glared up at me. Her deep red lipstick was smeared across her porcelain cheek. Her mouth gaped slightly as if still fighting for one last breath. A fight she'd been doomed to lose. An angry red welt ringed her neck.

I touched my own throat as Turner slowly shook his head. "It's a homicide," he said. "She's been strangled."

Turner, Steve, and Janie's gazes all turned to me . . . and my bruised throat.

CHAPTER THREE

With the three Secret Service agents watching me so gravely, my hand froze on the welt I could feel rising a few inches above my collarbone. I took a shaky breath as a dull buzzing sound filled my ears.

The stormy sky suddenly turned several shades grayer and much darker than it had looked just a few seconds earlier. I got a terrible sinking feeling that things were about to get worse.

Wait a blooming minute . . . I *was* sinking! That, or the ground had decided to surge up to smack me in the head.

Special Agent Turner grabbed my shoulders and gave a sharp tug, rescuing me from planting my face in the muddy ground. I was grateful. Ending up facedown in the mud even once in a day was one too many times in my estimation.

He set me back on my wobbly legs with about the same care the grounds crew takes when hauling sacks of topsoil off a wood pallet. Despite that, I started to thank him, but he ignored me.

"I'm going to get our gardener inside while she's still able to walk," he told Janie and Steve, "and before the press descends in full force." Turner gave a nod in the direction of the West Wing and the crowd of White House reporters pouring out the side door.

"Good idea, Jack," Janie said. "It's going to turn into a circus over here." She and Steve began organizing the agents who'd rushed over to help, their training evident as the group secured the crime scene and a large surrounding area long before any of the reporters would be able to get anywhere close.

"As for you" — Turner kept one hand on my shoulder as he guided me toward the White House — "if anyone wants to talk to you, you will say 'no comment' or nothing at all. Understood?"

The cool air and brisk walk helped to get some blood back into my dizzy head. My mind started whirling again. And with all that thinking going on up there, my gratitude toward Turner changed into aggravation. He had no right to treat me as if I were a certifiable flake.

"Give me a little credit," I told him. "This isn't my first day working for the White House."

He stabbed me with a sharp glance.

"Okay," I said, wincing at how red and puffy his eyes still looked and how much they kept watering from the lingering effects of the pepper spray. "I understand your point. I won't talk to anyone on our way back to the White House."

"Not even if you happen to bump into your mother, you say nothing. Do you understand?"

If only I could bump into Mom.

You were nearly given the opportunity, child, the voice in my head reminded me, sporting Aunt Willow's rich Southern drawl unique to residents of Charleston's posh South of Broad neighborhood.

"Well?" Turner asked.

I pressed my lips tightly together and nodded.

"What happened here? What's going on?" A woman dressed in an old shiny pale blue housecoat speckled with tiny pink, red, and white roses jogged up to us. A cardboard placard dangled from a silk cord around her neck with neatly handwritten letters that read, SEND THE BANKING CEOS TO JAIL. She was clearly one of the banking summit protesters.

Beneath the hideous housecoat was a striking woman with high cheekbones and beautifully arching eyebrows. Her light brown wavy easy-care hair brushed her slender shoulders. She looked like the kind of professional do-it-all woman who could take home the bacon, fry it up in a pan, and still find time to make her man happy. Her arching eyebrows rose a bit higher as she stared at my bruised and bloodied head. She stepped directly in front of us on the sidewalk.

"Did you beat her up?" she demanded of Turner with an agitated wave in my direction. "We have a permit to be protesting here today. You have no right to —"

"She's not part of your group," Turner said, trying but failing to skirt around her. He sighed deeply. "Please, ma'am, step out of the way."

Instead of moving, she dug around in her housecoat's large, square pocket and produced a business card that she handed to me. "I do pro bono work and have contacts with many lawyers in the D.C. area," she said softly. "Give me a call if you need anything."

"Um . . . thank you." Did she think I looked homeless? I glanced down at my clothes. The yellow rain slicker and skirt were caked in mud. My pantyhose were ripped. And my brown leather loafers didn't match anything I had on. This definitely wasn't my finest hour.

Her plain cream-colored business card read, JOANNA LOVELL, ATTORNEY-AT-LAW. On the line below her name was a phone number. No address or five- to ten-name law firm listed.

"Well?" Turner looked at me expectantly. I glanced at the card again. Did I need a lawyer? I had attacked a Secret Service agent. But it'd been a misunderstanding.

"Don't let him intimidate you," Joanna warned me. "You don't have to say anything without a lawyer present."

"Thank you. I'm fine," I assured her, but dropped her card in my pocket just in case. "And we're in a hurry."

Turner, tightening his grip on my arm, guided me around Joanna.

"Call me," she said in a crisp, professional tone that had me automatically nodding that I would call. "I can help you."

Turner stopped and turned back to her. His gaze hardened until he looked every inch the dangerous warrior. "Since you're so anxious to be helpful, I'm sure you won't mind answering the police's questions." He nodded to a pair of rapidly approaching United States Park policeman dressed in yellow and black.

Joanna held up her hands and took a step back, the hem of her housecoat flapping. "I won't let you bully me. You won't get rid of us that easily. As I said, I filled out the proper paperwork. We have the permits to hold this protest."

"Good," he said, and let the Park Police take over. Talking in low and unthreatening tones, one of the police officers asked Joanna what time she'd arrived at the park. Joanna crossed her arms over her slender chest but appeared to be willing to co-operate.

Part of me wanted to stay behind and question Joanna myself. Perhaps she could help explain what had happened to me and that poor woman in the trash can, and why.

Joanna's protesters had been standing around sipping their coffee on the opposite side of the park to where the attack had taken place. I doubted any of them had seen anything. Their attentions had been focused on the White House, not the seven acres of Lafayette Square behind them.

"Do you think one of them saw the murderer?" I asked Turner.

His grip on my arm tensed. "If they know

something, we'll find out. Let's go."

He picked up our already quick pace and hurried through the emerging press pool. We managed to bypass the reporters with only a few questions shouted in our direction. The press appeared much more interested in investigating why a crowd of Secret Service agents had gathered on the Lafayette Square lawn than in us. I didn't get the chance to utter "no comment" even once.

Not that I'd wanted the press corps to hound me, but I felt a certain need to show Turner I wasn't some half-crazed-pepper-spray-happy plant nut. I knew how to conduct myself in a professional manner without anyone's coaching.

"I don't usually go around fainting," I explained. "I'm not some clichéd Southern belle who wilts at the first sign of trouble. I can't remember the last time I'd even come close to fainting. And you're the first person I've ever doused with my pepper spray."

"Humph," Turner grunted.

A long line of White House employees had formed at the northwest gate. It didn't seem to be moving.

"What's going on? Why the line?" I whispered to Turner.

"Increased security. Slows things down to

a crawl. It's a standard precaution."

My heart dropped. I didn't have time to wait it out at the end of this line, not if I still had any hope of making it to my meeting with the First Lady.

I wasn't the only unlucky gardener stuck in the queue. Lorenzo Parisi, Gordon's other assistant, was standing close to the front of the line. He anxiously checked his watch, pulled a folded paper napkin from his pocket, and then checked his watch again.

While I'd known Lorenzo for three months now, I still hadn't figured him out. He dressed as if he belonged on the cover of *GQ* magazine. With his tanned, well-defined Mediterranean features, he had the looks to pull it off.

Today, probably because he'd planned on sitting in on the meeting, he wore a dark gray suit with razor-sharp creases, a crisply pressed white shirt, and a dark purple silk tie. I'd never known a gardener to be so fashion conscious. I mean, we spent our lives digging in the ground. Just look at how I'd completely ruined my new outfit after just a few minutes pulling weeds.

Lorenzo, on the other hand, could spend hours outside and not even have a smudge of dirt on him.

"Casey?" Lorenzo called as Turner marched me to the front of the stalled line. He dabbed the cuff of his jacket with his paper napkin. Could that be a stain? On Lorenzo's clothes? How odd. "What's going on?"

Turner tightened his grip on my arm as if he thought I'd rush over and run my mouth unfettered. I snorted. Like I needed to be reminded to keep quiet.

"I'll tell you later," I called to Lorenzo.

"What happened to 'no comment'?" Turner asked.

"He's a gardener, not a reporter."

"Ah. I stand corrected."

Fredrick stood outside the guardhouse with his hands on his hips, his cheeks nearly as red as his hair. Three additional guards had joined him.

"Where's your security pass?" Turner asked as we bypassed the line and headed straight toward Fredrick at the gate. "I've noticed most of the gardening staff wear them on lanyards around their necks."

"I do, too." I reached for mine. "We're in and out of the gates so often, it's more convenient. I keep it tucked into my shirt so it won't get in the way."

Where was it? I dug around in my blouse,

but I couldn't feel the plastic lanyard any-where.

"It's gone, isn't it?" Turner asked.

"It must have dropped off somewhere. We'll have to go back."

His grip on my arm remained firm. "It'd be a waste of time."

"What am I going to do? I can't —"

"Don't worry. I already suspected it was gone." Turner passed through the gate Fredrick had opened.

"Thatch is waiting for you," Fredrick told Turner, who nodded.

"Thatch? Who is Thatch?" I asked, but Turner hurried me past the guard hut and toward the West Wing before Fredrick could answer.

"Who's Thatch?" I asked Turner, but didn't get an answer.

"Good God, Jack, what happened to you?" demanded a burly Secret Service CAT agent with a shaved head who'd been waiting for us at the West Wing entrance. The agent swept open the door and followed us through the corridor and into the lobby.

"Nothing," Turner grumbled and tried to usher me toward the passageway to the left. But his colleague, who looked as if he'd played fullback in college, blocked him.

"No, something happened out there. You were attacked?"

"It's nothing."

Since we were both running short on time — Turner had a killer to track down and I had a meeting with the First Lady to get to — I decided to hurry this conversation along.

"I . . . er . . . might have shot him with pepper spray. Purely by accident, you understand. I thought *he* was attacking *me*. Now if you don't mind —" I tried to move him out of the way.

"Let me get this straight." The agent refused to budge. "You let her —" He bit his quivering lower lip, clearly struggling to hold back a laugh. "You let this itty-bitty thing get the jump on you? She's half your size, Jack. Just wait until the rest of the team hears about this."

"Hey, now!" I protested. I might not be built like a fullback, but I was by no means itty or bitty. I was taller than most women I knew. And I could take care of myself, thank you very much. And I would have told the agent just that if I hadn't caught sight of the murderous glare Turner had pinned on me.

"Right," I said. "We're in a hurry."

"Thatch is waiting for you in the main office." The agent stepped out of our way.

Turner grabbed my arm again and ushered me through a doorway to the left of the lobby. A deep chuckle followed us as we rushed down a narrow hallway.

I'd been in the West Wing only twice before. The first time was during the whirlwind tour Ambrose Jones, the White House chief usher, had given me on my first day.

The second time occurred on one of the rare days Gordon had called in sick. A potted pomegranate bush in the Chief of Staff's office had started dropping its leaves. I'd taken the call to go have a look.

The modest size of the West Wing struck me the same way it had on those two other occasions. Such big decisions were made on a daily basis in this intimate space. The history that had been made in these corridors was staggering, captured in photos decorating the walls we were passing. My step slowed.

"We don't have time for sightseeing." Turner rushed me down a rather utilitarian and narrow set of stairs leading to the basement.

"Look." He stopped at the bottom of the stairs and turned toward me. "Just answer the questions asked of you. Let me explain what happened with the pepper spray. We don't need to get distracted by irrelevant details. I need you to stay focused. A murder was committed."

"I know. I was there . . . apparently."

"Which makes you an important asset."

He wasn't kidding about that. If I'd suffered from the sin of pride, which I didn't, my head would have swelled from here to Charleston at the sight of the number of high-level staff members waiting for me in the Secret Service offices.

The long, windowless room was filled with agents working from several dozen sleek metal desks set up in three tight rows that reminded me of NASA's mission control. Large computer monitors flickered as pictures and data sped across the screens. The room had buzzed with activity until I stepped across the threshold. The activity ceased as the agents stopped work to turn and watch me.

Near the door stood Gordon, Ambrose, and Dr. Stan, the White House staff M.D. They were deep in conversation with a man I didn't recognize. He had a full head of silver hair and an air of unquestioned authority. Though dressed in a dark suit, the man looked as if he'd be more comfortable in military fatigues and lugging an assault rifle like Turner still had slung over his shoulder. Noticing our entrance, he picked up a thick folder from a nearby desk with my name printed on the tab.

"Mike Thatch, Special Agent in Charge of CAT," he said in greeting. "Please come with me to the conference room, Ms. Calhoun."

Before I could follow, Gordon pushed Thatch out of the way and grabbed my shoulders.

"When I heard that someone had attacked you and that there'd been a murder, I refused to believe it. Across the street from the White House? This is impossible! I should have never allowed you to go out there alone. It was too dark, too stormy. This is my fault that you're hurt. But I never imagined it would be dangerous. Look at you." He shook me in agitation. "You're bleeding."

"I — I'm okay." I had to pry his sweet but strong grip from my shoulders. My head simply couldn't take any more rattling about without great risk of seeing my breakfast again . . . all over Gordon's work boots. "Are those new? When did you get them?"

"These things?" Gordon frowned at the dark leather boots on his feet. "Last weekend. Thought today would be a good day to try them out."

Although he planned on attending the

presentation I'd prepared, not even an important meeting with the First Lady could get Gordon into a tie. But apparently he'd bought new boots for the occasion.

"I don't understand what you were doing out there at this time of morning, Casey," Ambrose said. "And all by yourself." His voice sounded tighter than usual. He looked me over from head to toe and rolled his eyes at my muddy self.

Ambrose's style hailed from an earlier, more formal era. He prided himself on running an efficient White House and had stressed to each and every employee working under him that he would not tolerate any behavior that disrupted the steady flow of day-to-day operations.

But instead of scolding me for working in the Lafayette Square flowerbeds alone and at such an early hour, as I'd expected, he pressed one of his starched, hand-embroidered handkerchiefs into my hand and raised it to my throbbing temple.

Tears sprang to my eyes. I'd never expected such kindness from him.

"Thanks," I said.

"You were about to drip blood on the carpet," he pointed out. The corner of his mouth twitched, a nervous tic I'd heard he developed whenever he was under considerable stress.

"Of course, the carpet. What had I been thinking?" I pressed the handkerchief firmly to my temple, wincing at the tender lump forming there.

"Here, let me have a look." Dr. Stan had come prepared with a first-aid kit complete with antiseptic wipes and bandages of all shapes and sizes. With a deft touch, he cleaned the mud from my face and wound and gently probed the bruised areas on my head and neck.

"I'm concerned about the blow she took to the head. She'd started to black out at the crime scene," Turner reported as Dr. Stan stuck a large bandage to the side of my face. "I've kept her on her feet and moving."

Really? Turner had insisted on that quick march to keep me from passing out? Had I mistaken concern for annoyance? Perhaps he didn't believe I was a flake after all.

I tried to turn and see if I could detect a change in him, a softening in his attitude toward me. But Dr. Stan grabbed my chin and shined a penlight in my eyes. He asked me to look up and down, left and right. When I finally had a chance to look at Jack Turner, the fearless and, I hoped, *forgiving* member of the elite Counter Attack Team, he was gone.

I'd spent many seasons in the garden. My time there had taught me the difficult art of patience, a trait that didn't come naturally. Plants grow and develop at their own rate with absolutely no regard to anyone's schedule. Some of my favorite cultivars can take years to mature to a point where they begin to produce fruits or flowers.

As I sat in the conference room, describing the attack, the loss of my security badge, and what I'd remembered seeing — which unfortunately was turning out to be very little — I wondered whether Special Agent in Charge Mike Thatch had been a slow-growing oak in a past life. Every few minutes he'd interrupt my narrative to ask seemingly irrelevant questions that mainly focused on my impressions of the banking protestors gathered near the northwest gate. He certainly had no regard for *my* schedule.

Dr. Stan had returned to his duties after his brief examination, making me promise I'd report to the medical center for a follow-up as soon as Thatch had finished questioning me. Ambrose had left with him.

Gordon had remained, his nerves badly shaken. Worry and stress had deepened the lines on his pale, stricken face. He looked worse than I felt, and that was saying something. When Mike Thatch had directed me to the conference room, he'd stopped Gordon from following us inside.

"I'll wait for you out here," Gordon had promised. "I still can't believe someone tried to hurt you. This has never happened."

With one eye on the round metal clock above the conference room door, I watched as my meeting with the First Lady grew nearer and nearer.

At eight thirty-eight, a little less than an hour before the Grounds Committee meeting was scheduled to start, Jack Turner slipped into the room.

The assault rifle and sidearm were gone. His eyes weren't quite as puffy. And his short hair looked damp, as if he'd showered. Without saying a word, he casually reached across the conference table and picked up a file folder with my name on the tab. He then dropped into a chair pushed up against the far wall. After listening for a few minutes, he started to flip through the contents of the folder.

"You'd mentioned you saw a black-and-white leather shoe with a lightning bolt design on the side?" Thatch asked me.

"Yes." The shoe had an old-fashioned look, like it belonged in a vintage clothing store. The toe was wide and rounded and the soles beefy. On the black leather, the cobbler had used white stitching. And on the white leather, black stitching had been used.

"And the man who attacked you, he was wearing this shoe?"

I rubbed my temples as if trying to conjure a genie. "I think so. Maybe." If I'd seen them on my attacker's feet, why only remember one shoe and not a pair? "I don't know. But I can tell you that the shoe had crushed three pink ruffled tulips."

Thatch didn't jot that vital piece of information in his notebook. But he'd written pages about the banking protesters who, for all I knew, hadn't molested a single tree or plant in Lafayette Square . . . much less have killed anyone.

"Excuse me for a minute." Thatch rose from the conference table and carried his notebook with him into the adjoining room. With a close eye on the clock, I drummed my fingers on the table.

Gordon stepped through the door Thatch had left open. "Casey, you look pale," he said. "You're not going to pass out, are you?" he asked, which caused Turner to look up from his reading.

"I feel fine," I lied.

"Perhaps I should call Dr. Stan and ask him to come back and take another look at you." Gordon came into the conference room and crouched down beside me to stare at the large bandage on my head. "I'm worried about you. I think you should go to the hospital."

And miss the meeting with the First Lady? I didn't think so. "Really, I'm fine. Give me a shovel and I'll head over to the White House greenhouses to turn the compost pile by myself."

Turner raised a brow at that and then returned to reading whatever had so captured his interest in the file with my name on it.

"Your health must come first, Casey," Gordon said softly.

Touched, I put my hand on his. "I'm shaken, not broken. But I am worried about making it to the First Lady's meeting."

Gordon gave my shoulder a gentle squeeze as he rose. "There's nothing for you to worry about. We can postpone the presentation, reschedule it for when you're feeling better."

"No, don't. Please, don't. I'm fine."

Gordon nodded, but creased his brows. "Okay. I need to get to the First Lady's office anyhow to set up for the meeting. I'll explain why you'll be running late. It won't be a problem, Casey. The Grounds Committee will understand. I'll make sure they do."

"Thank you, Gordon. That'll make me feel better."

As Gordon left, Thatch hurried back into the room. He reminded me of the movie version of General Patton prepared to charge headlong into battle.

"Let me summarize what we've got here." He flipped back a few pages in his notebook as he sat down. "You remember seeing a man in a suit wearing a baseball cap. But you don't think he was with the protestors. Is that correct?"

"He didn't seem to be heading toward them. And he wasn't dressed in old clothes like they were. I got the impression that he was hurrying to his office or something."

Thatch nodded. "And you said he was carrying a silver briefcase. He may or may not have been the man who attacked you."

"What about the security cameras we've got out there?" Turner glanced up from the folder in his lap to ask.

Thatch shook his head. "That's what I was checking just now. I'd hoped they'd be able to give us a good picture of our man. But the best we have is a partial image of a

66

shadowy figure who seemed very aware of the cameras and was doing his best to avoid them."

"Then not a mugging gone wrong," Turner said.

"No," Thatch agreed.

"What aren't you telling us?" I asked.

Thatch frowned at his notebook longer than I thought necessary before answering. "The murder might be part of a bigger plot against the President."

"What plot?" I hadn't heard anything about that.

"We don't have a clear picture of that. I assure you that if we did, the responsible parties would have been rounded up long before now."

"If this is something against the President, why kill that woman I found?"

Thatch shook his head. "He might have been after something she was carrying."

"Then why did he attack me?" I certainly wasn't carrying anything valuable or important with me.

"That's what we need to find out," Thatch said.

Turner had told me earlier that, as a White House employee, I was a link in the chain of security that protected the President. He'd wondered if the attack had caused a security breach.

"But it could have been just a mugging gone wrong, right?" I asked, grasping for an easy explanation. "I mean, maybe he wanted money?"

"A mugger wouldn't have worried about the security cameras like this guy did. And he wouldn't have left you with your backpack," Thatch said.

"Or stuffed our victim's purse in the trash can with her," Turner added.

My head buzzed and the room got fuzzy as I pictured the woman's lifeless face and how her flowered tote bag had been callously tucked against her chest. I gripped the edge of the table as it swayed a bit. "Have you identified her? Was she a White House employee?" I asked, determined not to embarrass myself and faint in front of Turner, who seemed to be watching me too closely.

"We don't think so." Thatch tapped his pen against his notebook. "But she might have had White House clearance. We'll know more as soon as we get a positive ID."

What if the murderer couldn't find what he'd wanted to steal from that poor woman? What if he'd attacked me with the hopes he'd get his hands on what he couldn't get from her? I reached for my backpack and started to riffle through it, looking to see if anything was missing, though I still couldn't imagine why anyone would think I had something worth stealing.

"What did he use to choke you?" Turner wondered aloud. "If he'd used piano wire or something like that, your neck would have been sliced open."

I pressed my hand to my throat. "What a gruesome thought."

"It's the truth." Turner got up and crossed the room to me. "It's the lanyard she wore around her neck that held her security badge."

"What about it?" Thatch asked.

"That's what he used to choke her. It was the closest thing on hand."

"But he didn't have to take her security card," Thatch pointed out.

"True," Turner agreed, but frowned. "I don't think our killer is a professional, and I don't think he set out to steal a White House security card."

"That may be true, but we have to prepare for the worst. We have to operate under the assumption that there's been a security breach."

"But no one can use my badge to get into the White House, right?" I asked.

"No. We've already canceled all of your

security credentials and have issued you a temporary card. It should be ready by now," Thatch said and hurried out of the room again.

When he returned, he handed me a bright red temporary security pass and turned me loose.

It was too late to worry about trying to do anything with my ruined outfit. But perhaps if I ran back to my office, I could grab my presentation boards and only be a few minutes late to the meeting. Like a bird set free from a cage, I dashed out the door and up the stairs.

I made it as far as the glass double doors leading to the West Wing Colonnade, the most direct route back to my office, when I hit a roadblock in the shape of a hawk-nosed bureaucrat.

"Ms. Calhoun!" Wilson Fisher, Ambrose's assistant usher, hurried down the covered colonnade toward me, his beady eyes bright with glee. His thin body swayed back and forth, and a stack of papers about as thick as *War and Peace* flapped in his arms with every quick step.

I'd bet dollars to daisies he'd compiled a hefty helping of forms for me to fill out. Wilson's favorite pastime was to bury me under his endless supply of paperwork that could never, ever wait. I'd never make it to my meeting if he caught hold of me.

"Ms. Calhoun!" He waved the forms in front of him. His shoes tapped a rapid tempo against the colonnade's stone tiles. "I urgently need to speak with you!"

CHAPTER FOUR

"Pretend you didn't see me," I told Turner, who was coming up the stairs behind me.

"Why? What's going on?"

"That." I hooked my thumb toward the colonnade beyond the double doors and the flapping paperwork dervish closing in on us. With the quiet stealth I'd picked up from reading a healthy heap of Miss Marple mysteries and the like, I turned on my heel and took off down the hall in the opposite direction.

With each step, my determination grew stronger. Yes, the meeting was scheduled to begin in less than ten minutes. And yes, my feet were taking me farther away from the First Lady's office, which was located upstairs in the *East* Wing. But if taking the longer route meant avoiding Wilson Fisher, then that's what I had to do.

I'd only briefly visited the First Lady's office once, but I could clearly picture its cheery canary yellow walls, the delicate Chippendale sofa with flowered upholstery that graced the far wall, and the half-dozen comfortable chairs to accommodate long meetings. Margaret Bradley, the President's soft-spoken wife, was well known for her love of the outdoors and gardening. I'd heard she never closed the blinds on the windows in her corner office that overlooked the intimate Jacqueline Kennedy Garden. If the sun came in too brightly during a meeting, she'd simply move the chairs around.

Gordon and I had taken all of this information, including the angle of the sun, into consideration when planning for this morning's presentation. Although I knew I'd found a kindred spirit with the First Lady, a few of the proposed changes might be viewed as radical by some of the long-standing members of the White House Grounds Committee who'd be present at this meeting and providing their input. They were the ones I needed to win over.

Past experience had taught me that many traditional gardeners still viewed proponents of organic gardening as those flaky hippie tree-hugger types. To them, we were an unreliable bunch who shouldn't be entrusted with the future of one of the nation's most revered gardens. A reporter named

Griffon Parker had written those exact words in an op-ed piece published in this morning's edition of *Media Today,* the print edition of the nation's largest news outlet.

It didn't matter that I'd been born in the seventies and had completely missed the hippie era. Forget my years of experience working in some of the most historic gardens in the heart of Charleston, South Carolina. Never mind that I'd never, ever walked away from any job, no matter how challenging. But I'm straying from my main point, which was: Being late or — even worse — not showing up to this crucial meeting would only feed the misconceptions about me.

"Organic gardening incorporates concepts such as balance and harmony. Unlike how many in Washington's partisan political environment approach their jobs, at the root of organic gardening is the belief that man can successfully work *with* the natural world instead of railing against it. It's this nonpartisan approach, which echoes the President's own style, I hope to implement." That was how I'd planned to start my presentation. Or, I should say, how I *still* planned to start it.

The First Lady had already stressed that she wouldn't approve any changes without the Grounds Committee's support.

Now that the Secret Service had finished taking my statement, no one but no one was going to get in the way of my making that meeting. Let Wilson dump his forms on me after the presentation.

I rounded a corner and met up with a small group of businesswomen and men all wearing red "Visitor" badges. They blocked the hallway while a young White House staffer with obviously no time pressures on *his* schedule showed off a photograph hanging on the wall depicting President Nixon's trip to China.

"Excuse me," I murmured, and tried to shimmy past them. As I'd mentioned before, the hallways in the West Wing were narrow, intimate even, and — at this particular moment — downright cramped.

I'd managed to wedge my way into the center of the group when an older woman with short gray hair stepped back and jammed her stiletto heel into the top of my shoe.

It hurt! A descriptive phrase quite unworthy of the proper manners my grandmother Faye had taken great pains to instill in me may have popped out of my overstressed mouth.

"Oh!" the older woman exclaimed, whirling toward me. She reminded me of someone I'd seen on TV. But who? "Did I step on you? I'm awfully sorry. I didn't see you back there."

"It's nothing." I gave my stinging foot a little shake and tried not to limp as I moved through the rest of the group.

A gentleman a head taller than the other two men in the group made a grand gesture with his arm and stepped clear out of my muddy way. He wore a deep gray three-piece suit that had clearly been tailored to hug his fit frame. His features were reminiscent of Greek god beauty, the kind of masculine beauty that had the power to steal the breath from a woman's chest.

His features were also very, very familiar.

Richard Templeton, only *the* richest bachelor in the United States, was a face anyone who owned a TV would recognize. "Tempting Templeton," a gossip maven had recently taken to calling him. He dated supermodels, Oscar-winning actresses, and heiresses. His breakups rarely went smoothly. The paparazzi followed him from party to party, hoping to catch footage of a nasty scene. News of his wild nightlife frequently made celebrity headlines in magazines such as *People, Us Weekly,* and *Time.*

Despite the prevalence of touched-up and

airbrushed photography that created perfection out of mere mortals, Richard Templeton looked even more handsome in person. His deep blue eyes sparkled with sharp intelligence and a smattering of mischief. As I passed him, a corner of his lips quirked up into a wicked grin, setting off a fluttering of soft-winged butterflies in my chest.

His dark brown hair, slightly long and untamed, made him look more like a rock star than a banker. But he wasn't a rock star. He sat at the helm of a "too big to fail" bank. His net worth rivaled Bill Gates's. He owned several islands and, I had heard, a small South American country. Not only that, but he'd been recently crowned by *Organic World Magazine* as Environmentalist of the Year in recognition of the work his charitable foundation had accomplished.

If I hadn't been in such a hurry or splattered in mud, I might have stopped and introduced myself. Okay, I wouldn't have. But I knew I'd have some lovely dreams tonight of what I *might* have said and what he *might* have said back.

For one thing, I could have asked him what he was doing at the White House. But then I remembered the President's banking summit, the same summit the raggedly dressed demonstrators were protesting.

The President had invited thirteen of the top banking CEOs to Washington. Congress was on the cusp of passing additional legislation to toughen banking regulations. It was legislation most of the large banks vehemently opposed. The President had called for this summit to bring the opposing parties together.

"If you'll come this way" — the staffer in charge of the small group pumped his arm and pointed with gusto in the opposite direction from where I was heading — "I could show you the rest of the West Wing while we wait for President Bradley." Apparently the staffer had suddenly remembered his schedule.

The woman with the stiletto heels, whom I still couldn't place, ignored the young man's directions and followed along beside me instead. She was smartly dressed in a dark blue suit with a straight skirt that hung a few inches below her knees. Her short gray hair curled out in such a way at the ends that it looked as if a low-hanging silver halo encircled her head.

The deep lines around her mouth and eyes gave her a look of experience and confidence, like a woman who expected to get her way no matter what. Her steely silver gaze latched on to the temporary security badge that dangled from the lanyard I'd hastily thrown on over my yellow rain slicker.

"Casey Calhoun," she read the name on my badge aloud. "You're the new gardener mentioned in this morning's op-ed piece."

"You mean the article that suggested hippies were plotting to take over the White House grounds?" the only other woman in the group asked. She looked about my age and had arctic blond hair that brushed the top of her shoulders. She was tanned and impeccably dressed in a lavender pantsuit.

"She doesn't look old enough to be a hippie, Lilly," a man who looked like a balding male version of the blonde pointed out.

"Thank you," I said.

"But she's muddy enough to be a hippie," he added.

Tempting Templeton chuckled.

"I had a little trouble this morning." I touched the bandage covering the side of my face.

"Uh, Senator Pendergast, we really should be going this way." The young staffer's voice wavered as his group of VIPs followed me instead as if I were the Pied Piper.

"Senator Edith Pendergast," I said as I realized why the woman with the sharp stilettos looked so familiar to me. She chaired the U.S. Senate Committee on Banking and had recently become one of the most powerful senators on the Hill. *She* was the senator spearheading the most current legislation to regulate both the banks and Wall Street. "I apologize for my . . . um . . . outburst."

"You should hear the senator when she gets in a bitch of a mood. I'm Brooks Keller, by the way." The banker with the receding hairline grabbed my hand and shook it, his smile dazzling.

I'd heard of him and his sister, the "wonder twins" of the financial world. Lillian Keller glared at her brother until he dropped my hand. She then rolled her eyes and planted herself between Brooks and me. "The trouble you mentioned, Ms. Calhoun, is that why Lafayette Square looks like a war zone this morning? What's going on?"

While I was waiting to be issued a temporary security pass, Thatch had stressed the importance of keeping tight control over the investigation. He'd instructed me not to mention the attack to anyone. The Secret Service and the White House communications director were to be the only points of contact for information.

So I didn't know what to say. "No comment" seemed somehow inappropriate. So I did what Grandmother Faye, the matriarch of the Calhoun family, had spent so many years trying to impress on me: I told the truth. "I was asked not to talk about it."

"But I understand everything is under control now?" Senator Pendergast asked.

"Was it those filthy-looking people protesting our summit who were making so much trouble?" Lillian shook her head with dismay, as if she couldn't imagine how anyone could be upset with the banking community.

"I don't know. Now if you'd excuse me, I hate to rush off, but —"

Though the bankers all nodded and let me go on my way, the senator continued to doggedly follow me. "I find the work that takes place on the White House grounds endlessly fascinating." She lowered her voice as if about to confess something truly scandalous. "I'm an avid gardener, you see."

"Splendid," I said, honestly pleased to meet someone who shared my passion for plants. "Then you must love working in D.C. and being surrounded by so many world-class public parks and gardens. Have you heard about what the National Arboretum is doing with their —"

"Yes, yes," she said impatiently. "I'd like to sit in on your presentation regarding the organic gardening proposal."

"I — I —" I stammered, not sure what to say. I didn't have the authority to invite guests to the First Lady's office, not even important senators like Edith Pendergast.

The senator raised her brows, obviously waiting for an invitation I had no right to give.

"You'll have to contact the First Lady's office. It's her meeting."

"Oh?" Her lips tightened, smoothing out many of the wrinkles surrounding her mouth. "Is that so?"

A chill spiraled up my legs from that icy stare of hers, slow and pervasive like a winter frost creeping into a flowerbed. I stopped in the middle of the hall and turned toward her. The chill continued to coil its way up my chest, tightening as it went. I'd made a tactical error with the senator, though I wasn't sure what else I could have said. Or what I should say now.

Early on in my career, when I'd worked for some of Charleston's most elite society ladies tending their gardens, I'd made a similar misstep that had nearly ruined me. Several of the ladies thought I was giving a certain Mrs. Harleston special treatment because I'd planted a rare variety of camellia in her garden. But truly, her garden had the southern exposure to support the plant's strict sunlight requirements that the other ladies' gardens lacked.

My, my, my, them ladies are so puffed up with pride, they can't help but get their peacock feathers ruffled, Aunt Alba had declared after I'd lost nearly half of my residential clients and was in danger of losing several more.

So to soothe bruised prides and salvage my fledging landscaping business, I scoured local nurseries and bribed camellia hobbyists to sell me some of their prize stock until I secured enough rare and individualized cultivars to give to each of my remaining clients. Every lady could now boast of the special treatment I'd given her, and only her, saving *her* pride and *my* career.

And that, I suspected, was exactly what I needed to do now. I lightly touched the senator's arm and leaned in toward her. Lowering my voice ever so slightly, I said, "Considering your experience with plants, I'm sure Mrs. Bradley will welcome any input you might be able to offer."

Her frigid glare warmed several degrees. "Splendid."

"If you contact her office, I'm sure —" I started to say.

"I'll let you go and get cleaned up for the

meeting," she interrupted.

"Thank you," I said with a big smile fueled almost completely by relief.

While I was busy congratulating myself for being ever so clever, the senator pushed her card into my hand. "Call my assistant and let her know when you have arranged for me to sit in on the meeting. She'll get the message to me."

"What? Wait, I hadn't . . . ."

Senator Pendergast patted my arm like she would a puppy's head and marched victoriously back to the bankers.

"But I hadn't . . ." I said to the suddenly empty hallway.

That didn't go as smoothly as it could have. And hell, it was one more task I needed to accomplish before the meeting could even get started. I dropped the senator's card into my rain slicker's pocket and trotted through the West Wing lobby, out the front entrance, and across the North Lawn toward my office.

I nearly jumped out of my skin when my cell phone started to belt out the words to "Stronger" by Kanye West. Nerves a bit on edge? Perhaps just a little.

The phone repeatedly sang the hip-hop version of Nietzsche's famous quote "what doesn't kill me" while I dug around in my soggy backpack. Naturally it had slipped to the bottom again and had lodged itself underneath the mystery novel I'd been reading. When I pulled the rose-colored phone free from my bag's clutches and flipped it open, I noticed not only the incoming number but also the time . . . or rather the lack of it. The meeting should have started five minutes ago!

"Lorenzo, thank goodness you called," I shouted into the phone. "Are you still in the office?"

"Yes, I am. Casey —"

"Great." I bypassed the passageway leading down to my office and headed straight for the East Wing. "As you can see, I'm running more than a little late. Could you please grab my presentation boards and bring them up to the First Lady's office?"

"Forget the First Lady. You need to get down here." He took a ragged breath. "Right now, Casey."

"Why? What's going on?"

"Just get down here," he said and hung up.

CHAPTER FIVE

Lorenzo Parisi, more than the rest of us, seemed to truly worry about appearances. I couldn't imagine any circumstance where he'd tell me to "forget the First Lady."

Something extraordinary must have happened. Something extraordinarily *bad*.

I dashed down the low, arching stone passageway underneath the North Portico that led to the offices and workshops. Something must have happened to my presentation boards. Why else would Lorenzo refuse to bring them to the First Lady's office?

A flood of water might have poured in from the ceiling, leaving the grounds offices in ruin. There might even be bits of carefully constructed presentation board scattered all over the desks and crushed underfoot on the floor with no regard to how much time I'd put into creating them.

My heart slammed against my ribs, and my bruised head pounded as I rounded the corner and slid to a stop at the doorway to the grounds offices.

Two men wearing similar off-the-rack suits, one tweed and the other gray, and red "Visitor" security badges around their necks stood just inside the door. They had the worn-down look of paperback novel police detectives.

"Lorenzo?" I called, craning to see around the two lugs so deep in conversation with each other they didn't seem to notice me bobbing up and down in a desperate effort to get past them.

Lorenzo was slumped in my desk chair, his head cradled in his hands. "Lorenzo? Why did you call me? Has something happened to my presentation boards?"

No, the boards were exactly where I'd left them.

"Ah, Ms. Calhoun." The stouter of the two men, the one dressed in the tweed suit, turned toward me. A slow, cautious smile spread across his wide mouth. "We need to speak with you." He introduced himself as Special Agent Cooper from the FBI and his taller, thinner buddy with a shaggy salt-and-pepper mustache as Detective Hernandez from the D.C. Police.

"Is there a problem?" I asked impatiently. I had a meeting to get to.

"Ms. Calhoun, I'm afraid you'll have to clear your schedule for the rest of the day." Cooper, who was several inches shorter than my five-foot-seven-inch height and built like a bulldog, gestured for me to come fully into the office. When I did, he shut the door and crossed his arms over his broad chest. "We need you to tell us everything you saw or heard this morning."

"But I thought that's what I'd just finished doing with the Secret Service."

"That may be true. But their duty is to the security of the President and the White House. We're in charge of investigating the murder. And as of right now, you're our only witness."

"Oh." That was a problem. I didn't want to be the only witness. Certainly they could find someone else in the park who'd seen more than I had. "I need to make a call."

Using my cell phone, I dialed the First Lady's office while secretly hoping Gordon or the First Lady would tell me that I was needed at the meeting and that the investigation could wait. Louise Fenton, the First Lady's secretary, put me on hold to fetch Gordon as soon as I'd explained the situation.

"Don't worry, Casey," Gordon said when he came on the line. "I'll handle things on this end for you. You know I can explain the basics of the proposal to the committee."

"But you don't have the presentation boards or my notes. And what if there are questions? I should be there. I should be the one giving the presentation."

Establishing an organic garden at the White House was pretty much my entire job description. The First Lady had hired me for my expertise in order to implement the plans I'd spent the past three months developing, plans that required the Grounds Committee's approval. The same Grounds Committee that convened only once a quarter.

"I agree," Gordon said. "This proposal is your baby. You should be the one to present it." He was quiet for a long time. "There are several other items on the Grounds Committee agenda. I'll work through those, give the basics of the proposal, and then schedule a time for the committee to reconvene before the end of the week when you can be here to explain how you propose we should implement the organic gardening practices."

"But —" The chance of shoehorning something into the First Lady's busy schedule tomorrow or the next day was about as likely as finding a rosebush in full bloom in the dead of winter.

It wasn't going to happen.

"It's the best we can hope for, Casey."

"I just . . ." I heaved a deep sigh. "I just wanted to be there. It's my job to be there, you know?"

"I know. Listen, I'll let you know what happened as soon as the meeting's over. I've got to go. The First Lady is waiting."

I ended the call and looked up to find Lorenzo and the two investigators staring at me.

Heat rose to my cheeks as I realized how coldhearted my single-minded obsession with getting to the meeting must have sounded to everyone else in the room. A woman had died this morning and I was worried about job security?

In my defense, it'd been easier to worry about the meeting than to shatter into a million pieces over what had happened — or what *could* have happened — this morning. Someone had died. And someone had tried to kill *me*.

Oh, God. I drew a shaky breath.

I should have stayed at my desk letting the tick, tick, tick of the office clock pick at my nerves while I waited for the meeting time to arrive. Or I could have delayed my trip out to Lafayette Square until a few of the grounds crew had clocked in that morning instead of venturing out into the public park alone. Maybe then all of this trouble could have been avoided.

For me.

The woman I'd found in the trash can, she'd still be dead.

"Do you know who she is yet?" I asked. "The woman I found?"

The FBI agent nodded. "We do," Cooper said. He seemed to be in charge. "Her name is Pauline Bonde."

At the mention of a name, Lorenzo vaulted out of my desk chair. His hands were shaking as he marched up to me. "What the hell were you doing out there? What was she doing?" he shouted. His face turned a deep red.

"Now, see here," Cooper said. "Let's stay calm."

Lorenzo pushed the FBI agent out of his way. "I don't know what you're even doing *here,* Casey." He threw open the door leading out of the office and disappeared down the hallway.

I tried to follow. I couldn't understand what had upset Lorenzo. Was he upset about the murder or the canceled meeting? It felt almost as if he blamed me for what had happened. That seemed terribly unfair.

Something else had to be going on. Although we'd only been working together for a short time and, well, his solution to almost any problem in the garden was to sprinkle pesticides or a heavy-duty fertilizer on it, I wanted to win Lorenzo over as a friend. And friends helped each other.

I tried to follow him but was blocked by the tall, hawk-nosed Wilson Fisher as he pushed his way into the office with the stack of paperwork tucked under his arm.

"Ms. Calhoun, it's imperative that you fill out these forms." His hooked nose twitched and his shoulders hunched like a vulture's. He dropped the bundle of papers on my desk. It landed with a thud. "Im-per-a-tive." He stabbed the stack with his finger with each syllable. "This form is for employees injured on the job. This form . . ."

I tuned out the rest.

"I've also included requisition forms for the truckload of mulch you still haven't filled out," he said when he got to the bottom of the stack. "All of these must be completed immediately. I expect to see them on my desk first thing in the morning, if not sooner."

With that he turned on his heel and, his nose still twitching, marched out of the office.

"Well, then." Cooper's brows furrowed as he watched Fisher go. "Well. Interesting . . . er . . . fellow. He seems very . . . thorough. Now, if you don't mind, I'd like to get started."

I kept my gaze on the door, not watching Fisher. I'd long given up trying to understand him. My concern was for Lorenzo.

Cooper cleared his throat when he realized I hadn't heard anything he'd been saying to me. "Ms. Calhoun, I understand you're busy, but we really need your cooperation."

"Of course." I tore my gaze from the door and forced myself to listen. "Was Pauline Bonde a White House employee?" If she was, Lorenzo might have known her.

"No. The victim worked for the Treasury Department. We're still trying to find out what she was doing in Lafayette Square so early in the morning. Was she heading to her office? Or was she going somewhere else? Do you remember seeing her?"

When I closed my eyes, I could clearly picture her. But not alive.

Should I have seen her? In my rush to pull the mile-a-minute weeds, had I missed the chance to notice Pauline or the man who must have been stalking her like a spider crawling down a dewy web in pursuit of its prey? Could I have stopped a murder? I shivered.

"No," I said. "I didn't see her. I wish I had."

He gave a curt nod and then gestured to the nearest chair. "Please, sit down."

I sat.

For the rest of the day, the two men took turns probing and prodding, teasing out details from my memories that had more holes in them than my grandmother's old lace handkerchiefs. They were persistent as they tried to pry some little gem loose from my fractured memories.

Like Mike Thatch, they seemed very interested in the banking protestors gathered in the park as well as in the businessman I'd seen carrying a metal briefcase.

A few hours after lunch, a sketch artist arrived with a sophisticated laptop computer that she set up on Lorenzo's desk. Lorenzo still hadn't returned.

Gordon had. He hovered and groaned as he listened to the retelling of my attack and subsequent discovery of Pauline Bonde's body, all the while blaming himself, poor sweet man. "I should have been out there with you," I heard him mutter more than once.

When the agents took a break to give the sketch artist time to set up her equipment, I cornered Gordon.

"What happened at the meeting? Were you able to reschedule?" I whispered. "Was Mrs. Bradley upset? How about the committee members? How did they seem? Should I expect another scathing opinion piece against me and my gardening plans to show up in tomorrow's edition of *Media Today*?"

Gordon waved away my concerns. "You have no reason to worry about the Grounds Committee or the missed meeting, Casey. Everything will be fine."

"Does that mean you were able to reschedule the presentation?"

Gordon scratched his chin and looked away. "Not yet. The First Lady's schedule this week is impossible," he complained, but quickly added, "She did express deep concern about your well-being. How is your head feeling?"

"I've got a throbbing headache, but I'm fine. What's going to happen with the presentation? What are we going to do if we can't reschedule?"

"I don't know. The committee insists on hearing the full details."

I groaned.

"Don't worry. I'm sure it'll work out. I

just don't know how yet."

I wished I shared his confidence.

"Have you seen Lorenzo?" Gordon asked. "He never made it to the committee meeting."

"He didn't?" I explained how he'd rushed from the office in a panic. "What do you think happened to him? Where did he go?"

Gordon, as concerned as I, had no idea where Lorenzo might have gone or what could have upset him.

We had just started to discuss where we might go looking for Lorenzo when the sketch artist announced she was ready to get started. Unfortunately, with my fuzzy memories she didn't have much to work with.

The man I'd seen carrying that silver briefcase was of average height, average weight, with a face that wouldn't stand out in a crowd, and that was if I could trust what little I could remember, which I didn't. Add to that he was wearing a hat, so I couldn't tell her anything about his hair or even if he had any.

"I really didn't get a good look at him. I was more concerned with pulling the vines out of my flowerbed," I admitted. "I only glanced in his direction once or twice. And I don't even know if he's the same man who hit me. Maybe Special Agent Turner saw him?"

I didn't mean to make that suggestion. Hell, I'd already figured it would be better if I kept my distance from the Secret Service for the next couple of days, especially from a certain grumpy CAT agent.

"That's a great idea!" The sketch artist's eyes brightened with the prospect of getting her hands on someone who could actually provide her with a workable description. "He's trained to remember details."

After Cooper made a few phone calls, Jack Turner arrived in the grounds offices. He wasn't carrying a gun, but that didn't make him appear any less dangerous. I slid down a little in my chair when I noticed the deep red spidery veins threading through his still red-rimmed eyes. It looked painful.

He wordlessly took a chair, pulling it as far away from mine as the small room would allow. Unfortunately, though Turner had spotted a man running toward H Street, he'd only seen the guy from behind and at a distance. So while he tried to be helpful, he really didn't have much to add to my rather vague description.

Throughout the process Turner impatiently tapped his foot and scowled. I got the feeling he was plotting ways to make my life at the White House miserable. But I was just being paranoid, *wasn't I?*

By the time we were finished, I felt so wrung out and achy I went straight home, took the maximum recommended dose of extra-strength painkillers, and crawled into a hot bath with the intention of floating in a cloud of lavender-scented bubbles until summer.

But oh, despite the thick pillows of steam rising from the lavender-perfumed water in the antique claw foot tub, the hot bath did nothing to wash away the chill that had crept into my bones. I shivered and sank a little deeper, submerging all but my nose in the water's warm embrace.

The gloriously renovated bathroom blended antique charm with modern luxuries such as towel warmers and radiant floor heating. The bath sat at the top of the stairs on the third story of the 1890s three-story brownstone where I lived in the Columbia Heights neighborhood. It was just two miles from the White House. Most days I walked to and from work.

My roommate, Alyssa Dunn, and I rented the upper two floors of this architectural treasure. The landlord had given us a reduced rate in exchange for my promise to revive the property's long-neglected garden.

I had plans to bring it back to the height of nineteenth-century elegance.

"Casey? Are you home?" The bathwater covering my submerged ears muffled my roommate's already gentle voice. "Casey?"

I sat up and sucked in a quick breath as the water clinging to my skin quivered in the sudden chill. "In the bathroom," I called.

"I brought home gado-gado salad."

"Really?" I reached for my towel and, rising like Venus from the ocean, wasted no time drying off. As I pulled on a floral pink satin pajama set, a decadent gift from Aunt Willow, my mouth watered at the thought of devouring the Indonesian vegetable salad of potatoes, cabbage, lettuce, cucumbers, and boiled eggs drenched in a spicy peanut sauce.

I loved it. Alyssa didn't. She must have purchased my favorite dish in hopes of bribing me.

Now don't misunderstand me. Alyssa, who hailed from bustling New York City, was the perfect roommate. I loved her to pieces. She always paid her half of the rent on time. She kept the apartment meticulously clean. And as a congressional aide to the elder statesman Senator Alfred Finnegan, also from New York, her hours at the office tended to run longer than my own.

But her idea of getting back to nature was watching a wildlife documentary on TV. And like the senator who'd employed her, she was somewhat ruthless in everything she did. So the fact that she'd brought home my favorite peanut-buttery Indonesian dish had me wondering. What did she want?

"I saw on the news there was some excitement at the White House this morning. A mugging-turned-murder in Lafayette Square? Finny seems to think there's more to the story than what the reporters are saying," Alyssa said as I entered the kitchen.

She leaned over a white take-out box and plunged a large serving spoon deep into the box's depths. Her shoulder-length black hair fell over her face like a curtain.

Her suit — very similar to the one she'd picked out for me, except hers was black and mine was gray — still had that fresh from the dry cleaners look despite the long day she'd put in at the senator's office.

She was about my height, five years younger, and constantly complaining about the fifteen extra pounds she'd gained since moving to D.C. three years ago.

She glanced up from the gado-gado she'd been spooning onto two plates from the take-out box. Her light brown eyes filled with expectation. "I don't suppose you know more about what happened than what's being reported on the news, do you?"

"Hmm, that smells delicious," I said. The cozy kitchen with its soaring ten-foot ceilings soaked up the exotic peanut and coconut scents. My stomach gurgled in happy anticipation. I took two forks from the silverware drawer and napkins from the holder next to the microwave.

"Good Lord." Alyssa dropped the serving spoon. It clattered on the counter as she lunged toward me. "What happened to you? You look as if you've been in a fight."

"The Secret Service asked me not to talk about it." I grabbed a plate of the gado-gado salad before she could hold it hostage.

"Ah-ha! Then you *do* know something," Alyssa crowed. "I told old Finny that you'd know. You've got a nose for finding things out. I bet no state secret goes unnoticed at the White House now that you're around."

"That's not true." I wasn't *that* nosy. I'm sure lots of stuff happened that I knew nothing about. Take for instance the trouble with the protestors. The Secret Service had acted truly worried about them. But did they tell me why? No. They'd stayed stubbornly close-mouthed about the whole affair.

I could have used that argument to make

the case that I wasn't a busybody. I didn't need to stick my nose into everyone's business. But I had no intention of arguing with a graduate from Yale Law School, especially not one who'd graduated at the top of her class.

Alyssa followed me into the living room with a tiny serving of the salad on her plate, proving how much she really didn't like the dish. She rarely skimped on meals.

On the occasions when we were both home for dinner, like tonight, we liked to eat our meals while vegging out in front of the TV.

I went straight for the TV's remote. Alyssa moved a bit faster. She snatched it up and then settled on the sofa next to me. Sending me a sly glance, she set her plate of food on the coffee table in front of us and tucked the remote control under her hip — and here I'd been looking forward to catching up on my favorite game shows. I huffed.

She snorted and turned toward me. Her wide, goofy smile did the talking for her. *You know you're going to tell me everything, so get on with it.*

I shoveled a forkful of gado-gado into my mouth. She couldn't twist information out of me if I kept my mouth full.

It wasn't as if I wanted to keep secrets

from my own roommate. Senator Finnegan regularly trusted Alyssa with all sorts of sensitive information, information she sometimes hinted at, but never talked about. I knew I could trust her, too.

I also knew she'd pester me until the cows came home, fully expecting me to spill my guts.

My stomach clenched at the thought of rehashing the events of this morning. I'd much rather spend my time working a fresh bed of warm fertile soil, letting the rhythm of the work soothe me as I helped life spring forth from a tiny seed.

Perhaps then I wouldn't see death when I closed my eyes, and I'd stop hearing that scream the killer must have silenced in Pauline Bonde's throat.

Suddenly my favorite blend of fresh vegetables soaked in my favorite spicy peanut sauce lost its appeal. I set the plate on the coffee table next to Alyssa's. She still had that goofy grin of hers trained on me. And damn, I don't know why, but it was persuasive. I decided to throw her a juicy tidbit to tide her over until I was ready to talk about the rest.

"I met Tempting Templeton today," I said, and raised my brows expectantly.

Alyssa didn't disappoint. "You didn't!"

She leapt to her feet. "Is he as hot in person as he is in pictures? How did he look? More importantly, how did *you* look?"

This was the same Alyssa who wore only designer clothes and believed that venturing outside without makeup was as obscene as running through the streets naked.

Just this morning she'd fervently protested my decision to walk to work in the drizzle wearing a top-of-the-line Ann Taylor suit. Not to mention the damage I'd inflicted on her eyes when I'd pulled my yellow slicker over the brand-new suit to protect it from the wet, freezing weather.

I'd committed such a vile fashion sin that the usually dignified Alyssa had actually blocked the front door until I threatened to walk to work without the rain slicker and let my suit get soggy.

"Well?" she asked. She'd adopted a very lawyerly stance with her hands clasped behind her back. She bounced lightly on her heels. "Tell me everything that happened, beginning with how you looked."

When I didn't answer her question right away, she rolled her eyes heavenward and sighed loudly. "Don't tell me you met him after you ended up battered and bruised."

"I did," I admitted.

Her gaze narrowed. "And what else?"

"I was caked in mud" — my voice dropped to a dramatic whisper — "from head to toe."

"Not in your brand-new Ann Taylor!"

I nodded.

She weaved as if on the verge of collapse. Alyssa knew how to put on a good act. With one hand pressed to her forehead, she cried, "You're killing me, Casey. Didn't I warn you that you shouldn't venture out in the wilderness while wearing new clothes? You should have taken a cab to work."

I laughed. "The D.C. streets are hardly the wilderness. And that's not where it happened."

Thanks to her overblown dramatics, the events of the day poured out of me. I told her everything, including my unfortunate assault on Special Agent Jack Turner.

"He sounds hunky," Alyssa said. "You should ask him out."

"I don't think he'd be interested."

"Why not?"

"Pepper spray. Remember? In his face? He didn't exactly think it was cute."

"That's nothing," Alyssa scoffed. "Most men I know would consider a little pepper spray a kind of kinky foreplay."

"Really? Remind me not to let you arrange any blind dates for me."

"You're missing out. I know some really

interesting guys who would —"

"No," I said. "No. No. No."

"Okay. Let's talk about something else, like why anyone would attack you so close to the White House. Either he's really stupid or that gutsy."

"The Secret Service seems to think that he's plotting to attack the President and that he murdered Pauline to get something. Perhaps a White House employee's security credentials?"

"That doesn't make sense. It's not like he could use them to get into the White House, right?"

"I don't know. I don't think so," I said.

"Besides, there are still guards to get past. And why not steal a security pass instead of killing someone so visibly and violently?"

"That's true."

"I don't think the Secret Service is being frank with you. There has to be a better explanation," Alyssa said, tapping her chin.

"I agree." All of this seemed to point back to that curious *something* that none of the agents were willing to talk about.

"I bet what happened today doesn't have anything to do with some sinister plot to assassinate the President. You know I recently read an article that said almost ninety percent of all murders are triggered by personal motives. Spurned and angry lovers topped the list."

"Really?" I wasn't sure it was true. Alyssa liked to spout "official statistics," even if she had to make them up. "Then why was I attacked? I'm not even dating anyone."

"I was just thinking the same thing." Alyssa wagged her finger in the air. "But you are a witness."

"Of sorts. I don't really remember having seen anything. He knocked me on the side of my head pretty hard." I rubbed my sore temple. "The Secret Service has asked me not to talk to anyone about what I do know. They want to keep a tight lid on the investigation."

"Good." Alyssa flopped back down on the sofa next to me. The cushions jumped. "If the press finds out you exist, we'll become prisoners in this apartment. News trucks will camp out on the street, reporters will call in the middle of the night in search of unguarded statements, and photographers will take unflattering pictures of us." She shuddered. "There should be a law against unauthorized photographs. I'll have to talk to Finny about that."

As if expecting a member of the paparazzi to pop through the window, she reached for her handbag, pulled out a small makeup case, and quickly reapplied her lipstick.

"So only your coworkers, the investigators, and the Secret Service know you're a witness?"

"I did call my family this afternoon. You know how they worry about me. But I didn't tell them about being a witness or finding the body, just that I'd been in the park around that time and that I was okay. I think Aunt Willow might have suspected I was holding back on them, but she didn't press me for more details."

"And that's it? No one else knows?" Alyssa thoughtfully tapped her chin again.

"No, there is someone else." I suddenly wondered whether the front door was locked. "The killer would know."

CHAPTER SIX

That night I'd hoped to dream of Tempting Templeton. I wanted to hear his liquid smooth voice, to see his rakish smile, to pretend he'd turn a blind eye to the super-models of the world and take notice of a plain Jane like me.

Heck, I'd have even welcomed a dream featuring that grumpy Jack Turner. Not as polished as Tempting Templeton, but Turner possessed the kind of rugged good looks that made me think of the mighty-fine models that regularly climbed their way through the pages of outback adventurer magazines.

Thinking about Turner that way made my heart race . . . just a bit.

Unfortunately I'd never had much luck controlling who showed up in my nighttime world. As I slept that night, no handsome men appeared, brandishing swords in valiant efforts to protect their fair maiden —

namely, me. Instead, a faceless figure lurked in the shadows of downtown D.C. wearing a pair of black-and-white leather shoes with a lightning bolt blazed down the side.

The latest fashion for the guilty?

I realized almost immediately I was dreaming, since all of the buildings appeared to be listing slightly to the left, as if they were slowly melting ice cream cones. It was a mental cue I'd learned shortly after Grandmother Faye took me into her home and the nighttime monsters started to come calling.

In the dream, the bustling D.C. streets bristled with danger. The swell of pride from being part of something bigger than myself had been pushed aside by a dark presence that made the hair on the back of my neck stand up.

I felt like a bug caught in a jar, unable to breathe.

"Nerves. Nothing more than overactive nerves," my dream-self whispered. Even so, I hugged my arms to my chest and picked up my pace. Where I was headed, I didn't know.

I frantically searched the faces of the people passing by. Would my memories kick in if I saw the killer's face? For all I knew, he could be walking beside me right now.

I hugged my chest a little tighter and pretended I didn't notice the threatening scrape of shoes against the pavement. It had grown louder. And closer. Someone was creeping up behind me.

I started to run.

I ran.

And ran.

Suddenly, I was back at the White House. I charged screaming for help down the hallway toward my office in the shadowy basement.

No one came to help me.

The muffled thump of the hard leather soles against the hard floor grew closer. Steady. Unerring. There was no escaping those black-and-white shoes . . . or the man wearing them.

He'd stolen my security pass, my identity, had nearly taken my life.

I wasn't safe. Nowhere was safe.

Not even the White House.

He grabbed me from behind. His fingers closed around my throat. I struggled helpless against his strong grip.

His fingers tightened.

Tighter. I couldn't breathe.

With a yelp, I jolted up in the bed. Gasping for air and so tangled in my blankets, I could barely move. My bruised temple throbbed with a devil's vengeance.

Thump. Thump. Thump.

What the devil? I shouldn't still be able to hear the footsteps from my dream. I pinched myself.

"Ouch!"

Thump. Thump. Thump.

It was coming from downstairs.

I unwound myself from the tangle of warm bedding and padded out into the hallway. My nervous heart crept up to my throat. The thumping sounded louder out here on the upstairs landing. Nearly as loud as the pounding in my chest.

I braced myself with a hand on the stairway newel post's large ball, timeworn and smooth, and listened.

Why would someone be pounding on the door at this time of night?

"Alyssa?" I called out. "Are you expecting anyone?"

Nothing.

My roommate could sleep through a nuclear war.

I rushed back into the bedroom and pulled on a pink satin robe decorated with delicate floral swirls that matched my pajamas. My hands shook as I tied the sash. My bare feet trembled on each tread of the stairs. The man who'd attacked me had stolen my security pass. He knew who I was. He knew where I lived. Every muscle in my body begged me to go back, go back up to my bedroom and hide under my covers. Which was silly. I needed to calm down. Killers didn't knock on front doors.

Breathe in: one, two.

Not even in the middle of the night.

The ornately carved front door loomed in front of me. Geometric patterns of crystal blues and sea foam greens splashed across the hardwood floor from the porch light shining through the door's art deco stained glass sidelights.

Breathe out: one, two.

The bright porch light would discourage any would-be killers lurking in the shadows of the street. Even so, by the time I'd reached the bottom of the stairs, my insides quivered like a big old bowl of muscadine jelly despite the deep-breathing exercises and pep talk.

A large shadow moved in front of the sidelight.

Bang! Bang! Bang!

I yelped.

And then I cursed myself for acting like a frightened mouse.

With a quick pull, I tore aside the heavy drape that covered the window in the top half of the door.

"Lorenzo?"

I quickly unlocked the door and threw it open.

"Lorenzo, what are you doing out there?"

He looked terrible. Worse than terrible. Dark bags sagged underneath his bloodshot eyes. His once freshly pressed suit looked as if it'd spent at least a week crumpled up into a tight ball on a floor somewhere. His tie was gone, his shirt untucked. Mud and grass stained his knees. The pocket of his coat had been ripped.

I knew he was my age, a youthful not-quite-forty. But seeing him slumping against the doorframe with his shoulders hunched against the world, I would have added at least ten years to that number. Under the bright porch light, his sharp Italian features appeared to be even more deeply etched.

I grabbed his arm and pulled him inside, closing and locking the door behind me.

"Lorenzo? Are you okay? What happened to you today? Where did you go?" I demanded.

He shook his head.

"Where did you go?" The sharpness of my voice surprised me. It must have surprised Lorenzo as well. His gaze snapped up from the spots of color from the stained glassed window on my hardwood floors that had captured his attention. His eyes met mine.

"I climbed a tree."

"A tree? You're joking." I shook my head. I could not — and believe me, my imagination lacked for nothing — but I couldn't picture Lorenzo perched up in a tree. Not under any circumstances. Not ever.

"What kind of tree?"

"A cherry tree near the Tidal Basin. An 'Okame,' I believe."

"That's illegal, not to mention how damaging climbing can be to those trees. Some of them are nearly a hundred years old."

Lorenzo shrugged. "I needed to think. It seemed like a good place."

We stared at each other for several minutes.

"What are you doing here?" I asked finally.

"I had to come." His eyes grew wide and more than a little wild. He took a step toward me.

I took a step back.

"You've got to tell me," he rasped. He took several more steps toward me.

I retreated until my back hit the foyer wall.

"What — what do I need to tell you?" I asked, desperate to sound calm. But failing miserably. My voice sounded breathless and weak. I hated that. I hated that I'd let myself get so frightened.

This was Lorenzo, for Pete's sake, soft-spoken, pesticide- and fertilizer-misguided Lorenzo. While he often sprayed indiscriminately for insects, beneficial or not, he wouldn't hurt me, a fellow gardener.

"I'll help you as long as you tell me what you need."

"That FBI agent said you were their only witness. You have to tell me. What exactly did you see?"

"What did I see? I — I'm not supposed to —"

"Dammit, Casey!" He slammed his fist against the wall beside my head with enough force the plaster cracked. "I'm not playing around here."

Good God, he'd lost his mind! I squeezed my eyes shut. Wincing, I turned my head away and braced myself, half expecting him to hit me.

"Look at me!" he shouted.

I looked. He must have seen the fear spiking through my body with such force that I was nearly doubling over from the pain of it. He cursed and stumbled backward as if he'd lost his balance.

"Dammit." He tunneled his fingers through his short dark brown hair. "I'm sorry, Casey. I don't mean to scare you."

His head dropped to his chest. "You don't understand."

I had to lean forward to hear what he whispered next.

"The woman you found, Pauline. She was my lover."

CHAPTER SEVEN

Well, shut my mouth, that explained why Lorenzo had run off in such a state this morning.

I dragged us both into the kitchen, scooped my favorite shade-grown Costa Rican ground coffee beans into Alyssa's French press, and started to heat a kettle of water while Lorenzo paced.

"She drove me crazy, Casey. When I was with her, I felt on top of the world one moment and as if I was losing my mind the next." He stopped at the refrigerator and, making himself right at home, opened the door and peered inside. Finding nothing of interest in there, he turned around and shuffled back toward the pantry.

"Are you looking for something?" I asked him.

"No." He seemed nervous, like he didn't know what to do with himself. "It's just that . . . I don't know. My world revolved around Pauline. She was everything to me. We'd been dating for nearly a year. I was going to ask her to marry me. What am I going to do now?"

"Why don't you sit down, Lorenzo?" His pacing was starting to make me dizzy. I breathed in the coffee's rich scents. It was like inhaling a thick dose of caffeine. "Tell me about Pauline."

"She was vibrant, a shooting star."

I poured the heated water into the French press. Then after swallowing a couple of pain tablets with a glass of tap water, I joined Lorenzo at the small maple kitchen table. He'd folded his arms over his rumpled shirt and had tilted his head back slightly. His eyes were closed.

Had he fallen asleep? I glanced at the clock on the stove. It was half past three in the morning. He must have been exhausted. I knew I still needed several hours of sleep before I could reasonably expect my mind to start functioning on all cylinders.

So I didn't try to think. I simply sat at the table with Lorenzo sharing his grief.

Five minutes passed. And then ten.

My muddy backpack was still on the kitchen table where I'd carelessly dropped it. The mud had dried and crumbled into a small mound.

Hadn't Alyssa recently complained about the amount of dirt I brought into the house? *Soil, not dirt,* I'd tried to explain to her. But she refused to acknowledge the difference.

I cleaned up the mess and then reached into the backpack. The mystery novel I'd been carrying around hadn't fared well from having spent the day in a soggy bag. Its pages were water stained, its cover slightly warped. But the promise of a mystery to be solved on its pages and justice demanding to be served called to me.

I hated feeling timid in my own skin. Heroines like Miss Marple knew how to keep a calm head on their shoulders despite their constant encounters with danger. And here I was shivering in my satin robe after a coworker — a man I wanted to consider my friend — unexpectedly showed up in the middle of night in search of comfort. And answers.

What would Miss Marple have done?

She'd do what any good friend would do. She would help him, of course.

I quietly stood and retrieved two coffee mugs from the cabinet.

"Did you see him?" Lorenzo asked. His eyes were still closed and his head tilted back as if in slumber.

"Yeah." I filled the pair of mugs with the

fresh coffee. "I saw him, but I don't know what I can tell you that would be helpful. I didn't get a good look at him." I placed a mug on the table in front of him and then fetched a carton of milk from the refrigerator. "The FBI, D.C. Police, Secret Service, and everyone else with a badge in the D.C. area are all using the information I gave them. Believe me, they want to find this guy as badly as you do."

"I understand that. But still —"

"Do you take sugar?" I asked.

He waved the sugar bowl away. After pouring a healthy serving of milk into his coffee, he took a sip.

"But you saw him, Casey? You saw the monster who killed Pauline?"

I remember seeing a shoe. A black-and-white shoe with a lightning bolt on one side.

If only I could remember his face. Did I even see his face?

"I don't know what or how much I saw," I admitted. "It's all hazy."

I looked away. I couldn't bear to watch his hopeful expression dissolve into disappointment. I'd already seen that happen with the Secret Service agents and then the FBI and the police. "Maybe when my head heals, I'll be able to remember more."

Lorenzo shifted uneasily. His shoe

bumped my foot.

"Sorry," he mumbled.

I moved my foot and instinctively glanced under the table to make sure my legs weren't intruding on his space.

"I can't wait, Casey. You need to remember it now. Think. Any bit of information might be helpful," he insisted. "I need to know what you know. You might have seen something that would identify him."

Like his shoes.

His black-and-white lightning bolt shoes.

Shoes exactly like the ones on Lorenzo's feet.

Why would Lorenzo be wearing the killer's shoes?

He wouldn't. Not unless the killer and Lorenzo were one and the —

In a panic I jumped up and grabbed the first thing that came to mind. A knife.

A satisfyingly large butcher's knife. I liked the weight of it in my hand.

"What are you doing?" Lorenzo asked as I whirled toward him, the knife pointed menacingly toward his chest.

"Um . . . um . . ." What did I think I was going to do with the knife? This was Lorenzo, for heaven's sake. "Oh, you know me. When I get nervous, I garden."

"With a butcher's knife?"

Right. That didn't make sense.

Desperate, I grabbed the closest thing at hand, a pineapple Alyssa had purchased a few days earlier and had left sitting out next to the bread box. The knife's sharp blade made a satisfying *thunk* as it cut through the top of the pineapple, freeing its bright green top. I raised the stalk of spiky leaves in the air as if it were a trophy. Bits of bright yellow pineapple flesh clung to it.

"I'm going to grow this pineapple top."

His brows crinkled. "Right now? In the kitchen?"

"Yes. Why not? They make great houseplants, you know."

"So I've heard." He didn't sound convinced.

Well, I didn't care whether he believed me or not. The knife wasn't going anywhere. I didn't feel safe with those shoes in the room with me.

"Are they new?" I asked, while pretending to concentrate on removing the bottom whorl of leaves on the pineapple stem, careful not to damage any of the roots that had already started to sprout. One by one I plucked off the lance-shaped leaves, my hand never straying far from the knife. "I've never seen you wear those shoes before. Have you had them long?"

"These things?" Much like Gordon had earlier, Lorenzo frowned at his feet as if he needed to see which pair of shoes he'd pulled from his closet that morning. "Oh, right. Pauline bought them for me last week."

"Were you wearing them when you came to work yesterday morning?"

"Yeah." He thought about it for a moment while still staring at his feet. "Yeah. I haven't been home since I found out about . . ."

"Of course not." This was the same Lorenzo who'd wear a dark green gardening apron and mud boots to protect his clothes whenever he worked out on the grounds. My gut tightened. "Pauline gave them to you. How were things between the two of you the last time you saw her?"

Alyssa's statistic that most motives for murder were personal came back to me like a slap in the face.

Did Lorenzo and Pauline have a lover's quarrel? Did an argument push him to attack Pauline? He'd admitted that she sometimes made him feel crazy. How crazy?

"How were things between us?" He shrugged his sagging shoulders. "I never knew. She kept me on edge all the time." A ghost of a smile loosened some of his tension as he kept his gaze latched on the black-and-white leather shoes.

I had to turn away. I couldn't bear to look at those shoes.

I reached for the knife again. "Did the two of you have an argument?"

"No. Pauline just stopped by my apartment with the shoebox wrapped in shiny silver paper. I wasn't expecting her. I didn't even know she was in town. She'd do that sometimes. Just buy me a gift out of the blue like that. The next day she had to leave again. That was the last time I saw her."

"She left town often. Why?"

"Her job. I hated that job. It took her to New York City almost every week for months now. She was an accountant for the Treasury Department, you know. She'd been investigating the books of several large banks. It took up most of her time. Such a waste."

"Her work was important to her?"

He made a rude sound. "Married to the job, she liked to say. I was hoping to change her mind and convince her that she had room in her life for her career and a husband. But she didn't want to hear it. Too ambitious for her own good, perhaps. I don't know. She told me she didn't want to be tied down. She made marriage sound like punishment. All she cared about lately was those lists of numbers she carried around with her on her laptop."

"Sounds like you were jealous."

He sat back in his chair and gazed at me, his dark eyes hard and untrusting. "I suppose at first I was," he finally admitted. "She'd come back from New York bragging about having lunch at some fancy restaurant with that rich Richard Templeton guy."

"Really? Richard Templeton, the banker?" I couldn't keep the excitement out of my voice.

"Yeah, that's the guy." Lorenzo grimaced. "Or partying all night with the Keller twins. Who wouldn't be jealous of that?"

"It sounds as if the two of you had been growing apart." I'd experienced that a time or two myself. Hearts slowly growing cold. The flame dimming. It was a painful experience. But had it led Lorenzo to *murder?*

"I'd thought Pauline and I were done." A faint smile returned. "I'd just started getting used to the idea that she'd moved on, but she dropped by last Friday and gave me these shoes. And she stayed the night. I loved her, Casey. She really knew how to —"

"Whoa, whoa. That's enough, Lorenzo." *Too much.* I didn't need to picture a coworker in that way. What I needed was to get him back on track. "So after that surprise visit she went to New York City? Did you see her when she returned to D.C.?"

"No, I never saw her again. I'd called her cell the night before she —" He leaned his head back and pressed his fists against his eyes.

"You called her?" Had they argued?

"Yeah. She was still in New York at her hotel. She'd sounded excited yet nervous. But she wouldn't say what was bothering her. You've got to help me, Casey. You were there that morning. You've got to help me understand why someone would do this to her."

Perhaps if I'd had a full night's sleep or if my head didn't still feel as if someone was playing the bongo drums inside it, I wouldn't have made the promise I'd made to him that night. Even as I spoke the words, I realized the mistake I was making. But that didn't stop me.

"I'll help you, Lorenzo." I placed my hand on the mystery novel in front of me as if swearing on a Bible. Despite my fears, I vowed to do something that would make the Miss Marples of the world proud. And who knew? Maybe someday people would write novels about me. "I'll find out why someone killed your Pauline."

CHAPTER EIGHT

"Hold up," Fredrick called from inside the guard hut as I approached the White House gate the next morning. A moment later, Fredrick, his red hair bright against the robin's egg blue sky, rushed out of the small white structure. He held up his ruddy hands when I started to wave my temporary security card in front of the reader. "I need you to wait out there."

"Is the White House still on high alert from yesterday?" I asked, but Fredrick wasn't listening.

Perhaps the banking summit protesters still had the Secret Service worried. I glanced behind me. The Secret Service and police had a larger presence than usual in the park today.

The protesters, dressed in old, tattered clothes, had also doubled in number from yesterday. Their angry shouts had grown louder, more frantic.

Joanna Lovell, attorney-at-law, was at the center of them with the hem of her shiny pale blue housecoat flapping. Many in her group waved oversized photo cutouts of the CEOs attending the White House meetings. Slogans such as WHERE'S MY BAILOUT? and CORPORATE GREED: STEAL FROM THE POOR AND GIVE TO THE RICH and THEY TAKE OUR MONEY AND GET RICH WHILE WE LOSE OUR JOBS had been scrawled in bold letters across cartoon moneybags the cutout bankers clutched in their hands.

"Fredrick? What's going on? What's the holdup?" I asked.

"I'm sorry, Ms. Calhoun —" he started to say.

"Casey," I corrected. He'd always called me Casey.

"Ms. Calhoun," he said, more firmly this time, his face mottling several shades of red. "I'm not to let you pass until you've been searched. Please wait there. I need to make a call." He started to duck back into the tiny wooden hut. "I'll try to make this quick," he tossed over his shoulder, and then was gone.

I leaned against the iron fence trying to look nonchalant while I waited for Fredrick to return. A West Wing staffer eyed me with caution as she passed through the gate. No one dashed out of the guard hut to stop her, which made me suspect my detention was personal.

Goodie.

"Excuse me." A dark-haired man dressed in a navy blue jogging suit brushed past me as he came through the first gate. He carried a briefcase up to the small white guard hut. "I need to get this to Richard Templeton. He's attending the banking summit," the man explained to Fredrick, who'd emerged from the hut to greet him. "I'm Wallace Clegg, Richard's personal assistant."

"I'll have to make a call," Fredrick said.

"Can you do it right away? These are important papers for this morning's meeting." Clegg's voice was strained, like the man was on the verge of a panic attack.

"Don't worry. Once I get clearance, I'll fetch a staffer to carry it to him directly."

When Fredrick disappeared into the guard hut, Clegg glanced back at me. He gave a nervous smile. "It's been one hell of a morning."

"Hopefully, it'll get better," I replied.

He nodded. "Hopefully." His hair was a shiny blue-black. His square features made him look like someone who spent more time in the gym than in a boardroom, like the kind of guy who'd been the star of his wrestling team in college. Not that he was large. But he did seem to be a bit muscular for a CEO's personal assistant. The ones I'd met in this town tended to be lean, nervous types who looked as if they didn't get out into the sunlight nearly enough. Instead, this guy was an odd combination of tanned skin, lean muscles, *and* jittery nerves. "I was supposed to make sure these files were with the rest of Richard's paperwork before he left the hotel this morning."

He started to tap his foot. We both seemed to be stuck in limbo between the White House outer gate and the inner gate that led onto the grounds. He leaned toward me. "Have we met somewhere before?" he asked me.

"I don't know. You do look kind of familiar."

"Were you at the —" he started to ask me when his cell phone rang. "Clegg here."

He frowned as he listened.

"I'm at the guard hut. You should get the files right away."

He made a face.

"Yes, Mr. Templeton. Of course it won't happen again."

Fredrick came out and gave Clegg a nod. "It's all set."

"Did you hear that?" he said into the phone. "They're sending a staffer to come and get it now. I'm going back to the hotel to get ready for our meeting with Senator Pendergast."

He smiled then. "Yeah, I'll keep out of your minibar."

He hung up, gave me a nod, and jogged off.

I drummed my fingers against the iron fence while wondering how much longer I was going to be kept waiting. I had a pile of work to get done, a meeting to reschedule, and I was running late already. Was this Special Agent Jack Turner's way of punishing me for embarrassing him yesterday?

Yeah, I was pretty certain that was the case when I spotted him, dressed in CAT team black complete with dark sunglasses and assault rifle slung over his shoulder, striding across the North Lawn toward the gate like an avenging angel.

My traitorous heart raced at the sight of him. I blamed *that* on Alyssa's bad influence. She was right. He *was* hunky. I mean, if you happen to like men with overbearing hero complexes.

He stopped on his side of the gate. A slow, self-satisfied smile spread across his lips. Determined not to give him any more pleasure at my expense than necessary, I greeted him as if I'd asked him to meet me.

"Good morning," I said brightly.

Truth be told, I was glad to see him. After the questions Alyssa had raised and Lorenzo's late-night revelations, I needed a partner to help me weed through the facts. Every good detective needed a capable sidekick. And considering how he'd probably saved my life yesterday, I couldn't think of anyone more capable.

"I see several members of the press are still camped out in Lafayette Park. They'll have a good day for their broadcasts. It's supposed to be at least ten degrees warmer today than yesterday. Look at the sky. Just a few wispy clouds. It's a good day for gardening, too. But I don't know how much of that I'll get done. As you can see, I'm running late."

I was babbling. But I couldn't seem to help myself. At least I had enough sense not to ask him how his eyes were faring.

With my arm propped lazily on the fence, I leaned forward and lowered my voice. "Any new leads?"

His smile tightened just a touch. "We've got the investigation under control." He opened the gate and gestured for me to follow him around the guard hut to a relatively

133

private spot under a littleleaf linden tree.

When we got there, he held out his hand.

I stared at his open palm.

"Your backpack," he prompted.

"Oh." I handed it over.

As he unzipped it and started to dig through its contents, I got to thinking. Fredrick was more than qualified to search my bag, so why the personal attention from a CAT agent who had better things to do with his time?

"How are you feeling this morning?" he asked, his voice softening a touch.

"I'm okay."

He looked up from digging through the backpack. "That's a nasty bruise on your temple. Have you been losing your balance or feeling dizzy? Experiencing any headaches?"

"No, I've been okay. Though as you can see, I'm coming in late this morning. Gordon insisted."

Turner nodded. "Your throat looks better today." He returned to pawing through my bag. "I'm glad to see that. You could have been seriously injured."

Alyssa seemed to think that any guy worth his salt would be turned on by my pepper spray mishap. Perhaps she was right. I did feel a certain tingly vibe growing between

Turner and me. He was standing a little closer than necessary. Close enough that his spicy sandalwood aftershave, a clean scent that reminded me of the woods after a spring rainstorm, made me feel a little giddy.

Had he contrived this pat down so he could ask me out on a date? My heart started pattering a little faster.

What was wrong with me? I didn't like guns. Or men with guns.

I wanted a sidekick, not a date. But there was something about Turner. He made me nervous as hell. Just the way he moved, like a predator tracking his prey, screamed danger. He probably knew how to kill a man at least seven different ways with his bare hands. But despite that, or perhaps because of it, I wanted Turner to stick close by me. He could protect me from the bad guys in the world. How crazy was that?

"No suspicious hairspray bottles in your bag today?" he asked and handed me my backpack.

"I didn't have the energy to make a refill last night." I hitched the backpack over my shoulder. "I was too busy trying to find out why Pauline was —"

"Wait a minute." Turner lifted his dark glasses. Rich hazel green eyes met mine. I hadn't noticed his stunning eye color yesterday. I'd been too busy worrying about how red they'd looked. "When you say Pauline, you mean Pauline Bonde, our murder victim?"

"Yes. And I've learned quite a bit about her. Did you know that she —"

"Ms. Calhoun!" he exclaimed and sucked in a deep breath. He took a second, much slower breath before continuing with a carefully modulated tone. "Casey, tell me you haven't been playing detective."

"You might say I've been poking around some bushes."

"I see." He pocketed his sunglasses and rubbed the bridge of his nose as if trying to ward off a wicked headache. "And despite express orders to keep quiet about our ongoing investigation, who exactly have you talked to so far?"

"I've been discreet," I assured him. He had nothing to worry about with me. "I've read enough mystery novels to know how to conduct myself."

He rolled his eyes.

Convinced he'd thank me for the information I'd uncovered so far, and hoping he'd share what the Secret Service had learned since yesterday, I told him about the doubts Alyssa and I had about why the killer had stolen my security pass.

"Why attack me, or anyone else, for a White House security pass? That doesn't make sense. It isn't as if he could use my pass to get access to the White House. There are too many redundant security procedures in place, such as the guards at the gate, to keep something like that from happening. He had to be after something else. And I have an idea of what that is."

"I see." Turner rubbed the bridge of his nose again.

Since he seemed willing to listen, I told him about Lorenzo's affair with Pauline and her involvement with some kind of investigation into the banking community. I left out the part about how Lorenzo's shoes matched the shoe I remembered seeing right before the attack. No need to get distracted by what must have been a coincidence.

It had to be a coincidence. I'd stared at my bedroom ceiling most of the night while trying to put all the pieces of this mystery together. Although it felt like I was working on a jigsaw puzzle where most of the pieces were missing, one piece stood out. Lorenzo wasn't a killer. I was sure of it.

"According to Lorenzo, Pauline Bonde had been auditing several banks' books for months now. I have to get some more information about that, but more than one of those banks she's been auditing have sent their CEOs to the President's summit. What if there's a connection?"

He leaned his arm against the wall of the guard's hut. "You're right about that. She'd been auditing three large banks. And yes, two of the three CEOs are at the summit."

"Really? Then it isn't a coincidence. One of them must have —"

"Stop right there."

"Why? I don't —"

"I like you, Casey," he said, not letting me finish a sentence. "You've got spunk. And you're attractive as hell. Most women I know would be an emotional wreck after what had happened to you yesterday, *not* leading their own personal investigation to catch the killer."

He thought I was attractive? "Um . . . thank you."

"But trust me on this. You need to stop."

"Stop? Why?"

"For one thing, you're on the wrong track."

"The wrong track?"

He nodded. "Remember Thatch told you about that suspected plot against the President yesterday? I can't talk about it, except to say that we're almost one hundred percent sure that the murder is connected to that."

"But why Pauline? Why her? It has to be something to do with her work."

"Not necessarily. She may have simply been in the wrong place at the wrong time."

"That can't be it." Her death couldn't have been so . . . so . . . meaningless.

"The assassin didn't take anything from her. Or from you."

"My security pass was gone," I reminded him.

"And as you pointed out, it's worthless to him. He used the lanyard attached to your security badge to strangle you. The cord probably snapped off in his hands and he bolted."

"That's why I'm still alive, because the lanyard cord broke? That doesn't make sense. Why kill Pauline and make such a fuss about hiding her body, but not me?"

"I don't know. Perhaps you didn't see what Pauline saw." He turned and started across the North Lawn back toward the White House. "About the pepper spray," he said over his shoulder, "you know you could be dismissed for bringing it onto White House grounds. I didn't send my report to Ambrose. Thatch agreed. It'll remain in our CAT files, though. And know this, CAT will be watching you. *I'll* be watching you."

"Wait." I jogged after him. So many questions churned in my head, all of them demanding answers. "Why was Pauline in the park so early in the morning? What was she doing?"

"Probably heading to work." He gave a nod to the large Treasury Building just off to the right of the White House. "Her office was on the third floor."

"Oh." I stopped to look. It was possible that she could have been cutting through the park on the way to work. I did. Still, I wasn't satisfied. Turner must have sensed it.

With a huff he pivoted around to face me. "Let it go, Casey. I know you think you're helping. But I assure you the Secret Service is more than capable of investigating a security breach. The FBI and police, also capable, are working tirelessly to solve this murder." He sliced his hand through the air in obvious frustration. "We do not need advice on how to do our jobs from an *assistant* gardener."

This time when he walked away, he made it clear that he didn't want to be followed. Who knew enlisting the help of a sidekick would prove so difficult?

Despite Turner's warning to keep my nose

out of the investigation, questions surrounding Pauline Bonde's murder kept worming their way back into my thoughts that morning. I couldn't accept that she'd been murdered simply for being in the wrong place at the wrong time.

When I arrived at the grounds office, I found Lorenzo sitting at his desk next to mine. He must have taken my advice and gone home after leaving my apartment last night. He'd washed and combed his deep brown hair. His khaki pants and white oxford shirt looked fresh and wrinkle-free. But dark purple smudges under his heavy-lidded eyes suggested he hadn't got any sleep at all. His shoulders slumped forward as if he needed to protect himself from a blow, while his listless gaze stared into a vast void of grief visible only to him.

Gordon and I tried to distract Lorenzo by discussing the Easter Egg Roll plans with him. He took part in the discussion and had agreed to take on several pressing tasks that day but had made no effort to get started. Instead he remained at his desk, his gaze staring again into his personal void of despair.

"Go home," Gordon had urged.

"I need to work," Lorenzo assured. "I need to be here."

Seeing him like that only added fuel to my desire to help him make sense of Pauline's murder. Was such a thing possible? Did murder ever make sense?

Sure, I didn't have the experience, the training, or access to the same information available to the Secret Service. And I understood why the Secret Service wanted to handle their part of the investigation in their own way. I got it. They had "Secret" in their organizational title for a reason.

Nor did I have the time. First and foremost on my to-do list was to convince the First Lady's personal assistant, Louise Fenton, to make room in Mrs. Bradley's impossibly tight schedule for another Grounds Committee meeting. As soon as I'd arrived that morning, I'd put in motion a plan to win over Louise's favor.

The White House has a greenhouse facility on the east side of town where we propagate and prepare plants for the gardens. About a month ago I'd started using a corner of one of the greenhouses for propagating small tropicals and houseplants for use inside the White House. Begonias propagate quite easily from cuttings and bloom readily in the humid greenhouse setting, making them a natural choice to grow in my special projects corner. I'd heard

Louise liked pretty flowering plants, so when I visited her office that morning, I brought along a begonia bursting with blooms to leave on her desk.

And I couldn't forget about the upcoming White House Easter Egg Roll. The First Lady's social secretary took the lead in the planning and coordination, but every department played an important role in making the event a success. This year, the new social secretary, Seth Donahue, had taken charge of the event with genuine enthusiasm. Planning events for the White House had been quite a change for him from running a private high-profile party-planning company that specialized in catering events for the stars. A sense of civic duty and deep admiration for President John Bradley had lured him into public service.

His heart seemed to be in the right place, even though some of his decisions had ruffled feathers.

Ambrose had objected quite firmly — but to no avail — when Seth had turned the White House Map Room on the ground floor into a temporary staging area for the event. As Ambrose had warned, the hallway leading to the room buzzed with deliveries.

On my way back from Louise Fenton's office in the East Wing, I skirted around two butlers as they maneuvered a large pallet of boxes down the hallway and through the room's narrow doorway. A bead of sweat had broken out on Ambrose's brow as he directed. "Watch the doorframe," he cried when the pallet came within a hairsbreadth of scraping it.

"Monday will be here soon," I assured him.

"Not soon enough." Ambrose dabbed his forehead with one of his crisp handkerchiefs. "I have just been informed that Mr. Donahue has decided to expand the Easter Egg Roll by three hours and expand the number of available tickets to thirty thousand."

"At this late date?" Today was Wednesday. And the Easter Egg Roll always took place on the Monday after Easter, less than a week away. "Can he do that?"

The corner of Ambrose's mouth quivered slightly. "Apparently he can do whatever he wants as long as he has the President's approval."

"And does he?"

"Why wouldn't he? This is the People's House. Why not open up the event to as many citizens as possible? Watch the wall!" he shouted to the butlers, who had managed to get the pallet through the door.

On the far side of the Map Room, I spotted Assistant Usher Wilson Fisher hunched over one of the cardboard boxes that had been stored there. With clipboard in hand and his hawkish nose twitching with delight, he pulled out an armload of oversized pastel plastic spoons. His pen scratched on his pad as he counted and sorted by color the spoons the children would use to propel their eggs down the South Lawn.

"And the other wall!" Ambrose called to his men. "Just — just leave it there." He heaved a deep sigh and turned toward me. "The increase in attendants would have been fine a month ago when we still had plenty of time to make adjustments, not to mention how busy I've been keeping up with the ever-changing demands from the banking summit. But that doesn't matter, does it? It's our duty to make sure the President's wishes, whatever they might be, are carried out in a timely and efficient manner."

"I know you're doing your best. You always do."

A smile almost made it to his lips. But he caught himself in time and straightened. "Thank you, Casey."

At the mention of my name, Fisher glanced up from his work. His gaze met mine and widened. He set down the spoons and started toward me.

Uh-oh. I'd only managed to get halfway through the pile of paperwork he'd left for me yesterday.

"I'd better make sure Gordon knows about these recent changes," I told Ambrose, and took off down the hall. "Tell Fisher that I haven't forgotten about his forms. I'll have them on his desk by tomorrow morning."

"I don't care how many green ones we have. Just increase the number of all the colored eggs as evenly as possible." I overheard the assistant chef's rising voice as I hurried past the kitchen on my way to find Gordon. He was standing in the doorway with a phone pressed to his ear. "Yes. Yes. I know." His tanned cheeks turned bright red. "It doesn't matter. We now need nineteen thousand hard-boiled eggs for the children. I know it's last minute."

Apparently Seth's decision to open the Easter Egg Roll to more families was causing problems for everyone on the White House staff. I wondered why he'd decided to do it.

Seth was still relatively new. We'd joined the White House team at about the same time, and although I'd only talked to him

146

once in the past three months, he'd seemed friendly enough.

Perhaps he hadn't taken the time to think about or even ask anyone how the increase of five thousand available tickets would impact the other departments.

As for the Grounds Office, the change meant there'd be five thousand extra pairs of feet trampling our meticulously groomed lawn and five thousand extra visitors we'd need to gently direct away from the flower-beds or keep from jumping into the fountain.

With less than a week to go, every member of the grounds crew had already focused much of their time and effort on preparing the lawn and the surrounding gardens for the coming assault.

Even now Gordon was out on the South Lawn overseeing the application of a preemergent crabgrass control and the pruning of the boxwood hedges. He also planned to inventory the snow fencing and various ropes and barriers stored in the maintenance shed. Seth still hadn't decided what he wanted to use to cordon off the different activity areas.

The first White House Easter Egg Roll, in 1878, had been an impromptu event. Before then, local families would celebrate Easter

Monday on the West Terrace of the Capitol grounds. But Congress, dismayed by the damage the children had caused to their lawn, passed a law banning Capitol grounds from being used as a playground.

A group of disappointed children had approached President Rutherford Hayes and explained the situation. Hayes, unable to control Congress, offered the kids the use of the White House lawn for their traditional Egg Roll.

On that Easter Monday in 1878, as families were turned away from the Capitol, word quickly spread that they should go to the White House.

Over the years the Easter Egg Roll had bloomed into an elaborate event with celebrities reading books to the children, musical performances, health and fitness demonstrations, arts and crafts stations, and the quintessential egg roll races.

The South Lawn's preparation had been primarily Lorenzo's responsibility, but since he had his own troubles to worry about, Gordon and I had divided the tasks between us.

Before I started work on the decorative planters for the display areas, I decided I should talk to Gordon about the increase in numbers attending. This was my first Easter

Egg Roll at the White House, and I wasn't sure if Seth's last-minute change put a monkey wrench in our preparations or not. Gordon would know.

Carrying my wide-brimmed straw hat, I crossed through the light-filled Palm Room that separated the White House from the West Wing. The small room had been decorated to resemble a gazebo. White lattice covered the walls. Potted citrus trees and President Bradley's favorite camellias brightened the corners. The three-foot blood orange tree I'd moved from the greenhouse last week had finally started to bloom. Tiny white flower buds dotted its dark green foliage.

As I passed through the door leading out to the South Lawn, I spotted Special Agent Janie Partners. Red highlights brightened her black hair today, and she was wearing a black pantsuit with a green silk scarf sporting a tiny dollar bill pattern tied around her neck. She gave me a friendly nod, glanced at the crowd behind her, and rolled her eyes.

"If you'll come this way, we have a tight schedule to keep." The young staffer I'd met in the hallway with the bankers yesterday waved a hand in the air as if swatting flies. The three bankers I'd meet yesterday meandered through the grass in the Rose

Garden along with about a half-dozen more professionally dressed men and women. None of them seemed to be paying the staffer any attention. Most had their Black-Berries pressed to their ears. A couple of them were wandering in the opposite direction toward the fountain.

"Ple-ease, this way." The young staffer waved his hand in the air with even more gusto.

"It's been like this all day. Take a break and they scatter. Makes herding cats look easy," Janie whispered before trotting after the straying bankers.

I spotted Lillian and Brooks Keller with their heads pressed together in deep conversation near the Jackson magnolia.

This particular tree, the oldest on White House grounds, was one of my favorite of the presidential commemorative trees. Andrew Jackson's wife, Rachel, died just two weeks after Jackson had won the presidential election. She never got to see him take the oath of office.

The grieving president planted two magnolias, Rachel's favorites, to flank the White House on its South Lawn. What a tribute to everlasting affection. For the past hundred-and-seventy-five years the pair of trees had thrived.

However it wasn't the tree that interested me today, but the drama unfolding underneath it. Lillian pushed a white cast iron chair out of her way. It made a loud scraping sound on the patio's concrete paving stone. She looked angry, though her voice remained too soft for anyone other than the stony-faced Brooks to hear her.

Lorenzo had mentioned last night that Pauline had been auditing Brooks and Lillian Keller's bank books and then would socialize with them at night. If that was the case, they might know what had made Pauline so excited the night before her death.

Before I could question them, Special Agent Steve Sallis stepped in my path. He gave me a hard look, his brows furrowing. "I hope you're keeping out of trouble."

"As much as possible," I said.

"Good." He chuckled, his expression lightening. "You're on CAT's radar this morning. And they don't sound especially happy about it."

"Lovely," I said with a sigh. I didn't need an entire division of the Secret Service thinking up ways to make my life miserable. "I didn't mean to cause trouble."

"I know that, Casey, and you know that. But CAT obviously doesn't. I suggest you keep a low profile for a while." He turned toward the bankers. "Break time's over, folks." He raised his voice just a bit so everyone could hear him. "The afternoon session is due to start in less than ten minutes."

Much to the young staffer's annoyance and relief, the bankers listened to Steve and started to file back inside the West Wing.

Lillian and Brooks Keller rushed past me. I started to intercept them, but the sight of Brooks's shoes hit me like a blow to the head. He was wearing the same black-and-white leather shoes with that lightning bolt on the side that I'd seen on the killer's feet. The wonder twins of banking hurried past as I stood frozen, staring at his shoes. "I don't care what you think." I overheard Lillian's sharp whisper.

"Go to hell!" Brooks shot back. He pushed the businessmen in front of them out of his way in his rush to get away from his sister and into the Palm Room. The hard soles of his shoes tapped against the pavement like a ticking time bomb.

Had a killer invaded the White House walls?

I grabbed Steve's sleeve. "Brooks Keller," I whispered. "His shoes."

"What about them?"

"The man who'd attacked me, he was wearing those shoes."

Steve peeled my hand from his arm. "Do you know who Brooks Keller is?"

I nodded and pointed toward the door Brooks had just blasted through.

"Apparently you don't know." His expression softened just a touch. "I'll quietly mention what you've told me to the lead investigator."

"Is that Mike Thatch?"

Steve nodded sharply and walked away.

"I wonder what that could have been about." Richard Templeton, as dangerously handsome as a rock star, came to stand next to me. He jammed his hands in his pants pocket and watched as Lillian glanced nervously around her while trying to pretend that nothing had happened. "Lillian and Brooks, they're an odd pair."

Richard kept his gaze trained on Lillian, which made me wonder if he realized I was standing next to him in the small niche under the magnolia tree. I discretely cleared my throat to give him fair warning.

"When our lunch break included a tour of the gardens," he said with a wry smile, "I was hoping to see you."

I looked over my shoulder, because he couldn't possibly be talking to *me.* But the only thing back there was the waxy-leafed magnolia.

"You're talking to me?" I asked, because it would make more sense if he was having a conversation with the famous Jackson magnolia tree than a plain Jane gardener like me.

"Yes." His dazzling gaze met mine. "I'm talking to you." His smile was irresistible.

CHAPTER NINE

A sudden breeze rattled the Jackson magnolia's thick leaves. Southern magnolias like this one graced nearly every plantation, grand estate, and suburban backyard in my native Lowcountry.

At the moment, though, I wasn't thinking of home. The charismatic Richard Templeton had completely captured my attention.

"I've been at my wit's end with a hydrangea bush in my garden. I've had it for years. But this past winter it's turned completely brown." His stylish light gray suit emphasized the lines of his fit body. He'd pinned a patriotic red, white, and blue flag to his lapel. "I thought perhaps you could give me some advice on what I can do to save it."

The rest of the bankers had slowly filed back inside, leaving me alone with Richard Templeton and Special Agent Steve Sallis.

Steve stayed a polite distance away. He crossed his arms over his chest and pretended disinterest, a skill the Secret Service had perfected to an art form.

"A hydrangea, you say?" Templeton had to be pulling my leg. "And you've had it for years?"

He nodded and gave me the most sincere look I'd ever seen. "I've lovingly tended it ever since it was just a little shoot."

That made me laugh.

"I don't understand," he said.

"Hydrangeas go dormant in the winter and drop their leaves, which you'd know if you actually had one in your yard for years."

He laughed, too. "Mental note to self — get my gardening facts straight before flirting with a gardener."

My jaw dropped open. "You're flirting with me?" I looked around again for another woman, because Richard Templeton, the man famous for dating supermodels, couldn't possibly be flirting with me.

He shrugged. "Why wouldn't I? You're a beautiful woman."

"You think so?" I beamed.

I'd once overheard my grandmother say that she thought my Aunt Willow's bulldog, Beauregard, had been hit one too many times with an ugly stick. But I'd never heard anyone mention getting hit with a pretty stick. And yet that must have been what had happened to me when I got hit on the side of my head, because I couldn't remember the last time two men complimented me on my looks in the same day.

"Er . . . thank you," I said graciously, remembering the manners Grandmother Faye had painstakingly drilled into me. I also remembered something else, something Lorenzo had said last night.

Pauline had told Lorenzo several weeks ago that she'd dined with Richard Templeton while in New York City.

I wanted to ask Templeton about it. But Turner had warned me not to talk about the investigation to anyone, and with the threat of the pepper spray incident hanging over my head, I didn't need to dig myself into an even deeper hole. I was very aware of Steve Sallis's presence nearby.

It was one thing to discuss Pauline's murder with Lorenzo. They'd been intimately involved.

Had Pauline also been involved with Richard Templeton?

I needed to find a way to work the question concerning Pauline's relationship with Templeton innocently into the conversation.

"I don't usually put my foot in my mouth around attractive women." Templeton rubbed the back of his neck. "Perhaps we could start over? I'm Richard Templeton. We met briefly in the hallway yesterday when Senator Pendergast stepped on your foot."

He extended a hand for me to take. I rather felt as if I should pinch myself because it didn't feel real. He cleared his throat and glanced pointedly at the hand I'd yet to take.

"Sorry." My cheeks burned a bit as I placed my hand in his. "I'm Casey Calhoun. It's a pleasure to make your acquaintance, Mr. Templeton. Have you been enjoying your visit to the nation's —"

"Please, call me Richard."

He kept hold of my hand. Not shaking it in greeting, just holding on to it as if he'd found a precious object. The soft-winged butterflies that had fluttered in my belly yesterday started whipping up a windstorm.

He lightly caressed the back of my hand with his thumb.

"I hope you're feeling better today. John told me what happened."

"John?"

"Bradley, the President. We were room-mates in boarding school. The stories I could tell." A wistful expression tugged at his lips as his gaze turned toward the Oval Office. "But I won't. I respect our friendship too much to want to embarrass him."

"President Bradley told you what happened yesterday?" I suppose when you have money and power and connections, those connections included access to state secrets.

Richard must have heard my frustrated huff. He turned all one hundred watts of his intense blue-eyed gaze back toward me. I could see why the tabloids called him "tempting."

"He gave some broad details. What is this world coming to? A woman murdered across the street from the White House." He shook his head. "And you were attacked."

I suppose if the President considered Richard a confidant, why shouldn't I? He obviously had more security clearance than I did.

Could a banking CEO work out as a gardener/part-time sleuth's sidekick? It might work.

I decided to test the waters with one of the questions I'd wanted to ask earlier. "It must have been upsetting for you, too, hearing about what happened to Pauline. Were the two of you close?"

"Pauline? Who is she?"

"Pauline Bonde, the woman who was murdered yesterday. I'd heard that she'd been auditing your company's books."

"Had she?"

"So you didn't know her?"

"No, I'm sorry. You say she'd been working in my office. That's terrible. We have federal auditors in and out all the time. It's a part of the banking business. It keeps our investors and depositors confident that their money is in safe hands. I assure you I have a team of employees who handle that end of things. I never meet the auditors."

"Yes, of course you wouldn't." Had Pauline been lying about having dinner with Richard just to make Lorenzo jealous? "After learning about how intimately involved Pauline had been in the banking audits, I couldn't help but wonder if someone killed her because of something she might have uncovered."

"I've not heard anything about that." He frowned as he considered the idea. "The Treasury Department audits were fairly benign. It's the SEC guys that tend to go for the jugular. Even so, I can't imagine anyone killing over anything an auditor might or might not have found."

"Oh." Turner had warned me that I was on the wrong track.

"I have to admit that you've got an interesting theory. With a killer lurking around the White House, I hope the Secret Service is investigating all angles," Richard said. "At least they seem to be making progress. Right before the break, I overheard that the FBI had picked up a suspect for questioning."

"They did?" Apparently Richard knew much more about what was going on than the few crumbs Turner had shared with me. "Do you know who?"

"No, but it sounded pretty serious. I mean, they might actually have their guy."

"I hope so." I touched my bandaged temple. My fingers were trembling.

"Perhaps I shouldn't have said anything. It's upset you."

"No, it's better that I know." Still, I felt shaken.

"At least you saw the killer," Richard said. "You can help the police identify him."

"I — I think so."

Richard's brows furrowed. He tightened his hold on my hand. "You're not sure?"

I closed my eyes, trying to remember. It felt as if some vital piece of information hovered at the edge of my consciousness. Every time I tried to grab it, the memory slithered farther out of reach.

I shook my head. "It's still a little fuzzy. But the memories are there." I hoped. "Give me a few days and I'm sure I'll be able to give an accurate description of him."

"That's good to know." He glanced at his watch. "I'd better go before your anxious Secret Service friend over there decides to use force to get me back to the Roosevelt Room. Would you consider meeting me for coffee after I get done for the day with this interminable summit? Say, five thirty at Capitol Perks?"

"Actually, I prefer the pastries at the Freedom of Espresso Café over on K Street."

"Why not? I'm always willing to try something new."

"Great. It's a date." I smiled so hard, I think I strained a muscle.

CHAPTER TEN

I rushed back to the grounds office underneath the North Portico anxious to find out what I could about who the FBI had picked up for questioning.

I was surprised to find Special Agent Cooper sitting at Lorenzo's desk with the ever-proper Ambrose standing watch behind him, arms crossed over his chest. The FBI agent with the thick, bulldog-like jowls had the middle drawer open and was riffling through its contents. The organized stacks of paperwork that always graced Lorenzo's desktop were spread across the floor in a messy jumble.

Loud whirling and banging noises could be heard through the thick concrete wall separating our office from the carpenter's shop next door.

"What's going on?" I demanded over the racket. "What are you doing in Lorenzo's desk?" I glanced over to my desk to see if

Cooper had sifted through my stuff. It was hard to tell if my disorganized mess of paperwork had been moved or not.

Cooper rose. "Good. You're here. I need to have a word with you." His tweed suit looked suspiciously like the one he'd worn yesterday, only more wrinkled.

"Casey," Ambrose said. His frown deepened when he turned to me. The corner of his tight mouth started to twitch.

"What's going on?" I asked again. "Does Gordon know about this?" I glanced pointedly at the paperwork that had been moved off Lorenzo's desk.

"They could have brought an entire team in here," Ambrose exclaimed. Tension put a squeak in his voice.

"We still might," Cooper added.

"A team for what?"

Cooper glared at me as if I should know.

"They've taken Lorenzo into custody to question him regarding his involvement in that woman's death." Ambrose took a deep breath. "I can't believe it. A White House employee being held under suspicion of murder. It's unthinkable."

I couldn't believe it either. I suddenly needed to sit down. "Lorenzo is a suspect?"

"Not yet," Cooper said, holding his stubby hands out. "You don't need to get upset.

We're only talking to him. He's not being held. No charges have been filed."

Still, the fact that the FBI had been concerned enough about Lorenzo's connection to Pauline that they'd sought a warrant to search his desk and to bring him in for questioning would be evidence enough to convict him in the eyes of many in the press. This could ruin Lorenzo's career.

"You should have told me that Mr. Parisi and the victim had been intimately involved," Cooper scolded. "I wasn't happy to learn that you'd shared that information with the Secret Service and not with us."

"That's what this is about? You're ruining Lorenzo's life because of something I told Turner this morning? I wish I had called you, because I would have told you unequivocally that Lorenzo didn't have anything to do with Pauline's death."

"I understand your loyalty to your coworker. I assure you that we're following several lines of investigation. But to be honest, many of them are leading us to Mr. Parisi." Cooper tilted his head and regarded me with close scrutiny. "Are there any other pertinent details you'd like to share with me?"

I pressed my lips together. I sure as hell wasn't going to tell him about Lorenzo's shoes, although I seemed to remember Lorenzo had been wearing them this morning and presumably still had them on. But that wasn't the point. I'd promised to help Lorenzo, not hurt him.

"Either you or Jack Turner have twisted my words around," I told him. "It's not Lorenzo's affair with Pauline that's suspicious. It's her involvement with the banking audits and the timing of her death that was worrying me. Did you know she was supposed to be part of a Senate hearing today to present her findings?" I held up today's paper. The cover story had provided that information along with some other interesting facts regarding her work with the Treasury Department.

"All avenues of investigation are being pursued. But as I've said, many of those avenues are leading to Mr. Parisi." Cooper stood directly in front of the office chair I'd landed in. He propped hands on his hips and puffed out his chest, straining the button on his tweed suit coat. "I ask you again, are you sure you don't know anything else? Have you remembered anything new about the attack?"

The door swung open as Gordon rushed into the office, his arms lightly coated with sweat, his face flushed from working in the gardens. The sweet scent of grass clippings clung to his khaki pants and white button-up shirt, the sleeves rolled up to his elbows.

"I was told there's a problem," he said, his gaze darting from Ambrose to Special Agent Cooper and then to me. "Has something happened, Casey? Has someone tried to hurt you again?"

"No," I assured him. "I'm fine. It's Lorenzo. We've got to help him."

"I don't understand."

"Neither do I." I bit my lower lip to keep it from quivering. "Apparently the FBI thinks Lorenzo killed Pauline and then attacked me."

"We're exploring several different —" Cooper started to say.

"Impossible!" Gordon exclaimed. "Preposterous! Who came up with such a crazy idea? What is this attack on my gardeners?"

"Ask Casey," Ambrose said. The corner of his mouth twitching. "She's the one who's been discussing his personal life."

"I didn't —" But I had.

I don't remember Miss Marple ever causing this much trouble for the friends she'd promised to help. Now what was I supposed to do?

■ ■ ■ ■

Gordon, Ambrose, and I spent the afternoon being grilled first by Special Agent Cooper, who was decidedly less friendly than yesterday, and then by Detective Hernandez, who'd arrived about fifteen minutes later and played the part of good cop. For a while *I* felt like a suspect. Acid burned in my stomach every time I thought about Lorenzo and how *he* must be feeling.

It was nearly four in the afternoon by the time Cooper and Hernandez left. Gordon had answered the rapid-fire questioning like a seasoned trooper. Ambrose, after a moment of panic, handled the crisis with the calm finesse that had made him an invaluable part of the White House staff.

And I ended up with aching muscles, a throbbing headache, and feeling like a wrung-out emotional wreck.

"I don't know how you held it all together so well," Gordon said once we were alone in the office again. He tunneled his timeworn fingers through his silver hair. "I'm on the verge of collapse. If we didn't have so much work to get done this week, I would call it a day and head straight home to bed."

"I'd almost forgotten, the Easter Egg Roll,

did you hear that Seth Donahue expanded —"

"I did," Gordon said. "That shouldn't cause us too much trouble. Despite everything, we have to stay focused. We can't neglect the spring planting and pruning. This is definitely the busiest time of the year."

Gordon was right. "They haven't arrested Lorenzo, so he might be back to work tomorrow."

"Of course he will be," Gordon said. "He's a hard worker. We need him here."

Gordon's phone rang on his desk. After answering it, he returned with a bewildered look on his face. "That was Louise Fenton."

"The First Lady's secretary?" I asked. My heart started to race. I hoped she liked the tropical begonia with bright yellow leaves I'd given her that morning. I'd selected a cheerful blue willow china pot for the plant, hoping the little gift would increase my chances that she could find an empty spot on the First Lady's impossibly tight schedule.

"She thanks you again for the begonia."

"And . . ." I glanced at the presentation boards propped against my desk, sadly unused.

"And she asked how you knew yellow was

her favorite color."

"She almost always wears yellow dresses. So I thought she might enjoy the bright yellow leaves of the tropical baby dress begonia to brighten her office.

"Was she pleased enough with the flowering plant to squeeze in another Grounds Committee meeting?" I pressed, trying not to sound too hopeful.

"With the banking summit and the Easter holidays, everybody's schedule is tight."

"I realize that." My shoulders slumped in defeat. "But it's already spring. The program should have been implemented months ago."

"Well then, we'd better get a move on," Gordon said, and shook his head in amazement. "The First Lady is assembling the committee right now. We have thirty minutes to make the presentation."

"Really?"

"No time to waste," he said.

I quickly pulled my hair into a ponytail, tried not to worry that I was wearing my usual khakis with a green-and-white-striped sweater instead of a professional suit, and scooped up the presentation boards.

Last-minute meetings were typical for the White House, where schedules tended to change like the breeze. Over the past couple of months, I'd learned to pay closer attention to the news and world events. Surprisingly, something as far away as a coup in the Middle East could affect how my day was going to unfold.

"What about Senator Pendergast?" I asked as we hurried down the hallway toward the East Wing. "She wanted to sit in on the meeting."

"According to Louise, the senator has already arrived."

Apparently, everyone had been gathered ahead of us. The entire Grounds Committee as well as the senator, a few of Mrs. Bradley's personal assistants, and the White House chef, who would have input on the proposed vegetable garden, had already assembled in the First Lady's large corner office on the second floor of the East Wing.

Margaret Bradley crossed the room to greet Gordon and me. At thirty-one years of age, she'd entered the White House as the third-youngest First Lady in U.S. history, narrowly edging Jacqueline Kennedy from that spot of honor by just one week.

Two years later, no one viewed her youth as inexperience. She wore her age like one would a fresh bloom on a lapel. Her light brown eyes sparkled with intelligence and cunning, leaving no doubt that she was perfectly suited to stand beside the leader of the free world. And her new short bob looked stunning with her dark auburn hair and had women all over the world copying her style.

Today she was wearing a simple tan skirt with matching pumps and a loose pale pink silk blouse that was belted low around her hips. The outfit accentuated her height and added color to her lightly tanned skin. I couldn't help being impressed as she shook our hands and thanked us for being able to fit *her* into *our* busy day.

"I'm the one who should be thanking you," I told her. Her slender hand felt soft and slightly chilled, but her grip conveyed a strength that many of her husband's opponents often overlooked. "I apologize for missing yesterday's meeting. I shouldn't have —"

"Never apologize for matters beyond your control," she advised quietly.

She then turned to face the gathered group. "I'm pleased to introduce the newest addition to the White House staff." Though her voice remained soft, she immediately captured the full attention of the men and women gathered in the room. As Gordon and I set up the presentation boards on the easels, the committee, staff members, and

Senator Pendergast took their places in the upholstered armchairs and sofa that had been placed in a semicircle at the front of the room.

"I have to confess," Mrs. Bradley continued, gesturing gracefully, "I lured the talented Cassandra Calhoun away from the glorious gardens in historic Charleston, South Carolina, by presenting her with an interesting challenge. I asked her to develop a plan that implements organic techniques in the care of the White House grounds. Additionally, I've asked her to design a vegetable garden that will provide our kitchen with the freshest organic vegetables."

She went on to describe my experience working in Charleston's public and private gardens and how she'd first met me at a fund-raising tea hosted by my grandmother's neighbor when the Bradleys were making the rounds on the campaign trail.

"As you know, my love of the outdoors and of gardening has been well publicized. Everyone I encountered in the Holy City kept telling me that I needed to meet this amazing woman who has a magical way of bringing new life and vigor to whatever garden she enters. And you know what? They were right. Ms. Calhoun is truly an amazing woman and we're lucky to have her."

The committee applauded politely.

I appreciated the First Lady's glowing introduction. Not only did her kind words cause me to flush with pleasure, but they also gave me a moment to catch my breath and gather my thoughts after Gordon's and my mad dash to her office.

"Thank you, Mrs. Bradley. And thank you, everyone, for making time to meet with us this afternoon," I said, and launched into my presentation.

As I spoke, the afternoon sun began to shine through a tall, west-facing window like a bright white laser beam streaming straight into my eyes. I squinted and pressed on.

Gordon, bless him, noticed my discomfort almost immediately and crossed the room to stand in front of the window to block the glare.

After a brief introduction, I provided a history of modern gardening practices. "This is information that surprised me when I first heard about it," I told the small audience. "After World War II and into the Vietnam War, chemical companies produced nerve agents, ammonium nitrate for use in explosive devices, and defoliants to give our brave soldiers in uniform a competitive edge in combat. However, these wartime companies made far more than any army could ever use and they needed to find a new consumer for their products.

"Nerve agents were repurposed as powerful insecticides. Explosive ammonium nitrate was packaged as fertilizer. And defoliants were now sold as effective herbicides. Out of these agents of war a new way of farming and backyard gardening had been born, one that creates a situation where strong chemicals are constantly required to maintain healthy-looking plants.

"Organic gardening practices involve taking care of the ecosystem of the garden as a whole. It's like adopting a healthy diet and lifestyle instead of constantly eating calorie-dense fast foods, which can sustain you, and expecting modern medicine and pills to fix the health consequences that arise from that fast-food diet.

"Chemicals may provide quick growth and quick fixes to problems, but the long-term health of the garden is ignored.

"Adopting organic gardening practices is more than simply substituting natural fertilizers and herbicides for their petrochemical counterparts. It's a complete change in how we think about gardening. Instead of reliance on chemicals derived from fossil fuels to produce vegetables and colorful flowers, organic gardening works to build fertility into the system, improve the soil, improve overall garden health, and decrease the need to apply artificial fertilizers, insecticides, and herbicides.

"The three biggest challenges that any gardener faces are weeds, insects, and fertility . . ." I launched into the details of the proposed changes, emphasizing the importance of beneficial insects and, yes, even beneficial *weeds.*

In my excitement, I strayed a bit — *quite* a bit — from the strict outline Gordon and I had created and poured out all of my passion for gardening and my love for my grandmother and aunts and the important lessons they'd taught me. Admittedly, the proposal involved some rather sweeping changes in the plants that were used and how the grounds crew cared for them. But the ideas were sound.

"I believe, if adopted, the organic gardening principles applied at the White House could become an important model in changing how gardening is practiced in backyards all across the United States."

I stepped away from the presentation boards and waited for the questions to begin. I'd prepared an extensive list of possible questions that the committee might ask along with thoroughly researched answers. I could quote studies conducted at the Rodale Institute or findings of papers written by some of the leading academic experts in the field of organic gardening. And I also had my own personal experience to draw upon. I was ready.

So I waited.

And waited.

Silence.

I glanced at Gordon, hoping he'd say something either to support what I'd proposed or to get the conversation moving. He pursed his lips and fixed his gaze on his shoes. Apparently I was on my own.

The ticking of an ornate gold clock sitting on a bookshelf seemed to drum louder and louder with each passing second.

"Well," Margaret Bradley said, breaking the awkward silence. She rose from her chair at the front of the room. "Thank you for that, Casey."

CHAPTER ELEVEN

My mouth dropped open. The committee members and staffers rose from their seats and started talking with one another as if my presentation had never happened. I glanced back at the presentation boards behind me. Yep, they were set up on their easels. I was standing in the First Lady's office. So why did I feel as if I were stuck in a nightmare?

What had just happened?

The White House chef patted my shoulder as she passed by me on her way out of the office.

Gordon laughed at something a large man with a full beard had said. Several members of the Grounds Committee joined Gordon and this other man as they headed toward the door.

I waited for a moment, expecting Gordon to return. The remaining committee members shuffled out, leaving me alone with my presentation boards.

"What am *I* to believe? It certainly feels like he's working against us." I recognized Senator Pendergast's crisp tone. The older woman had stationed herself a few feet outside Mrs. Bradley's office. Her hands propped on her hips, her cheeks flushed, she looked as if she was ready to take someone apart with her sharp-edged tongue.

"My husband would never do that." Margaret Bradley's gentle voice was harder to hear.

"How am I to know that? Everyone knows you attended college with several of them and how quickly you rose through the ranks to become the youngest vice president at BLK Investments."

"I resigned from that position a month before John and I wed."

"But you haven't cut your ties to the banking world."

"How can I? Brooks and Lillian are dear friends. I won't deny that. But you have to understand that my friendship with them has no bearing on what measures my husband will or will not support when it comes to banking reform."

"Then why is he spending so much time cozying up to your high-powered friends with this banking summit? I think it's because Wall Street has the President in their back pocket. Admit it, you and your cronies are exerting extraordinary pressure on him to yank the teeth out of my proposals."

"Obviously, you've already made up your mind about this matter, Senator, so I think you had better leave."

The senator's reply was quietly spoken. I couldn't make out the words, but her cool, staccato tone sent a shiver down my neck.

I quickly gathered up my presentation materials. Balancing the cumbersome boards in my arms, I rushed into the hallway. I wanted to talk with the First Lady. I needed to reassure her that I would work with the committee, find out their concerns and make certain they felt comfortable with the plan I'd proposed. But Mrs. Bradley was nowhere to be found. Though voices could be heard from behind the closed office doors to the left and right of me, the hallway was empty.

I gave myself a pep talk as I made my way down the stairs. I'd run into resistance plenty of times during the course of my career. People tended to shy away from change. Change meant taking risks. And risks were dangerous. I understood that. It was my job to prove to them how the rewards of this project outweighed the risks. I could do that.

"Oof," a man grunted, and gave my presentation boards a powerful shove that nearly sent me tumbling. "Watch where you're going!"

"Sorry. I didn't see you there." I doubt I would have spotted anything smaller than an elephant while carrying these boards. They were nearly as tall as I am and twice as wide. So it was tough going down the steps without Gordon's help. I stepped to one side of the stairway, lowered the boards, and was surprised to find Brooks and Lillian Keller being led by the same West Wing staffer who'd had so much trouble herding the banking officials back to the windowless Roosevelt Room after their lunch break and tour of the Rose Garden earlier that afternoon. He glared at me.

"Look Lillian, it's the hippie gardener from the newspaper, Casey Calhoun. We seem to be bumping into her quite often," Brooks said with a broad smile and twinkle in his eyes.

"She does seem to be everywhere," the staffer grumbled.

"Good afternoon, Ms. Calhoun." Lillian gave a nervous tug on Brooks's sleeve.

"We're in a hurry, brother dear."

"Run along without me. The gardener needs a hand carrying these atrociously large boards." Brooks reached out to help me.

"Thank you, but I can manage." Though I would have appreciated the assistance, if Ambrose saw or even heard about a guest at the White House being put to work because of me, my head would roll out the front door and across the North Lawn, never to be seen again.

I picked up the boards and started down the steps again, this time keeping to one side of the wide stairwell.

"See, she can manage quite well without you," Lillian chided.

"Quite nicely, indeed," Brooks drawled.

I channeled my inner Scarlett O'Hara and descended the steps with exquisite grace. I only wished I'd handled the situation with Lorenzo with the same degree of finesse. Because of me, the police had hung an umbrella of suspicion over his head.

Sure, he'd been wearing the same shoes as the killer. But maybe they were popular shoes for men. Even Brooks had them on.

And Brooks was a trusted friend of the First Lady.

No wonder Steve had reacted so strongly

when I'd suggested the Secret Service investigate Brooks's involvement in Pauline's death.

It wasn't only the shoes. He was about the same size as the man I'd seen wearing that baseball cap and carrying the silver briefcase yesterday morning in the park. But so was Lillian, for that matter. I propped the presentation boards against the wall and trotted back up the stairs in hopes of catching them.

Lorenzo had said that Pauline had gone to parties with the Keller twins. Perhaps I could use that information to help gather enough evidence to prove Lorenzo's innocence.

"I heard that the two of you were acquaintances of Pauline Bonde. I'm so sorry about what happened to her."

"I don't think —" Lillian started to say.

"Ah, Pauline," Brooks said at the same time. He lowered his gaze and slowly shook his head. "Lovely girl, Pauline. And smart. What happened to her was a tragedy. You were in the park at the same time and were attacked, too, we heard. It must have been terrible."

"I feel lucky to be alive," I admitted. "Were you close to Pauline?"

Brooks's face flushed a deep red.

"Our investment bank was on her audit circuit," Lillian answered before Brooks could say anything. "Auditors from the SEC and the Treasury come and go all the time. I believe she'd been conducting an off-cycle regulatory review?"

"I read in the newspaper that the Senate had asked for the audits to help get an accurate picture of how the banks are operating so they can draft effective banking reform legislation. What do you think about the proposals being discussed?" Were the Keller twins exerting pressure on the President to water down the reforms, as Senator Pendergast had charged?

Lillian leveled her sharp gaze on me and frowned.

"Oh, that?" Brooks rubbed his balding head. "I can't say that I agree with everything they want to put into that bill. It'll make it damned hard to do business. But I have to admit that there are guys out there who are only interested in making as much money as they can as fast as possible. They don't care if they're breaking the rules or creating problems down the line. As long as those bastards are out there, we need regulation."

"We've taken too much of your time, Ms. Calhoun." Lillian grabbed her brother's

184

sleeve again. The West Wing staffer let loose a deep sigh of relief. "Let's go. Margaret is waiting."

"Yes, if you'll follow me. I can show you the way."

"I suppose." Brooks wrinkled his nose at his sister. He then turned to me and flashed a devilish smile that took years off his slightly pudgy face. "I hope we bump into each other another again soon, Casey."

"Brooks, no." Lillian forced from behind clenched teeth. "We don't have time for this."

That was the second time Lillian had discouraged her brother from flirting with me. It wasn't as if I took him seriously. He just seemed like the type who flirted.

I puzzled over her unfriendly manner as the trio headed up the stairs to the second floor of the East Wing. At the landing, Lillian stopped and turned back toward me. She bit her lower lip and furrowed her blond brows before mouthing, "Watch yourself."

The constant whirl of saws and banging coming through the walls from the carpenter's shop sounded like an odd symphony in the background of the grounds office. I'd like to say that was why I couldn't concen-

185

trate, but it would have been a lie.

I couldn't stop thinking about Lillian's warning. Had that been a threat?

Also, no one had any news about Lorenzo. How long would it take for the FBI to come to their senses and release him?

I'd spent the past half hour mindlessly adding Seth Donahue's latest changes to a sketch plan for the Easter Egg Roll. He'd shuffled around where the various activities — such as the reading corner, the crafts booth, and the hot dog stand — were to be set up so many times that the pink and yellow pastel sketch plan of the South Lawn was slowly turning into an unrecognizable blob of orange ink.

"Will you be staying through the weekend?" I heard Gordon say a moment before the grounds office door swung open. "You owe me the chance to redeem myself on the golf course. My hand cramped up last time."

"I believe I can make time for that. Playing with you always makes me feel like a pro, Gordo."

The tall man with the thick brown beard who'd seemed so chummy with Gordon after the presentation entered the office and came to a stop in front of the presentation boards I'd left propped up against the wall beside my desk.

I jumped up to greet them. Perhaps I could salvage some of the organic gardening presentation. Clearly, the committee didn't understand what I was proposing.

"That was an interesting presentation you gave," the bearded man said to me. "You were certainly asking for the moon and stars in there, weren't you?"

"I don't think —" I protested.

"Barney," Gordon said, cutting me off, "meet Casey Calhoun."

A line of white teeth appeared from behind Barney's thick beard. I hoped that meant he was smiling.

"Barney, as in Barney Vetters?" Who just happened to be the chairman of the Grounds Committee and a leading authority on plant disease?

He nodded and showed more of his teeth. "Guilty."

"I don't think you understand what I'm proposing. The plans are really very modest. I mean —"

"You don't know what you've done, do you?"

"The First Lady directed me to —" I tried to say.

"You've suggested we make wholesale changes to a national treasure, a national treasure that most of the public feels an intimate connection to. You cannot expect the committee to approve such a proposal. It'd be like us recommending the Louvre paint the Mona Lisa's hair purple."

Gordon chuckled. "I'd like to see that, Barney."

I bit the inside of my cheek to keep from screaming. Barney Vetters, a renowned plant expert, should have known better. He, of all people, should have recognized that the proposed plan wouldn't *visually* change the White House grounds, not in any way that the visiting public would notice. I was merely suggesting a more environmentally sensitive way of taking care of the existing grounds.

"What do you want me to do?" I asked with my fists pressing against my thighs. I couldn't seem to keep my voice from trembling.

"Go home, Casey," Gordon suggested. He didn't look the least bit worried. And why should he? His career wasn't teetering on disaster. "Get some rest. We'll talk more about it tomorrow."

"What about Lorenzo?" I asked. "Have you heard any news about" — I glanced at Barney — "his situation?"

"I have. He was released about an hour ago. I told him to go home as well. He'll be back in the office tomorrow."

"So, he straightened everything out with" — I glanced at Barney again — *"everyone?"*

"Not completely. We'll talk more about it in the morning."

"We're heading out to grab an early dinner," Barney said as he pulled Gordon toward the door. "It was nice to meet you, Casey. Thanks for the laugh this afternoon." He wagged his finger at me. "Gordo was right. You really are something."

"Yeah." That was just the impression I'd hoped to make.

Damn.

Gordon leaned against the doorframe and told Barney to go on ahead without him. "Don't worry so much, Casey. It'll work out."

"Are you sure?" From where I was standing, without the chairman's support, the future of the White House's organic gardening program looked pretty damn bleak. "I only want to do what's right."

"I know you do."

"Then why didn't you support me at the meeting?"

"I would have spoken up if we'd had any hope of winning the committee's vote. We didn't. Not after you made it sound so . . ." Gordon sighed. "Barney's waiting. We'll talk

189

in the morning."

After Gordon left, I probably should have taken his advice and headed home, but leaving felt too much like giving up. I had to stay. I had to work.

Wilson Fisher's towering pile of forms taunted me from my desk. I sat and started to plod through them. At least this was one task I knew I could accomplish.

As I checked boxes and filled out endless lines of data on the forms, questions about Pauline's death gnawed at me. Why had she lied to Lorenzo? Why would she tell him she'd dined with Richard Templeton when, according to Richard, it wasn't true? Had she been deliberately trying to make Lorenzo jealous?

And how well did Lillian and Brooks know Pauline? Had Pauline been *too* friendly with the bankers she'd been auditing?

It seemed like too much of a coincidence that someone would murder her on the eve that she was to present her findings to the Congress. I wondered if there'd been something on her laptop that would prove damaging to someone.

Those questions had wrapped themselves around my brain so tightly that when I read the last sentence on page five of Fisher's

190

Form 4-AB-56 for the third time, I realized I had no idea what it wanted me to do. Frustrated, I set down my pen and rubbed my bruised temple.

Filling out meaningless paperwork wasn't getting me anywhere. I needed to get my hands dirty. I needed to be outside under the sun.

Since it was nearly five o'clock, I packed up my things for the day, grabbed my floppy straw hat, and headed outside. I always did my best thinking in the garden.

Earlier that afternoon, Ambrose had sent word to our office that the flowerbed where I'd been attacked was no longer roped off with crime scene tape. Since I didn't have time to attend to it myself — I rarely had time for the fun hands-on work — I'd asked a few members from the grounds crew to replace the damaged flowers, clean up the elm's broken branches, and repair whatever damage the reporters might have caused by stomping through Lafayette Square.

Joanna Lovell, still dressed in that ugly shiny blue housecoat, stood at the head of the banking protesters. She shook a cardboard cutout of Brooks Keller as if she were trying to kill it, while several in her group cheered.

A new protester had set up next to them

in front of the North Lawn. His camouflage hat pulled low on his head, he sat in a lawn chair with a handwritten sign propped up in his lap that read, EVERY AMERICAN DESERVES A SAFE WORKPLACE. He nodded in my direction as I passed.

Nearby, Connie was talking to a group of high school kids, showing off her antinuclear weapons posters. Tourists snapped pictures of every inch of the White House North Lawn and Lafayette Square as uniformed Secret Service agents stood by their cars parked on the closed-off Pennsylvania Avenue in front of the White House. A pair of U.S. Park Police officers rode ten-speed bicycles through the park as they kept a vigilant watch for trouble.

On the other side of the park, the National Park Service's three-man, one-woman grounds crew was finishing their work. An unbroken border of ruffled tulips and grape hyacinths waved happily in the late afternoon sun as if nothing had happened.

The elm's branches had been neatly trimmed back. In time the young tree would heal and would eventually grow to match the splendor of the older elms in the park. The scars left on its trunk, however, would forever mark the place where Pauline had died.

Sal Martin, a man in his late sixties, who acted and dressed as if he still lived in the swinging seventies, was raking in a small pile of mulch around the drip line of the elm. The heavy gold chain he wore around his neck jingled with each pull of the rake. He stopped when he saw me approach and propped his arm on the rake's handle as if he'd sidled up to a bar.

"Glad you moseyed your way o'er here, Miss Casey," he drawled. His heavy Texas accent always managed to startle me. If I closed my eyes, I could picture a man wearing chaps and a dusty old cowboy hat, not gold chains underneath his olive green park service uniform that looked two sizes too small. "Found this 'ere bauble buried in the flowerbed o'er yonder. Been thinking you must have dropped it."

He handed me a golden, diamond-studded charm with a broken clasp.

"Thank you," I said, frowning at the unfamiliar piece of jewelry. The charm, shaped like a large dollar sign, had diamond chips embedded in the double slashes bisecting an elaborate scrolling *S*. I turned it over and found *P* and *B* professionally engraved on the back. Underneath the letters someone had scratched in a phone number with a D.C. area code.

P and *B?* Could the charm have belonged to Pauline Bonde?

"You mean you found this near the elm?"

"No, ma'am." He pointed across the park to the bed of pink tulips where the killer had left me. "Found it plumb o'er there."

"I see. Thank you again, Sal."

"My pleasure," he said and winked. With his hips swaying to a funky beat only he could hear, he returned to his raking.

I was still puzzling over the charm — if it had fallen off Pauline's bracelet or necklace, how did it get across the park and into the flowerbed? That's when I noticed a young woman in her mid-twenties standing at the edge of Lafayette Square.

She wore a heavy cream wool sweater over a black turtleneck. Jeans hugged her waif-thin body before flaring like trumpet flowers at the bottom. A long black canvas tube I'd seen architects use to carry their plans was hanging from a strap over her shoulder. Her bleached blond hair tumbled in loose curls over her shoulders. Thick black eyeliner made her large eyes appear to occupy over half her face, like those paintings of sad children that were popular in the seventies.

She'd stopped at the edge of the grass, clasped her delicate hands together, and pressed them to her chest. As her gaze swept the park, tears welled up in her oversized eyes. She buried her face in her hands.

I crossed over to her while digging around in my backpack for the package of travel tissues I'd hoped had survived yesterday's dip in the mud. "Are you okay?" I asked the woman and handed her a — thankfully — dry tissue.

She raised her head from her hands. Her heavy eyeliner had not smeared, despite the tears streaming down her cheeks. Sniffling, she accepted the tissue. "She — she died here," her voice warbled.

"Pauline." I handed her the entire package of tissues. "You knew her?"

She nodded. Her shoulders shook as she cried even harder.

"I'm sorry for your loss," I said, not sure what to say or do to comfort her. If she'd been a friend, I would have pulled her into my arms. Heck, if this had been my hometown of Charleston, I wouldn't have thought twice about hugging a stranger. But since she didn't know me and I didn't know the mores of this city, I wasn't sure what would be acceptable. "It must have been quite a shock for you," I ended up saying.

"No." She blew her perfect nose on the wad of tissues in her fist while fighting off a new wave of tears. "No, it wasn't a shock. Not at all. I knew he'd kill her."

CHAPTER TWELVE

Much to my horror, the woman started to cry again. Not just dainty tears, but noisy, messy sobs. And I didn't have any more tissues to offer her.

I glanced over my shoulder at the gardening crew. They were packing up their equipment. Sal gave a small wave before hurrying away with a wheelbarrow.

"Please," I said and lightly touched the sobbing woman's arm. "I think you should sit down."

She nodded tearfully and followed me to a park bench under a willow oak. I'd purposefully selected a bench that put the crime scene behind us. We sat in silence watching the traffic rush by on H Street.

"I'm Casey Calhoun, assistant gardener for the White House." I drew a fortifying breath and gently explained how I'd discovered Pauline's body.

"Then — then you work with *him?*" She

wiped her nose with the wad of tissues in her hand and turned her large eyes toward me. "You know how obsessive he is."

"Who?"

"I'd warned Pauline not to play games with him, but she'd laughed at me, told me I had no sense of adventure, no imagination. Personally, I think she liked making him crazy. I think she liked the attention when he'd started to stalk her."

"Who?" I asked, more forcefully this time.

"Lorenzo Parisi, of course." A spurt of fresh anger stiffened her voice. "He killed her."

I drew back as if she'd slapped me. "No, I can't believe that. He's a good guy and a great gardener."

"Then you don't know anything about him."

"Perhaps you can help me understand. Perhaps you can tell me about Lorenzo and Pauline's relationship?"

"Oh, I can tell you everything, all right, because I lived with it. Pauline was my roommate."

She introduced herself as Isabella Cordray and, in between crying jags, described how she'd met Pauline. Isabella had recently graduated with a master's degree in architecture and had taken an internship at a well-known D.C. design firm. She'd found Pauline through a "roommate wanted" notice Pauline had posted on the Freedom of Espresso Café's bulletin board. The two women had immediately bonded.

As I listened to Isabella's recounting of her two-year history of sharing an apartment with Pauline, I couldn't help wondering about Lorenzo's role in this story. Isabella clearly disliked him.

"They'd been dating for about a year now. I never understood what she saw in him. Too slick for his own good. Too handsome. Too sure of himself. And much, much too arrogant. You know him, you know how he is."

When she looked to me for confirmation, I made a noncommittal sound that seemed to please her.

"About three weeks ago Pauline told Lorenzo they were over, that she'd moved on. Took her long enough. I told her to leave him after their first date, but she rarely listened to me. I thought at the time, good riddance. But the jerk kept turning up like a bad penny.

"He'd call. He'd drop by our apartment in the middle of the night, even when she was out of town. I knew from the first moment I set eyes on him he'd be trouble. I

199

have good instincts when it comes to men. It's like a fifth sense."

"You mean you can taste them?" That seemed odd.

"Taste? I don't understand."

"The fifth sense is taste."

"No, no. Not that." She waved her dainty hands in the air as if she was trying to erase her words. "I mean I can tell when trouble's brewing before it happens. Which sense is that?"

"The sixth sense, I believe." I had to bite my lower lip to keep from smiling. "Did Lorenzo ever threaten Pauline? Did she seem scared of him?"

"I don't think the devil himself could have scared Pauline. Like I said before, I think she liked the attention."

I closed my eyes and tried to picture Lorenzo, scorned lover, as a killer. Though I'd worked closely with him for the past three months, how well did anyone know a coworker? Could he have struck out at Pauline in a fit of passion?

I didn't think so. And even if he had, it still didn't explain why he would have attacked me.

Besides, the man I saw in the park, the man with the odd silver briefcase, had been wearing a baseball cap, something I'd never seen on top of Lorenzo's head.

I rubbed my bruised temple. There were too many details about the attack I needed to remember. As I'd told the police, the FBI, and the Secret Service, I couldn't remember seeing Mr. Baseball Cap — or anyone else — attack me. All I could remember seeing was that one black-and-white leather shoe with a lightning bolt down one side.

"Lorenzo told me that Pauline had visited him a week or so ago and given him a gift, a pair of shoes. Do you know anything about that?" I asked.

"I don't doubt that it had happened. He'd stopped coming over lately, probably because I'd threatened to call the cops on him. Pauline hated that. She liked the attention he gave her."

She leaned forward, buried her face in her hands, and moaned. "The lease was in Pauline's name. There's nothing stopping the building's super from kicking me out of the apartment at the end of the month. I know he'll do it. He hates me. Called me a whiny pain in the ass. And why? Because I'd complained about Lorenzo's aggressive behavior. I told Bill, that's the super, I told him that if he didn't hire a security guard for the front entrance, I'd call the owners and complain. Bill acted all put out about it. Now look what's happened. I don't know if I'll ever feel safe again."

"Have you talked with the FBI about this? Have you told them what you suspect?" I bet she was the one who had convinced Special Agent Cooper that Lorenzo had played a role in Pauline's murder.

Isabella blew out a sharp breath. "They're about as dense as Bill. Oh, the agent I'd talked to sounded very concerned and wrote down everything I'd said in his little notebook. He'd promised to look into it. When I called him this afternoon to see if they'd arrested Lorenzo, he assured me they were working diligently on the case. But I could tell from his condescending tone that he'd ignored everything I'd told him. I handed him all the evidence he needed to make an arrest, and he dismissed it. *He dismissed me.* It's a cut-and-dry case. I don't understand why they're dragging their feet. *Men!*"

I envied Isabella's unwavering certainty about what had happened to Pauline even if it did cast Lorenzo in the role of villain.

I knew from personal experience the turmoil of grief and fear, and — worst of all — a burning need for answers a violent death can cause for those left behind, who have to pick up their own shattered lives

Before reaching the edge of Lafayette Square, a disturbing sight caught my attention. A batch of mile-a-minute vines had invaded a second flowerbed near H Street. The weed's triangular leaves pointed at me like tiny mocking fingers as their spindly tendrils stretched up, entangling themselves around the length of over a half dozen tulip leaves, slowly but surely choking the plants to death. I slipped off my backpack and found my gardening gloves.

After pulling them on, I dropped to my knees and began the slow process of removing the weeds, roots and all, taking care that I didn't damage the tulips.

At about quarter to six I was just about finished with my task. Pulling weeds was just about the only progress I could claim so far that week. The tulips seemed to shiver with delight as I freed them from the strangling vines.

I'd stuffed the last of the limp weeds in a paper bag when I noticed Joanna Lovell a couple hundred feet away. She was standing toe-to-toe with the balding Brooks Keller. They were an odd pair, what with Joanna in that oversized pale blue flowered housecoat and Brooks in an expensive suit that had been pressed to razor-sharp creases.

I pulled off my muddy gardening gloves

and survive. More than three decades had passed since my mom had been taken from me in a violent flash, and the pain still burned in my chest with the same force as the day it had happened.

Last night Lorenzo had seemed shaken and desperate for answers. I knew the feeling. I'd been just as desperate for answers after my mom's death, answers I'd never been able to find. He'd become like me, a seeker. I had to help him, to clear his name, and to find answers for him.

And for myself.

I needed to understand why Pauline had died . . . and why I was still alive.

I handed Isabella the charm Sal had found. "Have you ever seen this?"

Tears welled up in her impossibly large eyes as she cradled the golden dollar sign in the palm of her hands. "Of course," she said. "Of course. This stupid thing. She'd come back with the charm from one of her New York trips. She got suddenly coy about the men in her life. But she was definitely seeing someone. I think he gave her this. I bet he's married. Men are such pigs."

"So the *P* and *B* on the back are her initials."

She flipped the charm over and ran her long, slender fingers over the engraving.

"Yes. And that's her cell phone number."

"Why would she scratch her own cell phone number onto a charm? Did she wear it on a bracelet or a necklace?"

"Neither. She hooked it to her laptop case. I suppose she added the phone number to protect it from loss." Isabella shrugged her dainty shoulders. "The charm clanked against the case when she walked. I told her that she sounded like a traveling one-woman band. But did she listen to me? She never listened to me."

I remembered the large flower-patterned bag that had been stuffed into the trash can with Pauline. Was that the laptop bag? And if so, how did the charm get into the flowerbed where I was weeding?

"Wait a minute. The charm clanked against the laptop case? Aren't laptop bags soft-sided like my backpack?"

"Not Pauline's. She carried this metal box like spies used to carry in the old James Bond movies."

"A silver briefcase?" Just thinking about it made my chest tighten.

"Yes, she carried the clanky thing everywhere with her."

It suddenly hit me. Actually, a *silver laptop case* had hit me. I remembered it clearly now. I saw that silver laptop case out of the

corner of my eye right before it slamm[ed] against the side of my head. The char[m] must have broken off from the force of th[e] violent impact. Which meant Mr. Baseba[ll] Cap *had* attacked me.

"Why would Lorenzo kill her and steal her laptop?" I wondered aloud. It couldn't be him.

"Who knows? He's crazy. Does anything he'd do need to make sense?"

Yes, it did.

Isabella didn't care. She started to complain about Lorenzo, her apartment's superintendent, and the police again. I was beginning to get the impression she didn't get along well with any of the men in her life. I stood rather abruptly and thanked her for talking to me.

I walked back to the flowerbed where I'd been attacked and where Sal had found the charm. I stared at the flowers in the bed as if they could tell me their secrets.

Turner had told me that nothing important had been stolen from either Pauline or me. Had he been lying to discourage me from asking more questions? Or did they not know about the laptop?

The flowers remained silent on the matter. So with the sun at my back, I headed home.

and gave them a shake as I watched Joanna poke Brooks several times in the chest with her slender finger. I was too far away to hear their conversation. But their body language seemed to speak volumes. Brooks leaned in toward Joanna and put his hand on her hip. At first she tensed. But as Brooks continued to talk, her pink lips relaxed into a smile.

Joanna said something and then laughed.

Brooks jerked back. Whatever she'd said, it must have been harsh. The balding CEO's smile dissolved. He jammed a hand in his pocket and pulled out a white envelope that he shoved against Joanna's chest.

"There!" he shouted and stalked off.

Joanna opened the envelope. As she peeked inside, her smile widened.

That's when I remembered.

And I ran.

CHAPTER THIRTEEN

My feet pounded as vigorously as my heart as I sprinted down the street, weaving deftly through the steady stream of commuters, apologizing for my rudeness as I went. I took a hard right onto K Street and blasted through the Freedom of Espresso Café doors, crashing to a stop at the front counter. My gaze flitted over the dozen or so round tables and the line of booths at the back of the café.

He wasn't there.

My shoulders dropped.

He must have already left.

According to the rooster-shaped clock hanging above the copper espresso machine, I'd missed my coffee date with "Tempting" Richard Templeton by no more than fifteen minutes.

"Are you okay?" the college-aged barista asked. She had a pierced nose and lip with a gold chain dangling between the two. She poured some water into a paper cup and handed it to me.

"Thank you," I croaked. I swallowed some water. "Richard — Richard Templeton?" I asked, still struggling to catch my breath. "Here?"

I gulped the rest of the water.

"So you heard about that, too? He left already." Her cheeks took on a rosy glow as her lips spread to form a mischievous grin, tugging on the chain hanging between her lip and nose. "You'll never believe what happened."

"I think I can guess," I said dryly, despite all that water I'd been drinking.

"No, not this. You're right, Richard Templeton, *the* Richard Templeton of National Tenure Bank, was in here. But that's not the exciting part. He was waiting for a woman . . . *who didn't show up.* Can you believe that?"

"Yeah, I can."

"I wish she had come in. I would have liked to have seen her. The women he dates are so incredibly beautiful and famous. They're always famous. I bet she's a model. My brother dated a model for a while. She was supposed to come to Thanksgiving dinner with him. But she stood him up at the last minute. Models are notoriously unreliable like that. If Richard Templeton had invited someone who looked more like you or me, he certainly wouldn't have been sitting at that table over there all by himself, staring into his steaming coffee."

"You might be surprised." I ordered a double espresso.

"I'm sure we'll hear more about this story." The machine behind the counter hissed as she made my drink. "The tabloids caught wind of Richard's embarrassment. Someone at the café must have tipped them off. When he left, he was seriously alone and pissed off, photographers hounded his every step. I'm sure it's already lighting up all the gossip blogs. I wouldn't be surprised if a TV show picks up the story, too."

"Goodie."

She handed me my espresso. As I sipped it, she swiped my credit card at the cash register. She bit her lower lip and swiped it again. With a huff, she handed the card back to me.

"You're going to have to pay cash. Your card's no good."

"Really?" I fumbled around in my backpack until I found enough loose change to pay for the drink.

"You must have forgotten to pay your bill," she said as she dropped the change into the cash register drawer.

"No, I don't think that's it." I frowned at the useless card. I might not remember yesterday's attack, but I clearly remembered paying my credit card bill last week.

I wondered if <u>Lillian Keller</u> had anything to do with this. Did she have the power to wreck my credit rating just because I'd asked a few innocent questions? Would she do that? And if so, I wondered how far she'd go to stop an unfavorable audit from going public. Would she commit murder to protect her bank?

A brutal wind pushed through the capital the next morning. Young trees bowed in submission to the harsh spring weather while the older trees swayed and creaked. Tender leaves and flower petals scattered through the early morning sky. Their pastel colors swirled and danced as they buzzed past streetlamps.

My hair, cool and slightly damp from the morning dew, slapped my face while I waited at the White House gate. I couldn't do anything about my hair. In each hand I held a reusable metal travel mug filled with steaming rich Kona coffee.

In this wind, I didn't dare set the mugs on the ground in order to finger-comb my hair or pull it back into a ponytail. With their tapering bottoms designed to fit in a car cup holder, the mugs were top-heavy.

I had important plans for both coffees, so I couldn't risk a spill. Biting my lower lip, I pretended I didn't care how tangled my hair looked by the time Special Agent Jack Turner emerged with his CAT-instilled stealth from the shadowy North Lawn.

"Good morning," I said brightly.

He gave a brisk nod and swung the gate open.

This morning when Fredrick had instructed me to wait while he disappeared into the guard hut to make a phone call, I had smiled with satisfaction.

With the wind blowing even stronger, I followed Turner to the far side of the guard hut under the littleleaf linden tree, where we were shielded from the worst of the spring gale storm, and I handed him my backpack even before he asked for it, which wasn't easy considering how I had to juggle the coffee mugs.

"How's the investigation going?" I asked him.

He did a fair impression of a deaf wall as he dug through my bag. I didn't let his silence discourage me.

"Pauline's roommate visited Lafayette

Square yesterday. We had a nice long chat. She thinks Lorenzo is guilty. *I* don't, in case you were confused about that. And I'm determined to prove it."

His hand stilled as he looked up from my bag. His green eyes met mine and then narrowed.

"I mean it, Turner. Lorenzo had nothing to do with Pauline's murder. And he certainly wouldn't have attacked me. You can tell Agent Cooper at the FBI that I said that. You can also tell him everything points back to the audits. I'm going to prove that as well, even if it means I have to talk with every banker from here to Wall Street."

"Does your career at the White House really mean so little to you?" He rolled his shoulders. "You seem to be doing everything possible to justify a swift dismissal. If that's what you want, I'll be happy to make it happen."

"I don't —"

"Really, Casey? All White House employees are expected to follow Secret Service directives. When I told you not to poke your nose where it doesn't belong, that wasn't a suggestion you could choose to ignore. Who knows what damage you've already done to our investigation, not to mention the damage to the hard work the FBI and D.C.

213

Police have put into this case?"

"Talking to Pauline's roommate to find out what she's been telling you and the FBI and lord knows who else is not interfering with anything you're doing."

"How do you know that?"

I wasn't going to win this argument, and since my position as assistant gardener was important to me, I decided to keep my mouth shut, but apparently he wasn't finished.

"You were also seen questioning Richard Templeton yesterday."

"Now hold on a minute." I held up my hand, but since I was holding those darn coffee mugs, I ended up looking like I was waving the mug around. "He was flirting with me. He asked me out to coffee."

"Really?" That seemed to take Turner by surprise.

I shrugged coyly, using a look every Southern lady worth her salt knows how to use to her benefit. The simple expression hinted at a multitude of secrets.

"Interesting," he said. "And did you?"

"Did I what?"

"Agree to go to coffee with him?"

"Of course." I blushed a bit as I thought about how I'd messed up that opportunity. Alyssa refused to talk to me after I'd told her what had happened. Actually, she'd called me an idiot before giving me the silent treatment. Not that I blamed her. I would have done the same if our roles had been reversed.

"I see." His dark brows furrowed slightly. "He's rich and good looking, quite a catch."

"It was just coffee." A coffee date that didn't even happen. "I brought *you* coffee. Kona coffee."

"I'm on duty."

"It's just coffee."

"It's a bribe. You want me to tell you what I know about the investigation."

"You could still take the coffee and not tell me anything."

"No, I can't."

"Well then, I'll tell you what I know and you can run and tell Cooper all about it." I set the coffee mugs on the ground next to the guard hut, where they'd be protected from the howling wind, and produced Pauline's charm from my jacket pocket. "A member of the grounds crew found this buried in the flowerbed yesterday where I was attacked."

He looped my backpack on one arm and took the golden dollar sign charm. His frown deepened as he turned it over in his hand.

"Pauline's roommate, Isabella, recognized it as belonging to Pauline. She said Pauline kept it hanging from the handle of a silver laptop case. Remember I saw a man with a silver briefcase?"

Turner nodded, offering nothing.

"Was Pauline's laptop stolen?" I asked.

"That's a good question."

"And do you have a good answer?"

"You're not part of this investigation, Casey. Nor should you be conducting your own investigation."

"My conversation with Isabella was very useful, though. Speaking with her sparked a memory. I saw that silver case right before it hit me. I'm sure of it. And the fact that my crew found the charm she kept on the laptop case only proves that what I'm remembering actually happened. Someone stole Pauline's laptop and hit me with its case. She might have even been killed because of something she had saved on its hard drive."

"I see." His expression remained inscrutable. "Have you remembered anything else?"

"No. But I'm sure I will. I have to."

"Let me know when you do."

"Of course I will."

"See that you do. And thank you for

bringing me this charm. It could be an important piece of evidence," he said. "Oh, don't go getting all smug on me. It might also be nothing."

Since we seemed to be done, I reached for my backpack.

"Hold up," he said, "you're not off the hook yet."

"I'm not? Why?"

"There's this." He held up the small green hairspray bottle I'd put in my backpack that morning. "More pepper spray? My God, you're a walking security risk. Tell me why I shouldn't report this to Ambrose with the recommendation that he dismiss you on the spot."

"I walk to and from work alone and often in the dark," I said quietly. "I need to be able to protect myself."

"Then you need to make arrangements. You can't just smuggle weapons into the White House. It will get you fired."

"Give me a little credit, Turner. I knew you were going to search my bag. I knew you were going to find the pepper spray. Perhaps you could return it at the end of the day so I don't have to walk home unprotected?"

My heart hammered while I waited for him to say something. Anything. He uncapped the bottle and sniffed the contents.

"It's potent stuff," I assured him. "But you already know that," the devil made me add.

"Yeah, I do." He pocketed the hairspray bottle. "Fredrick will return it to you when you leave for the day."

"Thank you. Are you sure you don't want the coffee?"

"Sorry. No."

"Your loss." I reached for my backpack, but Turner held it back.

"I read your security background check the other day while Thatch was questioning you," he said.

My insides clenched. "I was afraid that was what was in the folder you were reading."

"Those reports are thorough, you know. It had information about your parents, specifically about your mother's —"

"My paternal grandmother and my aunts raised me," I cut in rather forcefully. Everything that had happened before they took me in to live with them in the stately historic home located in Charleston's exclusive South of Broad neighborhood was kept securely bolted behind an iron door, never to be opened.

I'd never talked to anyone about what had

happened to me or to my mom. Not Grandmother Faye or either of my aunts. Not the soft-spoken child psychologist who sat with me in her office for an hour every Thursday for three years.

But ever since I woke up in the flowerbed two days ago, bloody and confused, memories from that dark time in my past had started to seep around my iron door.

"Have you considered that your need to ask so many questions about Pauline's murder stems back to what happened to you when you were six years old?"

"My past has nothing to do with what's happening now. Nothing at all. Do you understand me?"

Turner raised his hands in mock surrender and backed away. "Okay," he said. "Okay."

"I'll see you tomorrow." I snatched my backpack from him, scooped up the coffee he didn't want, and stalked away.

"Casey." Turner jogged after me. "Wait a minute."

I would have ignored him. I was in that much of a snit. But he added a plaintive "please."

"I'm busy," I said, though I slowed down a bit.

"I'm worried about you."

I squeezed my eyes closed. Tears seeped

out, which only made me more upset with him.

"Please, stop for a minute."

I did, but I wasn't happy about it. He'd touched a sore nerve by bringing up my past. I couldn't meet his gaze.

He knew. He'd pried into my past and learned of my darkest secret. My deepest fear.

He had no right.

"For whatever reason, you're not going to stop pushing your way into this investigation. You're not going to stop asking questions. Not even the threat of ruining your career is going to stop you. Am I right?"

I didn't say anything.

"This is a serious business you're getting yourself into, Casey. Why do you think we're going to such lengths to protect your identity from the press?"

"You don't want nosy reporters getting in the way of the investigation." My voice sounded unnaturally high.

"There is that," he agreed. "But we're more concerned about protecting you. You saw him, Casey. From the killer's point of view, that's a problem. And if he thinks you're getting close to identifying him, he'll stop you by any means possible."

I pressed my lips together and looked away.

"Dammit, I don't want to see you hurt. Here." He pulled a pen and a small notebook from a pocket of his flak jacket. The pen scratched noisily as he scribbled something on the paper. He ripped the page off the pad and handed it to me. "It's my personal cell number. Promise me you'll call if you ever feel like you've gotten yourself in over your head. Even if it's a hunch, call me."

"Fine." My hand shook as I jammed the slip of paper into my coat pocket.

My feet couldn't carry me fast enough away from him. I muttered angry words to myself as I stomped toward the grounds office, never once realizing that I'd just been handed exactly what I'd wanted.

Turner had agreed to help me.

CHAPTER FOURTEEN

"What do you mean, you can't tell me why my credit card's been canceled?" My voice quavered as I tried to keep my temper under control. I had more important things to do than to spar with the multinational bank that held my now useless credit card. The tip of my pen tapped a frustrated beat on the desk.

Turner had no right to bring up my past, blindsiding me like that. It had left my nerves badly shaken.

The woman on the other end of the call apologized and politely assured me that the bank never canceled credit cards without a good reason. "Have you recently moved?" she asked.

"About three months ago."

"That may be it. Please hold." I heard her typing on her keyboard.

As I waited, Gordon walked by and dropped a newspaper on my desk. The pages had been folded back to an inside section. The headline before the break on that page read: WHITE HOUSE GARDEN EXTRAVAGANCE STIRS OUTRAGE.

"While Congress penny-pinches, White House spending spirals out of control," proclaimed the article, written by Griffon Parker from *Media Today,* who probably disliked puppies, growled at children, and weighed down social events like a miserable storm cloud. *"The extravagances began with the wholly unnecessary addition of yet another assistant gardener to the White House staff. This new staff member, in a desperate attempt to make herself useful, has developed a complex and costly plan to 'green' the White House gardens."*

The article bemoaned several of the proposed gardening practices. He called my proposal to add native plants to the landscape *"a complete waste of time."* To my idea that the White House should alter its turfgrass management by replacing repeated applications of petroleum-based chemical fertilizers with compost and nutrient-rich compost tea, the report exclaimed, *"A disastrous idea that'll lead to a yellow-spotted, gangly lawn . . . not to mention the smell. Everyone knows compost is just a polite word for poop."*

And the cherry on top of his vitriolic rant was the reporter's response to my suggestion that in order to reduce pesticide use, the White House replace the current planting of roses in the Rose Garden with more sustainable varieties. He wrote, *"Remove the roses from the Rose Garden? This woman should be shot for* treason!"

"You're twisting my plans around to make them sound foolish. Do you even know anything?" I argued with the article. "If anyone should be shot, it should be jerks like you who can't get their facts straight."

"Excuse me?" the woman on the phone from the bank asked rather tersely.

"Sorry," I said. "I wasn't talking to you."

"Please be patient, I'm pulling up your credit report now."

"Thank you."

I pressed my lips together and forced myself to finish reading the libelous article. *" 'The new gardening position at the White House is not only unnecessary, but the organic gardening plan proposed by Cassandra Calhoun is a lavish experiment that will cost hardworking taxpayers money they can ill afford to lose,' said Senator Edith Pendergast, vowing to block the plans from being implemented."*

My jaw dropped. Senator Pendergast thought my position at the White House was a waste of money? What happened to her keen interest in gardening?

I put my hand over the telephone handset. "How did the reporter get this information?" I asked Gordon. "Do you think the senator talked to him?"

He shrugged.

I offered him the coffee Turner had refused. "It's Kona."

Gordon readily accepted the cup, but with none of his usual excitement, which made me even more worried about the damage the article had caused.

"Ms. Calhoun." The woman from the bank came back on the line. "I'm going to have to transfer you to our delinquent accounts department."

"But it's not a delinquent account."

"I understand, but I can't do anything for you from here. I have to transfer you."

"Forget it." I needed to talk to Gordon and find out what I had to do to combat the bad PR. "Just cancel the card and close the account."

"That's obviously already been done," she cheerfully informed me, and disconnected the call.

It took a great deal of self-control to hang up the phone without repeatedly slamming it against its cradle. I drew a slow, measured breath and, with the poise of a Southern debutante, rose from my desk chair. What extraordinary grace under pressure. I silently congratulated myself . . . until I noticed the crumpled edges of the newspaper inelegantly jutting at odd angles from between the fingers of my white-knuckled fist.

"This is outrageous." I shook my fist, rattling the paper. "How — how can this Griffon Parker get away with it? How can the paper get away with printing these lies?" My fingers itched to tear the newspaper into tiny bits and bury the unrecognizable remnants in the compost pile over at the greenhouses, a compost pile that contained no traces of poop or manure. Not that there was anything wrong with manure when used in the proper situation; the White House just didn't use manure in its compost. Leaves, grass clippings, vegetable food scraps, and yes, even libelous newspapers more than fulfilled the requirements for creating rich organic compost. "Most of what he wrote isn't even true."

"Welcome to D.C., Casey," Lorenzo said as he swept into the office. He looked well rested and very pleased with himself. He dropped several more copies of the newspaper article on my desk. "Nothing in this city is based on truths anymore. Don't forget this is the same place that just last year killed a program promoting healthy diets for children when a powerful senator called it a socialist takeover of our national school system. It only gets worse."

"Thanks a lot."

Was Lorenzo happy about my bad fortune? More likely, he was angry with me. I had anticipated that.

"I brought your favorite coffee," I said, holding up the cup. "I know it's not much, but I really didn't mean to cause trouble for you yesterday."

"Yesterday?" He took a sip of the coffee.

"I may have mentioned to a member of the Secret Service about your involvement with Pauline." Even if I hadn't said anything to Turner, I'm convinced Agent Cooper still would have picked up Lorenzo for questioning, thanks to Isabella's ranting that he was guilty of the crime. But still, I felt guilty.

"Oh, that." He took another sip of his coffee. "Don't worry about it. I'm not. I told Agent Cooper that I'm glad to help out in any way I can. I want to know probably more than anyone else why someone would kill Pauline."

"So everything's okay? You're not a suspect?"

"No." He laughed. "I think I was for a while. I can understand why. We had a tumultuous relationship. But I also had an ironclad alibi. Yesterday morning, I was dropping off my laundry at the dry cleaners. I have a ticket that proves it. Plus the clerk spilled scalding coffee all over my sleeve, a memorable experience for both her and me."

"Oh, I'm glad."

I was also confused. If he wasn't upset with me about that, why was he acting so damned pleased that the press had skewered my proposal? We were a team, the three of us. Gordon and Lorenzo had been working together for the past seven years. And although I was the new girl in the group, I never got the feeling that I wasn't welcome.

So why did I have a lump in my throat just now?

"Senator Pendergast has become a powerhouse lately," Lorenzo needlessly pointed out.

Gordon nodded. "I'd thought last night we'd have no trouble pushing some of your ideas through the committee, but that was before this. The overall proposal is on the verge of turning into a partisan hot potato, Casey."

"It's simply a gardening method," it hurt

me to admit. "There shouldn't be this much controversy."

Someone had purposefully stirred up trouble for me.

Someone who didn't want me around.

Special Agent Jack Turner had warned me the killer would want me out of the way, especially if he thought my memories were returning.

Well, I wasn't going to give up my life's work that easily.

"What do I do?" I asked, ready to fight for my job and this project. My grandmother didn't raise a coward. Southern ladies, especially the lucky ones born into the Calhoun family, may appear demure on the surface, but anyone who cares to dig deeper will find a backbone of high-grade steel and a temper as hot and steamy as the long Lowcountry summers.

"There's nothing you can do," Gordon cautioned. "The organic garden is the First Lady's idea. She's its public face and the only one who can fight for it."

Margaret Bradley might be the garden's spokeswoman, but that didn't mean I couldn't help build a compelling case for it from behind the scenes.

"Excuse me for a minute." I scooped up the pile of newspapers and carried them down the hall. Since setting them on fire in the White House's basement would cause about a trillion times more trouble than attacking a Secret Service agent with pepper spray, I dropped the pile in a large blue recycling bin. That's when I spotted the other article, the one that got my heart really pounding.

"Casey?" Ambrose said. "Why are you climbing into the recycling bin?"

I ripped the second, and much more interesting, article from the newspaper and carefully folded it in half before dropping back down onto my feet. It was a rather large recycling bin. "I accidentally tossed something in there I needed to keep." I tucked the page into my pocket.

"He wants to see you," Ambrose said cryptically.

"Who?"

Ambrose raised his brows and gave me a look as if I'd just asked the difference between grass and a tree.

"Oh. Him." I still hadn't gotten used to the rule that the President should always be called "he" and the First Lady "she." We weren't supposed to use their actual names. "*Oh!* Why would the President want to speak with me?"

"You don't want to keep him waiting," Ambrose said.

"No, of course not."

I still didn't move.

"Do you . . . um . . . know what he wants?"

Was he going to grill me about the pepper spray? Or worse, the newspaper article?

Ambrose put a hand on my shoulder. "Don't be nervous, Casey. He's a busy man. He doesn't call employees into his office to scold or sack anyone. He has staff members to handle that for him . . . like me."

I swallowed hard and tried to remember the rules of protocol for dealing with the President that Ambrose had explained in rapid-fire succession during that quick tour of the West Wing on my first day. Although a White House employee might pass PO-TUS or FLOTUS in the hallway, only a few worked directly with either member of the First Family.

Under normal circumstances, a summons to the President's office would have made me giddy with excitement. I blamed the dread I was feeling on Turner. He'd planted a bumper crop of doubt in my head this morning with his threats and warnings.

He had no right talking about my mom.

I wiped my suddenly sweaty palms on my khaki pants, which made me notice what I

231

was wearing. The khakis were clean and pressed, but a dress or suit would have been much better. And my top, gracious, why had Alyssa let me leave the apartment this morning wearing a V-neck cream-colored cardigan sweater over a plain light blue blouse? I looked like a female Mr. Rogers.

Unlike everyone else on the staff, the gardeners had a pretty lax dress code. Perhaps I should have followed Lorenzo's example and dressed as if I worked in an office instead of under the bright sun with dirt caked under my nails.

At least I'd taken extra care with my makeup this morning. The bruising on my temple was hardly noticeable, and my eyelids sparkled with shimmering champagne and honey tones. My hair was another matter.

"Stop tugging at it. You're making it look worse." Ambrose wrinkled his nose as he grimaced at the top of my head. Walking with his usual dignified, straight-back bearing, he accompanied me down the North Hall and through the heart of the White House's busy center.

All the while, I had a devil of a time keeping my hands out of my hair. Every time we passed a window or a piece of furniture with the slightest mirrored surface, I slowed down and, peering at myself in the glass's reflection, tried to tame the stray strands that had decided to stick straight out to one side or the other.

"Ms. Calhoun!" Wilson Fisher spotted me as we passed the Map Room. His hard-soled shoes clacked on the floor as he hurried after us. "The forms, I need them —"

"Later," Ambrose calmly informed his assistant, without altering his stride. "She has an appointment."

At the far end of the light-filled Palm Room, Ambrose held open the door to the West Colonnade for me. The vigorous spring gale whipped down the narrow walkway, tangling my hair and completely undoing all the hasty finger-styling I'd done to make my hair look halfway presentable. A nervous giggle snuck out as I headed out into the wind. After the terrible morning I'd had, a little messy hair really didn't matter.

At the other side of the walkway, I passed through the glass doors that led into the West Wing. Without Ambrose rushing me along, I took a detour to the nearest ladies' room to make sure I looked presentable.

I opened the ladies' room door and nearly smacked heads with Senator Pendergast, who had just declared my position at the White House a frivolous extravagance.

233

"Good morning, Senator," I said amicably. I'd dealt with enough problem clients in my career to know that the surest path to losing a disagreement was to let your emotions show.

"Oh! Ms. Calhoun, I'm surprised to see you." Judging by the way her eyes widened and the quick step she took away from me, I'd say she was more startled than surprised. She swiftly regained her composure and narrowed her gaze suspiciously. "Does your work take you to the West Wing often?"

"Not usually. Important business with POTUS," I said, feeling damn glad the President had summoned me, even though I still had no clue why he wanted to see me.

"Well, I'll not keep you," she said.

Mirroring her behavior the other day, I followed along the hallway beside the senator. I wanted to ask her about something I'd read in that newspaper article.

No, not *that* article, but the other one, the one I'd crawled into the recycling bin to retrieve.

"Perhaps you can answer a question for me," I said.

"I don't know," she returned coolly. "I'm afraid I'm in a hurry."

"This shouldn't take long." I pulled the newspaper article from my pocket. "It's about this."

"I was afraid you were going to bring that up," she said. "You understand that it's nothing personal against —"

"According to this article, you've withdrawn your sponsorship of the Banking and Finance Stabilization Bill." I tapped my forefinger to the headline: BANKING REFORM BELLIES UP ON THE HILL.

"Oh, that article. What about it?" Bless her heart, her usually tight lips gaped just a bit. She glared at me as if she thought I were half a bubble off plumb. "I don't see —"

"The text explains that you pulled your support for the bill after the Office of Domestic Finance's audits came back with no evidence that any of the banks have shuttled more toxic assets into the derivatives market. Now I know how reporters don't always get their facts straight. So I wanted to make sure that what I've read was true."

"I still don't see how —"

"Please, indulge me a minute," I said, feeling every inch like my favorite heroine, Miss Marple. "Wasn't Pauline Bonde a senior policy accountant with the Office of Domestic Finance? And wasn't she one of the main auditors working on the banking investigation that spurred you to author the Banking

235

and Finance Stabilization Bill in the first place?"

"Yes. I believe she was. But I was told that her death had nothing to do with her position at the Treasury Department."

"I'd been told that as well. But the article claims that the audits were completed and reviewed by not only Treasury officials, but also by the Senate committee."

"That's true."

"How do you know that you had all of the reports when Pauline's laptop was stolen on the day of her murder?"

Senator Pendergast shook her head. "No one told me that."

"She kept her computer in a silver hard-sided briefcase, which the killer took from her."

"But I'd been led to believe that we had all of the completed reports. But if what you say is true . . ."

I rubbed my bruised temple. "I'm sure it's true. I wonder what was on her laptop. Perhaps there was information on it that someone didn't want you to see."

"I'd been under the impression that Ms. Bonde's reports had been recovered. I'll be sure to look into this."

"Good. Oh, and Senator, I do hope you'll give me the chance to explain in further detail the First Lady's organic gardening plans. I assure you, the reporter who worked on that story didn't get even half his facts straight."

"About that —" the senator started to say.

"You'll have to excuse me," I cut her off. "The President is waiting."

CHAPTER FIFTEEN

I rushed back toward the ladies' room to check my hair. As much as I hated to keep President Bradley waiting any longer than I had already, I didn't need the added worry that my hair might be sticking up at odd angles. I was nervous enough just trying to guess why the President of the United States wanted to meet with *me* and not Gordon or Lorenzo.

Before I made it halfway down the hallway, Jack Turner, the last person I wanted to see, rounded a corner and put himself directly in my path. Since I was still reeling from our earlier confrontation, his sudden appearance upset my generally unshakable balance. That, and the fact that I'd tripped over one of his black combat boots.

He caught my arms just long enough to steady me.

"What do you think you are doing?" he demanded.

I glanced meaningfully at the restroom door down the hall behind him. "I think that would be obvious."

"I mean with the senator."

"Senator Pendergast? We met the other day and started talking gardening. She's a plant nut like me. We're becoming fast friends."

"I'm sure the two of you are like sisters." He paused a beat. "I read the article."

My face heated just a bit. "Reporters are notorious for mangling stories."

"True. But I've never seen one get a quote quite so wrong. 'The new gardening position at the White House is not only unnecessary, but the organic gardening plan proposed by Cassandra Calhoun is a lavish experiment that will cost hardworking taxpayers money they can ill afford to lose.' "

He'd memorized the article?

"Doesn't sound too friendly to me," Turner said. "So what were you *really* doing with the senator, Casey? I hope you aren't pursuing your unauthorized and unwelcomed investigation right here in the West Wing just a few hours after I'd warned you not to do so."

"It's not what you think," I tried to explain, kicking myself for getting caught in

239

that little white lie about being friendly with the senator. I'd never had much luck with white lies. Now big whoppers, well, that's another story.

"Come on now, just admit you couldn't stop yourself from talking to the senator about the murder."

"How do you know what we were talking about? Are you lurking around corners spying on me?"

"I assure you I *do* have better things to do than to follow the gardeners around. But I did happen to hear you tell the senator that Pauline's laptop had been stolen."

"I felt she had a right to know that the killer stole a huge chunk of potentially important information, considering how the banking legislation Senator Pendergast had been drafting relied so heavily on what Pauline and her colleagues had gathered." I handed him the article that I'd retrieved from the recycling bin.

Turner glanced at it and handed it back to me. "It wasn't stolen," he said.

"What wasn't?"

"The reports. Pauline had downloaded all of them to the Treasury's server the night before her death."

"What?" That didn't make sense. "Then why did the killer steal her computer?"

"That's a puzzle for the experts to solve." He spun me around toward the hallway that led back to my office. "I'm sure you have soils to test, weeds to pull, roses to spray, or whatever it is you do around here."

"As a matter of fact," I said, "the President is waiting for me in the Oval Office. If you'd let go of my arm, I'd like to check my hair before meeting with him."

"Of course." He released me.

I dashed into the restroom and hastily tucked my hair behind my ears and patted down an errant curl on the top of my head. It was the best I was going to manage without a comb or hairspray.

My mind kept circling around the stolen laptop that hadn't been stolen. Did the killer take the case but not the laptop? That didn't make sense. Or did the killer take the case, hit me with it, and then return it to where he'd left Pauline's body? That made even less sense.

Then again, nothing about Pauline's death made any sense.

When I emerged from the restroom, I found Turner waiting for me. He was beginning to remind me of a persistent weed. A strong, healthy, and rather handsome weed with a crooked grin. "Ready?" he asked.

"In addition to the embarrassing searches

at the gate, am I now required to have an armed escort everywhere I go?"

"I'm just making sure you arrive safely at the Oval Office, if that's really where you're heading."

I rolled my eyes.

"You're sure about the reports on her laptop?" I asked him as we headed down the hallway again. "Perhaps she found something important at the last minute that she hadn't had a chance to download."

"Let it go, Casey."

"But — but there has to be a reason why the laptop was stolen. It had to be because of the audits."

"No, it doesn't. Let the professionals do their jobs."

"But I think you're missing an important point —"

"As I've told you again and again, you're not part of this investigation. You don't know what we do and do not know."

"But I do know —"

"Here we are." He gave my shoulder a gentle squeeze at the door to the President's outer office. He opened his mouth to say something else, but stopped himself. "Keep out of trouble," he finally said and walked away.

I turned the brass handle on the mahogany

door that led into the secretary's office, which served as the gateway to the Oval Office. This outer office had a pair of arched glass garden doors that led out to the Rose Garden. From this angle there was a lovely view of the Jackson magnolia and the south side of the White House beyond.

Inside the cream-colored walls of the office were two large desks. The President's personal secretary was seated at the desk closest to the door. Seated at the other desk was the President's personal assistant. Both men were on the phone. Piles of papers, folders, and notebooks crowded the personal assistant's desk. Bright yellow sticky notes almost completely covered his computer monitor. The secretary's desk, in contrast, was the picture of organization with a small pile of paperwork in a clearly marked in-box and a slightly larger stack of papers waiting in the matching out-box. I wondered how the two men managed to share the same workspace.

On top of a filing cabinet near one of the glass doors that led out to the garden sat a television tuned to a twenty-four-hour news station. As I waited for the secretary to finish his call, I took a seat on the office's leather sofa and watched the news program. After a lighthearted report on a new dog

243

breed, the news turned to the banking summit. A pretty blond-haired reporter frowned as she explained that without Senator Pendergast's support of the Banking and Finance Stabilization Bill, she doubted any meaningful reforms would come out of the summit, leaving the American public vulnerable to another financial collapse.

The camera cut away to a shot of Lafayette Square on one side of the screen and a photograph of a smiling and very much alive Pauline on the other.

"Pauline Bonde, the Treasury Department employee, had been one of the key investigators working tirelessly to assess the health and stability of our largest banks." The reporter's voice took a serious tone. "On the day she was to present her reports to the Congress, her life was cut short by a vicious attack. The FBI and D.C. Police are conducting a joint investigation."

"We are looking into the matter from all angles," Special Agent Cooper said to the two dozen or more microphones that had been thrust into his face on the front steps of the austere Hoover Building.

"What about Brooks Keller?" one of the reporters shouted.

Brooks Keller?

I leaned forward.

One of the banking wonder twins? What about him?

"We are looking into the matter," Cooper repeated and pushed several of the microphones away.

"Questions remain whether Brooks Keller" — the camera returned to the reporter in the studio — "financial wizard and head of —"

"Ms. Calhoun." The President's secretary had circled around from his desk and blocked the TV. "He's expecting you."

Although I had a mind to shush him and push him out of the way so I could listen to the end of the news story, courtesy won out. "Thank you," I said and stood, craning as far as I could to the left so I could find out why the press was talking about Brooks Keller.

"— fervently denies the allegation," the reporter concluded before the program moved on to a new story.

"This way," the secretary said. He crossed the room to a door that sat at an odd angle to the rest of the perfectly rectangular room. He leaned up against the slanted door and peered through a peephole. With a nod, he knocked twice before pushing it open.

"Mr. President, Ms. Cassandra Calhoun has arrived," he announced, using my full name as he entered the room. He stepped out of the doorway and gestured that I should follow him.

The Oval Office struck me as surprisingly . . . oval. Light streamed in from a bank of three windows located behind a very presidential-looking desk flanked by the U.S. flag on the left side and the President's flag on the right. Personally, I'd have turned the desk around so I could look out over the South Lawn when working. But that was just me.

With a nod, the secretary returned to his office, closing the door behind him. From inside the Oval Office, the door had been designed to disappear into the room's surrounding walls. There was no doorframe. The bottom half of the door had the same bright white paneled wainscoting as the rest of the room, and the top half of the door had been painted the same cream color as the walls.

To my left, a glass door between two large windows with scalloped shell lintels led out to the Rose Garden. Directly opposite, an ornate solid door was located between a pair of built-in shelves with scalloped shell lintels that matched the windows. I wondered where the second door led.

Two sofas the color of butter and several

blue-and-cream-striped armchairs created an informal meeting space in the middle of the room. President John Bradley, dressed in his signature dark gray suit with red tie, sat on one of the sofas with his right ankle propped on his left knee. A fluffy golden puppy with one white leg and a white chest wiggled on his lap.

Across from him sat Richard Templeton. He was dressed more causally than he had been the other day. Instead of a suit, he wore black pants and a dark gray golf shirt with an asymmetric black-and-red argyle pattern running down the right side.

At my entrance, Richard glanced in my direction and frowned.

He'd mentioned that he and the President were old friends. However, at the moment neither man looked particularly friendly nor happy, which I found surprising. The little puppy appeared to be doing his best to entertain the men. President Bradley had had to pry his red paisley tie from the pup's mouth twice already. Puppies and their antics never failed to make me smile.

"We'll talk about this more later," the President said.

"We certainly will," Richard replied sharply.

A look of tension passed between the two

men as they rose to greet me.

"It's a pleasure to meet you, Mr. President," I said, my smile widened. The puppy wiggled even more, its tail beating an excited tempo against President Bradley's chest as it tried to jump down so it could investigate me, the new person in the room.

"Hello, Richard," I said. I wanted to say more, to explain why I'd missed our date, but that wouldn't have been appropriate.

"Casey," Richard replied with a quick nod.

"Ms. Calhoun, it's a pleasure to finally meet you. Margaret is looking forward to implementing the organic gardening plans. That's why I asked to speak with you. You need to understand how important it is that Margaret gets what she wants. Don't let politics or personal agendas railroad her work. I'm expecting you to smooth the way for her."

"Yes, sir. I'll do my best," I assured him.

"You will do what it takes to get the job done," he corrected and flashed his trademark smile.

During the campaign two years ago the press had discussed ad nauseam President Bradley's charismatic personality. It was a trait that didn't come through in his speeches on TV. Sure, his public appearances were well crafted and delivered with the skill of a trained orator. But I hadn't understood what had so enamored the press until this moment.

When the President spoke, it felt as if the air around me hummed with bright energy.

"I have a suspicion, Ms. Calhoun, you'll not rest until you win the critics over. I bet you'll end up breaking new ground at the same time."

His vote of confidence ignited a renewed sense of purpose. I drank up his encouraging smile. The President and First Lady were my clients. And my first and foremost duty was to keep my clients happy. "I know just what needs to be done," I promised him.

"Good. Good. Ah, here's Margaret now."

The First Lady came through the door on the other side of the room. She looked radiant in a flowing knee-length dress made from a silvery-colored material with a subtle paisley design. She greeted me and then hurried over to the President to kiss him on the cheek. The President, who was clearly in love with his wife, beamed.

"A puppy, Richard?" She tickled the pup's fuzzy ear. I detected a hint of strain in her voice as she addressed her husband's friend. "You cause us too much trouble."

"Every family needs a dog," Richard

insisted, "especially ones with kids."

"We're not talking about that." President Bradley gave Richard another one of his tense looks.

"Oh, let's tell Casey," the First Lady said. "I think she should know."

"Are you sure, Mags?" The President clearly didn't want his wife to tell me whatever private bit of information they'd shared with Richard.

"I am, John. Besides, if we wait too long, the newspapers will start to report on how the stress of the office is making me fat. I'm not fat," Mrs. Bradley turned to tell me. "I'm pregnant. We're expecting twins."

"My word! Congratulations!" Forgetting decorum or that she was the First Lady and not a neighbor back in Charleston, I threw my arms around her in a great big Southern hug. As soon as I realized what I'd done and where I was, I released her and backed off. "That is wonderful news."

"After so many years of trying, I'd all but given up." She gave my hand a squeeze as if we were girlfriends.

"We don't plan to go public with the news until next week. I expect you'll respect our privacy," the President said.

"Naturally." I'd yet to meet a White House

employee who wasn't the model of discretion.

"Call me a nervous mom-to-be, but I want the White House grounds to be as natural and safe as possible for my little ones when they arrive in the fall. That's why we brought you here in the first place. I want the organic gardening program to work." She turned and gazed lovingly at her husband. "And yet, I won't push the plan if it looks like it'll hurt John politically."

"Honey!" the President cried. "You know you come first."

Mrs. Bradley raised her hands in protest. "Still, you don't need me causing trouble. You're having a difficult time of it already with these nasty rumors that you're trying to kill the banking legislation."

"I'll do whatever it takes working behind the scenes to smooth the way," I offered.

"I know you will, Casey. I believe in you," she said.

President Bradley flicked a glance at his watch, which wasn't easy considering he had to juggle the approximately twenty-pound squirming puppy in his arms to manage it. "I wish we had more time to chat, Ms. Calhoun, but I have a very busy schedule. Could you please take this little guy to Gordon?" He handed me the golden puppy.

The little fluff ball gave an excited yip and started to lick my face. "I've been told Gordon has taken care of the White House pets for nearly thirty years."

"Yes, he has." And I'd heard Gordon grumble more than once at the current administration's lack of pets. "He'll be thrilled to meet . . . What's his name?"

"Milo," Richard supplied. "Ms. Calhoun, may I have a word with you?"

"The two of you can talk out in the Rose Garden," the President suggested. "I've got a phone call to make before Margaret steals me away for lunch."

"Are you sure you won't be able to make it to the golf course with the rest of us this afternoon?"

President Bradley shook his head. "Regretfully, no. My schedule is packed all week."

I led Richard out to the Rose Garden. The garden was tucked in between the White House and the Oval Office in the West Wing. Bordering the grassy space in the center, where Presidents liked to give press conferences, were wide flowerbeds planted in the French style of mixing a profusion of colors, textures, and heights in a single space. Edged with a low boxwood hedge, the four corners of the garden were marked with showy saucer magnolias that were in full bloom with their large waxy pink-and-white flowers.

Crabapples and littleleaf lindens stood as silent sentinels down the center of the flowerbed. The crabapples had recently been replaced with younger, smaller specimens. Since it was spring, the bed was filled with jonquils, daffodils, grape hyacinths, tulips, and several other flowering bulbs.

And of course, there were the rosebushes. The hybrid tea rose and grandiflora rosebushes looked lush and healthy, too healthy for this early in the season. They looked that way because they'd been grown in a greenhouse and planted once the blooms had set.

I'd been surprised to learn that the roses were treated like annuals in the garden, pulled out and replaced with new plants the White House purchased every spring. Part of my proposal, a definite cost-*saving* measure, was to plant antique rosebushes, hardier varieties that weren't chemically dependent or quite so short-lived.

With the President's trust in me to help quiet the controversy swirling around the garden's plans, I knew I needed to rethink my approach for convincing the Grounds Committee and the press to accept the proposed changes.

Milo wiggled and whimpered in my arms,

insisting I pay attention to him. He was making so much of a fuss that I set him down. As soon as the pup's feet hit the grass, he trotted over to the nearest flower-bed, hopped over a low boxwood hedge, and immediately started to dig up a meticulously trimmed geometric hedge of thyme that bordered the flowering crabapples with their explosion of white blooms.

"Stop that." I clapped my hands. Milo glanced up at me and then returned to his digging.

"You'd better get him to start listening to you now," Richard warned. He chuckled as I chased after the naughty puppy. "We think he's a goldendoodle and will grow up to be about seventy pounds or so. Look at the size of his paws. I had him sent over from a rescue organization I support. John took one look at him and fell in love. I don't remember a time when John didn't have a dog. I think it makes him tense not to have a dog around."

"Dogs can be stress relievers," I agreed as I hopped over the boxwood hedge into the flowerbed. I reached down to pick up the muddy little scamp. Before I could grab him, he darted between my legs and was off and running, dirt and bits of thyme flying into the air with each bouncy leap. I'd never met a puppy I didn't like, but I was beginning to wonder about this one. He ran over to Richard and patted his pants leg with his paw.

"That's a good boy." Richard scooped the puppy up for me. As he straightened, his gaze met mine. "Well, then."

Richard and I stood in the middle of the Rose Garden not saying anything, just staring at each other.

"I'm glad John sent for you," Richard admitted finally. "I don't know what to do to get your attention. I don't usually have to work this hard with women." He shook his head with dismay. "I don't know what to say."

"You don't have to say anything. I need to apologize about yesterday. I wanted to call to explain, but I didn't have your number."

"I had wondered why you didn't show up."

"I did show up! Just not on time. You see, I met Pauline's roommate."

"You did? Why?"

"It wasn't on purpose." I explained how Isabella had come to Lafayette Square, what she'd told me, and why I thought the killer had stolen Pauline's laptop.

"What do you think it all means?"

"I think . . ." I rubbed my bruised temple. "I don't know. Perhaps she held back a vital piece of information from the audit report she'd submitted, but had kept it on her laptop?"

"That doesn't make sense. Why would she do that?"

"I don't know. Perhaps she wanted to surprise everyone when she presented her findings to Congress?"

"That doesn't seem very professional."

"No, it doesn't. But there has to be a reason why the killer stole her laptop. There simply has to be."

Richard nodded thoughtfully. "You know, I wish the police would find the laptop to prove that Pauline wasn't holding back anything. If you're wondering about it, I'm sure members of Congress are wondering about it, too, which makes my job of protecting my bank that much more difficult."

"I didn't realize. So why else would someone want her laptop gone? What do you know about Brooks Keller?" I asked, thinking about the news report. "Do you know if he was involved with Pauline?"

"You have to remember I never actually met her. I didn't even know she'd been conducting an off-cycle regulatory review of my bank until after her death."

"Oh, right."

"But I do know Brooks has a reputation

for . . . um . . . fooling around with employees and the like. I seem to remember a scandal erupting a few weeks ago when he got involved with his sister's legal counsel. I don't know the details."

"Hmm . . . I wonder if that's why the press is asking about Brooks Keller in relationship with Pauline Bonde's death."

"They are?"

"I just saw part of a news report. They mentioned him."

"That's interesting. Perhaps they've found something important." He handed me the puppy. "I'm sorry, Casey, I've got a tee time I can't miss. Lots of important deals happen on the links. But I'd really like to talk about this more."

"I would, too. If you're brave enough, we could meet for coffee again."

"I don't think so."

"Oh. I understand."

"I was thinking more along the lines of taking you out for dinner. Tonight? At eight?"

I practically had to stand on my own foot to keep from dancing a jig. "You have my word I won't be late this time."

"How about I make sure of that and send a car to pick you up?"

Milo barked.

"I would like that," I said, and gave Richard my address.

"Until tonight then."

"Until tonight."

CHAPTER SIXTEEN

"There's no time to wait, Ms. Calhoun. It's imperative that the grounds crew paint the snow fencing green." Seth Donahue, the First Lady's social secretary, had the gall to smile at me.

I zipped up my backpack and slung it over my shoulder as I rose from my desk. "I thought they finished painting it green yesterday."

"Dark green," Seth said. He sniffed as if he'd caught whiff of a horrible scent. "The Easter Egg Roll is supposed to be a celebration. The color is too bleak."

"But I thought you'd selected it?"

"I did." He waved his hands as if the change meant nothing. "It needs to be a lighter shade. I'm picturing a festive apple green."

"You'll need to talk with Gordon. I'm sure he can work out something for tomorrow. If you'll excuse me, I need to get going." I tried to sidestep Seth, but he blocked me.

"Perhaps you didn't understand. You need to get them started on the project today."

"No," I said, and squeezed between him and the doorframe. "Sal Martin and the other available members from the National Park Service grounds crew are coming with me to the greenhouse facilities. We're going to be working on the flower containers for the Easter Egg Roll."

"They can work on that later," Seth said. Tension crinkled the skin around his eyes. "I need them to paint the fencing."

"You do, do you?" Considering the day I'd been having — despite Richard's unexpected dinner invitation — I was in no mood to let some upstart steal my grounds crew away from me for some frivolous task. The dark green fencing would serve its purpose just fine. The gardeners didn't need to spend hours repainting it because Seth, on a whim, had changed his mind. If he wanted a battle, I was more than prepared to give him one. "Now see here, Mr. Donahue —"

"Um, Casey," Gordon called from the hallway. He'd been taking Milo around to introduce the pup to the other staff members. The puppy yipped a greeting as he bounded up to me. "Seth," Gordon said coolly, "I'll send the crew out to work on the fencing this afternoon, but we'll need them working on our projects exclusively after that."

"See?" Seth said with a broad gesture in Gordon's direction. "I don't understand why you were making this so difficult, Ms. Calhoun." He hurried down the hallway but paused. He spun back around. "Don't forget, when you get around to making the flower containers, I'll need fifty extra for the displays."

"Fifty!"

He smiled again and, nodding happily, rounded the corner to no doubt terrorize some other hardworking White House staff member.

"Gordon, how can you let him get away with that?"

"How could I not? He's got it bad," Gordon said, sounding as if he felt bad for the social secretary.

"Got what?" I asked.

"*White House-itis.* Poor guy has all the symptoms — a swelled sense of self-importance and a burning need for more and more assistants."

"That doesn't mean he can swoop in and conscript our staff."

"Let it go for now, Casey. You've got

enough going on. You don't need to add a war with Mr. Donahue."

"But I need to get the containers planted. I was hoping to get started on them this afternoon."

"You still can. Have Lorenzo help you."

"Help Casey with what?" Lorenzo grumbled as he returned from lunch. "You know I have a lot of work to do."

"I want you to go to the greenhouses with Casey. She needs help planting the flower containers for Monday. Seth has asked for fifty more."

"But I —" Lorenzo took one look at Milo and pinched his nose. "Whad — whad is *dhat* doing in here?"

As if the pup knew it was being talked about, Milo loped over and, while wagging his tail like a helicopter blade, untied Lorenzo's shoelaces with his sharp puppy teeth.

"Stop dhat!" Lorenzo pushed Milo away.

"Milo is the new First Dog," Gordon said, puffing out his chest like a proud papa. "Isn't he a handsome fellow? The members of the press are going to fall all over themselves, fighting over who can get the best pictures of him."

"I'm." *Sneeze*. "Allergic." *Sneeze*. "To." *Sneeze*. "Dogs." Lorenzo turned to me.

"I'm." *Sneeze.* "Going." *Sneeze.* "Wid." *Sneeze.* "You."

I had held up my hands in protest. "No. No. No. I would never dream of taking you away from your work. I can handle the containers on my own. I'll do as much as I can today and get the crew to finish them in the morning."

"No." Gordon stood his ground. Milo picked up on the older man's stern tone and started to bark at me. "You will not be going anywhere by yourself. Not after . . ." He huffed. "Quiet, Milo."

Although Gordon hadn't even raised his voice, the floppy puppy stopped barking and plopped down at Gordon's feet.

And that had been that. Lorenzo and I left Gordon to manage the unruly Milo, who had already gnawed shallow grooves in the legs of Gordon's desk. The way Gordon was grinning at the pup, you'd think I'd handed him a baby to love, not a destructive garden gnome. I drove to the greenhouses with Lorenzo sitting beside me in the nondescript white van, sniffling unhappily.

The greenhouses, seven in all, were located on the outskirts of D.C. Within these long, domed structures, we grew out many of our plants for the gardens and various special projects, such as creating a hundred and fifty Easter planters to mark the boundaries of the various activity areas on the South Lawn and to act as friendly Jersey barriers during the Easter Egg Roll.

"You're humming again," Lorenzo complained about an hour later. He dropped his trowel onto the workbench inside the greenhouse with a clatter. "I can't work with all this humming."

"Sorry," I said, biting back a grin.

Into each of the concrete Grecian urn–shaped containers, we planted two dozen egg-yolk yellow tulips surrounded by a bed of bright pink English daisies.

It was hot and humid inside the building, which would have been fine if I didn't have to also deal with Lorenzo's heated mood. I wiped a rivulet of sweat from my eyes with my sleeve just as the large fans on the far wall turned on. The metal vents slammed as they opened.

"What do you have to be so happy about?" Lorenzo demanded, raising his voice above the fans. "I'd think you'd be crying in the potting soil, what with the way the press is skewering your organic gardening plans and how your position is in jeopardy of being cut along with the rest of the government waste."

"Yes, I suppose I should be crying." I pressed a flowering tulip bulb into the container's black soil. "But right now I can't help feeling happy, deliriously happy. I have a date tonight. An honest to God, he's picking me up at the door, date. Do you know how long it's been since I've been on a date? No, don't try to guess. You'll just depress me. Let's just say it's been a very long time. So long, in fact, I'm afraid I'm going to be rusty."

"Is that so?" Lorenzo's jaw tightened, a sure sign his patience was just about gone. "Aren't you the lucky one? So pretty and so *alive.*"

"And I'm grateful for it." Many people dealt with their grief through anger. Some more forcefully than others. "I'm sorry about Pauline."

"Not sorry enough to remember what the killer looks like. You promised to help me, Casey. But you haven't done anything."

"That's not true." I carefully placed a large red-leaf lettuce, the next plant to go into the pot, back on the workbench. Losing my temper would serve no purpose. What Lorenzo needed was my compassion . . . and space. "I'm going to fetch another wheelbarrow of potting soil."

"Sure, run off. Pretend no one got killed

the other day. Live your life as if nothing happened. Because it didn't, did it? Not to *you.* You survived. And now you're the center of attention, being all coy. 'Oh heavens to Betsy, I can't remember what I saw,' " he said, raising his voice several octaves while feigning a ridiculous Southern accent. " 'But I'm sure I will remember, so you'd better keep your attention on me, sugar pie.' And it's working. You were called to the Oval Office to meet with the President. All I want is a few answers about what the hell happened out there. And here you are showboating all over the place, making this tragedy all about you. Poor helpless Casey. I think I'm going to vomit."

"That's enough."

I firmly told myself not to sink to his level. He was hurting and vulnerable. Ignore his anger, I told myself. But hell, he'd been needling me and needling me all day. No, that wasn't quite right. Ever since the day Gordon had introduced us, Lorenzo would slip in a snide comment here and there about my abilities or my role at the White House.

I'd made apologies for him time and again, overlooking his addiction to chemical fertilizers and herbicides, telling myself that he'd come around. He was a holdover from another time, I'd told myself, even though we were the same age. But enough was enough.

I went straight for the jugular.

"I'll have you know I've put my career on the line to find answers about this murder. I've been asking questions even though I've been warned not to. And you know what? You won't like what I've learned, because I know Pauline would have never stayed with you. She'd moved on."

"That's a lie."

"It's not. She was having an affair with a man in New York, quite probably with the rich and powerful Brooks Keller, who is everything you're not," I said, and immediately regretted it.

Lorenzo ripped off his gardening gloves. "I'm out of here."

"Wait," I called after him.

The muscles in his tense back twitched, but he didn't stop. With an unimaginative curse, he yanked open the greenhouse door with enough force that it slammed against the metal framed wall.

I dropped my head against the worktable. I should have handled that better. I should have been more sensitive to his feelings and realized my good mood would bother him.

Hopefully, after blowing off some steam,

Lorenzo would return ready to work and put his anger to good use in finishing planting these pots. We still had over a hundred to complete.

Outside the van's engine roared to life.

He wouldn't.

I sprinted toward the greenhouse exit, hoping to stop him. The metal door crashed against the greenhouse's metal frame when I tossed it aside. "Lorenzo!"

A chilly wind slapped my face as I emerged from the greenhouse's steamy interior. Taking off at a hard run, I made it to the front of the property in record time.

We'd driven out here together. And with the rush to prepare the White House grounds for the Easter Egg Roll, we were the only two people working at the greenhouse facilities today.

I dashed around a storage shed and stumbled into the parking lot just in time to watch the nondescript white government van peel down the long asphalt drive.

"Lorenzo!" I bent over and grabbed my knees. He'd stranded me in the middle of an unfamiliar D.C. suburb. Alone.

Don't panic. I had my cell phone. Once I'd finished with the planters, I could call a cab . . . only, I had no way to pay the fare because the bank had canceled my credit card. And I rarely carried much more than fifteen dollars in my purse.

Practicing the deep breathing exercises my therapist all those years ago had taught me, I returned to the greenhouse to fetch my cell phone. I could call Alyssa or Gordon or — I pulled the crumpled slip of paper from my pocket with a phone number hastily scrawled across it — I could even call Special Agent Jack Turner. He had guns.

Nothing to worry about. I looked around my workbench for my backpack, where I kept my cell phone. It wasn't there. I went back to the door and retraced my steps from the moment Lorenzo and I first arrived. No backpack.

I must have left it in the van. I'd done that before when I didn't want to get it dirty.

Still, no reason to panic. I could use the phone in the small office near the gate.

The greenhouse fan high on the far wall shut down. The vents slammed shut with a loud clang. At the same time the lights in the grow lamps went dark.

I picked up my pace just a bit. If worse came to worse, I could always walk over to the nearby aquatic gardens and ask for their assistance.

Being stranded in the greenhouses was truly more of a hassle than a danger.

But as Grandmother Faye likes to tell me, the Calhoun backbone of high-grade steel has gotten the family through some pretty tough times, but it's also led us into heaps of trouble. Trouble such as finding myself stuck at the greenhouses with no phone and no ride home.

Luckily, the National Park Service staff kept an extra key to the small red clapboard office underneath a large potted persimmon tree. I retrieved it and unlocked the door. As in the greenhouse, the power was off.

I picked up the phone's receiver in the shadowy wood-paneled office and listened for the dial tone.

Nothing.

Both the power and the phone lines were down?

More curious than worried, I headed back outside and studied the overhead wires as if I could find the problem and fix it. I also liked to open the hood and stare at the engine whenever my car broke down. It made no sense to do it, but it seemed to make me feel better.

As expected, I didn't see any obvious loose electrical wires dangling from the poles. But the wind had been gusting around like an uptight harridan all day. There was bound to be some damage as a result.

So I squinted up at the lines one more time, just to make sure.

That's when I spotted something moving between two of the greenhouses. Fear prickled at the back of my neck. I slowly backed away from the greenhouses until my backside bumped up against the office building's metal door.

A few seconds passed. And then I saw it — *him* — again. A man. He darted between the next two greenhouses closer to me.

Oh.

Lordy.

I wasn't alone.

CHAPTER SEVENTEEN

I'd read enough mystery novels to know that women who venture into dark basements in search of murderers or wander into shady forests where dangerous beasts have been hunting rarely survive to see the next chapter. I didn't want to be *that* character.

So instead of confronting the man I'd seen running around the facility and explaining to him that this is restricted government property, I raced inside the facility's office and locked the metal door behind me.

I checked three times to make sure the lock's bolt had driven firmly into the door-frame before I sank to the floor.

A quick glance around the small office had me noticing things I'd never noticed before about the building. For example, each wall had at least two rather large windows. Anyone could peek in and see me with my back pressed against the door hugging my knees to my chest.

If I was spotted, the man could easily break one of these large windows to get to me.

Not caring how stupid I might have looked — the man wandering the grounds out there could be anyone from a member of the maintenance crew to a tourist who'd strayed from the nearby aquatic gardens — I crawled on my hands and knees across the floor.

I barely had a chance to squeeze underneath the administrative desk in the middle of the room when someone jiggled and pulled on the doorknob. The sound of scraping metal clanked in my ears. When that stopped, the door shuddered and gonged as someone pounded on it.

Holding myself very still while my heart hammered in my throat, I closed my eyes.

He couldn't get to me. He couldn't even know for certain that I'd taken refuge inside the building. If he peeped in any of the windows, he'd now find an empty room.

The pounding stopped.

In the silence that followed, I blew out the breath I'd been holding.

Hopefully someone would notice I was missing and come searching. And soon. My right hip started to throb. I shifted around in the small space under the desk in a fruitless effort to find a comfortable spot. The wait for rescue could take hours. Who knew, I might even have to stay tucked in this tight position long into the night.

Richard would think I'd stood him up . . . again.

Across the room someone had placed on top of a filing cabinet three very healthy potted plants — a spider plant, a mother-in-law's tongue, and a small African violet with a bud that was on the verge of breaking. The plants had clearly received constant care and attention, especially the African violet, which took more work than the other two plants for it to thrive. Maybe the plant's caretaker would return this afternoon and find me.

But at the same time I didn't want an innocent bystander to accidentally bump into a murderer. I'd much rather handle this on my own, even if it meant waiting all night for the man outside to give up and leave.

After what felt like many, many tense hours listening for the movements of the man outside, but hearing nothing other than an occasional scraping sound, I heard the deep roar of an engine and the crunch of tires as a vehicle slowly drove over some loose gravel on the asphalt pavement. The brakes whined just a bit. And then the engine fell silent.

A car door creaked as it opened and then was slammed shut. The *shush-shush* of footsteps grew fainter and fainter. A short time later, a metal greenhouse door clanged.

My ears strained in the sudden stillness. Who was out there? Had the man darting between the greenhouses left? Or was he stalking the person who'd arrived in the car?

I needed to warn whoever was out there. I popped out from under the desk. But before I could make it to the door, a shout of pain rippled through the silence.

Dammit, I was too late. My shaky fingers struggled with the lock on the door. It finally popped open. The White House van was parked in front of the office as if it and Lorenzo had never left. My backpack sat on the seat exactly where I'd put it. I grabbed the bag and, as I took off toward the greenhouses, dug out my cell phone and dialed.

"Nine-one-one, what's your emergency?" the dispatcher asked.

"Uh . . . uh . . ." I skidded to a stop outside the greenhouse where Lorenzo and I had been working. Lorenzo's body sprawled across the greenhouse's threshold, his legs spread at an unnatural angle outside the building's green transparent walls, and the rest of his body was inside the building.

"Oh God, I need an ambulance." I recited the greenhouse facility's address and, at the dispatcher's urging, repeated it.

"An ambulance is on the way," the 911 operator assured me. "What's going on?"

"My coworker, Lorenzo Parisi, is unconscious." I stepped over him to get inside the greenhouse. "He's bleeding from a head wound."

"Do you know what happened?" the operator asked, her voice concerned but comforting, like a friend's.

"No, I didn't see what happened."

A four-foot landscaping timber lay on the ground beside him. "I think someone hit him. You'd better send the police," I said, amazed at how calm I sounded, when I felt anything but. "The attacker may still be around."

The operator quickly relayed that information to the dispatcher.

"Is your coworker breathing? Do you see his chest rising?"

He was lying on his stomach, and I didn't want to move him in case his neck or back had been injured. So I crouched down beside him and put my face near his mouth. A faint but steady breath brushed my ear. "Yes, he's breathing."

The operator relayed that information to

the dispatcher as well.

"Someone's coming." I could hear movements around outside. "I need to set down the phone."

"Someone's coming? You mean the police?"

"No, I didn't hear a siren. Lordy, I think he's returning. I'm setting the phone on the ground."

"Wait. Don't —" the operator said. But I didn't have time to discuss this with her. I set the phone next to Lorenzo and picked up the landscaping timber. It was heavy and took both hands to carry it.

If that bastard thought he could get the upper hand on me, he shouldn't have left the landscaping timber behind. I stepped over Lorenzo, which wasn't easy since he was lying lengthwise across the door's threshold. My balance faltered when through the door's green-tinted Plexiglas, which made everyone look distorted and fuzzy, I saw the figure of a man.

With a battle yell, I tossed aside the door and swung the heavy landscaping timber.

The wood connected with the man's middle with a satisfying *thunk*. He stumbled back a step, teetered, and then landed on his backside.

"Don't move," I warned, poised to hit him again.

The man on the ground held up a hand. "Remind me to stop charging to your rescue," he wheezed. "It's too damn dangerous."

"Turner? How did you —" I dropped the timber.

It landed on his foot.

The U.S. Park Service Police, D.C. Police, and EMS all came screaming into the facility at just about the same time. I jogged over to the parking lot and directed them to where both Lorenzo and Turner had fallen.

By the time I returned with a pair of EMTs following in my wake, Turner had managed to pull himself back to his feet. Hugging an arm to his ribs, he limped over to check on Lorenzo, who'd rolled himself over and was clutching his head and groaning.

The pair of emergency medical technicians dressed in dark blue uniforms took charge, while I gave the police officers the details of what had happened. "I can't imagine why someone would follow us here," I told the officers. "I don't see how it can be connected, but . . ." In truth, I didn't want to connect this attack with Pauline's murder, but what other choice did I have? "I'm pretty sure the man who came after me here is the same man who killed Pauline Bonde in Lafayette Square. It must be."

"I agree," Turner said. He limped over and identified himself to the officers.

None of the D.C. police officers looked happy about the revelation. One of them swore and then radioed for Detective Hernandez to be called to the scene.

While the EMTs focused on Turner and Lorenzo, the officers fanned out and began a search of the area. They were joined by more officers. Police cars, marked and unmarked, seemed to keep coming, taking up every available space in the facility's small parking lot and overflowing onto the median beside the greenhouse's long driveway.

It would only be a matter of time before news vans arrived packed with curious reporters and persistent cameramen.

With so much activity going on, I felt like a housecat left out in a rainstorm. I didn't know where to go.

The EMTs had moved Lorenzo onto a stretcher. The front of his shirt was splotched with blood. His once crisply pressed trousers now had a rip in the leg and several dirt stains. And his dark brown hair, which stood straight up in several places, was matted with clotted blood.

His olive skin tone had paled several shades and had a green tinge. His eyes were closed, but his brows furrowed as if he was lost in a cloud of pain.

"Is he going to be okay?" I whispered to the EMT standing closest to me. I thought I'd lowered my voice enough that Lorenzo wouldn't hear me. But in response to my question, Lorenzo's eyes snapped open.

"Of course I'm going to be okay." His tone was sharp as ever, but there was no mistaking the raspy sound of pain in his voice. "Did they catch the guy who did this?"

"No, they're searching the area. Did you see him?"

Lorenzo closed his eyes and turned his head away from me.

"We've got the bleeding under control, but he's going to need stitches and an MRI." The EMT bent over Lorenzo and tightened a strap on the stretcher.

"I want to come along. Do you mind if I ride in the ambulance?" I wanted to hear what Lorenzo had seen or heard. Together, we might be able to figure out who attacked us, if it was indeed the same guy. I started to follow behind the EMTs as they carefully wheeled the stretcher to the ambulance.

"Wait." Turner caught my arm. "You're needed here."

"But I —"

"Hernandez and Cooper are already on their way. They'll want you to show them what happened. I'd like to hear what happened, too."

Staying behind while the ambulance rushed Lorenzo to the hospital didn't seem right. I now understood why Gordon had acted so upset the other day. I was on the verge of turning into a leaky watering pot.

I needed to let Gordon know what was going on. I found my phone on the ground where I'd dropped it. I dialed Gordon's number and gently explained the situation.

Gordon already knew. Ambrose had told him. How Ambrose knew, I had no clue. But Gordon assured me he was already heading over to the hospital to personally make sure Lorenzo received the best possible care.

After hanging up, I dialed the number for Rosebrook, the antebellum Charleston home where my two aunts and grandmother lived. I wanted to assure them that I was safe . . . and to be honest, I wanted to hear their voices.

Before I could type in the last number, Turner put his hand on my phone and snapped it closed.

"You can make your phone calls later," he said. "You need to tell me exactly what you did this morning, everyone you talked to, everyone who saw you. Even if it seems harmless, apparently you did something today to get this guy worked up enough to come after you."

"I resent that. I didn't do anything to deserve this."

"I didn't mean it that way." Turner huffed and then grabbed his ribs. "Dammit, that hurt." Breathing short shallow breaths, he continued more calmly. "I'm trying to keep you safe."

"How did you get on the scene so quickly?" I demanded. "How did you know Lorenzo and I were in danger?"

"The facility's security system automatically sends an alert to the U.S. Park Police when there's a disruption to the power. It's a red flag that there's a problem. Whenever something like that happens, they send an officer out to check on things."

"But that doesn't explain why *you're* here."

"I already told you CAT would be keeping an eye on you." His gaze hardened. "I wasn't kidding."

"I don't know what to say."

"You could thank me."

"I'm not sure I'm happy to know that my every move is being watched."

"You don't like being watched by the Secret Service, but you're okay with being stalked by a killer?"

I shrugged.

"You could at least apologize for bruising my ribs."

"I am sorry for that and for dropping that board on your foot."

The second EMT returned. "Jack, those injuries need to be looked at. You need to go to the hospital." He seemed to know Turner. I wondered how. "Your ribs need to be x-rayed. And your foot is probably sprained. It might even be broken."

"No. I'm not leaving."

"Be reasonable. There's enough police here to protect her and then some." The EMT gestured toward the parking lot filled with cop cars. "They don't need you."

"I'm not leaving."

The EMT sighed and thrust a clipboard at Turner. "Then sign this form."

Turner quickly scribbled his name at the bottom of the sheet and handed it back.

"Is he a friend of yours?" I asked after the EMT stormed off.

"No. He's my younger brother."

"Really? You have a brother?"

"What? You think I was hatched out of a pod?"

I laughed. "Yeah, I think so. You know, I am sorry for hitting you and dropping that board on your foot. Are you sure you don't want to go with them? I could go, too." I still wanted to hear Lorenzo's version of what had happened.

"This is nothing compared to the pepper spray."

"Oh." Embarrassment scorched my cheeks. "Sorry. I shouldn't have acted —"

"However wrongly, you thought you were protecting yourself," Turner said rather tersely. He limped over to a bench in the shade and, wincing, started to sit.

"Dammit, Jack, what the hell happened to you this time?" The silver-haired Special Agent in Charge Mike Thatch grumbled as he hurried toward us. I could tell by the fire in his eyes that there was going to be hell to pay.

If Turner got his way, I was sure I'd be the one making those payments.

CHAPTER EIGHTEEN

Like a good soldier, Turner shot up from the bench to stand straight and tall in front of his boss. He slowly lowered his hand from his ribs.

"Nothing happened to me, sir," I was surprised to hear him say. I'd expected him to present a blistering report of how I'd attacked him again.

Thatch turned toward me and raised his brows. "What happened?"

I shrugged.

Sure, I could've spilled my guts about what I'd done. But doing so would only make me look rather stupid and make Turner more upset with me than he needed to be. If he wanted to keep quiet about what happened, who was I to question him?

Thatch continued to press his deceptively innocent silvery gaze on me. I think he'd missed his calling. He would have made an excellent interrogator. Even though I'd turned my attention to an overgrown concord grape vine growing up one side of the greenhouse doorframe, my skin felt itchy. I wanted to say something. I *needed* to say something.

"There may have been" — I started to say when I couldn't stand Thatch's wide-eyed scrutiny a moment longer — "a landscaping timber —"

"I'm fine," Turner insisted. And as if to prove his health, he paced. Even though his foot had to be hurting, he managed to bear weight on it without limping. But it wasn't without a cost. With each step, his jaw muscles grew tauter and tauter. His fingers curled into fists he held so tight that, as my Aunt Willow would say, he scared all the color out of his knuckles.

"Sit the hell down, Jack, and get off that foot." Thatch turned to me again. "I passed an ambulance on the way out. Did my agent at least let them take a look at him?"

"He did," I said, which earned me a glare from Turner that, I swear, had enough heat to incinerate the hair right off the top my head. Thatch hadn't missed the look, either.

"I think I don't really want to hear the rest."

"Probably not," I agreed and returned my attention to the grape vine. It was in dire need of pruning.

"From the looks of it, our killer targeted Ms. Calhoun. He cut the power and phone lines to the facility," Turner said, still on his feet. But at least he'd stopped that idiotic pacing. He shifted his weight off his injured foot.

"Apparently, you've not been doing a very good job of keeping our witness out of trouble, Turner. Do I need to assign someone else to handle her?"

"Excuse me? You assigned him to *handle* me?"

"I meant no offense, Ms. Calhoun," Thatch said smoothly. He smiled like a snake. I'd met less than a handful of people who'd rubbed me the wrong way. Today, I added one more name to that short list. But he was Turner's superior and had the power to make his life and *my* life at the White House miserable. So I pressed my lips together and swallowed the hundred or more choice words begging to be said. He thought I needed a minder? Ohhhh . . .

"As I was saying, Jack, do I need to assign someone else to take care of this" — he glanced at me — "*delicate* task?"

Turner's Adam's apple bobbed as he swallowed deeply. The muscles in his jaw tightened again. "No, sir. Of course not, sir."

Thatch's silver brows rose again. The older man tilted his head slightly toward me. "See that I don't."

Turner stuck by my side as Special Agent Cooper and Detective Hernandez questioned me at length. Not wanting to get Lorenzo into trouble — he had returned with the van after all — I remained vague about why Lorenzo had left.

"And as soon as Mr. Parisi had gone on his errand, the electricity was cut off?" Cooper asked as he ran through the details for the third time.

"It all happened in less than a minute." The sun, deep red and large, sat low on the horizon.

Richard had said he'd pick me up from my apartment at eight. I needed at least an hour to shower and put on some makeup, not to mention pick out an outfit to wear. It was stressful enough going out on a date after a long, dry spell. Add to it that I was dating a man who had a long-standing habit of dating gorgeous supermodels and actresses who draped themselves in the most expensive designer clothes. Knowing that didn't help my self-confidence.

"I need to clean up for the night. Would it bother you if I worked and answered your questions at the same time?"

"This won't take much longer," Cooper assured. "But go ahead and do what you need to do."

The three men followed me into the greenhouse, where I found the pots and plants exactly as Lorenzo and I had left them earlier. I stacked empty planters while the two detectives fired questions at me.

Turner, I was glad to see, had found a chair and was able to get his weight off his injured foot.

By the time I'd finished straightening up, Cooper and Hernandez seemed satisfied that I'd answered all of their questions. Naturally they reminded me that they might call for follow-up questions as the investigation proceeded.

Hernandez rubbed his grizzled, salt-and-pepper mustache and shifted uneasily. He put a fatherly hand on my shoulder.

"Be careful, Casey. This guy has you in his sights and you don't even know what he looks like. He could walk right up to you, and you wouldn't know your life was in danger."

I hadn't thought of it that way, and that worried me.

I'd have to take extra care in the future. Not just for my own protection, but for the safety of those around me. Lorenzo could have been killed.

"I'll see you tomorrow morning, then," I told Turner, who limped silently behind me as I headed back to the van. "I'm beginning to look forward to our meetings at the White House gate." I reached for the van's door handle.

Turner put his hand on mine. "One of the Secret Service agents will return the van to the White House. I'm driving you home."

He tightened his grip as if bracing for an argument.

"I'd appreciate that," I said, which must have shocked him.

When he didn't let go of my hand, I gave his shoulder a nudge. "If you don't mind, I'm sort of in a hurry."

About half an hour later Turner leaned back in a kitchen chair and took a sip of the herbal tea I'd brewed for him. He looked at home in my kitchen.

"You sure have a lot of plants."

"Occupational hazard," I said while I rooted around in the pantry. Next to a half-empty bag of potting soil and below a stack of two-gallon pots, I found the first-aid kit Aunt Alba had given me the day before I'd left for D.C. She believed all Northern cities were festering pits of depravity. So she'd bought me the deluxe first-aid kit from Charleston's last corner five-and-dime store.

When I emerged from the pantry with the kit in hand, I'd noticed Turner's expression had soured. He wrinkled his nose. "They look so harmless on the shelf up there."

"What does?" I followed his line of sight. "Oh, the peppers?" I'd built the glass plant shelves myself. They ran the length of the south-facing window above the sink. On the top shelf were my habaneras. They were a little bit leggy from having to reach for the winter sun, but they were producing a nice crop of spicy fruit.

"They're not even red."

"Not yet. Those aren't ripe." A few had turned light orange, but I liked to pick them when they took on a bright reddish-orange hue and the surface of the skin had wrinkled just a bit. That's when this variety of pepper, in my opinion, was at its peak of potency.

"And what do you have growing on the shelf beneath them, deadly nightshade?"

"Close. Tomato seedlings."

I placed the first-aid kit on the kitchen table and dug around in its contents, searching for something that would help ease the soreness in Turner's ribs and foot.

He'd already turned down pain relievers.

"Do we wrap the ribs?" I asked when I found an Ace bandage.

"No. I'll just ice it down when I get home." He started to get up. All the color in his face drained away. He groaned and landed back in the chair with a thump.

I groaned in sympathy. "Your muscles must have tightened up. Let me help you." I found an ice pack in the back of the freezer. "If you drove home now, you'd probably end up getting in an accident."

He nodded and gritted his teeth.

Since the temperature in the house was warm, he'd shed his flak jacket as soon as he'd checked the apartment for signs of intruders. Underneath, he was wearing a black T-shirt that hugged his impressive muscles. Now I could have handed him the ice pack and let him place it where he thought it would do the most work. But the devil led me to mischief.

I was being helpful — right, *helpful* — when I said, "I think we need to get your T-shirt off so I can inspect your injury." As if I'd know what a broken rib would look like.

"No offense, but I already have enough injuries thanks to you," Turner protested.

"I'll be careful," I promised.

"No. I'm good. Really."

"Please, it's obvious that you're hurting, and it's my fault."

The corner of his mouth tilted up. "You're right. This is your fault. You ambushed me with that freaking log." He pushed his chair away from the kitchen table and slid it around so it faced me. He spread his arms in mock surrender. "I guess you do owe me."

"Glad to know you can be reasonable." I set the ice pack on the kitchen table and, straddling his legs, helped him pull his black T-shirt off over his head. Our hands brushed.

Turner's gaze locked on mine.

I licked my lips and swallowed.

His shirt slipped from my fingers and fell in an untidy pile on the tile floor.

We both seemed to be holding our breath.

"Casey? Casey, where are you? I know just the dress you should wear!" Alyssa shouted as she breezed through the apartment. She halted with one foot in the kitchen and one in the living room. Her eyes widened and then, after sweeping her gaze over Turner's delightfully broad chest, widened even more. "I — I didn't realize you were . . ."

"I'm not," I said, but jumped away from Turner as if I was guilty of . . . *something*. Which I wasn't.

Alyssa yelped and grabbed my arm. Her grip tightened as she pulled me toward the living room. She paused just long enough to take another hard look at Turner. Her frown deepened.

"Who is that? And what are you doing with him?" she demanded in a harsh whisper as soon as she'd dragged me over to the far side of the small living room. "Didn't you tell me you had a date with Tempting Templeton in" — she glanced at the ornate French Rococo clock on the mantle — "less than an hour?"

"Oh! Is it that late? I should start getting ready."

Alyssa grabbed my arm again when I tried to escape.

"You — you have a half-naked man *in the kitchen!*" She jabbed her finger toward the cased opening. "You were nearly sitting on his lap *in the kitchen!*" I wondered if she'd have made such a fuss if I'd hidden Turner in my bedroom.

I *wasn't* hiding him, because we weren't doing anything wrong.

"It's not what you think," I explained. "I was helping him."

"That's *exactly* what I'm thinking."

"No." I glanced over my shoulder to make sure Turner was still in the kitchen and then lowered my voice. "Remember the Secret Service agent I . . . um . . . sort of attacked in Lafayette Square?"

"Is that him?" She hurried across the room to the kitchen and leaned through the cased opening. After a moment she wiggled her fingers in a demure wave. "He's cute, really cute," she said when she returned. "But that's still no excuse. We're talking about Tempting Templeton. He's a powerful man, and you've already stood him up once. I wouldn't risk crossing him twice. Who knows what he might do."

"Like cancel my credit card?"

"Exactly."

I swallowed hard. "You don't think he actually canceled my credit card, do you?"

"Damn, I'd forgotten about that."

"I haven't. That cranky bank representative couldn't explain why they'd canceled my account. Perhaps Richard made some phone calls when he was stewing about why I'd missed our date."

"It's possible. But then again, if he was that upset, why ask you out for dinner?"

"A change of heart?" I suggested.

Alyssa shook her head. "I don't think he had anything to do with your credit card. But you do need to be careful around powerful men. Don't give him a reason to want to destroy your career or your reputation. If you make the most of this opportunity, maybe Tempting Templeton will pull some strings and get you a new credit card with a fabulous interest rate."

"You're right. I hadn't thought of that."

"What's the use of dating a banker if not to take advantage of some of the perks?"

"Personality? Compatibility?"

"And the fact that he's so sexy he can charm the panties right off a woman just by looking at her?"

"Oh yeah, that, too." I giggled.

"Now what are you going to do about hunk number two?" Alyssa hooked her thumb toward the kitchen. "You've got to get yourself upstairs and cleaned up or else you'll be looking more like a pumpkin than a princess by the time your Prince Charming arrives."

"Oh goodness, I don't even know what I'm going to wear!"

"Don't worry. As I was saying when I came in, I have the perfect dress you can borrow."

"Thank you!" I hugged her and started to dart up the stairs.

"Don't forget about the hunk you have stashed in the kitchen."

"I didn't stash him —"

"If you ask me nicely, I suppose I could take him off your hands for you." She swished her hips in a suggestive manner.

"It's not what you think."

"He sure has nice, tight abs."

"I was *helping* him."

"I don't think *I've* ever gotten a man to take off his shirt so quickly."

I blew out a frustrated breath. Alyssa wasn't going to stop until she got it all out of her system. "I need to get in the shower. Please, just help him with his ribs. And don't do anything else. No touching. No seducing. And absolutely no kissing."

"You're no fun." Alyssa swished her hips again.

"I mean it, Alyssa. You need to leave him alone. I have enough trouble on my hands right now. Please don't do anything that would make things between Turner and me any more . . . um . . . awkward."

"Said the one who'd peeled off his shirt," she sang over her shoulder before disappearing into the kitchen.

Chapter Nineteen

Before getting into the shower, I called to get an update on Lorenzo's condition. "He's home," Gordon told me.

I sighed a breath of relief.

"He's growling at me to leave. So I guess that means he's feeling better. I plan on staying with him this evening and watching some TV. I'll see you in the morning."

"Tell him that I'm thinking about him?"

"I will, Casey. And Casey?"

"Yes?"

"Be careful. I don't think my heart can survive anything else happening."

"I will. Thank you, Gordon."

Next, I called my family. All the major news channels had arrived at the greenhouses before Turner and I had left. And since I'd never known my grandmother to miss the evening news, I could guarantee that the mood at Rosebrook would be tense while my aunts and grandmother fretted over my safety.

Tears welled in my eyes as I explained to my grandmother what had happened, assuring her that I was okay. I could clearly hear my lively aunts shouting advice in the background. Lord, how I missed them. I could have talked with them all night, but I didn't want to keep Richard waiting.

I spoke briefly with Aunt Alba — she offered all sorts of creative advice on how to disable a man — before Aunt Willow wrestled the phone away from her. As soon as I told Aunt Willow that I needed to get ready for my date, she hung up.

About an hour later I descended the stairs feeling a bit like Scarlet O'Hara or Cinderella or perhaps a strange mix of the two women, strong but extremely lucky and more than a bit in over my head with Richard. My feet were stuffed into a pair of slingback heels so high I felt like I could touch the ceiling. The slinky black dress Alyssa had left lying on my bed hugged every curve and dipped low in the cleavage. Tugging at the shoulder straps only raised my breasts. It didn't cover me more.

My mother's diamond and emerald necklace graced my throat. Heavy makeup hid the bruises still visible on my neck and temple. My lips glittered with cherry roses and my eyes shimmered in honey hues. Thanks to Alyssa's styling prowess, romantic blond curls framed my face. I barely recognized myself in the mirror.

Both a fully dressed Turner and a beaming Alyssa waited for me at the bottom of the steps. Turner's hazel green eyes widened as I came to a stop in front of him.

"You look . . ." His gaze swept slowly from my head all the way down to my toes.

"Yes?"

He gave his head a hard shake. "I've got to go."

"You could stay and have dinner with me," Alyssa suggested, batting her long, black eyelashes.

"No." Turner grabbed the door handle and gave it a vicious yank. "Thank you, but no." He rushed out of the apartment as if escaping one of Dante's circles of hell.

"What did you do to him?" I demanded as Alyssa and I watched Turner limp-hop down the front steps.

Alyssa, smiling coyly, shrugged.

Turner had just reached the bottom of the slate steps when a shiny black town car pulled up to the curb in front of the brownstone. As soon as it stopped moving, Richard's assistant emerged from the driver's side. After carefully scanning the area, he jogged up the steps.

"Ms. Calhoun?" His deep voice rumbled low in his chest. "I'm Wallace Clegg, Mr. Templeton's personal assistant."

"Is that what they're calling bodyguards nowadays?" Alyssa whispered in my ear.

I batted Alyssa away. "Yes, I remember you, Mr. Clegg. We met at the White House gate yesterday. It's good to see you again."

"Did we meet before?" He looked me over from head to toe. "You'll have to forgive me. I never remember faces."

"Some people don't," I said. But the other day Clegg had mentioned he thought he'd recognized me. Perhaps he was distracted this evening. Otherwise, I'm sure he would have remembered talking with me.

His nose pointed down like an arrowhead to the thin lips he had pressed tightly together. His gaze narrowed as he watched me.

"Mr. Templeton is waiting for you at the restaurant." He stepped aside and gestured that I should precede him down the stairs to the waiting car.

I didn't move.

It wasn't my feet that stopped me. It was *his.*

His *shoes,* to be exact.

"Yes, I'm looking forward to dinner," I

301

said to those black-and-white shoes with the lightning design that were becoming a very familiar sight lately.

"Er, Ms. Calhoun, you are ready to go, aren't you? Mr. Templeton is waiting."

"Am I ready?" I asked Alyssa.

Alyssa must have noticed the shoes and recognized them. I'd described the design to her all the way down to the shoe's white stitching enough times that she'd told me she's been dreaming about them. But the fact they were on Clegg's feet didn't seem to bother her.

She gave me a not-so-gentle push. "Get going already. You don't want him to think you're having second thoughts."

I suppose she was right. Besides, I'd seen those shoes all over D.C. lately. Apparently, they'd become an overnight hit.

I grabbed my purse, a small beaded black clutch, from the console table beside the door. "I'm ready."

"Don't do anything I wouldn't do," Alyssa called from the front door as I slipped into the town car's dark interior.

Dinner at the historic Old Ebbitt Grill was exquisite. Richard had a sharp wit that kept me laughing as the courses were served. He presented a mighty fine view to boot.

So why, at the end of the night after he'd walked me up the brownstone's steps and to my front door, did I not feel those soft-winged butterflies fluttering around in my belly? And why, when he leaned in to kiss me, did I turn my head?

He crossed his arms and frowned at me. "Okay," he said quietly, as if he understood. "Good night."

"Wait." I caught his arm when he turned to head down the stairs. "It's not you. I've had a crazy day. First, my credit card was canceled. I still don't know why. Then Senator Pendergast goes to the newspaper to attack my organic gardening proposal. You'd think I was suggesting that we pave over the South Lawn. And . . . and . . ." Tears welled up in my eyes. "And then there's Pauline Bonde. I cannot get her out of my head. It's not as if I know anything, but that didn't stop someone from trying to kill me today. That is, if it's the same guy. And Lorenzo certainly doesn't know anything. So why would anyone want to hurt him?"

"Wait a minute." Richard grabbed my hands. "Someone came after you today?"

"Didn't I mention that?"

"Don't you think I'd have remembered it? What happened?"

"It wasn't my finest hour," I warned.

"I don't care. What happened?"

Richard listened patiently as we stood under the lamplight on my front stoop. I told him about the man stalking me at the greenhouse facility and how he'd attacked Lorenzo. I even admitted to how I'd attacked Jack Turner . . . again. When I finished, Richard cursed under his breath.

"Did you get a good look at him?"

I shook my head. "No. Hopefully Lorenzo saw something. I haven't been able to talk to him yet."

"God, this is terrible." His hold on my hands tightened. "I'm going to stay here tonight to protect you."

Exactly where was he expecting to stay? The apartment I shared with Alyssa had only two bedrooms. I certainly didn't want to spend the night sleeping on a lumpy sofa. I'm sure Richard wouldn't want to sleep on a lumpy sofa.

And he wasn't going to stay in my —

I wasn't ready to go *there.*

Not yet. Not this quickly.

"I'll be fine." I freed my hands from his grasp. "I'll lock the door and sleep with the phone under my pillow."

"No, that won't work. I'm not going to leave without providing you some degree of protection. Here's what I'll do, I'll send

Clegg back here to watch the place after he drops me off at the hotel."

I opened my mouth to protest. I don't know why, but Clegg, with his nervous twitches, gave me the willies.

"You will do this," Richard said rather sharply. He then held up his hands and smiled. "Otherwise, I won't get any sleep and will be in a fog tomorrow morning. Do you want that on your conscience?"

"I'm not sure how I feel about letting a strange man into the apartment," I admitted. "I'm sure Clegg is capable and trustworthy. But I don't know him."

"You don't have to let him in. I'll have him watch the place from outside. He'll be more effective that way. And I won't listen to any more arguments."

He caressed my cheek. "Don't you worry about your credit card or the senator. I'm sure all of that will work out. Good night, Casey." Richard kissed me on the cheek. This time that was the spot he'd been aiming for. And then, with a blazing smile bright enough to light up the night sky, he rushed down the stairs and back into the waiting town car.

After Wallace Clegg closed the door for his employer, he turned to glare up at where I was standing. When our gazes met, his upper lip twitched.

This was the guy who'd be standing guard outside my front door all night? Perhaps I'd sleep with the phone under my pillow after all.

CHAPTER TWENTY

The next morning I poked my head out the front door to find Wallace slouched in the driver's seat of a black sedan parked at the curb. He grunted when I tapped on the passenger-side window.

"Coffee?" I held up a steaming cup.

"No, thanks. It'll only make me have to pee."

"Oh." I hadn't thought of that. "Do you need to come inside?"

"Yeah, for like about the past five hours," he grumbled. "And it's cold out here."

I really didn't feel comfortable letting him in, but what else could I do? According to Aunt Alba, hospitality was a cornerstone of society. "I'll make oatmeal."

"Knock yourself out."

While I wrung my hands and kept a close watch on Richard's twitchy personal assistant, who looked as if he'd spent hours in a gym lifting weights, Alyssa flirted. She poured him several more cups of coffee and even suggested he try her gourmet vanilla creamer.

"I really need to get to work," I said after he'd finished his breakfast, hoping he'd take the hint and leave with me.

"Okay, bye." Alyssa waved at me without taking her gaze off Wallace's squared features. He leaned back in the kitchen chair as if he had no plans of leaving . . . ever.

I walked toward the door. "Alyssa?"

"Bye," she called.

"Can I have a word with you?"

Silence.

"In the living room?"

After a few minutes Alyssa came out of the kitchen with her hands on her hips and a cross expression on her face. "Since when did you become so selfish?" she demanded.

"Selfish?"

"You have Richard Templeton and that hunky Secret Service agent. What do you need this guy for?" She gestured back to the kitchen.

"I don't need him for anything."

"Then leave him here with me."

"I can't!" I pressed the heels of my hands to my eyes. "I don't," I continued in a softer voice, "I don't trust him. I don't want him in our apartment. I don't want you to be alone with him."

"You don't trust Wallace? He's Richard's right-hand man."

"I know. I know." Was it fair that I didn't trust him because of the shoes he wore? And was that really the only reason? "Richard wanted to stay the night last night to protect me. I — I wasn't ready for *you know.* That's why he parked Wallace outside our door."

"Have you lost your freaking mind?" Alyssa shrieked. "You turned down a night of passion with *the* Richard Templeton. So, yes, that must be it. You're certifiable." She waved her hands in the air for emphasis. "Cer — ti — fi — able. Get the net, boys. We've got a live one this time."

"Are you done?"

Alyssa nodded.

"I need to get to work. So do you."

"I suppose." She headed for the stairs. "Tell lover boy in there that I would have rocked his world."

Yeah, right. I could so see me telling someone that. Instead, I told him that Alyssa sent her regrets, but she remembered that she — wonder of wonders — actually had a job to get to.

"A shame," Wallace grumbled. But he left the house with me.

"Good-bye," I said to him at the bottom

309

of the town house steps, and hurried down the sidewalk. Because I'd had to feed and care for Wallace, I was running late. The sun was already up and so were most of my neighbors. I waved to Mrs. Coomby, my elderly neighbor with the silver-blue hair, as she puttered among her roses next door.

"Aphids," she complained, shaking her head.

"Try washing the leaves with dish soap and a sponge," I offered as I passed by her small front yard. "That should take care of them."

"Thanks, doll." She waved her garden-gloved hand. "I'll give that a go."

I started to continue down the sidewalk but noticed Wallace standing beside Richard's town car, glaring at me.

"Is something wrong?" I called to him.

He glanced at my neighbor and shrugged. "I'm supposed to drive you to work," he said, making it sound like he'd rather do anything of the sort. "Richard will be upset if I don't."

I was going to tell Wallace he didn't need to bother, but I didn't want to get him into trouble. Besides, I needed to get to work as soon as possible. Seth Donahue had called me at three this morning raging about some sprigs of crabgrass he'd found popping up in the Rose Garden flowerbeds.

He'd made it sound as if the free world wouldn't survive the shock of spotting a weed poking out from behind a rosebush during this afternoon's press conference to introduce Milo to the world. I'd promised him I'd handle it first thing in the morning.

"Very well," I said to Wallace. "But I need to stop at the Freedom of Espresso Café." I wanted to do something nice for Turner by bringing another mug of gourmet coffee. Perhaps this time he'd accept my gesture of goodwill. And if, as a consequence, he happened to share some details about the investigation, so much the better.

When the town car pulled up at Lafayette Square, I quickly got out of the sedan. "Thanks for the ride and for stopping at the coffee shop."

Wallace wasn't listening. He was staring at the group of banking protesters setting up in Lafayette Square.

"What the hell is *she* doing here?" he said. "Unbelievable. I should have known she'd follow us to D.C."

"Who?" I asked.

"Joanna Lovell!" He spat her name.

There must have been over fifty banking summit protesters gathered in the square that morning. Joanna stood in the center of the crowd. I almost didn't recognize her. She'd exchanged the pale blue housecoat for a steel gray power pantsuit and looked every inch the lawyer this morning. She pointed to the North Lawn, and someone in the group started a steady tempo on a drum. The protesters chanted to the beat, "Financial regulation, financial legislation. Put the crooks in jail," with the last part getting a shrill note.

"You know her?"

"Who doesn't? She's been trying to stir up trouble for every banker east of the Mississippi. It's a personal vendetta for her."

"Really? Why?"

"Joanna used to head up the legal department at BLK Investments. That was until Lillian wandered into Brooks's bedroom one night and found Joanna in bed with him."

Richard had mentioned that Brooks had been involved with a scandal. I watched Joanna as she led a cheer with enough vigor to turn her cheeks red.

"Lillian not only fired Joanna on the spot. She made it her crusade to ruin the woman. All sorts of vicious stories about Joanna's personal and professional life have surfaced since the affair went public."

"Out of those ashes rose a firebrand set

on destroying the industry she once loved?" I asked.

"Something like that. I'd bet my entire portfolio that she's the one we can thank for the senator's renewed interest in financial reform."

"Renewed interest? What do you mean?"

"Haven't you heard? Senator Pendergast announced yesterday afternoon that she was reopening the banking hearings."

I wondered if my little chat with her yesterday had anything to do with that. "I didn't know."

"Now you do." He started to walk away.

"Thank you for watching my apartment last night, Wallace. You must have been very uncomfortable. I do appreciate it."

"Don't thank me. I did it for Richard. I'd do anything for him. He's going places in this world, and I intend to go there with him." He reached over and slammed the town car's passenger door closed, barely missing my side as I jumped out of the way.

A shiver traveled up my spine as I watched him drive away. I knew it was wrong of me to hold a grudge against someone simply because of the shoes he wore. But I couldn't help it. Wallace made me uneasy.

I wound my way through the crowd of protesters to get to the White House gates, skirting between Joanna Lovell and a large cutout of Lillian Brooks, but then stopped and turned back around.

"Joanna, do you have a minute?"

"Of course." She walked alongside me. "Keep them going," she said to a young man with shaggy blond hair who was dressed in overalls with holes in both knees. "I'll be back in ten."

We ended up at the same park bench where I'd comforted Pauline's roommate, Isabella.

"What can I do for you?"

"I saw you talking with Brooks Keller a couple of days ago." I sat down on the bench.

Joanna remained standing. Her lips compressed to a tight line.

I rushed to finish. "I also heard what happened between the two of you and what his sister did afterwards. I can't imagine what that must have been like."

"No, I don't suppose you can." She started to pace. "No law firm in New York will even take my calls thanks to the lies Lillian has spread about me. I can't get a job. I'm teetering on homelessness, but neither of the Wonder Twins cares what happens in their wake. They just take, take, take. Look out if you dare get in their glorious way, because they'll roll right over you."

"I'm sorry for that."

"If that's all you wanted to know —" She started to walk away.

"When you were talking with Brooks the other day" — Brooks had also handed her an envelope — "what was that about?"

"You saw that?"

I nodded.

"I suppose we weren't being discreet. Well, I'll tell you what the sticky bastard was doing. Why shouldn't I? I'm sick of everyone thinking he's so squeaky clean and honest. He was trying to pay me off. Can you believe him? He wanted the protesters gone, especially me." She gave a throaty chuckle. "I took his wad of cash. Oh, yeah, I took it. But I'm not going anywhere. Now if that's all —"

"There is one more thing. It's about Pauline," I said, hoping to channel some of Miss Marple's smooth questioning style. "The news had reported that the FBI had questioned Brooks Keller about her death. Was Pauline involved with Brooks, too? Is that why the press is trying to draw connections between him and her murder?"

Joanna sat down beside me. "Pauline, Pauline . . . that unsophisticated fool. She craved attention like a neglected puppy. And

Brooks, you know, was only too eager to provide it."

"But wouldn't getting involved with him be considered a conflict of interest? Pauline was auditing BLK's financial records."

Joanna shrugged. "They're bankers. Do you think ethics ever enters into their greedy minds?"

"I would hope —"

"Then you're as naive as Pauline. She should have kept her nose in those bank books. I wish I'd never introduced her to Brooks and the like."

"Wait a minute. You introduced them?"

"That was before my downfall." She sighed wistfully. "Seems like a lifetime ago. Once a month I'd host an intimate salon at my Manhattan apartment. Pauline was gorgeous, smart, and ambitious. Of course I invited her. In order to attract the best sort of men, I had to invite the most interesting and eye-catching women. I didn't realize how ambitious Pauline was until after that party. It was the last one I ever held."

"And that's where she met Brooks?"

"She had her eye on Richard Templeton, but he only dates celebrities with boobs out to here." She demonstrated with her hands.

"Really? I heard she had lunch with Richard while in New York City."

"Impossible." She repeated her demonstration of his preference for large-breasted women. "At the party, when she'd tried to start up a conversation with him, he'd crinkled his nose and looked as if he'd spotted a cockroach. Believe me, he wasn't interested and she knew it. That's when she turned her sights on Brooks."

"*Your* Brooks."

"I knew going in that monogamy wasn't his thing."

"Still, that didn't bother you?"

She waved her hand and looked away.

"So if she was sleeping with Brooks and found something in the BLK account books, something that might make the Wonder Twins look bad, do you think she might have mentioned that to him?"

"It's a possibility."

"Do you think he would have killed her to keep her quiet?"

"Not Brooks. Lillian, perhaps. She's the shark in the family."

But the shoes I saw, they were the same shoes Brooks was wearing. Still, everything seemed to be pointing me back to my original theory that Pauline had been murdered because of something she'd found in those audits of hers. It might have been something damaging enough to win widespread support for Senator Pendergast's proposed legislation.

"What do you think about Senator Pendergast's ideas about how to regulate the banks?"

"They're tough, but needed. Some bankers are more interested in hitting the jackpot year after year with their profits than they are in making good long-term decisions." Joanna cursed and jumped up from the bench. "What does the Secret Service think they're doing now? I've got to go put a stop to it."

She jogged down the path back to where two uniformed Secret Service agents were talking to a couple of her protesters, her high heels clacking against the pavement. "We've got a permit to be here!" she shouted.

Brooks. Everything so far pointed back to Brooks Keller.

Perhaps Pauline had warned Brooks that she'd found some compromising information during the audit, and he needed to stop her from making that information public. He needed to kill her and steal her laptop.

Or perhaps he didn't care about the audit. Perhaps there was something else on that computer of hers, like a racy e-mail that

318

Pauline had threatened to use against him. I could imagine the PR disaster that would erupt if it got out that Brooks was sleeping with the government employee who was supposed to be making sure his bank's accounts were in order.

I hurried to the White House gate and waved to Fredrick.

After my surprise meeting with the President and First Lady yesterday, I was beginning to understand why Lorenzo dressed so formally. This morning I'd decided to wear a dark gray tailored pantsuit with a white silk blouse that was more fitting for the office than the garden.

"Could you let Special Agent Turner know that I need to see him right away?"

"Only if I want him to move more slowly," Fredrick replied.

I tapped my foot impatiently while I waited. I was anxious to tell Turner my new theory. It had to be Brooks. Or his sister.

"Come on, come on." I didn't have time to stand around waiting like this. Spring was the busiest time of year for a gardener. Working at the White House only increased the workload by, oh, one hundred and ten percent or so.

There were plans to be approved, soils to be amended, plants to get into the ground, shrubs to be pruned, and not enough hours in the day to do it all.

Not to mention the string of outside public events and the expectation that the grounds always look immaculate.

I checked the clock on my cell phone. Five minutes had passed. And then ten.

Finally I spotted a dark shadow lumbering down a tree-lined walkway. Unless Jack Turner had grown a few inches both in height and girth, the Secret Service agent heading my way was not the understanding agent I kept accidentally assaulting.

As he got closer, I recognized the CAT agent as the same one who'd given Turner a tough time in the West Wing lobby after the — *um* — pepper spray incident. He'd insulted me. I am *neither* itty *nor* bitty.

"Where's Turner?" I demanded.

Perhaps Turner had wised up and decided to keep his distance, regardless of his supervisor's orders to *handle* me. Or perhaps he was more seriously injured than he'd let on yesterday.

He shrugged. "Don't know. It's his day off. That coffee for me?"

"Yeah, sure." I handed him the mug. "But Turner's okay, right?"

"Don't rightly know. I suppose so."

I detected a Southern twang in his accent.

"Where are you from originally?"

He regarded me for a long moment before answering. "Mississippi, ma'am."

"Imagine that. I'm from Charleston, South Carolina. We were once practically neighbors."

"I have a cousin in Charleston. Nice place," he commented, and then asked for my backpack.

While he searched my belongings, I decided to see if all Secret Service agents were as close-mouthed as Turner.

"I heard that the investigation is moving forward, that an arrest might be made any day now."

He grunted.

"What about Brooks Keller? Did you know he was involved with Pauline even though she was conducting a financial review of his bank? Sounds a mite suspicious if you ask me."

He grunted again.

"And have you heard about the cows?"

"Cows?" He kept searching my bag.

"Congress voted to send a colony of them up to live on the moon."

He looked up and stared at me for a moment. "Ha! That's a good one." He zipped up the backpack and thrust it at me. "Keep out of trouble," he said, turning away. "Oh, and thanks for the coffee."

"Wait! What about a little tit-for-tat? That's the best coffee in town."

He took a sip and let the coffee's rich flavors bathe his palette. "Yeah, it's much better than the muddy crap in our coffeepot. Wouldn't call that coffee, but we drink it because that's all we've got." He took another sip and smiled. "Thanks."

"And?" I prompted.

"And I'd mind my own business where this investigation is concerned. You might have Turner wrapped around that pretty pinky of yours, but I'm from the South, missy. I know how you Southern women use your charms to trick us men into looking like fools. And you've done plenty of that with Turner-boy, but you'll not be doing that with me."

"Now see here —"

"I know you're fixing to say that I don't know you and blah, blah, blah. Save it for someone who cares."

Stunned, I closed my mouth and stepped back. This guy was really something else.

And he wasn't finished. "How or why you managed to make a straight-shooter like Jack look incompetent — to make the entire CAT team look incompetent — is beyond me. But I do know one thing, you're damned lucky Jack took his damned babysitting gig so seriously. You'd be dead right now if he'd let those crazy protesters get their hands on you yesterday."

"You mean the banking protesters out on Lafayette Square? You think one of them followed me to the greenhouse?"

The Secret Service had been suspicious of the protesters even before Pauline's body had been found. "You think one of them murdered Pauline Bonde?"

"Damn. You didn't know that?"

"Apparently, I don't know much of anything. My life is on the line, and yet no one cared to tell me who is trying to kill me."

"Why else do you think Thatch put Jack on babysitting detail? Jack's responsible for keeping you alive."

I glanced out at the protesters chanting fervently. They didn't look so harmless anymore.

I lowered my voice. "And you suspect that one of the protesters out there has been plotting to attack the President?"

"You know about that already?"

"Thatch told me."

"Well, then." He cleared his throat. "Now you know everything."

"I don't know who killed Pauline, or why.

I don't even know — Wait! How'd he get out?"

A not-so-small fluffy ball of golden and white fur bounded toward us at full speed, clumps of mud flying in every direction.

"Milo!"

Why wasn't anyone watching the puppy? He could easily slip out of a gate or get into something he shouldn't.

Like the Rose Garden.

The naughty pup plowed into my legs and would have knocked me over if Turner's stand-in hadn't caught my arm. Not to be deterred, Milo reared up. His muddy front paws landed with a squishy splash on my expensive tailored pants. His tail thudded with unleashed excitement against the ground as he showed off his treasure.

Milo was carrying a rosebush, roots and all, in his mouth.

The naughty puppy hadn't dug up just any rosebush. The plant hanging from his drooling mouth, a floribunda "Pat Nixon" rosebush, was covered with delicate buds that would have produced rich burgundy red blooms. The only place on the White House grounds where this particular variety grew was in the Rose Garden.

I shuddered to think about the extent of damage Milo might have wrecked in the planting beds. Seth had lost sleep worrying over a few sprigs of crabgrass in the Rose Garden? Just wait until he discovered the new First Puppy had ripped out part of the plantings a few hours before the press conference was to begin.

CHAPTER TWENTY-ONE

I reached down to snatch the bush away from Milo, but before I could get a good grip on the prickly plant, the gangly puppy gave a muffled woof. He shook his large head and ripped the branch I'd grabbed out of my grasp. He took off with an amazingly quick bouncy gait toward the East Wing, dropping a trail of twigs, leaves, and rose-buds in his wake.

"Excuse me," I said, and took off running after him.

In retrospect, chasing after a puppy wasn't a good idea. He *woof-woofed* as he played hide-and-seek, darting between the parked cars in the east lot of the White House grounds. He jumped over a low hedge and darted left and right under a thick canopy of trees on the South Lawn. For a moment it looked as if he'd run right back up to the house. But he heard a car behind him and made a sharp turn back toward the south gates. The fences were open. And the traffic in the streets was hectic as usual.

If he went much farther, I feared the worst.

"Milo!" I clapped my hands.

He ignored me.

The guard hut was only a few yards away. I called for the uniformed Secret Service officers manning the gate to help me stop Milo, because once he ran past that point, he'd either take off into the fifty-two acre park behind the White House known as the Ellipse or dash out onto the street. I could see the headline now: WHITE HOUSE GAR-DENER LOSES FIRST PUP.

Forget the headlines, forget that in a few hours the President planned to hold a press conference to introduce Milo to the country, I couldn't let anything bad happen to the oversized puppy. To him, he was simply playing a game. He didn't know the dangers lurking beyond the iron fence.

"Come on, Milo. Let's go." I ran in the opposite direction.

That got the puppy's attention. He crouched down on the grass with his tail end up in the air and watched me running around like a lunatic before deciding to join in on the fun.

"Got him!" Janie Partners crowed. I don't

know where the Secret Service agent had appeared from or how she'd managed to grab Milo's bright blue collar, but she had.

Milo's entire rear half wiggled with delight as I jogged over to them.

Today, Janie was wearing a jet-black suit with a sedate brown scarf tied around her neck. When I got closer, I noticed the scarf was decorated with tiny paw prints.

"Thank you for catching the scamp. Where did you come from? How'd you know I needed a hand?"

"It's not every day someone runs suspicious zigzag patterns full speed across the White House lawn. You attracted a lot of attention." She gestured behind me.

I turned to look. About a dozen Secret Service agents, most of them from the uniformed Emergency Response Team with their beefy P90 assault rifles that could blast through armored vehicles, had fanned out across the lawn. They were all staring at me. Even the snipers on the roof had trained their binoculars in my direction.

Biting my lower lip, I gave a small wave.

"They're not going to let me forget this, are they?" I murmured.

"Not on your life." She turned to Milo. "And what do you have there, mister? You haven't been into Miss Calhoun's hybrid teas, have you?"

Still happily thumping his tail, he dropped the bush. His bright pink tongue lolled out the side of his mouth. I scooped up the plant before he decided to grab it again.

"Actually, it's a floribunda rose, which is a little bit different from the hybrid teas. For one thing, they're hardier. Their flowers form in dense clusters. See here and here?" I pointed that out on a part of the bush that wasn't too damaged. "All those blooms will open at about the same time and continue to bloom over a longer period of time than a hybrid tea. And you don't care about any of that, do you?"

"Not really. I heard you've come up with yet another theory about what happened out in Lafayette Square." She lowered her voice. "You might want to think twice before throwing around accusations that involve friends of the First Lady like Brooks Keller."

"Do you Secret Service types have nothing better to do than to sit down in your basement lair and gossip?"

"We don't have to go to our lair." She pointed to her earpiece. "Radio chatter."

"I'll have to remember that. What evidence do y'all have on the banking protesters? Do you have any idea which one of them is the prime suspect in Pauline's murder?"

"I'm not sure I can talk about that."

"Don't you think I deserve to know who I should be worried about?"

Janie thought about that for a moment. "Yeah, you're right. I'd want to know when I needed to watch my back. *Reader's Digest* version is this: We don't know who it is, but we've picked up some intel that there's a person or persons involved with the banking reform protests who is so angry with the President's ties to Wall Street that he or she is plotting an attack."

"So I've heard. But if that's the case, why not cancel the permit and send them away?"

"We can't punish everyone in a group just because we suspect — but have no proof, mind you — that one of them might, and I stress the word *might,* be planning something."

"And you also believe this is the same guy who killed Pauline and then attacked me in the park and again at the greenhouse?"

Janie nodded. "That's the working theory. Uh-oh, don't look now. Seth Donahue is heading this way." She pushed Milo over to me. I grabbed his collar before he could take off again. "I'm out of here."

"You're not going to leave me, an unarmed woman, alone with him?"

Janie didn't seem to care. She trotted off

through the trees toward the south gates without a backward glance.

"Looks like it's just you and me, Milo."

"Ms. Calhoun." Seth's crisp voice cut through morning air. "The Rose Garden is in shambles, and the President and First Lady are scheduled to hold their press conference there in less than two hours."

"Have you talked with Gordon about this?"

"I'm talking to you."

"Yes, I see that. Here, you can give me a hand." I picked up Milo and dropped the muddy puppy into Seth's arms. He gave a startled yelp. Milo yipped.

I ignored both of them and started to walk up the sloping lawn toward the White House.

"Ms. Calhoun! You have to do something. When I contacted you last evening —"

"At three in the morning."

"You promised to have the crabgrass out of the gardens. And yet, the crabgrass is still there and several of the plants have been dug up."

"I'll get the crew working on it right away."

"You do that. When I took this position, I'd expected a higher degree of professionalism. No one seems to understand how to do anything around here." He practically threw Milo back at me and stalked off.

"No, Seth, you're the one who doesn't seem to understand. You're making everyone change how they've operated for years," I said even though he'd already disappeared through the entrance at the South Portico. "You should be listening to how things are done and then suggest gradual adjustments."

Child, what do they say about pots calling out kettles? my inner voice chided.

Gracious, I could have slapped myself in my forehead for not heeding my own advice. No wonder Gordon had refused to support my gardening plans the other day. I'd stood in front of a room of his peers and declared that everything he'd been doing for the past quarter century was wrong.

Milo whined as I tucked him, all mud-coated and everything, under my arm.

"You look as if you've been out rolling in the marsh, little gnome." He was going to need a bath before his debut in front of the world press, but that would have to wait. With the rosebush in one hand and the puppy in the other, I set out to find Gordon and make things right.

"What have you done to my sweet puppy?" Gordon exclaimed the moment he spotted us coming through the Diplomatic Reception Room.

"What about your helpless rosebush?" The plant's small green leaves rattled as I shook it for emphasis. A mistake. Clumps of mud landed on my once pristine white blouse and on the robin's-egg blue and gold rug under my feet. Emblems representing all fifty states encircled the one-of-a-kind rug's border. I planned to apologize profusely to the maid charged with cleaning up the clumps of mud now staining it.

Thanks to muddy puppy paws, my blouse already looked as if I'd been rolling in the mud along with Milo.

"The rosebush doesn't have a press conference in a few hours." Gordon grabbed Milo and started cooing over the pup that had been entrusted to his care. He didn't seem to mind that his forest green polo shirt was getting just about as muddy as my blouse.

The oval Diplomatic Reception Room, which had once served as a boiler and furnace room and later as the site of FDR's Fireside Chats, was elegantly furnished in the Federal style. It was not a place for an unruly puppy.

Jacqueline Kennedy had installed a fanciful mural wallpaper called "Views of North

America," featuring vignettes of American landscapes. Although the original wallpaper had been printed in 1834, the images had a colorful and timeless feel to them.

"I found Milo running through the North Lawn with the rosebush in his mouth. No one was watching him," I explained to Gordon as we headed out into the vaulted Center Hall.

"What! That's unforgivable." He glanced at a group of primary school children taking the White House tour heading our way and pursed his lips. We quickly crossed into the basement hall that led to the grounds office and, thankfully, was not part of the White House tour.

"He could have gotten lost," Gordon continued more softly, though not with any less passion. "Or even killed. I'm going to have to have some sharp words with the Secret Service about this. They need to keep as close an eye on this little fellow as they would any other member of the First Family."

"I agree," I said, relieved to hear that Gordon planned to take charge and speak to the Secret Service. Keeping out of their way appeared to be necessary for my own job preservation now more than ever. "And give them hell," I whispered.

"There you are." Margaret Bradley hurried toward us. The fabric of her lavender silk dress swished around her legs with each step.

I was surprised to see her coming from the direction of the offices and shops located underneath the North Portico. Members from those offices would go to *her,* not the other way around.

Milo wiggled happily the moment he saw her.

"Mrs. Bradley," Gordon said as he jogged over to her. "As you can see, he's been found."

"Thank goodness." She gave my disheveled state a once-over. Her warm smile grew wider. "You found him, then?"

"He's been digging up the Rose Garden, I'm afraid." I held up the damaged rosebush as evidence.

"What a mess. He's quite coated in mud, too," she observed, and patted Milo's head. "There's not much time to get him cleaned up, either."

"We'll see to it," Gordon offered.

We would? I supposed we could use the hoses outside to give him a quick bath. But would we be able to get him dried off in time for the press conference?

"No, I wouldn't hear of it. The two of you

have enough to do. Give him to me." She held out her arms.

"He'll ruin your dress," Gordon protested.

"I can put on another one. Now, hand him to me. I'll see to him. You look after the Rose Garden. Our social secretary is on the brink of a nervous breakdown already. I don't want him to find out that the puppy has been digging up —"

"Seth already knows," I told her.

"Oh, dear." Her impeccable poise slipped for a second, causing her lower lip to tremble. She swiftly bit down on it and forced a smile. "Well, it can't be helped. We'll simply have to deal with this as it comes. Two of the upstairs maids are a whiz with hair. I'm sure they'll be able to wash and fluff this little guy back into shape."

She hugged Milo to her chest, his huge puppy paws smearing mud on yet another outfit that morning.

"Don't worry about the Rose Garden," Gordon told her. "The grounds crew is out there already."

"They are?" I asked. Gordon never ceased to amaze me with his efficiency.

"Sprucing up the area is standard procedure before a press conference, even last-minute press conferences," Gordon explained. "It'll look perfect."

"I'm glad to hear it. Thank you again," Mrs. Bradley said as she hurried off.

Back at the grounds office, I was surprised to find Lorenzo at his desk filling out a stack of paperwork that rivaled the pile Fisher had left for me. A large white bandage stood out in stark contrast to his dark brown hair. Other than that, he looked like the freshly pressed, perfectly groomed gardening assistant I'd grown used to seeing every day.

I couldn't be happier.

"Lorenzo! You're okay!" The muscles in his shoulders tightened as I gave him a great big hug. After questioning him on how he was feeling — his head throbbed — and Gordon had a chance to scold him for not taking the day to rest and recover, I finally got the chance to ask the question that had been burning on my mind since the attack.

"Do you remember what happened? Did you see the guy who did this?"

"Or was it a lady?" Gordon put in.

"As I told both the police and the FBI, I barely remember being attacked." Lorenzo pressed his hands against the sides of his head and pinched his eyes closed. "I didn't see anyone."

"Not even a pair of shoes?" Gordon asked with a glance in my direction.

Lorenzo opened his eyes and stared intently at me. "No. I'm sorry, Casey. I shouldn't have blamed you for not getting a good look at your attacker. I didn't understand that something like this" — he rubbed the back of his neck — "could happen so unexpectedly or so quickly. I didn't see a damned thing. I didn't really understand what had happened until it was explained to me at the hospital."

"I'm still convinced I can help identify Pauline's killer. I haven't given up, Lorenzo." A promise was a promise.

"Thanks, Casey, I appreciate that." Lorenzo said.

After this morning's revelations, my mind whirled with scenarios and possibilities. Pauline had been intimately involved with Brooks. So had Joanna.

Joanna had expressed regret at introducing the pair.

Did she regret it because Pauline had been murdered? Or did she regret introducing Pauline to Brooks because Pauline had caught her lover's roving eye?

Joanna had been present in the park the morning Pauline had been murdered.

Brooks and Lillian may have ruined Joanna, but Pauline had betrayed their friendship by taking Joanna's lover to her own bed. Perhaps the murder didn't have anything to do with the banking reform legislation after all. Perhaps I was completely wrong about everything.

"Have you seen this?" Lorenzo handed me the newspaper.

The headline stopped me cold: SENATOR PENDERGAST'S BRUSH WITH DISASTER. I quickly scanned the article. Last night, while I enjoyed dinner with Richard, a car had swerved onto the sidewalk and nearly run down Edith Pendergast as she walked her dog near her house in the Dupont Circle neighborhood. Both she and her small white dog, Churchill, were shaken but had sustained only minor cuts and bruises. The FBI was investigating.

"No, not that." Lorenzo snatched the paper away, flipped to the last page of the first section, and slapped it down on the desk in front of me. He tapped his finger on the corner of an editorial cartoon at the top of the page.

Gordon leaned over my shoulder to look. "This could prove problematic."

Building on the scathing article Griffon Parker had written, the national newspaper, *Media Today,* had run an editorial cartoon envisioning an overgrown White House grounds that resembled an abandoned city lot with weedy flowerbeds and an unkempt lawn littered with kitchen waste, including banana peels and rotting tomatoes. A cartoon depiction of me, complete with floppy straw hat, stood at the center of the drawing with her hands on her freakishly wide hips. The caption at the bottom of the cartoon read *Organic Gardener Runs Amok.*

"About that," I said, looking up at Gordon. My heart pounded in my chest. I wasn't used to eating crow. And boy, did I have a lot of stringy bird to eat this morning. "I am so sorry about the presentation the other day. I got totally carried away and, well, I didn't mean to make it sound as if I was criticizing the way things have been done around here. I have nothing but the utmost respect for both you and Lorenzo. I honestly didn't mean to steamroll over either of you." I sighed and pulled a hand through my hair. "I messed up."

"You sure did," Lorenzo agreed.

Gordon crossed his arms over his chest. "What do you plan to do about it?"

I closed my eyes and sighed deeply. If I wanted their forgiveness, I needed to prove that I wasn't going to act like Seth Donahue anymore. "I suggest that we take things more slowly. Change doesn't have to happen overnight. The implementation of the program should be gradual. Take the lawn, for instance. The tall fescue grass is well suited to the climate and use. There's no reason to change it. But perhaps we could raise the mower height from two and a half inches to three. The taller the leaf blade, the stronger the roots, which means it'll need less water and be less susceptible to weeds, insects, and disease. I also suggest that we should water deeply and less frequently and always in the morning, when there's no wind, to give the grass roots the best chance to absorb the water."

"There's nothing controversial about raising the mowing height an inch or altering the watering schedule," Gordon agreed. "We don't even need committee approval for something like that."

"Right. And by doing this over the summer season, hopefully we can wean the lawn off its dependence on chemical fertilizers, herbicides, and insecticides."

Gordon nodded thoughtfully. "That could work."

"As for the vegetable garden," I continued, "that's the First Lady's project. I've not really heard anyone criticize growing a few vegetables in the South Lawn. So that can still go forward as planned."

"No one can fault the family for wanting to have fresh backyard vegetables," Gordon agreed. "It's an American tradition."

"Okay. So do we have a plan?" I asked.

"Sounds like one to me," Gordon said.

"The rest we can add in over the next couple of years. It'll be gradual. If something doesn't work, we'll stop and reconsider. Do you think the committee will go for that?"

"With my support they will," Gordon said.

"Will you support it?"

I held my breath, waiting.

When Gordon nodded, I threw my arms around him and gave him a hug big enough to cover the entire south coast and left him blushing a bright red that extended deep into his hairline.

"Don't forget about Griffon Parker." Lorenzo tapped the cartoon. "It doesn't matter what the committee thinks. If public opinion swings against the plan, it's done."

"What can I do to fix that end of things?"

"Nothing publicly," Gordon reminded me. "This is the First Lady's house. But you might try giving Senator Pendergast a call."

"I did talk to her a little bit yesterday."

"Good. Keep working that angle. I'm sure that's where Parker is getting his information. No one on the committee would be foolish enough to talk to the press about White House affairs, not without prior approval. As you know, Senator Pendergast has been unhappy with both the President and the First Lady because of their deep friendships in the banking world."

I remembered the senator making those rather sharp accusations to the First Lady the other day. "And yet, she's kept quiet about those accusations to the press."

"Have you seen her approval numbers? They're not good. She's up for reelection and facing a tough battle," Gordon pointed out. "The President, on the other hand, is riding high with his approval numbers right now, especially in the senator's home district. It'd be political suicide to attack either him or his wife directly."

"So she's attacking me?"

"I'm sure that's not all she's doing. But it's her most visible attack, and safest. She's mainly complaining about the cost of the program."

"But it's not costly!"

"Doesn't matter. All she has to do is put the question out there in order to swing public opinion. Don't forget all the special news reports that have been questioning whether or not the President will support strong regulations against an industry that seems to have him in their pocket."

"You think the senator is behind those

negative news reports as well?"

Gordon shrugged. "Your guess is as good as mine. If you want to try and swing public opinion back our way, keep working on the senator. See if you can't win her over with this new plan of ours. And I'll talk with the committee."

"Okay, we can do this." I hoped.

While Gordon went to oversee the crew working in the Rose Garden, I found the business card Senator Pendergast had given me and dialed her number, hoping I could also find out about what had happened to her yesterday evening.

Did she think the driver of the car was angry about her renewed efforts on the financial reform bill?

Did the police?

Unfortunately the senator wasn't taking calls this morning, her chipper secretary informed me.

"Could you give her a message?" I asked. "It's important. I'm working with Mrs. Bradley on the White House garden plans. I understand that the senator has some concerns with the proposal, and I'd like to discuss —"

"You're calling from the First Lady's office? You should have told me that right away." The secretary put me on hold. A few minutes later she came back on the line. "The senator has already made her position clear. She also suggested" — the secretary hesitated — "I'm sorry, she wants me to tell you that you should consider seeking other employment alternatives. I'm sorry."

So was I. I stared at the phone, not sure what to do. With the senator working so diligently to embarrass the First Lady, I feared the organic garden plan, no matter how much Mrs. Bradley wanted it, would soon become a casualty of the battle being waged between the two powerful women.

Despite Gordon's promise to help me, I doubted my future at the White House could look any bleaker.

"Casey." Lorenzo swiveled around in his office chair to face me. He was smiling for the first time this morning. "That was Mike Thatch on the phone. He sounded really angry. He said he needs to see you right away."

My heart sank.

Forget about having to survive the senator's attacks on my job — that was nothing compared to facing an entire division of the Secret Service who appeared eager to see me gone.

CHAPTER TWENTY-TWO

Squeezing my hands together in my lap, I fought an urge to brush at the mud caked on the front of my white blouse or pick at the tiny dirt blobs speckling my gray pants as I sat in the plastic chair across from Mike Thatch's desk. The white walls, the long stretches of silence, and Thatch's grim expression brought back the same gut-sinking queasiness I'd suffered with every trip to my high school principal's office.

Thatch sat behind a large mahogany desk with a laptop open in front of him. Like his salt-and-pepper hair, his office didn't have even a stray piece of paper out of place.

He leaned back in his burgundy leather chair and beat the tip of his pen against the desk while he listened to my story, the rhythm of his tapping increasing when I got to the part where Turner had arrived.

Line by line, Thatch went over the statement I'd made at the greenhouses. He'd read a section and then would pause, look up, and wait for me to comment.

"Yes, that's what happened," I'd answer meekly.

He'd sniff and read on.

His quiet demeanor did nothing to quell my rattling nerves. I figured that as soon as he finished reviewing the statement, he'd yell at me for interfering in the investigation or for causing that ruckus this morning when I'd chased after Milo. Or worse, he'd call in Ambrose and have me fired. My hands tightened on the chair's arms as the scenarios playing in my mind of what might happen grew increasingly worse as the minutes stretched into an hour.

"And you're sure Turner is okay? I mean, you spoke with him personally this morning?"

Thatch stopped tapping his pen and looked up from the statement in front of him. "All my agents are tough. I assure you it would take much more than a scrawny gardener to put one of them out of action. Now where were we?"

After an hour and a half of his quiet torture, my nerves had frayed so much that when the assistant director in charge of Protective Operations, William Bryce, stuck his head into Thatch's office to let him know the press conference in the Rose Garden was about to begin, I jumped out of the plastic chair with a startled yelp.

Thatch had nodded and rushed through a couple more questions, not touching on the banking reform legislation except to mention the protesters. My foot jangled with impatience.

"Do you think the driver who tried to run down Senator Pendergast last night is linked to Pauline's murder and yesterday's attack at the greenhouse?" I finally built up the courage to ask.

"What do you think?" he asked.

Brooks Keller had motive. His shoes matched the ones I'd remembered seeing at the scene of the crime. And the senator's proposed bill put the squeeze on banking institutions.

Without the senator pushing so fiercely for the bill's success, I doubted many of its most stringent regulations would make it to the final version.

Aunt Willow had told me more times than I cared to count not to look a gift horse in the mouth. I never really did understand what that meant — I grew up in a city with absolutely no interaction with horses, unless you counted the workhorses that would ramble up and down Charleston's historic streets pulling carriages filled with tourists hoping to catch a glimpse of a bygone era.

And yet suddenly I knew what Aunt Willow had been telling me. This was one mouth I didn't want to pry open.

"Well?" Thatch pressed.

"I don't know," I lied.

"Good," he said as he stood. "Keep it that way."

He put his hand on my shoulder as he walked me through the Secret Service offices. "Stay clear of this, Casey. We're going to make an arrest . . . and soon."

"Who? One of the banking protesters?"

"Perhaps." He squeezed my shoulder. "If you don't stop meddling in the investigation and in Secret Service affairs, I'll have to report you to Ambrose. No one wants that, right?"

"Right."

A sense of dread followed me as I left the Secret Service offices. I was supposed to stay out of the investigation, but no matter how many times I worked out the scenario in my mind, I kept coming back to the same thing — the Secret Service was looking for their killer in the wrong place. The protesters had gained nothing with Pauline's death. And why would they attack the senator? She was on their side.

Still, the Secret Service knew what they were doing. They were experts at recognizing threats. Who was I to question them?

I rubbed my suddenly throbbing temples and decided to focus on my job. With the Easter Egg Roll just three days away, my to-do list wasn't growing any shorter, not when Seth kept adding items to it.

The press conference was under way in the Rose Garden. President John Bradley stood at his official podium in front of the doors that led into the West Wing. Margaret Bradley, dressed in a light green pantsuit, stood to his right. Milo sat between them, his clean, glossy coat gleaming. He tilted his little puppy head to one side. His ears were tipped forward as he watched with a bemused expression at how everyone was staring at him.

There were rows and rows of the press sitting in the folding chairs that had been set up on the grass. Hordes of cameramen filled every available space behind a rope barrier on the left side of the seating area. On a raised platform behind the seated reporters, cameramen snapped still photos with ridiculously large lenses and filmed every aspect of the press conference.

A smattering of Secret Service agents were spread out across the garden. While looking deceptively relaxed and slightly bored with the entire affair, they kept a close watch on every movement.

Seth Donahue stood watch near the back of the group. He kept his hands clasped behind him as he bounced nervously on the balls of his feet.

I don't know what he had to worry about. The pink, yellow, and white tulips were in their peak of bloom. The rosebushes looked healthy and ready to burst forth with an impressive show within a month or so. And there wasn't a weed in sight.

I weaved through the West Wing staff members who had gathered on the colonnade that connected the West Wing to the White House to watch the proceedings. Gordon stood next to a column with his arms crossed, smiling like a proud papa.

Everyone clapped when President Bradley reached down and shook the paw of the star of the show.

"Just think, a week ago he was locked in a cage in an animal shelter with a bleak future. Now he's living in the White House as the nation's First Dog, the Commander in Leash," President Bradley mused, much to the delight of the reporters. "I'd say this little guy is the epitome of the American dream."

When the President opened the press conference up for questions, a lanky man with leathery tanned skin was the first person to jump up.

His stark black hair had obviously been dyed. His narrowed gaze made him look as if he was too proud to admit that he needed glasses. "Griffon Parker with *Media Today.*"

So this was the weasel who'd been writing all those critical articles about my organic gardening program? I stopped to watch.

"Mr. President, is it not true that your puppy was a gift from your friend, the banking CEO, Richard Templeton?" the reporter demanded. "How can you stand up there and say that you support stringent banking regulations when you not only accept campaign contributions from Wall Street but also welcome top executives to the White House, call them your friends, and accept their gifts and bribes?"

Everyone in the audience seemed to hold their breaths, waiting to see how President Bradley would respond to such a pointed attack.

Relaxed and looking completely in control of the situation, President Bradley placed his arm on the podium and leaned forward slightly. "I'm glad you asked that, Parker. You raise a very good point. What is the role of friendship in government? We've seen friendships abused so often in politics that the very idea has become tainted. To say that someone is friends with a politician often is code for them receiving special favors. And that may be true for some people.

"To some, friendship may merely mean helping out the other person, no matter the cost. For others, friendship may mean being supportive and not speaking up even if he believes his friend is doing something wrong.

"For me, friendship is about honesty. It's about speaking the hard truth, especially when no one else around you is brave enough to speak it. I'm sure plenty of people out there know what I'm talking about. Whether your friend is addicted to drugs or alcohol, is engaged in some sort of unethical behavior, or is simply acting like a jerk, it's the mark of a true friend to pull the offender aside and say, 'Hey, what you're doing is stupid and wrong. You need to stop. And if you don't stop, I will do everything in my power to stop this for you.'

"So in answer to your question, can I have friends in the banking industry and still support strong regulations on how banks conduct their business? Absolutely, I can. I wouldn't consider myself a very good friend if I didn't."

"Do you have any more magic tricks up your sleeve?" a man standing behind me whispered.

"I don't know what you're talking about." I recognized Richard's voice.

I turned and spotted him walking with another of the banking CEOs. Led by the young White House staffer — who crinkled his nose when he spotted me — and three Secret Service agents, nearly all of the banking CEOs who'd been attending the summit spread out along the colonnade to watch the Q&A portion of the press conference. Noticeably absent were the Wonder Twins.

"Come on now, Richard, you can't tell me that you're not using your friendship with the President to your own benefit. I know you better than that. You gave him a dog? The PR value of that alone is priceless. I wish I'd thought of that. With Senator Pendergast acting like she's on a holy mission to get this new and improved financial reform bill of hers passed, you've got to be up to something," the other man whispered.

"Believe what you want," Richard said with a shrug. He spotted me and smiled. "I see you've been busy this morning, Casey," he said, giving my muddy outfit a once-over.

"Occupational hazard." I picked at some of the worst of the clumps. They dropped to the pavers and shattered into piles of gray dust. "It looks as if the Bradleys are enjoying your gift."

One reporter asked whether the President was going to handle the middle-of-the-night walks. Another asked about the rescue organization that had saved Milo. But quickly, the questions returned to the appropriateness of the First Family accepting a gift from a banker at this point in time.

"You do one nice thing for someone, and everyone gets suspicious," Richard said with a sigh.

"Yeah, I heard you talking to that guy."

"I was afraid of that. He's an idiot."

"Do you know where Brooks and Lillian Keller are?"

Richard shook his head. "Haven't seen them all morning. No one has."

"That's odd. I wonder where they could be."

"They might be busy with damage control. The news won't let go of the reports that Brooks dated the murdered Treasury official. It looks bad for him. Speaking of bad things, there's a Wildlife Diversity Preservation League charity dinner tomorrow night.

It'll be a bunch of boring business executives, stuffy old society mavens, and even stuffier members of Congress all trying to impress each other. I don't suppose you'd be interested in going with me?"

"Are you kidding? I'd love to go."

"Wonderful. I'll call later today and let you know what time I'll be by to pick you up."

The thought of a second date with Richard Templeton didn't excite me as much as the first time. Still, it was enough of a thrill that for the rest of the day I didn't think once about Pauline's murder or where Brooks and Lillian might have gone or why the Secret Service was so certain that someone involved with Joanna Lovell's group was plotting to kill the President.

CHAPTER TWENTY-THREE

At around five that evening my cell phone chirped out the hip-hop beats to "Stronger." I was sitting at my desk at the time, half-buried under Wilson Fisher's forms, determined to get them off my desk — and Fisher off my back — before heading home for the evening.

"Hello, this is Casey."

I didn't recognize the incoming number on the caller ID, and I'd given Senator Pendergast's office my cell number, hoping beyond hope that hell would freeze over and the senator would agree to meet with me so I could explain to her the merits of organic gardening. This could be her. *Please be her.*

"Casey." It wasn't the senator or even her cheery secretary.

"Jack Turner?" Why was he calling me?

"What time do you plan to walk home tonight? I'm going to accompany you," he said.

"I thought it was your day off."

"It is."

I waited for him to clarify. Silly me. Turner never gave out useful information.

"If I had the day off, I'm not sure I'd spend it thinking about the White House." A lie. With my work on the organic gardening proposal, I'd thought of little else these past several months.

There was silence on the line again.

"Look," he said, "after what happened yesterday, I'm worried. I don't think you should be walking anywhere alone."

"You're right. I was already planning to ask Gordon if he'd drive me home."

"Oh. Well, in that case —"

"Wait. If you don't mind coming in on your day off, I would appreciate a member of the Secret Service's elite military arm protecting my back." And I wouldn't mind taking advantage of the opportunity to try to wring some small tidbit of information out of Turner.

"Good. What time do you plan to leave for the day?"

I checked my watch. Gordon, Lorenzo, and I had managed to check off several important items from our task list. I just had Fisher's forms to finish. "How about in a half hour?"

"I'll meet you in Lafayette Square," he said and hung up.

I stared at the cell phone for a moment, wondering how he got this number. Sure, he was Secret Service, but still. It wasn't as if I handed out my cell phone number to everyone. No one at the White House other than Ambrose, Gordon, and Lorenzo had access to it.

Apparently, the Secret Service had done a thorough job poking into every aspect of my life.

I didn't like it. Not one bit.

Turner knew too much about me already.

I'd long ago pushed those memories of my mom and my past deep into the recesses of my mind. What had happened to my mother had no bearing on my life today. That was ancient history. It had nothing to do with —

I gripped the edge of the desk with both hands as a wave of panic hit me.

Breathe in. One. Two.

Breathe out. One. Two.

The panic attacks would go away as soon as I helped bring Pauline's murderer to justice. Thatch had said that the FBI was getting close to making an arrest.

Once that happened, I'd feel whole again. Safe.

I did a few more breathing exercises. My heart still beat a bit too fast. I ignored it and turned my attention back to the towering stack of forms. I needed to get them done and off my desk.

A half hour later I dropped the forms off at the usher's office on the first floor of the residence and headed outside to meet Jack Turner.

The cool spring air felt crisp against my face. After sunset, the temperatures were forecasted to drop into the thirties. I shivered as I crossed Pennsylvania Avenue on my way to Lafayette Square.

With the President's banking summit reaching its end and the intrigue surrounding Pauline's involvement with Brooks, Joanna's protesters had drawn the attention of the press. Bright camera lights shone on the face of Joanna's curly-haired assistant as he spoke animatedly with a reporter.

Except for a higher than normal number of uniformed Secret Service agents on hand, everything seemed to be normal in the park.

Ever since the murder, my shoulders tensed up every time I entered Lafayette Square. My gaze never rested but remained on constant lookout for danger.

There was nothing suspicious to find, just Joanna as she rushed toward the Treasury

Building. Still dressed in her skirt and suit, she'd exchanged her heels for running shoes.

She passed the front gate of the Treasury without slowing down. Once she reached 15th Street, she glanced over her shoulder several times before hurrying toward the Washington Monument.

Honey, if you don't want to be followed, you shouldn't act so suspiciously.

I had to find out where she was headed. I'd be wrong not to. Chewing on my bottom lip, I chased after her.

She went about a hundred yards, stopped, and glanced behind her again.

I quickly turned around. After a few moments, I resumed my pursuit, hanging back about a block to keep her from noticing me. I kept my stride casual, my hands jammed into my pockets. Joanna led me down the gently sloping hill that led past the Washington Monument and to the famous Tidal Basin located on the banks of the Potomac River.

The cherry trees coated with their pale pink-and-white blossoms formed a colorful canopy over the walking trails that wound around the basin. Petals floated on the wind in delicate spirals, much to the delight of the tourists that flocked to the basin in great numbers like migratory geese.

Several rows of bright blue paddleboats bobbed lightly on the water as they sat docked at the boathouse. The Jefferson Memorial stood watch on the far side of the basin. Its stately columns looked as if they reached deep into the evening shadows draped across the water.

With her head down and her body slightly hunched inward, Joanna skirted around a tour group of about fifty, each snapping away with their cameras, pointing, and talking excitedly. She was moving so quickly, I nearly lost sight of her as the tour group swallowed her up.

I rose up on my tiptoes, searching. When I spotted her, I picked up my pace, weaving through the tourists with the deft skill that would have made a native Washingtonian proud.

She'd stopped in a heavily treed pocket of the park. I watched from a distance as she pulled out her cell phone. Her lips moved too fast for me to try to read them. Before I knew it, she returned the phone to her purse and started to pace.

Several minutes later, a man wearing a black baseball cap low on his head, large sunglasses, a black windbreaker zipped up to his neck, and dark blue jeans approached

Joanna. As soon as she saw him, she crossed the distance between them and grabbed his arm.

He looked vaguely familiar all the way down to his black-and-white leather shoes with a lightning bolt shooting down the side.

Those shoes.

The breath caught in my throat. I ripped my backpack off my shoulders and dug around in the bag for my cell phone. It was on the bottom, of course.

My fingers trembled so much that I had to dial Turner's number three times to get it right.

"Where are you?" he demanded. "You were supposed to meet me at —"

"H-He's here," I whispered.

"Where are you?" he repeated. The aggravation in his voice was replaced with a cool detachment.

"The man. Lafayette Square. Mr. Baseball Cap. He's here." I couldn't catch my breath, couldn't form a sentence. I wanted to run, but I didn't dare take my eyes off him.

"Did he follow you?"

"No."

"Is he watching you?"

"No . . . I'm watching him. With Joanna."

"Casey, listen to me." Turner's voice grew even quieter and more detached. "Tell me where you are right now."

"Tidal Basin," I answered, still unable to utter a coherent sentence.

Joanna and the man, whose face I couldn't see — *was that Brooks?* — had moved farther away from me. They moved to stand deep among the trees, where the growing evening shadows were the darkest.

Large groups of tourists kept wandering in front of me, blocking my view, but I didn't dare move closer for fear that either Joanna or Mr. Baseball Cap would notice they were being watched.

"Okay," Turner said after a long pause. "I'm going to hang up for a minute. I want you to stay out of sight. Do you understand?"

I nodded.

Joanna made a sharp gesture with her hand. Mr. Baseball Cap backed up a step. I wished I could hear what they were saying.

"Casey?" Turner asked.

I nodded again. I wasn't going to move from the safety of this crowded spot, even though it meant the tourists would have to flow around me like water around a stone in a stream.

I wondered what Joanna was doing meeting with a murderer.

Was she in danger, or had she been involved with Pauline's murder all along?

Or had she been involved with the murder plot, but was now in danger?

The few times I'd spoken with her, she'd seemed so efficient, so helpful. Bitter, yes. But Brooks had ruined her career. Of course she'd be bitter.

"Casey!" Turner shouted into the phone.

I jumped. "I'm here," I whispered. I held the phone so tightly my fingers ached.

"Good." Turner sounded out of breath. "Stay put. I'm going to hang up for a second."

I continued to clutch the phone to my ear. The silence on the other end seemed to push away the roar of rush-hour traffic and the excited conversations of the tourists.

At this time of year, more than half a million people poured into the Tidal Basin to admire the spectacle of thousands of trees exploding with color and perfuming the air with their light almond scent.

With so many people milling around, I seriously didn't think there was any way either Joanna or Mr. Baseball Cap would notice me.

Even so, when Joanna looked suddenly in my direction, I held my breath, waiting. She shrugged and turned back to her dangerous companion. Her brow wrinkled with consternation. She gestured passionately with her hands as she spoke.

Unnerved that I might be spotted, I moved a few feet off the sidewalk to stand in the shadow of one of the original 1912 Yoshino cherry trees on the north bank of the Tidal Basin. It had been a gift from the Japanese ambassador to President and Mrs. Taft. Although the tree with its snowy white blossoms had long outlived its forty-year lifespan, it looked as healthy as its younger counterparts.

From this viewpoint, I could still watch Joanna and her companion. The man grew dangerously still while Joanna continued to gesture and argue. Her voice rose louder and louder until I could make out bits and pieces of what she was saying.

". . . betrayal . . . revenge . . . mistake."

The man raised a hand. I couldn't see his face, but I assumed he was talking, since Joanna had pressed her lips together.

She shook her head.

That only seemed to anger Mr. Baseball Cap. With a jerking motion, he reached into an inside pocket of his windbreaker jacket.

My muscles tensed. Was he reaching for a gun?

Should I shout a warning?

Before I could react, he thrust a lunch-sized brown paper bag toward Joanna.

She stepped back.

"Excuse me," I said to the couple who stopped directly in front of me to kiss, blocking my view completely. The lovers didn't hear me.

By the time I'd maneuvered back onto the sidewalk where I could see Joanna and Mr. Baseball Cap, Joanna had crossed her arms over her chest. Her muscles were tense. She looked ready to bolt.

"Do it." His deep voice caused several heads to turn in their direction. He lowered his head and turned more fully away from the crowd on the sidewalk.

Joanna continued to shake her head, but she took the paper bag and clutched it to her breasts. Her lips moved rapidly.

Suddenly, Joanna's head snapped in my direction.

Her eyes grew wide as we stared at each other.

She said my name.

Mr. Baseball Cap turned toward me as well. His shoulders jerked.

The three of us stood frozen while the world seemed to move at a frenetic pace around us. With his dark sunglasses and baseball cap pulled low on his head, I couldn't get a good look at the killer's face.

He could have been anyone.

All of a sudden Joanna started to shake her head with agitation. She grabbed Mr. Baseball Cap's arm again, shaking her head more furiously.

"Hey!" I sprinted toward them, worried that Mr. Baseball Cap might hurt her.

Before I could reach them, he shoved Joanna toward me and took off running toward the road.

I caught Joanna's arms as she stumbled. "Who was that guy?"

She struggled against me, twisting and turning. The paper bag the man had given her dropped to the ground.

"What are you doing here? You shouldn't be here." She kicked my shin with enough force that my leg collapsed beneath me. I tumbled to the ground.

"I'm trying to help you," I said from the dirt. She was acting as if she thought I wanted to hurt her. Balancing on my hands and knees, I picked up the paper bag Mr. Baseball Cap had forced upon her. "Let me help you."

"You don't understand." She kicked my wrist.

I toppled over, landing hard on a knobby tree root. For a petite woman, Joanna had incredible strength. I'd unfairly misjudged her in the same way others misjudged me based on my slender body frame.

Before I knew what was happening, she snatched the paper bag from my hand.

"You shouldn't be here," she repeated and took off in the same direction that Mr. Baseball Cap had gone.

"Wait!" I scrambled to my feet and ran after her.

She knew who'd killed Pauline. I had to stop her.

CHAPTER TWENTY-FOUR

Joanna sprinted through the trees weaving left and right with amazing agility. I barely managed to keep up, and I'm no couch potato.

Excitement thrummed through my veins. Joanna held the key to catching Pauline's killer. Hell, she'd been plotting with him.

It had to be Brooks.

The Tidal Basin was bordered on three sides by busy roadways and the Potomac River to its south, so as long as I could keep Joanna in view, she was trapped.

Or so I thought.

Joanna stopped at a busy crossroads and glanced over her shoulder at me. It'd be suicide to dive into rush-hour traffic. The safe route would be to run toward the river-bank.

Hoping to close the distance between us or even get in front of her, I sprinted across the grass to cut her off as she rounded the corner. I was skirting around a park bench when I heard a car horn blare. Brakes squealed. Metal smashed. I spun around in time to watch Joanna slide across the hood of a car.

"No!" She needed to tell me who killed Pauline. I needed her to end this. I ran toward the road.

She hit the ground, landing on her hands and knees, but didn't stay down long. She darted between traffic toward the bridge.

I couldn't let her get away.

I dashed after her into the traffic and jumped back as a sedan approached, going faster than it should. The driver blared his horn at me.

Joanna had made it across the four-lane road and kept running toward the Washington Monument.

With my toes hanging off the edge of the sidewalk, I jumped up and down, desperate to keep her in view. But with the setting sun shining brightly in my eyes, if I didn't do something soon, she'd get away.

I waited for a break in the traffic. But the cars just kept coming and coming. If I was going to act, I'd have to take a chance. Hell, if Joanna could get across without getting killed, I figured I could, too.

It was now or never. I drew a deep breath

and tossed myself into traffic. I made it halfway across the first lane without getting hit and was about to sprint into the next lane when an arm grabbed me around the waist. With a sharp yank that knocked me off my feet, I went sailing through the air and landed back on the sidewalk where I'd started.

"Hey! She's getting —"

Brakes screamed. A whoosh of air slapped my cheeks as a large delivery van skidded to a sideways stop several yards beyond where I'd been standing.

If that arm hadn't tugged me from the road, I'd probably be as flat as a pancake right about now.

"Are you trying to get yourself killed?" Turner roared as he picked me up from the sidewalk.

"Let go of me. She's getting away!"

I tried to twist out of his grasp. Turner tightened his hold, squeezing my middle.

"Stop fighting me. She won't get far." He gestured to the Park Police descending in full force. A D.C. Police cruiser, its lights flashing and siren blaring, was winding its way through traffic.

But was that going to be enough? I couldn't see where Joanna had gone. I needed to find her, to keep her in my sights.

Turner held firm his hold around my waist. I could feel his chest rise and fall in rapid succession.

"You ran here?" I twisted around in his arms to face him. "That's a long way."

"You were in danger."

"I had it —" I started to explain that I had it under control. I wasn't ever in any kind of danger. I knew how to be careful. But Turner's tense expression stopped me cold.

He was frightened.

Well, I was frightened, too. Frightened that I wouldn't get the chance to find out what Joanna knew, frightened that Pauline's murder, just like my mom's, would forever remain a question mark branded on my heart.

"Don't you see? I have to stop her." I gave his chest a push. "She knows who killed Pauline. She spoke with him. She saw his face."

He gripped my shoulders. "We'll find her."

"But —" The officers were scattering, but there was no sign of either Joanna or Mr. Baseball Cap.

"Casey, listen to me. You're not alone in this. We will find her. This doesn't involve your mother and you're not responsible."

Angry tears sprang to my eyes as I twisted away.

I hugged my arms to my chest and danced away from him when he tried to touch me. "You don't have to protect me. I won't charge out into traffic again."

He seemed startled by my angry tears. "Casey —"

"Leave me alone."

His gaze searched mine. I made damn certain he wouldn't find any vulnerability in them.

He huffed and turned away. I watched as he walked over to confer with the officers and uniformed Secret Service agents gathering in the area.

He was wrong.

This wasn't about my mother.

It was about justice.

Later that evening I stood next to Detective Hernandez and gazed across the Tidal Basin, the reflection of park lights swirling in the dark water.

"Why don't you go home?" the detective asked.

I shook my head.

He rubbed his salt-and-pepper mustache. "We've issued a BOLO for Joanna, and officers are stationed at her hotel. It's only a matter of time."

"A BOLO?"

"Copspeak for 'be on the lookout for.' "

I nodded, but the longer Joanna remained missing, the more I despaired that she'd ever be found. The number of officers canvassing the park had dropped dramatically. Also, tourists still packed the sidewalks, making the search that much more challenging. Joanna could be anywhere. This was a large city filled with unfamiliar faces.

It would be easy to disappear.

I should have been more aggressive with her. Perhaps if I'd hit her or kicked her when I'd had the chance, she wouldn't have gotten away.

Why had she run? How was she involved in all this?

"It's late." Turner emerged soundlessly from the shadows. "I'm going to take Casey home."

"It's not even seven thirty yet," I protested.

"Go on," Detective Hernandez said and rubbed his stomach. "Get him to buy you some dinner."

"I'm not hungry." I didn't want to leave. That would be admitting defeat, but I had to face the truth. "Joanna's not in the park anymore, is she?"

"I doubt it," Hernandez said.

I nodded.

Turner stayed several feet away as he waited. Since he had the day off, he wasn't wearing his uniform. It didn't matter. Even out of uniform, he looked like a warrior. Tough. Dangerous.

"If you're not hungry, at least let me buy you a coffee," he offered.

"Go on, Casey. Give the guy a break." Hernandez nudged my shoulder.

"Better make it decaf. I think I'm nervous enough already."

Turner nodded.

We walked in silence. From the Tidal Basin, it was a fair distance to the Freedom of Espresso Café. We were still at least three blocks away when Turner started to favor his injured foot.

I slowed down. "Do you need to take a break?"

"I'm fine." His muscles tightened and the limp disappeared.

At the café he opened the door and waited for me to walk inside before following. The barista at the counter flirted shamelessly with him as he placed an order for two decaf coffees.

Once we had our mugs, he led the way to a small corner table at the back of the café that gave him a clear view of the door and the rest of the tables.

"They're going to find her," he assured.

"I hope so."

"They are." He sounded so sure of himself.

"What do you know that you aren't telling me? Was Joanna the target of the Secret Service's investigation?"

"Ongoing investigation," he corrected.

"So?" When he didn't say anything, I added, "Was the FBI getting ready to arrest her?"

He sipped his black coffee.

"She didn't murder Pauline, you know. The man Joanna met at the Tidal Basin this afternoon was responsible for Pauline's death. I'm sure of it. So I wonder where Joanna fits in with all this."

I waited.

He continued to drink his coffee.

"You're not going to tell me what you know, are you?"

"Sorry. No."

I added a little bit of nonfat creamer and a packet of sugar to my steaming white ceramic mug. "Joanna told me that Pauline was having an affair with Brooks Keller. I also know that Joanna was sleeping with Brooks, too. I asked her about it and she pretended that it didn't bother her that

Brooks had taken up with Pauline. But how could she not be jealous?"

"Perhaps it wasn't a serious relationship?"

"No. Even if Joanna didn't care for Brooks, even if it was just sex, a woman's pride would still take a beating."

I tapped my chin. "Alyssa had said the other day that most murders are crimes of passion, or something like that. I'd been thinking that Pauline had been killed because of something she found during the audit. But what if I'm wrong? What if this was a crime of passion?"

"How do you mean?"

"Joanna told me how Pauline had met Brooks at the last party she'd held. Pauline had arrived at the party hoping to get her hooks into a powerful man. She went after Richard Templeton first. But he turned her down."

"Really? I wonder why. From what I've heard, he's the kind of guy who has to have a new woman on his arm every night."

"I think that's just his media image. I haven't seen that."

Turner rolled his eyes.

"For whatever reason, he turned Pauline down. Undaunted, she charmed Brooks. It wouldn't be difficult. He seems like a shameless flirt and has a reputation of taking up with women in the workplace, much to his sister's horror."

"Don't you women follow something like the guy code, where you don't hit on your friend's girlfriend?"

"We do. I'm starting to think Pauline didn't care. From what I've heard, she seemed to like drama in her relationships."

"I've met a few women like that. They're not worth the trouble."

"I wouldn't think so," I agreed. "Brooks either didn't care or didn't notice the trouble he was getting himself into when he started to sleep with both Pauline and Joanna at the same time. But I'm starting to think both Pauline and Joanna noticed *and* cared."

"Two strong women fighting over the same man. It could get messy."

"I think it did. Shortly after Pauline arrived on the scene, Lillian learned about Brooks's relationship with Joanna. How did she learn about it? We don't know. But Lillian exploded and did everything in her power to ruin Joanna's career. I wonder if Pauline could have been the little bird whispering in Lillian's ear."

"That would be a motive for murder." He leaned forward. "Who was the mystery man with her in the park, though?"

"It could be Brooks."

"Why would he kill Pauline? What's his motive?"

"Perhaps Pauline was threatening to go public with their relationship. Seducing the woman auditing his bank must be breaking at least a few ethics rules."

"That's a possibility. But then why team up with Joanna? And why would Joanna agree to conspire with him? He and his sister ruined her career and her life."

My shoulders dropped as I slumped over my coffee mug. "I don't know."

Turner reached across the table and tilted my chin up. The corner of his lips lifted. "You have good instincts. I think you might be on to something. We just need more information."

"Really?"

"Have you known me to lie?"

That made me smile. "My grandmother keeps telling me that reading murder mysteries is a waste of time. I keep telling her that it's research and training."

"I don't know about that."

"Well, I do." My back straightened and my heart picked up just a bit. "Every mystery I've ever read tells me that whoever Joanna met in the park was a regular at her monthly salons. Did the Secret Service compile a list of the men she'd invite to her parties? We could go through the list and see who's in town."

"Now, Casey, you should know by now that I can't talk about the investigation."

"What good is having a sidekick if —"

"Whoa . . . sidekick?"

I waved away his aggravation. "Every modern-day amateur sleuth has a sidekick."

"Sidekick?"

"Pick up any mystery novel, and you'll see that I'm right."

"I'm *not* a sidekick."

"It's either you or Richard Templeton."

"You shouldn't be talking about this case with Templeton. For all we know, he's involved."

"He's not involved. He doesn't have the right kind of shoes."

"What?"

"You know, the shoes that the man who'd attacked me was wearing. Brooks Keller owns a pair."

"How do you know Templeton doesn't? Don't tell me you've been so cozy with him that you were able to search his bags at his hotel."

"Of course not." My face heated.

"Then you don't know. Be careful around him."

381

"Don't be jealous, Turner. I prefer you as my sidekick over Richard. You have guns. Not that I like guns. I don't. I think the world would be much better off if they'd never been invented. But — but —" I sighed. "But since there are guns in the world and there are people who see nothing wrong with hurting someone else, it's nice having someone around who can handle himself in a fight."

"I'm not your sidekick."

"I know. You keep too much important information to yourself to be of any use."

He must have sensed my frustration. It wasn't as if I tried to keep it hidden.

"Listen, we don't know much about Joanna beyond what you know. Not anything that would really help," he said, pitching his voice low. He was probably breaking a half-dozen rules by telling me this. "If we had anything concrete on her, the FBI would have picked her up days ago. As you said, she didn't kill Pauline. Is she involved? We simply don't know."

"And does the Secret Service have a list of the men who attended her parties?"

He refused to answer, which only increased my level of frustration.

"Then we don't have much to talk about, do we?"

"I think we do." His voice softened. "I think you should tell me about your mother and that night you lost her."

I stared into the creamy depths of my coffee mug. "I've never talked about her with anyone."

Not even Grandmother Faye. We'd work side by side in the garden for hours without speaking a word. Sometimes in the comforting silence, I'd let my thoughts drift back to the time before I came to live with my grandmother, to memories of my parents.

I wasn't about to discuss her now.

Turner's rough hands rested loosely on his coffee mug. His chest rose and fell in a slow, even pattern.

Sure, he'd read my background check, a background check I'd been warned would be thorough and would include any major childhood incidents . . . *like a murder.*

More than once he'd mentioned that he believed the ghosts from my past drove my need to find Pauline's killer. *He knew.* He might not know the entire story. I doubt anyone did. But he knew what had happened that night.

"I think my parents were criminals," I said while watching the swirling eddies of steam rising from my coffee mug. I glanced up and met Turner's steady gaze.

There was no reading his expression.

"They lived like criminals. Always moving from place to place. Always coming up with new names. They told me it was a game they liked to play. What did I know? I was only six."

"Kids pick up on a lot of things adults are doing." He sighed. "I know I did."

I waited to see if he'd offer anything else about himself, about his background, his family. I'm sure he was waiting for me to do the same.

I went back to staring into my coffee mug.

"One morning I woke up to discover Dad was gone," I said. "I clearly remember that morning. We were living in the United States for the first time in my life. Phoenix, Arizona. Mom wore this big, fake smile as she made chocolate chip pancakes — a treat reserved for birthdays and holidays. But it wasn't my birthday, and Christmas was months away. Her smile never wavered as she tried to convince me Dad would return, but her hands shook when she'd flipped the pancakes. Looking back, I think Dad must have known trouble was coming our way and he fled." I swallowed hard. "He deserted us."

"Has he ever tried to contact you?" Turner asked.

I shook my head. "He was Grandmother Faye's youngest child and only son. For her sake, I wish he would damn the consequences and reach out to her. As for me, I don't want or need him in my life." I shrugged. "I doubt he's even still alive."

Turner nodded. Did he know something? Did my background check include information about what had happened to my father?

I swirled the coffee in my mug. Some of it sloshed over the ceramic rim and splashed onto the table. I grabbed a napkin and wiped up the spill. "I don't care. I don't want to know."

"So you were alone with your mom?"

"Not for long. The next night I was upset that Dad had left." My insides clenched. I tried to stop the memories from replaying like a silent movie inside my head. Images of my mom flickered in and out of focus.

She'd been wearing a blue dress with little white flowers on the hem that morning. I'd forgotten about that dress. It'd looked so pretty on her.

"I'd whined and complained. I wanted ice cream. What a brat I was. Mom finally agreed to take me to the ice cream parlor I liked, even though it was on the other side of town. I manipulated her by using Dad's abandonment as an excuse to get my own way. I did everything I could to make her feel guilty that he was no longer around for me."

"You missed him," Turner corrected. He reached across the table and unclenched my fist. His warm hand closed over mine. "You were just a kid acting like a kid."

"But if I hadn't . . ." I couldn't bring myself to finish that thought.

"On the way home from the ice cream parlor, your mother's car was forced off the road?" he prompted.

"Is that what the police report said?" I nodded. "A car slammed into the side of Mom's van. It jolted me out of the seat. We crashed into a brick building. Smoke poured out of the van's hood. Mom told me to get down on the floor and to keep quiet. If I had obeyed . . ."

I squeezed my eyes closed.

"A man pulled open the driver's-side door. He grabbed Mom and dragged her from the van. More men were shouting in a language I couldn't understand. They sounded so angry.

"I was frightened. They'd taken my mom. I needed to know what was going on, so I disobeyed her. I peeked out the window to see what was happening. That's when I saw the guns. They were pointed at my mother.

"I screamed. I screamed and screamed. One of the men, the one with stubble on his chin, reached back into the van and grabbed me. I kicked and squirmed, but he only squeezed me tighter. Holding on to my hair, he dangled me like a helpless puppy in front of my mom and laughed."

Emotions as real and raw as when it had happened returned like a punch to the gut. The man with the stubble on his face frightened me more than the others. I had to open my eyes to get his face out of my head.

"I wanted to kill him." My voice shook as I admitted it.

To this day, nothing had changed. I still wanted to kill him. How could I feel that way? Why cling to some childish and un-healthy desire to put an end to someone's life? I abhorred violence. And yet all through college I'd taken one self-defense course after another. Had it been defense I'd been looking to learn or something else, some-thing darker?

"You wanted to protect your mom and yourself. It's nothing to feel ashamed about."

If they had been simply feelings from the past, I don't think they would have worried me as much as they did. But I knew if I met that stubble-bearded man today, I'd go for his throat. I'd squeeze, squeeze, squeeze until . . .

No, I couldn't think about that.

"The men switched to speaking English. I think they wanted me to understand them. They shouted at Mom, demanding she tell them where Dad had gone. They wanted something he'd stolen from them and they wanted to know who had helped him steal it. Mom told them to go to hell. That was the first time I'd ever heard her swear. She was usually so gentle, so soft-spoken. I barely recognized this new tough lady."

"A lioness fighting to protect her cub?"

"No. She was protecting *him*." Tears filled my eyes. I blinked them away. "The man with the long face and stubbly beard hit her again and again. I screamed for him to stop, but he laughed at me and kept on hurting her. I was helpless to stop him.

"He told her that he'd let us go if she'd tell them where Dad had gone. But she refused. He demanded that she tell him what she knew and hit her until blood ran down her face. She still refused to talk, so he turned to me.

"He grabbed a fistful of my hair and caressed my cheek with his calloused hand. 'So young,' he said. 'So innocent. I'd hate

to have to hurt her.' Mom didn't say anything."

I pressed a hand to my stomach and bent
forward slightly, unable to save myself from
drowning in a torrent of emotions. My own
mother had refused to even look at me. I'd
cried out for her. I'd needed her more than
life, and she'd turned her head away . . .
she'd turned away from me, her only child.

"The man roared with anger and frustration, screaming at her that he'd shoot me if
she didn't tell them what they wanted to
know. I sobbed when he waved his big, ugly
gun in my face."

The words my mom had said next echoed
like an unholy wind in my ears. "I'm so
sorry, pumpkin." I pushed her apology deep
into the recesses of my memories where I
wouldn't have to hear them ever again.

"Her voice was cold as she told the man
to stop stalling and go ahead and get it over
with. She told him to shoot me. So he did.
He shot me three times in the stomach."

"God." Turner's eyes had grown dark.

"I was conscious long enough to watch
him turn the gun on Mom."

Mommy. Please, don't leave me.

"He squeezed off just one shot." My voice
cracked. "The bullet hit her in the head."

I touched the center of my own forehead.

"I know," Turner said, his voice gruff. "I know."

"She was dead. Even as young as I was at the time, I knew that she'd left me, that she'd never be around to tuck me in my bed or to hug me or to . . ." I shook my head and muttered, "Or to be there for me when I needed her the most."

"What happened to you?" Turner asked.

"Those bastards left me there to die with her, but I didn't. I used to wish that I had. Surviving can be harder than dying, you know? But a Good Samaritan found me and called the police. When I woke up in the hospital, I was all alone in the world, trusted no one, spoke to no one. The authorities only knew me by the false name my mom and dad had started using only a few days before Dad's disappearance. I think it was Melissa Baker or something like that. It took over a year for my grandmother to realize what had happened and to rescue me from foster care."

I pulled my hand from Turner's and took a sip of coffee. The warm liquid burned in my tight throat. I set the mug back down.

Who were those men, and why did they want to find my dad so desperately? Those two unanswered questions still haunted me. No one should have to live like this, never knowing why a loved one had been taken so violently. No one should have to endure this kind of pain.

"I've got an early morning," I said and stood up so quickly the chair almost toppled over.

Turner jumped up. He took my hand as we walked out of the café. He didn't hold my hand the same way Richard had. His thumb didn't caress my knuckles. He'd merely wrapped his calloused fingers around mine.

He slowed his step to match my pace as we walked side by side toward my apartment.

"Thank you," Turner said after a long span of silence. "I know it couldn't have been easy to talk about it."

I nodded.

"I believe your mother said what she did to protect *you,* not your father."

I must have flinched, because his fingers tightened around my hand.

"You're smart, Casey. Think about it. If she acted as if she might break, who knows what those monsters might have done to you. Do you really think they would have let you or your mom escape alive even if she'd told them what they wanted to hear?"

But hadn't that been the fantasy that had

haunted my dreams even to this day? Mom would have told them where to find Dad and . . .

A stupid fantasy.

"No, I suppose not," I said.

Turner stopped walking. He dropped my hand.

I looked around, startled to realize we were standing in front of my apartment.

"I've never told anyone about that night," I felt the need to explain. "I'm not sure why I told you."

"I think you did it because on some level you knew I could hear what happened and not go to pieces with pity for you." He tilted up my chin and leaned in close as if he was going to kiss me. "Maybe you wanted me to pity you. Maybe somewhere in that conniving mind of yours you thought you could use your past to get me to open up to you about the investigation."

"Did it work?"

"Do I look open?"

I rolled my eyes and then raced up the stairs.

"Casey?" Turner called to me after I opened the front door.

"Yes?"

"Your parents weren't —" he started to say and then shook his head.

"What? What do you know about them?"

"Nothing. Be sure to lock the door behind you."

"If you know something —"

"It's nothing. Good night."

CHAPTER TWENTY-FIVE

"Ms. Calhoun, what do you think you're doing?" Seth Donahue's crisp voice assaulted my ears the next morning as he trotted up with his self-important swagger.

I'd taken Milo for a walk in the Jacqueline Kennedy Garden outside the East Wing, both to get him accustomed to me while he was still a manageable size and also to check on some of our most recent arrivals in the garden beds. Just a few days ago we'd planted a spring crop of rosemary, thyme, and a hardy variety of basil under the holly trees at the chef's request, and I was worried that they'd suffered damage in last night's cold snap. The basil worried me the most, since even a little bit of frost would knock it out completely. Thankfully, the hollies had protected the tender herbs. Some of the leaves showed a few black spots from the cold, but the stems were fine.

I wasn't.

Last night had left me badly shaken. I'd never opened up so completely to anyone. I'd ended up tossing and turning all night, worrying about how Turner might use my vulnerability against me.

Not that I thought he would . . . just that I knew he *could.*

And Joanna was still missing.

Seeing Seth bearing down on me with his Hollywood swagger and the devil shining bright in his eyes wasn't comforting either.

"We have a major event coming up," he jabbed with his sharp tone, "and here you are for the second day in a row spending all of your time playing with the President's dog."

"Excuse me?"

I tightened my grip on Milo's leash. The puppy had lowered his head and body in a primitive move very similar to a wild predator stalking its prey. A low growl rumbled in his throat.

"I directed Sal Martin to have his men paint the snow fencing. The green is too bright. I think a soft yellow would be more tasteful. And you know what he told me? He said that I'd have to talk to you. To *you!*" Seth repeated, his voice growing not louder but sharper. "The incompetence I've encountered these last few days staggers me.

No one seems capable to act without my direct supervision. And even then, it's a struggle."

With everything that had been going on with the investigation into Pauline's murder, the upcoming Easter Egg Roll wasn't at the forefront of my thoughts that morning. Nor did it need to be.

Lorenzo, Gordon, and I, along with the grounds crew and the greenhouse staff, had worked long and hard to prepare the planters, grow the seedlings for the gardening booth, and polish the landscape until the grass shimmered and the hedges formed perfect geometrical shapes. Hell, we'd even come to work today, a Saturday, to make sure all the small details had been properly handled. We'd done our part and we did it while running around in a hectic race to keep Seth happy.

Seth came to a stop directly in front of me, invading my personal space — and Milo's. He propped his hands on his hips. His face had turned dark red. A prominent vein throbbed in his neck.

His explosions were growing more and more frequent. To my knowledge, no one had dared stand up to him.

We'd mumble.

We'd agree.

We'd do whatever it took to get the hell away from this madman.

But no one pushed back.

Until this morning.

I didn't have the time or the patience for Seth's chronically bad temper. Shouting and ranting might be his management style. Perhaps it worked for him.

I didn't care.

I should have been over the moon with anticipation about tonight. I'd be attending one of the hottest events of the season. All of the power players of Washington and Wall Street would be there. I'd be the envy of every red-blooded American woman as I floated into the ballroom on the arm of the nation's most eligible, most delectable bachelor.

Alyssa and I had an early afternoon lunch date to hit the boutiques in search of the perfect dress. It was last-minute and nerve-wracking and wonderful.

But thanks to yesterday, a bad cloud had come up and washed out all my happiness, as Aunt Willow would say.

There'd been no sign of Joanna at her hotel or anywhere else. Pauline's killer still lurked in the shadows. Alyssa had driven me to work, because I no longer felt safe walking the D.C. streets.

The banking protesters had turned out on Lafayette Square in full force, but without Joanna's leadership, they'd been standing around like lost chicks. Fredrick had waved me through the gates without calling Turner to search my backpack. I still didn't know what to think about that. Although I'd been nervous about having to face him, *not* seeing him seemed even worse.

And to top it all off, Senator Pendergast continued to refuse to take my calls. I needed to talk to her about both the organic gardening proposal and whether the car that had run her off the road could be linked back to Pauline's murder.

All my troubles seemed to go back to Pauline.

My mind wouldn't find any rest until her killer was brought to justice. Move over, Miss Marple, and look out, Brooks Keller, I planned to catch the killer, whoever he may be, and make sure he took responsibility for what he'd done.

I would let no one get in my way. Certainly, not an overhyped event planner with an ego the size of Texas.

"Seth Donahue" — I drew in a deep breath — "if'n you think you can come over to me and raise sand whenever you plumb well like, well then, you must be dumber than a stump." Generations of Calhoun pride came pouring out of my mouth while Milo barked his agreement. "Everyone, and I mean everyone, has been tiptoeing so much around you that their legs are about to give out. We're bending over backward to make you happy. But no matter what anyone does, you're perpetually *un*happy.

"You'll do well to remember that the White House staff has executed the Easter Egg Roll flawlessly ever since the first one way back in 1878. Not once did they need your yammering to get it done. You're the problem, Seth Donahue, you and your endless changes."

I stopped only because I'd run out of breath. And yet, I'd said all that needed to be said. I felt cleansed, relaxed even.

"The bright green fence will look great," I said calmly. "I'm not going to ask the grounds crew to change its color for a third time. Neither will Gordon."

Seth glared at me. He pressed his fists to the sides of his thighs. If he'd been a cartoon character, I suppose steam would have been pouring out of his ears right about now.

"I just thought you should know the unvarnished truth." I beamed a Southern-sized smile. Milo, worked up from my impassioned speech, pulled on the leash and barked, anxious to get into the middle of the action. "You're making us all crazy, Seth. Work with us, not against us. That's all you need to do."

Seth opened his mouth. Shut it. Opened it again.

"A package arrived this morning for you. Ambrose is holding on to it in his office," he said and walked away.

"Well," I said to Milo, "that felt good."

Milo, prancing happily alongside me as we returned inside, seemed to agree.

"Casey, there you are." Gordon bent down to rub Milo's scruff. "What a good boy you are."

Milo tugged at Gordon's pant leg, and then did a little bow, a clear indication that he was anxious to play. Gordon chuckled and gently pushed on the puppy's side, eliciting happy growly barks.

"Have you seen today's edition of *Media Today*?" Gordon asked.

"I've decided not to read that trash anymore."

"You might want to see this article."

More interested in playing with the puppy than talking with me, Gordon handed me the first section without pausing in the roughhousing game he'd started with Milo.

The pup flopped over on his back and nipped at Gordon's arm.

The newspaper had been folded open to the editorial page.

My heart sank as I read the title of the op-ed piece: ORGANIC GARDENING AT THE WHITE HOUSE, written not by *Media Today*'s star reporter Griffon Parker, but by Barney Vetters, the chairman of the Grounds Committee.

"I don't need to read this to know I've got a lot of repair work to do." I tried to hand the newspaper back to Gordon.

"I think you should read this one," he said.

Holding my breath, I scanned the first paragraph. And then the second.

The article compared my seven-point organic lawn care proposal to Harvard University's sustainable landscape management program. Over a series of years, the university had transitioned away from chemical fertilizers and pesticides to a holistic and natural approach that my proposal echoed. Barney lauded Harvard's Facility Maintenance team for spearheading a program that he called a stunning success.

"The program produced healthier grasses with deeper roots that thrive with less water and less intensive care," Barney had written.

He'd concluded the article by saying, *"I believe the time has come for the White House to follow in the footsteps of the most prestigious of institutions in the adoption of organic lawn care. It's not only good for the environment, it's good for the nation."*

I looked up at Gordon. "You did this?"

"Barney wrote it. He sought and received approval from the First Lady's office for the article, of course."

"Right, of course. But did you prod him to write it?"

Gordon kept his attention on Milo, who was trying his best to jump up and bite the head gardener's ear. "I may have talked with a few members of the committee."

"Are there any new articles written by Griffon Parker in here?" I couldn't bring myself to look.

Gordon shook his head and smiled. "He's moved on to greener pastures. The President and First Lady's connection with Wall Street has grabbed the rabid reporter's interest."

"Oh dear, Mrs. Bradley doesn't need this kind of stress, especially not now."

"What do you mean?"

I'd forgotten I was among a small circle who knew of Mrs. Bradley's pregnancy.

"Nothing. It's just a bad time for this to happen, what with the banking summit coming to a close and Senator Pendergast on a rampage."

Gordon's eyes narrowed. "I see."

"What else would I be talking about?"

He clearly sensed that I was holding back on him, but he didn't push the matter.

"Ambrose is looking for you," he said, changing the subject.

"I heard. Apparently a package arrived for me?"

"Curious, isn't it?" Gordon took Milo's leash and, rising from his crouched position, followed me to the chief usher's office located up the stairs on the main floor.

Not only was it curious, it was unheard of. Packages didn't simply show up at Ambrose's office for the White House staff. The usher was responsible for a great many things that happened at the White House, but deliveries and mailings weren't among them.

"I suppose I can't return it," I heard Margaret Bradley say, her generally gentle voice growing tight with tension as we approached Ambrose's office.

Ambrose responded in that deep, steady voice of his, too low to be clearly heard.

"Thank you, Ambrose. That's a wonderful idea."

The chief usher's door stood open. Still,

since the First Lady was obviously engaged in a serious conversation with Ambrose — it was extraordinary enough that Mrs. Bradley would come down to his office, instead of the other way around — I didn't feel as if we should stroll in unannounced. I rapped on the white painted wooden door.

"Ms. Calhoun, Gordon," Ambrose said in greeting. If he shared any of the First Lady's anxieties, he didn't let it show. "As you can see" — he gestured behind him — "I'm in a meeting. But I do have a package for you, Ms. Calhoun. Let me get it."

"Is that from him as well?" Mrs. Bradley asked.

"It is," Ambrose confirmed.

"He's been busy," she quipped. She spotted Milo. A smile brightened her cheeks. She bent down and clapped her hands. She was casually dressed in a pair of jeans and a long-sleeve turtleneck sweater with blue and aqua stripes. The puppy, excited to see his owner, bounded over to her, his tail wagging like a flag caught in a gale storm.

Ambrose disappeared behind the door for a moment and retrieved a garment bag.

"What's this?" Gordon asked with a sparkle in his eyes.

When I unzipped the bag, a river of champagne silk poured out.

"It's lovely," both Gordon and I crooned.

"So Richard is trying to control everyone, is he?" Mrs. Bradley asked between puppy kisses.

"I don't understand." The floor-length silk gown, the kind one would see on fashion runways and worn by the most glamorous celebrities gracing the red carpet, shimmered in the light. "Richard picked this out for me? How thoughtful of him."

I checked the tag. He'd even gotten the size right.

Mrs. Bradley gave an inelegant snort. "You'll have to forgive me, but any gift from that man has a certain taint about it."

"How's that?" I asked.

Mrs. Bradley sighed. "Richard is a control freak. He uses his power and his money to get what he wants. He's ruthless, really. Did you know John and Richard were roommates in boarding school? They came from a similar background. According to John, they were once inseparable friends."

I nodded. "That's what Richard told me."

"Did he also tell you about how he became the captain of the lacrosse team? In school, everything had to be about Richard. Once he got an idea in his head or saw something he wanted, he'd stop at nothing to get it. Their senior year, John and Richard were both competing to become lacrosse captain. In the end, the coach picked John to lead the team. Not a half hour into the first practice session of the year, Richard's play turned aggressive. He slammed into John during a long run down the field. John went down hard, his ankle broken. The injury sidelined him for the rest of the season, and Richard ended up captain."

"But Richard was just a boy at the time," Gordon pointed out. "Boys are apt to do stupid things."

Ambrose nodded in agreement.

"John thinks the same thing. He'd hoped to rekindle his friendship with Richard. That's one of the reasons my husband spent so much time with him this past week. He'd hoped things could be different between them. But all I see is tension and competition between them. And these gifts." She gestured to a large box behind them. "It feels like he's trying to buy my husband's friendship and manipulate the banking reform package."

"But he speaks so highly of President Bradley," I said. "I'm sure it's a gesture of friendship, not some calculating game."

"I hope you're right." She stood and placed her hand on my shoulder. "I'm telling you this so you'll know to be careful tonight. Once Richard leaves, I'd be surprised if he's ever invited back."

I wondered if hormones were making the First Lady overly suspicious. Richard appeared to be the best of the group. After spending a week with the bankers, I was quickly learning that they were all ruthless in one form or another. Just take a look at the Keller twins. Lillian had ruined Joanna, pushed the poor woman into something dangerous, something that might get her killed.

And Brooks.

He had the shoes. The motive. And I planned to find out tonight if he had had the opportunity to kill Pauline.

CHAPTER TWENTY-SIX

"What's wrong with you, Casey? You seem more excited about questioning potential murder suspects than you are about your date with America's most eligible bachelor," Alyssa accused that afternoon while she tamed my blond locks into large, soft curls.

I sat at a dressing table in her bedroom facing a mirror while she stood behind me, wielding her curling iron like a weapon.

"I'm not more excited about . . ." I started to protest, but she was right. Beyond the initial excitement over the dress, I'd barely thought about Richard. He was my entrance to the party, my way to get direct access to Brooks and Lillian, not the main attraction for the evening.

"You want to know what I think?" Alyssa asked. I ducked as she waved the hot curling iron for emphasis.

I didn't answer, since I knew she'd tell me whether I wanted her to or not.

"I think you've got the hots for that sexy Secret Service agent of yours."

"If you believe that, you're the one who's crazy," I told her. "Turner is arrogant, he follows me around like some deranged stalker, and he lacks any kind of a sense of humor."

He also knew my deepest, darkest secret.

"I don't want anything to do with him," I said, hugging my arms across my chest. "I don't even want him as my sidekick anymore."

"That's good to hear, because I don't think you could handle him."

"What?" I twisted around to face her. "Why?"

"Hold still." Alyssa turned my head back toward the mirror. "You're going to get the curling iron tangled in your hair."

She did a little more work before declaring I was ready. I rose from the dressing table and slipped on the gown that Richard had sent over. It fit like a glove.

Varying shades of champagne-colored silk ribbons crisscrossed the bodice, enhancing all the areas around my chest that could use a little enhancing. The same silk ribbons that hugged my body in the bodice hung loose to create a full skirt that swirled like eddies in a stream when I moved.

I felt myself standing taller.

"You look like a fairy-tale princess," Alyssa whispered.

"Thanks to you." When I reached out to hug her, she threw up her arms in protest.

"Don't get all mushy. You'll ruin all that hard work I put into your makeup and hair. Besides, I didn't do all that much. It's the dress. Do you know how much an original design like that costs?"

The first thing Alyssa had done when I'd shown her the gown was to check the label. She'd shrieked the designer's name, a name I didn't recognize, and had swooned on my bed.

"No, I don't know how much this dress is worth and don't tell me. It'll make me nervous and I'll end up spilling red wine down the front."

"Have you ever done that?"

"No, but considering the week I've had, I wouldn't be surprised if I ended up wearing an entire bottle tonight."

Or mud. Between the unruly Milo and being stalked by a killer, just about every outfit I'd worn this week was mud stained to the point of ruin.

I would hate for something to happen to this gown. "It really is a work of art." I swished my hips, enjoying how the gown seemed to flow over my legs. "It was thoughtful of Richard to pick it out for me."

In the short time that I'd known him, he'd been nothing but attentive and thoughtful. He was every woman's dream. So why didn't I feel more excitement about spending time with him?

It had to be because of my obsession with finding Pauline's murderer. Once I knew the killer was locked behind bars, maybe then I could move on with my life and enjoy the attentions of a handsome man without fretting.

"Don't get all emotional on me, Casey," Alyssa scolded.

A knock on the front door broke the tension. Alyssa squeaked with excitement and took my hand as we hurried down the stairs. "A man like Tempting Templeton doesn't do his own shopping, no CEO would. He has staff to handle tasks like that. He most likely called his secretary, who called a designer dress shop, who directed a knowledgeable clerk to select a dress. So you don't have to feel overly indebted or nervous. Just have fun tonight."

"You're right. I will." I drew a deep breath and opened the front door.

Richard smiled when he saw me. A few inches taller than me, even with the ridiculously high heels on my feet, he made quite an impression in a jet-black tuxedo. His dark brown hair, slightly long and untamed, made quite a contrast with the tuxedo's perfect lines. He blended rock star rogue with clean-cut billionaire with polished ease.

"You look lovely, my dear." He took my hand and brushed a kiss on my knuckle that turned my mouth dry.

Alyssa sighed loudly in the background.

"Thank you." I invited Richard inside and introduced him to Alyssa, who despite her excitement, acted aloof and dignified, as if she met handsome billionaires every day.

I wasn't feeling nearly as composed. My mind buzzed with excitement. Brooks would be at the party, which meant this would be my best chance to force his hand, to catch him in an unguarded moment. I was sure I'd be able see it in his eyes and know what evil he hid. It wouldn't be easy, or without danger.

To keep from fidgeting, I clutched with both hands the cream-colored beaded purse Alyssa had loaned me.

Alyssa had turned to one of her favorite topics, fashion. She gushed over the gown, praising the designer. "She is a genius when it comes to evening wear. Just look at how naturally the lines fall."

"Yes, thank you," I said, embarrassed that I hadn't thanked him right away. "As you can see, it fits perfectly." I twirled around for him.

"I'm glad you like it. Oh, before I forget." He patted his pockets. He smiled when his hand touched the inside pocket of his tux. "I brought a small gift for you."

From his pocket he produced a small golden box, which he held out for me to take. That size box might hold a necklace or earrings or jewels.

"You didn't need to do this, Richard. You've done too much already," I protested, although common courtesy and, hell, good old curiosity had me lifting the box from his hands.

Alyssa leaned over my shoulder, her breath quick and hot on my neck, as I opened the lid. Inside, nestled in a soft bed of black velvet, I found a platinum credit card with my name emblazoned in raised letters on it.

"It's to replace the one that had been canceled," he explained. "I had my bank issue you the best card available. It gives you cash back and has an impressive interest rate."

"Thank you." I turned the card over in my hand. "Now I'll be forever in your debt."

He chuckled politely. Alyssa, not as polite,

nudged me in the side with her elbow. She never did like my puns.

"If you're ready" — he held out his arm for me to take — "we should be going."

Alyssa, cautious of my makeup, air-kissed me on the cheek and told me to be daring tonight.

Instead of the black town car, a two-door silver Italian Maserati, with low, sleek, sporty lines, sat parked at the curb.

When Richard opened the passenger-side door for me, I realized Wallace wasn't along to chauffeur. "What happened to the town car?"

"Nothing happened to it. It's Wallace. He's back at the hotel, said he'd throw up all over my suit and your dress if he had to go out tonight."

"I'm sorry to hear that. I hope it's simply a stomach bug and nothing too serious."

"Personally, I suspect he got carried away at the minibar." He sighed before adding, *"Again."*

"At least you get the chance to drive this beauty. Is it a rental?" The car shimmered so brightly it had to be off the showroom floor new.

"Why rent when you can buy?" He ran his hand along the roof's sporty line. "I had a local dealer deliver this, their latest model, to the hotel. Shall we go?"

"Yes, of course." I slid into the Maserati's luxurious leather seat, an updated version of Cinderella's carriage, to rush me off to the ball.

And to my date with a killer.

CHAPTER TWENTY-SEVEN

Casey, if you go running off like a headless chicken, that's how you're likely to end up, Grandmother Faye used to warn me when I was in high school. I rarely listened to her back then and more often than not landed in heaps of trouble because of it.

You'd think I'd have learned my lesson by now and come up with a solid plan for the evening.

I hadn't.

It wasn't for a lack of effort, mind you. I would have thought a lifetime of reading mystery novels would have prepared me for this, but life wasn't anything like a mystery novel. There was no guarantee that justice would be served at the end of this tale.

I pondered this as Richard and I waited at a security checkpoint. Because the President and First Lady planned to attend the event, it took nearly fifteen minutes standing in line in front of La Pasta Ria, the restaurant in Dupont Circle hosting the Wildlife Diversity Preservation League charity dinner, to pass through security and get inside.

As soon as we entered the quaint Italian restaurant's banquet room with frescoed walls covered with murals depicting southern Italy, candles flickering on the tables, and tiny white lights that shimmered like stars hanging from the ceiling, all thoughts about my quest to find proof of Brooks's guilt faded away.

I fought an urge to pinch myself. Standing next to Richard, who looked as if he belonged on the cover of a fashion magazine, and with me dressed in such a beautiful gown, I felt like a princess who'd just found her glass slipper. Heads turned to watch us, while gentle strains of chamber music provided by a string quartet seemed to float through the air all around me.

The wildlife event had brought out many of Washington's power players. I spotted Alyssa's boss, Senator Finnegan, having a conversation with Senator Pendergast. Other congressmen were mingling with lobbyists from various nonprofit organizations. Every now and then I'd recognize a celebrity from the Discovery Channel.

The only group noticeably absent were members of the press.

Richard was clearly in his element. Keeping me at his side, he worked the room, shaking hands with everyone he encountered. I was surprised at how many people he knew. It wasn't as if D.C. was his hometown.

A hush descended over the crowd, signaling the President and First Lady's entrance. The President matched all the other men in the room, who were similarly dressed in tuxedo and black tie, but he seemed to stand taller, prouder. Margaret Bradley was dressed in a silver gown that accentuated her graceful figure. They greeted the event organizers, who'd been waiting near the entrance. One of the organizers, a gray-haired man wearing a tuxedo that was too tight in the arms and too long in the legs, broke away and hurried up to a podium that had been set up on the far side of the round room and started to explain what the Wildlife Diversity Preservation League had accomplished over the course of the past year.

I followed as Richard moved away from the podium and struck up a conversation with Senator Finnegan. While the two men talked, I searched the crowd for familiar faces.

Near the entrance, I spotted Agent Cooper dressed in his familiar tweed suit. He must have arrived after the First Family. He seemed to be people-watching as well. His gaze never stopped as he stood with his arms crossed over his chest.

Lillian and Brooks Keller were standing in a crowd near the buffet tables. I almost didn't recognize Lillian at first. She was dressed in a tuxedo that matched her brother's, and she'd pulled her arctic blond hair back into a tight bun. She stiffened when she noticed Cooper by the door. Glancing nervously around, she grabbed her brother's arm, skirted around a buffet table draped in a white tablecloth, and disappeared through curtained French doors that led outside to a walled-off patio.

Richard and Senator Finnegan's discussion turned to the technical aspect of hedges — and not the kind of hedges that got pruned. My attention kept going back to the French doors through which Lillian and Brooks had disappeared.

There were two more sets of doors that led out to the same patio. I edged toward the one closest to me and slipped through.

The night sky looked dark against the glow of the city. A jet engine roared in the distance as a plane approached nearby Reagan National Airport.

Because of a vine-covered wooden pergola

in the middle of the patio, I couldn't see either Brooks or Lillian. I nodded to a Secret Service agent standing guard and then moved quietly in the direction of the door the twins had gone through.

"I don't know why I shouldn't talk with them," I heard Brooks say. I peered around the corner of the pergola and found Brooks and Lillian standing toe-to-toe a few feet away from me. "All the major news agencies are running pictures of Pauline and me together. Where did they get them?"

"Joanna, most likely."

"No, not Joanna. She wouldn't do that to me. She's too . . . too . . ."

"She's a thief and a liar. She'd do anything to hurt you and me."

"That FBI agent, what's his name . . ."

"Cooper," Lillian supplied.

"Yeah, him. He grabbed my arm on the way out of the hotel tonight. He said they're gathering evidence against me and that they're getting close to making an arrest. An arrest, Lillian! What evidence could they possibly have? He suggested that if I had nothing to hide, he'd appreciate it if I came in and answered some questions."

"God, tell me you didn't say anything to him."

"I'm not a moron, but he got me to thinking. If I went down there and explained —"

"Nothing would change. Nothing. Don't you see what's happening? They're looking for someone to blame, a convenient scapegoat. A murdered lover makes for a good story."

"But perhaps if they understood —"

"They'd arrest you, and the court of public opinion would convict you." Lillian huffed loudly. "Keep your mouth shut and let the FBI look elsewhere. Pauline dug deep into National Tenure's accounts, deep enough that I'm sure she found a skeleton or two. No one benefitted more from her death and the loss of her precious laptop than Richard. If you had managed to stay out of her bed, I bet the FBI would be all over that angle right now instead of bothering with you."

"You don't think he killed her, do you?" Brooks sounded appalled by the idea.

"I don't care what he's done. As long as it takes the focus off you, I'm willing to drop a few hints here and there."

"Now, Lillian." It was Brooks's turn to sound wary. "You're about as subtle as a bulldozer in a china shop."

"You mean a bull."

"What?" Brooks shook his head in confusion. "No, not a bull. I mean you, Lillian.

You're too aggressive when it comes to —"

"I protect what's important to me."

"But Joanna —" Brooks protested.

"Had her fingers where they didn't be-long." Lillian shivered. "Let's get back inside and try to act as if nothing has hap-pened, because it hasn't."

My heart banged in my chest. Could I let them return inside without saying anything? The banking summit was over and the CEOs would be heading back to New York. I might never get another chance to ques-tion either Brooks or Lillian again.

"Excuse me," I called, and hurried over to them.

Lillian turned around to glare while Brooks got a goofy grin on his face.

"Ms. Calhoun, what a pleasure," he said, closing the distance between us.

"Yes," Lillian said, her expression tighten-ing, "a pleasure."

"Lovely evening," I said, turning toward the edge of the patio to deflect Brooks's at-tempt to kiss my hand or anything else.

"We were just going inside." Lillian moved toward the French doors.

"I couldn't help but overhear the two of you talking about Pauline. You know, the other day I found a charm that had been on her laptop case, the same metal case the killer used to knock me unconscious."

I rubbed my temple as if it still pained me and turned to face them.

"I was wondering if you knew anything about that charm. Pauline's roommate had mentioned to me the other day that someone she knew in New York had given that charm to Pauline, someone *very* close to her. Was that you, Brooks?"

"I don't know what you're talking about."

"You mean to say you didn't give her a golden charm, like the kind you'd hang on a necklace or a bracelet?"

"What charm? I didn't give her a charm, did I, Lil?"

"Of course you didn't." Lillian turned toward me. "You have to understand that my brother doesn't actually shop for gifts for his lady friends. Jeffery, his personal assistant, handles details like that, and ever since he spent a fortune buying jewels for that conniving Joanna Lovell, I've been going over the books, making a list of all the gifts Jeffery's purchased."

"Are you certain?" If not Brooks, then who gave the charm to her? "It looked like a dollar sign encrusted with gems. Her initials had been engraved on the back."

"No. I don't know what you're talking about." Brooks shook his head with obvious distress.

"Of course he doesn't," Lillian cut in. "He's a wizard with numbers but clueless when it comes to women. Pauline was just like you, darling brother. She'd sleep with anyone who'd let her into his bed." She turned to me. "I bet that stupid charm came from one of her other lovers."

"There was more than one?" That surprised me. "In New York? Are you sure?"

"No," Brooks protested.

"I'm sure," Lillian said. She'd started to drag her brother back inside, but she stopped. "The people involved in this affair aren't as lily white as the press portrays them to be, Ms. Calhoun. Pauline craved attention and drama. She came to me with a crazy story about Joanna's hold on Brooks, hoping to cause friction."

"Lillian," Brooks hissed. This time he was the one tugging on his sister's arm, anxious to leave.

Lillian batted his hands away. "Turned out Pauline had been right about Joanna being trouble, but it wasn't the affair that was the problem. After reviewing the accounts, I discovered Joanna, my trusted personal attorney, had embezzled nearly half a million dollars from me. I suppose the lavish gifts she'd been getting from Brooks weren't enough."

"I didn't realize."

"We didn't prosecute." Lillian glared at her brother.

"She had photographs," Brooks grumbled.

"I'm so sorry."

"So are we, aren't we, Brooks?" Lillian said, and dragged Brooks inside.

I returned to the restaurant feeling sorry for Brooks.

Guilt had been written all over his face when his sister had mentioned Joanna. But when I'd asked him about Pauline, he'd crinkled his nose and brows and looked simply confused.

So if not Brooks, then who strangled Pauline?

And why would Lillian think Richard had the most to gain from Pauline's death?

"There you are." Richard brushed a kiss on my cheek. He was holding two plates piled with hors d'oeuvres. A small stack of tiny crab cakes caught my attention.

"For me?" I took the plate and popped a crab cake in my mouth, savoring its creamy sweet taste. "Thank you."

"What's bothering you?" Richard asked. He smoothed out the crease between my eyes with his thumb. "I don't think I've seen anyone frown so hard."

I popped another crab cake in my mouth before answering. "I thought you'd said the other day that you wanted the police to find Pauline's stolen laptop, because it could prove to the senate committee that added regulations weren't needed."

"That's right. I do." He glanced around the room. "Who have you been talking to?"

"Lillian Keller."

His lips pulled into an unfriendly smile. "Figures. She's a shark and she sits at the helm of my bank's toughest competitor. She'd love to hurt me."

"I didn't realize. But —"

"Come here." He took the plate and set it on a nearby table. He then took me into his arms and kissed me.

Oh boy, Richard could kiss.

The tingling started in my toes and worked its way to the top of my head before he'd finished making love to my lips. Before today, I didn't understand that phrase.

Joanna must have been wrong when she'd told me that Richard exclusively dated supermodels and celebrities, since I was neither. Or perhaps he'd grown tired of the gorgeous, leggy, and well-endowed types and was looking for a real woman, because the way he kissed me made me think of weddings and forever and towheaded little . . .

I grabbed his lapels and peeled my lips from his.

"Um . . . um . . ." What had we been talking about?

"Have I told you yet how beautiful you look tonight?" he whispered in my ear.

"No, but I like how you express your approval." Excitement bubbled in my chest. If his kiss had the power to knock me breathless, what would happen if I invited him up to my bedroom and let him do more than kiss?

"What's that?" A commotion at the entrance had caught Richard's attention. "John's in trouble." The Secret Service agents seemed to have all converged in one spot. Richard and I moved closer to get a better view of what was happening.

Was that the head of CAT, Mike Thatch, arguing with President Bradley?

The First Lady spotted me and directed the Secret Service to allow us to come closer. Because there was really no danger to the President and First Lady, just a minor disagreement, Richard and I easily squeezed through the tight circle the Secret Service agents had formed around the First Family.

"What's going on?" I asked Mrs. Bradley

when I reached her side.

She hooked her arm in mine. A sparkle of excitement lit her eyes. "We're springing a little surprise for the press pool. They follow John and me everywhere, dutifully recording our movements. But we've been attending many private events like these lately where the press pool is banned from coming inside and watching the proceedings. They're stuck in a stuffy van for hours, waiting to follow us back home with really nothing to report. But not tonight. Come on."

"Give us five minutes to secure the area," Thatch told the President, who nodded.

It actually took more than ten minutes for the Secret Service to give the okay. By that time, nearly everyone at the event was speculating on what President Bradley planned to do.

"He's going to sing," someone whispered behind me.

I doubted that.

"We know what this is about," Richard whispered in my ear.

I nodded as we preceded the President and First Lady outside. The press pool had gathered around the restaurant's entrance along with Dupont Circle residents, who'd lined the street in order to catch a glimpse of the First Family.

Uniformed and Secret Service agents dressed in dark suits eyed the crowd suspiciously and moved quickly to intercept anyone who tried to get too close. I spotted a few CAT agents patrolling in the background.

The President's limousine stood running at the front door, ready to whisk the First Family away as soon as the surprise had been sprung.

Richard stood behind me with his hands on my shoulder. The First Family took their place in front of the press pool. Senators Pendergast and Finnegan pushed their way through the crowd to stand at the President's elbow.

Once everyone had settled down, President Bradley cleared his throat. Photographers began snapping nonstop, their flashbulbs blinding.

"Many of you in the press pool have become as close to me as family. We practically all live together at the White House."

Several members of the press pool chuckled.

Mrs. Bradley squeezed her husband's hand. When he continued, he gazed lovingly at his wife. "There's going to be a new addition coming to live with us at the White

House. *Two* new additions, actually."

A collective gasp rose from within the press pool.

"Margaret has given me the best gift a wife can give her husband." His smile grew wider. So did the First Lady's.

"We're having twins," she said.

Someone started to clap. Others joined in. Cheers and whistles filled the street.

"John's a crafty man," Richard said, shaking his head. "Just like me, he'll do anything to win. The morning news will be about the pregnancy, not about how he spent the week butting heads with senators and Wall Street without accomplishing anything."

"I'm sure that's not why —" I'd started to say.

The rest of that thought got caught in my throat as I spotted Joanna Lovell. What was she doing here? She stood at the edge of the crowd gathered from the surrounding neighborhood.

She wore the same suit and running shoes from two days ago, but they looked freshly pressed and clean. She'd pulled her hair back into a ponytail, and her face had been cleaned of makeup.

A large flowered bag was slung over her shoulder, as if she'd spent the day shopping. She looked so harmless that when I first spotted her, recognition didn't fully kick in until I saw her reach into that bag and pull out a —

"Gun!" I broke away from Richard and lurched toward her. "There! She's there!"

But I was too late.

The Secret Service agents who dove toward her were also too late. The gun had been fired but I don't remember hearing it go off.

Senator Pendergast went down first.

And then Brooks.

A CAT agent jumped in front of me. Bullets that would have struck me peppered his chest. He fell backward, knocking me down with him.

Other Secret Service agents swarmed the area with their guns drawn. The Presidential limousine's tires screeched as it sped away from the curb followed by several black SUVs. I prayed the President and First Lady had escaped unharmed.

As I pulled myself up, I noticed the CAT agent who had saved me remained crumbled like a broken toy soldier on the sidewalk. Grabbing his shoulders, I rolled him over onto his back.

"Turner!"

CHAPTER TWENTY-EIGHT

I ran my hands over Jack Turner's chest. He wasn't my sidekick and wasn't even my friend. So why was I crying? I pressed my hands against the three dark bullet holes that had torn through his uniform in an effort to stanch the flow of blood.

But there wasn't any blood.

A heart has to beat for a bullet wound to bleed. Thanks to Turner for bringing up memories I had hoped to leave buried in my past, I remembered that grisly detail from my mother's death.

No heartbeat. No blood. No life.

Turner was dead.

"No." Tears clogged my throat. I cradled his lifeless body in my lap and buried my face in his chest. He'd saved me. He didn't have to do it. He didn't have to fling himself into the line of fire for me. But Turner had that damned hero complex, and that's what heroes did — they sacrificed themselves.

"Oh, Turner."

"What the hell are you doing?" a raspy voice asked.

I raised my head, expecting to find Richard.

I didn't expect to see that the dead guy I'd been cradling in my arms had opened his eyes.

I yelped and dropped him on the pavement. "You — you're okay?"

"Yeah." He rubbed the back of his head. "Bulletproof vest."

"Of course." I patted his ruined vest.

He pushed my hand away. "The bullets still pack one hell of a punch. Come morning my chest will be a rainbow of bruises, but you don't have to cry. I'm fine." He jumped to his feet and thumped the vest's ceramic insert. "These really are top-of-the-line, military-grade body armor."

"Wait," I called.

"They've got the shooter." He pointed to his earpiece as he trotted away. "It was Joanna."

The Secret Service corralled everyone who'd attended the wildlife charity event back into the restaurant while a pair of ambulances roared away with their sirens blaring, rushing Senator Pendergast and

433

Brooks Keller to the nearest hospital. So far, no one I'd asked knew the extent of either of their injuries. They'd both been shot, but no one else had been hurt.

"I don't understand what's going on. Why would Joanna want to shoot at the President?" I asked Agent Cooper, hoping he could answer at least that question for me.

An uncomfortable hush had descended in the room. A couple of people were whispering as if they were attending a funeral. Most looked shell-shocked, staring blankly at nothing.

I followed Agent Cooper as he took charge of the investigation, giving orders to the officers on duty. Looking sorely out of place with his tweed suit in the midst of black-and-white tuxedos, he snatched a crab cake as he passed the buffet table.

"Didn't have dinner," he explained.

"Didn't eat much tonight myself," I said, and popped a crab cake in my mouth. They were excellent. "Joanna had a grudge against Brooks. I understand that. But President Bradley and Senator Pendergast were both pressing hard on passing the kind of banking legislation that Joanna and her gang of protesters wanted."

Cooper shook his head as he chewed. "Don't know. But she's in custody, so you can bet we'll find out."

"Will you?" I wasn't so sure.

Richard came over with his BlackBerry glued to his ear. "How much longer before they let us go home?" he asked Cooper.

"I'm wondering the same thing," Senator Finnegan agreed as he joined us.

"Well, we'll need to take everyone's statement. Once that's done, I suppose you can go."

Several partygoers standing near us seemed to wake up from their state of shock. One man shifted nervously from foot to foot. A few others sighed loudly. The volume of the conversations increased sharply.

Janie Partners must have noticed the rising tension, too. She had a short conversation with the string quartet. A few minutes later they started to play one of Beethoven's opuses.

Detective Hernandez arrived not long after with his team of detectives. After conferring with the FBI and Secret Service, Hernandez directed his men to spread out across the room with notebooks in hand to assist in taking statements from everyone in the room.

Lucky me, I got the special treatment. Detective Hernandez, Agent Cooper, and the Secret Service's top man at the White House, the Assistant Director in charge of Protective Operations, William Bryce, all wanted to personally talk to me.

"Are the President and Mrs. Bradley okay?" I asked as soon as the men had settled around one of the buffet tables that had been cleared.

"Thanks to your sounding the alarm and taking quick action, they're safe," William Bryce said.

"Really?" I beamed not only because I was happy to know that the First Family was safe, but also because this was the first time the Secret Service hadn't scolded me for something I'd done. "How about Senator Pendergast and Brooks Keller? Have you heard about how they're doing?"

Bryce nodded. "The senator only suffered a superficial wound in her arm. It bled like the devil, but she'll be home by tomorrow morning. I heard she's still planning on bringing her grandchildren to Monday's Easter Egg Roll and that she's giving her doctors at the hospital hell."

"That's good to hear. And Brooks?"

"The last I heard, he was still in surgery. He took a bullet to the stomach."

"God, he's going to be in a world of pain

for a long time to come." I winced, remembering.

"You sound like you know what you're talking about," Cooper said, frowning at me. "Why? Did something —"

"Let's go over what happened." Bryce, who knew my past from my security clearance check, didn't let the FBI agent finish his question.

The four of us reviewed the events as they'd happened in great detail. Because Detective Hernandez wasn't on hand when the shooting started, he asked the most questions.

By the time we'd finished, I had a sinking feeling that they were missing an important piece of the puzzle.

"You don't think Joanna killed Pauline?" I asked Agent Cooper.

He flicked his pen several times. "I think she was involved, yes. You knew that both Pauline and Joanna were sleeping with Brooks. We have reason to believe that Pauline may have been responsible for Joanna getting fired and blacklisted."

"Yes. I'd heard that, too."

"That's more than enough motive for me." The other men nodded.

"But what about Senator Pendergast?"

"What about her?" Agent Cooper asked.

437

"Why would Joanna try to run her down with a car the other day? What's her motive there?"

"There's no evidence connecting the hit-and-run to any of this," Cooper pointed out.

"If that's true, why did Joanna shoot the senator tonight?"

Bryce sighed. "Bullets were flying everywhere. Until we get a clear picture of what Joanna had planned, if she ever gives us one, we don't know who she targeted. My money's on President Bradley. If she'd been gunning for anyone else, she could have picked an easier place to do it."

But the only people who had been shot were Senator Pendergast and Brooks Keller. And those last bullets seemed to have been aimed at me. If not for Turner's heroic dive, I doubt I would have survived the night. I hugged my arms to my chest and leaned forward in the chair.

And yet, Joanna had no apparent reason to want to kill the senator, the president, or me. Perhaps Bryce was right and her spray of bullets had been random. But why would she open fire like that? What had made her snap? Did Mr. Baseball Cap push her into something that she couldn't control?

Detective Hernandez patted my shoulder as he rubbed his salt-and-pepper mustache.

"It's been one hell of a week, Casey."

I nodded.

"But it's all over now."

"Is it?"

I wished I shared their confidence that, come morning, all the loose ends would be tied up in a neat bow.

Since the trio was done questioning me, I left them and went in search of Richard. I found him just inside the restaurant's entrance, sipping a cocktail.

"Shall we go?" I asked, hoping we could pick up where the kissing had left off earlier. I could use the comfort of his arms around me right about now.

Richard set the drink on a nearby table and turned toward me. His slow gaze lingered on the top of my head. I could tell from the hunk of limp hair that kept falling across half my face that the careful curls Alyssa had styled were now a mass of unruly tangles. Conscious of his scrutiny, I tried to finger-style it back into submission.

That's when I noticed my gown, my beautiful designer gown.

"Oh, dear," I examined a large rip down the side of the skirt and the grime from kneeling on the sidewalk with Turner. "It's ruined, isn't it?"

Richard wrinkled his nose. "Yeah, looks

like it is."

He glanced back out the door and at the dozens of reporters and cameras that had descended on the crime scene. Getting past them to reach Richard's waiting car at the curb would involve walking through that gauntlet.

"Uh," he said, pitching his voice low. He looked pointedly back at the crowd of reporters. "Under the circumstances, I think it would be best if we left separately. You wouldn't mind finding another way home, would you?"

Perhaps he was trying to protect me. Lord knew I didn't need any more bad press. Still, I could hear it in his voice. He was embarrassed to be seen with me looking like this.

A mess.

I *was* a mess.

"Oh. Yes. Of course. I understand." I straightened my shoulders and made sure I kept my back straight and my chin up, as Grandmother Faye had taught me a proud Calhoun acted in times like these. "Good night, Richard."

He gave a brisk nod. Flashbulbs exploded with their quick blinding white lights when he emerged from the restaurant. Reporters shouted questions. He ignored it all like a

440

seasoned pro. At the end of the gauntlet, Richard raised a hand, smiled for the cameras, and then was gone.

"It's for the best," I told myself and sank into a nearby chair, using my cell phone to call for a cab.

"What are you still doing here?"

I glanced up to find Turner standing directly in front of me with his hands on his hips.

"Waiting for my ride home. You?"

"I'm on duty for another three hours."

"No time off for good behavior?" I joked.

The corner of his mouth tilted up, which I considered as good as a knee-slapping laugh from a member of the highly trained, terminally serious CAT team.

"I don't know how to thank you for jumping into the line of fire for me," I gushed. "You — you saved my life out there. I —"

"Casey —"

"No, let me finish. That was awfully foolish and awfully brave."

"Casey —" he said more forcefully this time.

"You don't have to be modest. You're a hero. I'll forever be in your debt."

"Don't be," he grumbled. "I didn't save you. I was jumping in front of the President, who just happened to be standing directly behind you. So please, don't thank me."

"You mean Joanna wasn't aiming for me?"

"I don't think so."

"And you weren't trying to save me?" I bit my lower lip as my cheeks burned with embarrassment.

"Look. I'm glad you're okay." Turner glanced around. "Where's lover boy?"

I shrugged. "At his hotel, I suppose."

"Really?" Turner sat down beside me. "How are you getting home? Do you need a ride?"

"The cab company said they'd have a car out here in about fifteen minutes."

"A cab?"

I nodded.

"I'd be glad to drive you home. Or at least arrange for someone to drive you."

"I'm fine." I angrily swiped at the tears that had misted in my eyes. It had been a long, hard day. And his concern for how I planned to get home threatened the rather tenuous hold I had on my emotions. "Joanna didn't kill Pauline," I said, expecting a fight.

"I know," he said. "Come with me."

CHAPTER TWENTY-NINE

That darn curiosity of mine had me following Turner out a back door of the restaurant despite my better judgment. Sure, he'd saved my life. But it had been by default.

"Where are we going?" I asked.

Turner stopped beside an unmarked Secret Service black sedan.

"I'm giving you a ride home." He held the door open for me. I put my hand on the car's roof.

"I thought you were still on duty," I pointed out.

"I am."

I stared at him. He stared back.

"You and I both know Joanna wasn't the one who attacked you at Lafayette Square or at the greenhouse," he explained. "That means there's still a killer on the loose, a killer looking to hurt you."

"So you're on babysitting duty and not letting me out of your sight?"

"Something like that. With Joanna in jail, her accomplice might get desperate and try to get rid of loose ends — like you — before getting out of town."

"I think you've got it backwards. I think Joanna's the accomplice and a dupe at that."

I slid into the car and waited for him to start the car before continuing.

"I don't think Joanna will be able to explain to the FBI why Pauline was murdered, because I don't think she ever had the full picture of what Pauline's killer really intended to do. If she did, if she knew that the end goal was to stop the banking reform bill, I don't think she'd have agreed to do what she did."

When we reached my brownstone apartment, Turner pulled to a stop at the curb. I thanked him for the ride and started to open the door, but he caught my wrist. Turning in his seat to face me, he smiled.

"You wanted me as your sidekick so you could have someone to bounce ideas off of. So here I am. Start bouncing."

I snatched my wrist out of his grasp. "I've changed my mind. I don't need anybody."

Petty, I knew. And yet when I looked at Turner, I couldn't stop myself from cringing inside. I shouldn't have told him so much last night. That was the one secret I'd thought I'd guard to the end of my days.

I'd been responsible for my mom's death. And now he knew it.

I closed my eyes and practiced my deep breathing exercises. Even so, the regrets came flooding back. I shouldn't have been such a brat. If I hadn't insisted that my mom leave the safety of our house that night for ice cream, she'd still be alive.

"You must be exhausted," he said, unruffled by my rejection. "We can talk later. After everything that's happened this week, I don't know anyone who could keep their chin up and keep pushing like you have."

"It's a family trait," I said with a burst of pride. "Calhouns aren't born. We're forged from the toughest of steel."

"Forged, eh? Didn't you accuse me of being hatched from a pod?"

I opened my eyes to find him still smiling at me.

"Is this a trick?" I whispered.

"I've never tried to trick you." His lazy grin faded. "I'm asking for your help, Casey. You've been poking your nose into every nook and cranny in this case. I want to hear you try and connect the dots. Perhaps, and I know it's a long shot, you might be seeing something the rest of us have missed."

I knew I was seeing something they had

overlooked.

"Senator Pendergast," I said.

"What about her?"

"That's what you're missing. A car tried to run her down just a few hours after I told her about the missing laptop. Because of me, she publicly renewed her determination to push her version of the banking reform bill through the Senate. Because of me, the killer was forced to act again."

Turner, I noticed with a spurt of irritation, didn't seem to be listening to a word I was saying. His gaze was glued to the side view mirror. I peered over my shoulder just as a car turned onto my street. It rolled slowly toward us.

"Let's get you inside." The muscles in his shoulders tightened just a bit. When I started to open the door, he caught my wrist again. "Wait."

My body went still. I didn't even breathe, didn't dare turn my head to look at the dark sedan that was approaching from behind.

It drew up directly beside us and stopped.

Turner released my wrist and reached for his sidearm. "Get down on the floorboard." His lips barely moved as he spoke.

I slid down in the seat, lower and lower, loudly popping stitches out of the seam of my gown while my heart battered my throat as it tried to leap right out of my mouth.

A car door squeaked as it opened. Turner cursed, which did nothing good for my already fraying nerves.

"What is Steve Sallis doing here?" he asked. The Secret Service agent hadn't been at the wildlife charity event tonight, so why would he show up at my place?

"Bryce asked me to swing by to keep an eye on things," Steve explained after Turner had rolled down the car window. "But I see that you beat me to it, Jack. What are you doing on the floor there, Casey? Are you okay?"

I nodded, too nervous to form words.

"Hey, look. She's speechless," Steve said, poking his head into the window.

"You scared the hell out of the both of us," Turner snapped. "Back up, so I can open this door."

"Wait," I said. Steve's driving up like that had reminded me of something, something besides my vulnerability out on the D.C. streets. Wallace had scared me the same way when he'd come to pick me up for my first date with Richard.

"What is it?" Turner asked.

"Wallace Clegg."

"Who?"

"Richard's assistant. He was wearing a

447

pair of those black-and-white leather shoes the other day, the same shoes the man who attacked me was wearing." I pulled myself back up to the car's seat. "It was Wallace." I banged the dashboard for emphasis. "That's who I saw in the park arguing with Joanna. I'm sure of it. He killed Pauline."

"I'll call the FBI and ask them to look into this new angle," Steve said, pulling out his cell phone.

I suddenly couldn't sit still. "Don't you see? It now makes sense how he got Joanna involved. Oh, she'd told me that she didn't care that Pauline had slept with Brooks. And maybe she didn't. But she wouldn't have forgiven Pauline for getting her fired and blacklisted."

"Cooper said he'll look into it in the morning," Steve reported, glancing at his watch. "It's late, Casey. After everything that's happened, you've got to be exhausted."

I'm sure it was a lack of sleep in combination with a shot of adrenaline that made my eyes feel too bright and my skin tingly with excitement. "We can't wait until morning. Once he finds out the FBI has Joanna, he's going to run. We've got to get over to Richard's hotel."

Turner stared forward, his expression

frustratingly inscrutable.

"Please, Turner, we have to stop him before he gets away."

He turned the key in the ignition.

"Get Cooper back on the cell," he instructed Steve. "Tell him where we're going and ask for FBI and police backup."

"Have you lost your mind?" Steve shouted as Turner mashed his foot on the gas pedal, sending the unmarked sedan tearing away from the curb.

"You were talking about your theory regarding Senator Pendergast," Turner prompted as he drove at top speed down the narrow residential streets.

"I — I didn't think you were listening." I yanked the seatbelt over my chest and snapped it into its holder.

"What can I say? I'm a multitasker." He careened around a corner without even slowing down. "How does Wallace fit in with that? And how is he connected to Joanna? Do you think Joanna tried to run down the senator with a car?"

"Why would she? What would be her motive? I'd put my money on Wallace. He killed Pauline and stole her laptop. It's probably destroyed by now." I yelped as he ran a red light and had to swerve to avoid hitting a cab. "At first, I was sure Brooks

Keller was responsible. His shoes matched the ones I saw on the man who hit me."

"But because Joanna shot him tonight, you think he's innocent?"

"No, it wasn't that, although that does kind of take him out of the suspect pool. How do I explain this? I spoke with him tonight, and he's . . . he's not a killer."

"How can you be sure? If the shoes matched, then why not him? Perhaps Joanna double-crossed him."

I shook my head. "It's not him. Those shoes had to have been a gift from Pauline. She gave a pair to Lorenzo and I bet she gave the same pair to Brooks. They were both her lovers. I learned tonight from Lillian that Pauline had recently taken a third lover in New York. So why wouldn't he also have a pair of the same shoes? I saw Wallace wearing them the other day. It has to be him."

"You're sure about this?" Turner asked. He pulled the sedan to a cockeyed stop in front of the hotel.

Lillian had said that Richard had the most to benefit from Pauline's death. Wallace had dedicated his life to protecting his employer. He'd said it himself. That chilly morning after spending the night in a car watching my apartment he'd said that he'd do anything for Richard. *Anything.*

"I'm sure Wallace is the one," I said. "He has to be."

"I hope so." Turner blasted through the revolving door and charged up to the front desk.

I had to hike my gown's ruined skirt to catch up to him.

"Secret Service," Turner said and flashed a badge. "I need you to get me into Wallace Clegg's room."

The heavyset clerk took one look at Turner with his imposing CAT uniform with three fresh bullet holes in the chest and then ran his eyes over me, with my hair in tangles and my dress muddy and torn. "Does this have something to do with that lady who shot at the President this evening?" the clerk asked, paling at the thought.

"I can't say" — Turner paused a millisecond to read the clerk's name tag — "Frank."

"Do you have the authority to do this?" I whispered.

Turner shushed me and turned back to the clerk.

Frank typed something into his keyboard. "He's in an adjoining room to the penthouse suite. Let me get a keycard."

With Frank leading the way, we rode the

elevator to the top floor, where there were three doors. "It's this one," Frank said.

Turner pulled out his gun and knocked on the door.

No one answered.

"Open it," he told Frank.

Beads of sweat formed on the clerk's brow as he swiped the card in the door and jumped back.

Turner held up his arm, indicating that Frank and I should stay back before he pushed the door open. Frank stayed in the hallway where Turner had indicated. I tried to wait with him, but I felt too anxious. I needed to see for myself if Wallace had fled.

He hadn't.

I followed Turner into the hotel suite. In the room just beyond the suite's foyer, we found Wallace sprawled facedown across a king-sized bed. Holding my breath, I watched as Turner pressed two fingers to Richard's personal assistant's throat.

Turner didn't have to say anything. I could tell just by looking at him. Wallace was dead.

"It's over," Detective Hernandez assured us as we stood in the hotel lobby swarming with uniformed policemen.

Everyone kept telling me that. That it was

over. So why didn't I feel better?

The police had found a note. Wallace, wracked with guilt over killing Pauline, had taken his own life.

Supposedly.

"I don't know why you can't accept it, Casey." Hernandez clicked his pen shut and slid his notebook into his blazer's inside pocket. For him the case was over. He leaned against the lobby's marble wall and watched as the coroner wheeled Wallace's body out to the waiting van. "We found an empty bottle of sleeping pills on the bedside table along with three empty minibottles of vodka and the note. He clearly died of an overdose."

I wrapped my arms around my middle, hugging myself. "I know."

Richard had confirmed that Wallace had been acting troubled, drinking too much and forgetting things. "I should have done more," I'd overheard him telling Agent Cooper in the hallway outside Wallace's room. "I can't say I'm surprised this happened. I could tell he was getting in over his head. God, I should have done more."

"It's late." Turner appeared at my side and directed my shoulders toward the hotel's revolving door. "The car's still parked outside. Let me take you home."

"What about Senator Pendergast?" I asked with a jaw-cracking yawn as I let myself be led away. There was no reason to stay at the hotel. Richard refused to even look at me. And Wallace, he was dead.

"What about the senator?" Turner opened the sedan's door for me.

"The banking legislation is supposed to come out of committee on Tuesday, and the senator has the power to get a majority of votes on her side to get the bill passed. Don't you see what that means? If the killer wants to stop the bill, he'll strike either tomorrow or Monday." How could I have forgotten? "Monday is the White House Easter Egg Roll. Senator Pendergast is planning to be there. That'll probably be the only time she'll be making a public appearance before Tuesday's hearing."

"You're forgetting something important, Casey."

"What's that?" I leaned my head against the passenger-side window's cool glass and closed my eyes.

"Wallace is dead and Joanna is in jail. It's over."

"Is it?"

"According to Agent Cooper, now that Joanna knows Wallace killed himself, she's started talking up a storm." Turner's voice sounded like a faraway voice in a dream. "She's explained that Wallace was jealous of Pauline's relationship with Brooks Keller — just as you'd suspected. Joanna was out of her head with jealousy, too. Pauline had practically stolen her lover out of Joanna's own bed and then had ruined her career and her life. That's a pretty strong motive for murder."

"Don't forget that Joanna embezzled from BLK Investments," I added sleepily.

"That's an even stronger motive, then."

"It's a nice story. Jealousy breeds murder. Too bad it's not true." More asleep than awake, I yawned. "That's not why Wallace killed Pauline, you know. It wasn't about a lover's spat. It was about what she'd saved on her laptop and how it would fuel the banking reform legislation."

"But, Casey, all her reports were down-loaded to the mainframe. No data was lost."

"Hmm . . . She could have held something back. Everyone I talked to told me how ambitious and power hungry Pauline seemed. What if she was trying to leverage something with Wallace or even with Richard, but it backfired? Whatever she had on that laptop got her killed."

"Still, Wallace is dead."

"Yes, he's dead. Richard won't have Wallace to run his errands or buy his gifts, like this lovely gown I've ruined."

"What are you saying?"

"No CEO handles mundane tasks. That's why they have personal assistants and whatnot." I yawned again. "Goodness, I'm tired. Are we almost home?"

"We're parked outside your front door."

I opened my eyes and was surprised to see my apartment's familiar mahogany door. "Do you know what time Wallace died?" I wondered if Wallace was already dead when Richard picked me up driving his new car.

"I don't know. No one will until the autopsy results come back. Why?"

"I don't know." I was too tired to think straight, much less hope to make any sense.

Turner walked me to the door and waited while I unlocked and pushed open the door.

"Will I see you at the Easter Egg Roll?" I asked.

"Are you kidding me? I don't have any desire to babysit thousands of screaming kids on Monday. I made sure I had the day off."

"Meaning you've been on a babysitting assignment ever since you met me, and you've had enough?"

"That's not what I said."

"It sure sounded that way." I hated the shrill tone in my voice.

"Don't worry, Casey." He leaned against the doorframe. "Joanna is in custody. Wallace is dead. Nothing is going to happen to the senator . . . or to you. Go to bed. Get a good night's sleep. You're safe now."

Was I?

I didn't feel safe.

CHAPTER THIRTY

Monday morning rolled in along with a thick white mist that hugged the White House's South Lawn. I sipped my mug of coffee and watched workers dressed in blue jumpsuits carry displays, folding tables, and chairs to their designated spots for the Easter Egg Roll. As they moved silently through the haze, they'd intermittently disappear and reappear.

In a few hours, the southeast gate would open to admit the first group of ticketholders.

From my first day at the White House, I'd looked forward to the Easter Egg Roll with great enthusiasm. I loved Easter with its brightly colored hard-boiled eggs, chocolate bunnies covered in golden foil, marshmallow chicks, and the scent of spring flowers in the air.

Trays of English pea and romaine lettuce seedlings we'd grown in the greenhouses had been carried to the bottom of the South Lawn to the gardening display under a green tent. Gordon had dubbed them our presidential crop, since we'd purchased the seeds from Thomas Jefferson's kitchen garden at Monticello.

Excitement should have been thrumming through my veins. Today had promised to be a treat, the cherry on top of the proverbial cake. But Saturday's tragedy hung heavy on my mind.

According to the local news reports and tidbits I could get out of Cooper and Hernandez, Brooks had been airlifted to a hospital in New York City and was expected to make a full recovery. Senator Pendergast had been discharged from the hospital early Sunday morning and had spent the day taking her grandchildren to church services and to a picnic on the National Mall.

Although she'd been out in the open and vulnerable for hours, no one had attacked or threatened her. And Joanna continued talking, despite her lawyer's warnings to keep quiet.

Wallace had approached Joanna a week ago to discuss their mutual enemy, Pauline. Nothing had come out of that initial meeting, but Wallace continued to call Joanna. He constantly reminded her how Pauline and Brooks had ruined her.

According to her, she had nothing to do with Pauline's murder, but she'd immediately suspected Wallace. He kept calling and reminding Joanna how Brooks and Pauline had hurt her. He told her that she should do something about it. He pushed and pushed until Joanna's anger had grown to a point that she couldn't stand it any longer. Suddenly, revenge was worth more to her than her own life. That's when she agreed to meet with Wallace. He gave her the gun and told her about the charity dinner.

If her purpose that night was to shoot the President, Senator Pendergast, or even me, Joanna wouldn't say. Her confession, while not complete, should have been enough for me. With Joanna's arrest and Wallace's death, the nightmare truly appeared to be over.

Turner believed it.

Detective Hernandez had been adamant about it.

So had Alyssa. She couldn't understand why I'd asked her to drive me to work this morning. I seemed to be the only one still nervously searching every unfamiliar face for signs of danger.

According to everyone I'd talked to and everything I'd read, Pauline had been killed because she'd visited too many men's beds. Why Wallace also stole her laptop and what he'd done with it, we'd probably never know.

Even Lorenzo had accepted that explanation with quiet dignity.

So why couldn't I? Why couldn't I find peace knowing that justice had prevailed?

I causally sipped my coffee — decaf, since my nerves were already jumpy enough — and wished I felt as relaxed as I pretended to be. Perhaps by the end of the day, things would start to feel normal again.

A blurry figure emerged from the mists and shadows with a gait I recognized immediately.

"Jack Turner, what are you doing here on your day off?"

Dressed in his black CAT uniform complete with the large assault rifle slung over his shoulder and a menacing pistol jutting out from a black leather leg holster, Turner headed straight toward me. My heart sped at the sight of him. I'm sure it was because of his guns.

"After this weekend, I volunteered for duty in case I was needed," he said with a shrug that ended with him wincing.

"Always good to be needed," I said, wondering just how badly his chest had bruised after Saturday night's shooting. "If I'd known you'd be here, I would have brought you a mug of gourmet coffee."

"Why?" He glanced around him with a dramatic flair. "Don't tell me you've latched on to another intrigue. You know I can't be bribed."

"I think I've had enough intrigue to last me a lifetime. From now on, I'm going to leave the sleuthing to my paperback heroines." Why was I smiling at him?

Thank goodness he smiled back. "I'm glad to hear it. It'll save me some sleepless nights. But that's not why I'm looking for you." Turner reached into a pocket of his flak jacket and pulled out the bottle of pepper spray I'd left with Fredrick at the gate.

"What are you doing with that? Please don't tell me I'm being banned from even leaving it at the gate. You know I need it when I walk to and from work."

"Nothing's changed. You can still leave the bottle at the gate."

"Then what's going on? Did something happen?"

"No, nothing's happened."

"Then what's this about? Aren't you afraid I might pepper spray the First Dog or the

President?" I joked to cover up my confusion.

He pressed the bottle into my hand and curled my fingers around it. "I want you to keep the pepper spray on you and . . . just . . . just be careful."

"Be careful? Why?"

"I don't know." He ventured back into the mist and shadows. "It's nothing in particular, Casey, just a bad feeling. You should be fine."

I stared at the spray bottle, my brows scrunched so hard it started to make my head pound.

"There you are!" Gordon boomed from directly behind me.

Startled, I spun around with my finger at the ready on the bottle's plunger and a millimeter away from spraying a healthy dose of hot pepper oil in Gordon's face. I quickly jammed the bottle into my jacket pocket before I accidentally assaulted someone.

"Good morning, Gordon. Don't you think that once this mist burns off, the weather will be perfect?"

"Absolutely. Couldn't ask for anything better," he agreed. Gordon was dressed in his usual khaki pants with a navy blue windbreaker zipped up to his neck. "I need you to do something for me."

"What?" I didn't trust the goofy tilt of his head or the excitement brightening his eyes. "Why am I getting an itchy feeling that I'm not going to like this?"

"It's Easter Monday." He sounded like a kid with a new toy. "It's going to be a fun day. Come on."

I followed him through the White House and down the steps to the bottom floor of the two-story basement, where a small crowd had gathered. I recognized several high-ranking staffers from the West Wing standing around in the hallway.

"What are they doing down here?" I whispered to Gordon. Very few West Wing employees ever came into the residence and certainly not into the basement.

"You'll see."

The door to a small storage room I'd never noticed before sat open. Fisher stood in the doorway with a clipboard and pen held at the ready.

He glanced up. His gaze latched on to Gordon and me.

"Ah, you're here. We can begin." His long nose twitched as he pinched his lips together in an odd, twisted smile.

"Cassandra Calhoun," he called needlessly, since he'd obviously seen me walking toward him. "Cassandra Calhoun," he repeated when I failed to say anything.

"Uh, here . . . I guess."

"Good." He made a checkmark on the clipboard and disappeared into the storage room. He returned carrying a bulging garment bag.

"Try not to get dirt on it," he said, and then called the next name on his list.

"Gordon? What's this?" I had a sinking feeling I already knew.

"Think of it as your initiation."

"No, you didn't."

He nodded.

"The costumes? You signed me up to be a costumed character?" Sure, I was as fun-loving as the next person. But a girl had to have her standards. She had to know where to draw her line.

No member of the Calhoun family had ever paraded about in a goofy character costume. I didn't wish to be the first. "You wear it."

Gordon held up his hands as I tried to hand over the fat garment bag. "I can't. It's . . . er . . . feminine."

"Don't tell me," I groaned. "You signed me up to be a baby chick."

"Nope. Better."

"Better?" I didn't want to know.

I took the costume into the women's

locker room located just down the hall and donned the delightful contraption.

I took one look at it and started envying the staff members who'd gotten one of those cute fluffy baby chick costumes.

The body of *this* costume was shaped like a giant white egg. It covered my body, stopping just above my knees, where frilly bloomers hung out the bottom.

A feathered collar decorated the egg's neck opening. Oversized layered puffy sleeves in varying shades of pastel paisley ran the length of my arms. White gloves capped my hands. A wide-brimmed white hat sat on top of my head with a pastel blue ribbon tied at my chin.

I was to carry a frilly lace parasol and a basket of decorated eggs, which seemed a bit odd, an egg handing out eggs for the children to eat.

The costume was hideous. It was heavy and hot and damned difficult to walk in without falling on my face.

I nearly did fall flat on my face as I hobbled out of the locker room.

Gordon, who'd been waiting for me in the hallway, clapped with delight. "The children are going to love it!"

CHAPTER THIRTY-ONE

The costume, as Gordon had predicted, was a hit, attracting giggly children as effectively as the Pied Piper's pipe.

By midmorning, the sun had burned off the last signs of the early morning mists. The temperature was still springlike with a brisk bite in the air. Parents led smiling kiddies dressed in their Sunday best to take part in the various activities.

A favorite author from my childhood who wrote adventure stories set at the White House perched on the edge of a chair at the center of the reading corner and read from his latest book to a small group who listened in riveted silence. I stood outside the bright green snow fencing, reveling in the moment. My dream of having adventures of my own at the White House had actually come true.

A little too true.

The back of my neck tingled. Thanks to Turner and the bottle of pepper spray tucked up my frilly sleeve, I didn't feel safe at what had to be the most secure place on earth.

As the crowds moved toward the area around the South Portico to where President Bradley was scheduled to make a short speech, I perfected a spinning hop-dance across the South Lawn while twirling my lacy white parasol, figuring if I had to look foolish, I might as well put my heart into it.

The First Family, with Milo yipping his approval, were received with a roar of relieved applause when they emerged on the first floor of the South Portico to welcome the Easter Bunny and declare an official start to the celebration.

It had been the first time since the shooting that anyone had seen Mrs. Bradley. I was relieved to see that she was looking well.

While the First Family mingled, I continued to entertain the kids who flocked to me. An hour later, my dance had slowed a bit, so I retreated to the bottom of the lawn and to the gardening display under the green tent.

"Oh. My. God. Casey, you look" — Lorenzo snorted — "stupid. Really and truly stupid."

"Thank you. That was the look I was after," I said with as much dignity as I could muster, and started to hand out the small paper cups for use as temporary planters for the seedlings.

While Lorenzo, who got along surprisingly well with the kids, gave instructions on the proper way to plant the seedlings, I stood back and watched the crowd. Senator Pendergast, her arm in a dark blue sling, chased after three of her grandchildren, a toddling boy and girl and an older boy, as they charged up to the Easter Bunny.

The six-foot white fleece bunny had a fixed, slightly surprised, gaping smile. Small wire-rimmed glasses perched on the end of his terminally cute pink nose. He hopped in delight when the senator's grandchildren ran up to greet him.

He patted the tops of their blond heads with his oversized paw, messing up their hair. He then lifted his hands to his mouth in a broad cartoonish gesture, pantomiming laughter. The youngest boy giggled.

The bunny moved to mess up the senator's hair. Laughing, she batted his oversized paws away. I'd never seen her look so relaxed.

"I'll be back in a minute," I told Lorenzo. After handing a paper cup to a smiling little boy, I set the remaining stack of cups on the table. Waddling as fast as my huge egg body would let me, I made a beeline toward the senator. Seeing how she was already set against both the gardening plan and my position at the White House, I couldn't see how it would hurt to try to convince her to change her mind.

Before I could reach her, the Easter Bunny bent down and whispered something in the children's ears. The kids jumped up and down with excitement.

The bunny put his paws over his mouth and shook with laughter as the children darted over to take part in the next heat of the egg race.

The senator started to head in that direction as well, but the Easter Bunny tapped her shoulder. Like the bunny did with the children, he leaned over and whispered into the senator's ear.

Instead of laughing, Edith Pendergast violently jerked back.

The Easter Bunny, giving a dramatic shrug, bounded away.

I hurried toward the senator to find out what that was about, but before I could reach her, she chased after the giant white bunny as he wove through the crowd, patting curly-headed tots on their heads as he went.

The two of them were moving much faster

than I could while wearing the stupid egg suit. And with the large number of families milling about, I was afraid I'd lose sight of them.

There was one way to catch up. The hop-dance I'd perfected made much better time than slow waddling. So I did my spring dance, twirling my parasol, as I followed the odd pair.

First the Easter Bunny and then the senator skirted behind the gardening display and toward a thick planting of trees and bushes that formed a barrier between the South Lawn and the back part of the secluded Children's Garden.

Secret Service agents had blocked off the entrance to the Children's Garden using the bright green snow fencing. No one should have been back there.

The bunny reached a line of hedges and stopped. He waved at Senator Pendergast, pantomiming that she should hurry up. Using his giant rabbit's feet, he blazed a path through the thick branches that skirted the edge of the tennis court.

The senator followed.

More curious than concerned, I ducked under a low-hanging tree branch and blazed my own trail through the bushes.

In addition to the thick planting of trees

and bushes and the tennis court, the Children's Garden was blocked off with an eight-foot-tall, semiopaque black fabric fencing intended to create a secure and private space within. I figured the bunny would hit that fence and be forced to turn back.

I hadn't expected to find a tear in the fencing encircling the Children's Garden tall enough for a man — or giant bunny — to pass through. I stepped into the slit in the fence and started to slide through.

I got halfway into the Children's Garden. The bottom part of the egg costume had wedged itself into the fence and refused to budge. I was stuck like a bug in a spider web. As quietly as possible, I tugged at both my costume and the fence, hoping to tug myself free before either the senator or the bunny noticed me.

"I don't know what you want." I heard Senator Pendergast's tense whisper from inside the Children's Garden. "Money?"

The bunny, with its eerily fixed smile, shook his head. Moving with amazing speed considering the weight of that costume, he grabbed the senator by the neck.

Oh, Lordy, he was going to kill her!

Forget being quiet — with a grinding rip, I forced my way through the fabric fencing to stumble through the knee-high pittosporum bushes and onto the stone walkway. With a grand swing, I walloped the Easter Bunny over the head with my parasol. The wooden handle snapped in two.

The bunny didn't flinch.

The senator's face turned an alarming purple tone. Her head fell forward and her body went limp.

With a shout of panic, I jumped on the oversized bunny's back and pulled at his arms. Numerous self-defense courses guided my motions as I delivered a chop to a spot on his arm where several nerves converged.

It disabled him long enough that he dropped the senator. She landed like a rock on the hard stone walkway.

He threw his hands up and spun around with enough force to send me flying off his back. I landed facedown in the garden's small goldfish pond. The icy water stung my cheeks.

Before I could pull my cumbersome egg-self back onto my feet, he landed on top of me. His large paws pressed on the back of my head, forcing my face into the water.

Gurgling, I reached behind me and grabbed the first thing I could get my hands on — his long bunny ears — and gave a hard yank.

Instead of knocking him off balance, the costume head came off in my hands. I hit my attacker with the giant rabbit head and twisted out from under him.

"Richard!" A burst of adrenaline got my feet under me in record time despite the weight of the soggy costume.

I could barely believe what I was seeing. The incredibly handsome human head sticking out the top of the bunny suit belonged to Tempting Templeton, with his untamed rock star hair as slick and tempting as ever.

"What — what are you doing?" I still couldn't believe Richard had tried to kill me just now. With my hands raised defensively in front of me, I inched toward the long winding walkway that led out of the garden, prepared to make a dash for help. "Is this about the banking audits and what was on Pauline's laptop?"

"You already know it is. You've been hinting for days how you suspected Pauline had found evidence that I'd been shuttling toxic assets into dummy accounts. She knew that if she took that information to the Senate Banking Committee, Pendergast's draconian bill would fly through the Congress without debate and I'd find myself facing indictment. So she held it back to use for blackmail."

"So you killed her?"

"Not me, Wallace."

The senator, I was glad to see, had sat up. I reached down to help her to her feet. She looked too weak to manage it on her own. With an irritated grunt, she waved me away. *"Go,"* she rasped. *"Get help."*

She was right. I needed to get the Secret Service down here. Shouting for help, I made a mad dash toward the walkway.

Richard lunged forward and grabbed my neck before much of a squeak escaped my lips. Those large bunny paws were more powerful than they looked as he squeezed, cutting off the air and blood flow to my head.

"I should have let Wallace kill you." His grip tightened. "He wanted to, you know. He knew you saw him. But every extra body would only increase the chances he'd be caught."

"So . . . why . . . now?" I managed to get out.

"Don't be conceited. I didn't come here to kill you. It's the senator I'm after. Thanks to your prodding, she won't give up on that damn legislation of hers." He pressed his face to mine. "I never lose."

My oxygen-starved brain suddenly remembered the pepper spray. I reached up my sleeve searching for the bottle.

"As for you, you're an afterthought, a footnote. Did you really think I was attracted to you . . . *to you?*" His grip on my neck tightened despite those silly fleece bunny paws covering his hands and my attempts to pry him loose.

"I had hoped we could be friends," I wheezed.

He laughed. "You're constantly covered in dirt and mud. I wasn't dating you. I was keeping an eye on you, making sure you didn't get your memories back. But I'm glad I get to kill you, because you, Casey Calhoun, repulse me."

My fingers curled around the small plastic hairspray bottle I'd tucked up my sleeve. With a yank that ripped the sleeve and cracked the egg open, I pulled it out and squirted.

And missed.

I pressed the plunger again. I had to get away so I could get help and save the senator.

The world around me disappeared as I began to lose consciousness.

I kept pressing the plunger, praying he'd let go.

Richard finally shouted an ear-blistering curse and dropped me.

"Some dream guy you turned out to be," I whispered as I crumbled to the ground, thrilled that the pepper spray had actually worked this time.

Frantically rubbing his eyes with his giant rabbit's paw, he hopped around blindly. I tried to roll out of his way, but I couldn't move fast enough. He stumbled and fell on top of me.

His grasping hands grabbed my arms in a bruising hold, pulling me toward him. I kicked and fought, but his determination gave him a maddening strength that was no match for my woozy half-strangled self.

I could feel the cold hand of death in his ever-tightening grip. He'd worked his way up my arms and had grabbed my neck again.

"Die, dammit, die already," he groaned in my ear.

In a desperate move to protect myself, I hugged my legs to my chest and tucked my head between my knees, to make myself as compact and small as possible. Too late, too late, though. His fingers pressed against my windpipe in a crushing grip.

"Take your hands off the gardener or I'll blow your damned head clean off your neck," a low, unnaturally calm voice warned.

Richard's grip around my neck loosened.

Shivering from head to toe, I slowly uncurled my body and raised my head. The first thing I saw was a shiny black combat boot grinding into Richard's back, the barrel of an assault rifle pressed menacingly against his temple.

My gaze traveled a little higher.

"Turner," I whispered. "Thank God."

His jaw was set. His gaze locked on Richard's face. His finger held at the ready on his rifle's trigger.

"What took you so long?" I asked as I wiggled out from under Richard.

"It took some time to chase down and secure the senator's grandchildren," Turner explained in his deadpan voice. "And then we had to figure out where you'd disappeared to."

The entire CAT team flanked Turner, their rifles held at the ready, their expressions as deadly as his. What a wonderful sight.

"Thank you for saving me," I said to them. My voice sounded as if I'd swallowed a bag of gravel. "Now, could you please get out of the flowerbeds? Y'all are crushing my grape hyacinths."

EPILOGUE

A week had passed since Richard's arrest. The newspapers still buzzed about his meteoric rise and violent downfall as the SEC took apart his bank's books piece by piece. As a result of the scandal, Senator Pendergast's banking legislation sailed through the Senate without much debate and looked as if it'd soon pass the House as well.

Gordon and I silently flanked Lorenzo as we sat in the back row while Pauline Bonde's family and friends hugged and cried after the graveside service. Gradually, everyone left the cemetery.

Lorenzo remained, so we stayed with him.

"I know she would have never married me," Lorenzo said. He sat with his hands clasped between his knees and stared at the lightning bolt down the side of his leather shoes. "It was over between us. I knew that, but that doesn't stop me from loving her or grieving the life we might have had if she hadn't been married to her job or grasping so desperately for the next powerful man to head her way. But isn't that what we're all doing in this town? Grasping for power?"

"Not all of us." I gave his clasped hands a gentle squeeze.

"Thank you, Casey." He turned toward me. "Thank you for finding out why this happened. I'm grateful for that."

I nodded with a lump in my throat.

"Let me take you home," Gordon said to Lorenzo. "I'll fix you my secret recipe for macaroni and cheese."

Lorenzo nodded jerkily and rose from his chair.

"You're welcome to come, too, Casey," Gordon said as he stood as well.

"I think I need to be alone for a bit."

"If you change your mind, you know where I live," Gordon said. He put his hand on Lorenzo's shoulder and led him toward the cemetery's parking lot.

Tears stained my cheeks as I gazed at the open grave and lonely granite marker, an inadequate reminder of the life that had left this world too soon. I'd cried not only for Pauline and for her family, but also for my mother and the questions surrounding her murder that would never be answered.

A piece of me had believed that if I could find Pauline's murderer, if I could find justice for her, a piece of my heart would be healed and I'd begin to be whole again. And yet on this crisp clear spring morning I felt worse.

This tragedy had only forced the grief I'd buried deep in my heart to bubble up to the surface. It tore at me as raw and real as the day I'd lost my mom. I turned my stinging face to the pale blue sky and inhaled the cool fragrant air.

I needed someone to hold me and to tell me that it was okay to feel lost and alone and frightened. My grandmother, with her gentle wisdom and strong embrace, would know the right words to say to soothe my battered heart. Too bad she was a day's drive away. Too far.

I should have never left Charleston or the loving embrace of my family at Rosebrook.

The white plastic folding chair the funeral home had set up at the graveside creaked as I stood. When I turned around, I discovered that I wasn't alone.

Special Agent Jack Turner stood underneath a poplar tree a hundred feet away. Dressed in a black suit and matching tie, he looked trim and professional and not at all like the knight errant image he played so well.

My heart raced at the sight of him. Now that Pauline's murder had been solved, I'd assumed Turner would disappear back into the shadows with the rest of the secretive CAT agents.

We stood there staring at each other for I don't know how long.

The corners of his lips kicked up into a half grin.

That got my legs working again. The thick fescue grass swished under my feet as I crossed the distance between us at a careful, measured pace.

"Don't tell me you're still on babysitting duty," I said.

"No reason to be. Everyone who was involved is either dead or in jail. I even heard that Senator Pendergast is now campaigning for your organic gardening program."

"She was awfully grateful that I'd saved her life."

He nodded.

"If you're not on assignment, Turner, what are you doing here?"

"Don't know. Bad habit, I suppose." He crossed his arms over his chest and bumped his shoulder against mine. "Do you mind that I came?"

"Not at all."

"How about I buy you a coffee?"

"That would be . . . would be . . ." A sob tore from my throat.

Why did he have to go and pull this nice act? It was just too much.

Turner pulled me close and wrapped his arms around me. I pressed my cheek against his strong chest and wept. As soon as I felt safe and strong again, I pushed him away and wiped at my eyes, trying my best to pretend that nothing had happened.

"Brace yourself, Casey," he said as we walked toward the road. "I do have some bad news."

My muscles instinctively tightened. "What now? Wait, don't tell me. I don't want to know."

We walked a little farther.

"Okay. I can't stand it. Spit it out. What happened?"

"Milo got into the Rose Garden again this morning. He dug up two more rosebushes."

"No! I hope whoever was supposed to be watching him gets fired."

"Now that's unfair. He *was* being watched."

"How do you know?"

"Because *I* was watching Milo. I watched

him dig up the one bush and then the other."

"Agent Turner!"

He threw his arm over my shoulder as we headed toward the parking lot. "I think you should call me Jack."

"Well, Jack, you should be ashamed. Those poor, defenseless roses. I don't know how they're going to survive Milo's puppyhood. I don't know how *I'm* going to survive it."

And yet I knew I would survive Milo's antics, Seth's nervous ranting, and anything else that might be thrown my way because I loved the excitement of gardening at the White House.

"Aren't you going to say something about this being the beginning of a beautiful friendship?" Jack asked, interrupting my train of thought.

Our eyes met, and I laughed. "I think you already did."

A PAGE FROM CASEY'S SPRING GARDENER'S NOTEBOOK

March

Week 1

PLANTING: Planted 35 varieties of tulips (an even mix of early, mid, and late bloomers to ensure a steady show of colorful blooms). 3,000 bulbs planted in the Rose Garden, bordered by 8,000 grape hyacinths. 8,000 tulip bulbs planted around the South Fountain, bordered by 16,000 grape hyacinths. 4,000 tulip bulbs planted around the North Fountain, bordered by 8,000 grape hyacinths. Next week: Plant tulips and grape hyacinths in Lafayette Square park.

SOWING: Started tomatoes (5 heirloom varieties), green bell peppers (the First Lady's favorite), and cucumbers in the White House greenhouse.

CULTIVATING: None this week. Hopefully,

we'll be cultivating organically grown beets this time next year.

FERTILIZING: With the warmer weather on its way and the new leaves beginning to appear on the roses, it's time to start fertilizing. I've talked Gordon into an organic alternative this year with a half-and-half mix of alfalfa and cottonseed meals, 10 cups per plant. The fertilizer was carefully mixed into the top inch or two of soil in the Rose Garden. The application will be repeated every 10 weeks.

Applied liquid seaweed using a hose-end sprayer to the South Lawn to give a quick boost of green to the tall fescue turf.

PRUNING: Early spring is the time to prune perennials. Removed old foliage from the perennials in the Children's Garden, making room for the new growth that's about to appear. To avoid sour grapes, we vigorously pruned the Concord grape vines in the East Garden, cutting new shoots back to the third or fourth leaf. Next week: Prune roses in Rose Garden.

WEATHER: Warmer days have made everyone anxious to get to work in earnest in all the gardens. Gordon has been reminding us daily that it's early in the season. There's still the danger of freezes and frost. It's been a rainy week. I took a handful of soil in my hand and squeezed. The dirt formed large clumps, which means it's too wet to work. Soil prep for the First Lady's vegetable garden will have to wait.

NOTES: Keeping an eye out for weeds. Turned compost pile at the White House greenhouse facility. Ordered diatomaceous earth, a natural barrier against ants and other harmful insects, for use in the spring garden.

QUICK AND EASY GUIDE FOR GROWING A PINEAPPLE TOP

Fresh pineapple
Small pot
Perlite, vermiculite, or coarse sand
Knife

Purchase a fresh pineapple with a large, bright green top. If you can find a pineapple that already has roots sprouting, get that one. Check between the leaves for root growth. Roots will be brown filaments growing off the stalk between the leaves.

Remove the green stalk from the pineapple. You can do this one of two ways: Twist off the stalk or cut off the top of the pineapple. I prefer to chop off the top of the pineapple, because twisting can damage the leaves.

Remove all pineapple meat from the stalk. Be sure the stalk is clean of any pineapple residue. Even a small bit of meat left on the stalk will rot, which may cause the plant to rot and die.

Peel off the bottom whorl of leaves to expose approximately an inch of stalk. Take care not to damage any existing roots when removing the leaves.

Place in a dark, dry spot for three to seven days to allow the stalk to dry out and form a callus.

Once the stalk has dried, plant in a small pot with perlite, vermiculite, coarse sand, or any combination of these. Bury the stalk up just above the first leaf. The pineapple will want to be in a dry, well-drained environment. If the planting medium stays too damp, the pineapple stalk will rot. If the center of the pineapple stalk rots, don't panic. Remove the rotted material and let dry out. With some extra care, the pineapple can still produce roots and form offshoots from the stalk.

Alternative to potting: Root the pineapple in a glass of water. Place pineapple stalk in a glass of water, with the end of the stalk submerged in the water at a depth of a quarter to a half inch. Change the water every two to three days.

Set pot or glass in indirect light. It takes six to eight weeks for the stalk to root.

Once the roots have set, repot in a well-drained potting soil and gradually move to direct sunlight. Feed the established plant a 10-10-10 fertilizer. Do not overwater.

It will take approximately three years before the plant will flower and fruit. Until then, enjoy the look of the tropics within your own home.

ABOUT THE AUTHOR

Dorothy St. James lives a charmed life at the beach just outside Charleston, South Carolina, with her husband, two slightly needy dogs, and a contemplative cat. She earned her bachelor of science in aquaculture, fisheries, and wildlife biology from Clemson University's School of Agriculture, graduating at the top of her class. She went on to receive a master of public administration from the University of Charleston with an emphasis on environmental urban planning.